Richard Lepsius

Standard Alphabet for reducing unwritten languages and foreign graphic systems to a uniform orthography in European letters

Second edition

SALZWASSER VERLAG

Richard Lepsius

Standard Alphabet for reducing unwritten languages and foreign graphic systems to a uniform orthography in European letters

Second edition

Reprint of the original, first published in 1863.

1st Edition 2022 | ISBN: 978-3-37500-505-4

Verlag (Publisher): Salzwasser Verlag GmbH, Zeilweg 44, 60439 Frankfurt, Deutschland
Vertretungsberechtigt (Authorized to represent): E. Roepke, Zeilweg 44, 60439 Frankfurt, Deutschland
Druck (Print): Books on Demand GmbH, In de Tarpen 42, 22848 Norderstedt, Deutschland

STANDARD ALPHABET.

STANDARD ALPHABET

FOR

REDUCING UNWRITTEN LANGUAGES AND FOREIGN GRAPHIC SYSTEMS

TO A

UNIFORM ORTHOGRAPHY IN EUROPEAN LETTERS

BY C. R. LEPSIUS, D. PH. & D. D.

RECOMMENDED FOR ADOPTION BY

THE CHURCH MISSIONARY SOCIETY

SECOND EDITION.

LONDON.

1863.

ADVERTISEMENT
TO THE FIRST EDITION.

THE need of a fixed system of orthography induced several of the missionary societies of London, a few years ago, to agree upon "Rules of reducing unwritten languages to alphabetical writing in Roman characters." These Rules, though imperfect, have been already applied with success to several African languages. The societies were assisted in this work by the late Professor Lee of Cambridge, by Mr. Norris of London, and by Professor Lepsius of Berlin; but feeling it to be necessary for the establishment of any *Standard* system that an alphabet should be presented in a more complete form, and that the scientific principles should be explained upon which it was constructed, Professor Lepsius, at their request, kindly undertook this work, and has furnished the following admirable treatise, which will prove, it is hoped, an invaluable help to missionaries. The clear and scientific exhibition of vocal sounds which it contains will relieve Missionaries from many of their first difficulties in studying a foreign language, and will spare future translators much painful uncertainty respecting the powers of the letters which they employ. It has therefore been adopted by the Church Missionary Society as A STANDARD ALPHABET.

It is not expected that those who have already adopted a different system of orthography will at once conform to all the recommendations of Professor Lepsius, and in some minor points the genius of a language may possibly require a departure from the general standard. But such exceptions need not annul the *standard* character of this alphabet as one to which all parties may refer. Attention is particularly directed to the observations of Professor Lepsius upon this point at page 23 (45).

Founts of letters and matrixes are provided for printing according to this alphabet, and though its adoption may thus involve in the first instance some trouble and expense, these will be counterbalanced by the great and permanent advantage of a fixed orthography.

The object of this treatise concerns not only missionaries, but also the interests of the natives whose language is to be reduced to writing. It is most desirable that a nation should be furnished with an alphabet combining simplicity and precision to the utmost degree in which they are attainable. The art of reading will be thus greatly facilitated, and the natives will themselves teach one another to read and write without the perpetual aid of European teachers. In illustration of this remark, we may refer to the following instances:—In West Africa the Vei tribe invented a syllabic alphabet, in which every sign had its fixed sound, and the people taught one another to write without the aid of European teachers or the knowledge of European alphabets. Similar instances of natives teaching one another to read and write by a syllabic alphabet have occurred among the Indians in America. In New Zealand a very simple alphabet was carefully prepared by Professor Lee, and many tribes learned to read and write by the help of instructed natives before they were visited by Europeans.

In respect of Africa it is especially important to take every step which may facilitate the mutual instruction, and supersede the labours of European teachers. In this way only can we hope for the Evangelization of that vast continent.

It is a matter of much satisfaction, that in this, as in other instances, science lends its aid to the Christian zeal of missionaries for communicating to mankind the highest benefits; and the work is commended under this aspect to the blessing of Almighty God for the furtherance of the Kingdom of Christ among the nations of the earth.

H. VENN, B.D. Hon. Sec.
J. CHAPMAN, B.D. Sec,
Late Missionary in South India, and Principal of the Syrian College, Travancore.
H. STRAITH, Hon. Lay Sec.
C. GRAHAM, Lay Sec.,
Late Persian Interpreter to the Commander-in-Chief in India.
Church Missionary Society.

Having been concerned in the preparation of the Rules, &c., referred to above, which have been successfully employed in our West African languages — where the want of a uniform system was especially felt, — we express our cordial approval of this treatise, in which Professor Lepsius clearly explains the scientific principles upon which a *standard* alphabet must be constructed, and renders it, in its complete form, capable of the most extensive application.

JOHN BEECHAM, D.D. Sec.
ELIJAH HOOLE, Sec.,
Formerly Missionary in South India.
Wesleyan Missionary Society.

(Extract from a letter to the author.)

Société der Missions Evangéliques.

Paris le 7 juin 1855.

„J'ai le plaisir de vous annoncer que dans sa séance mensuelle d'hier, le Comité de la Société des Missions a décidé d'envoyer à nos Missionaires au Sud de l'Afrique le "*Standard Alphabet*" et de recommander à leur plus sérieuse attention le système qui est proposé pour arriver à une manière uniforme d'écrire les langues étrangères qui n'ont point encore de littérature.

En outre, il désire vivement qu'après avoir étudié ce système les Missionaires de notre Société puissent en faire l'application à la langue Séchuana.

Il serait utile pour cela, que notre Comité pût avoir une vingtaine d'exemplaires de la traduction anglaise du *Standard Alphabet*, pour les envoyer au Sud de l'Afrique."

Au nom du Comité:
GRANDPIERRE,
Directeur.

London Missionary Society.

London, June 28th 1855.

The importance of the object proposed by Dr. Lepsius will be deeply felt by every individual conversant in any degree with the difficulties to be encountered in the formation of a language previously unwritten, and with the want of harmony which has hitherto been found in such attempts. I cannot therefore but rejoice in the result of Dr. L.'s close and profound attention to this subject, as exhibited in his pamphlet and I most earnestly hope that it may greatly tend hereafter to secure substantial agreement, and if possible, uniformity in the practice of Christian Missionaries who are labouring to give the Word of God to tribes and nations among whom the symbols of thought have been previously unknown

ARTHUR TIDMAN,
Foreign Secretary L. M. S.

Moravian Missions.

London, June 1855.

I beg to give my cordial assent to the general principles which Professor Lepsius has so ably sketched in his Treatise. That the adoption of his system, however modified in some of its details, will be of the greatest service to Missionaries in every part of the world and especially to English Missionaries, can hardly admit of a doubt. Had such a system been originally applied to the languages of the Greenlanders and Esquimaux and to those of the Indian tribes of North and South America, much uncertainty and difficulty would have been avoided.

P. LA TROBE,
Secretary in England to the
Moravian Missions.

Barmen, den 30. Juli 1855.

Die Deputation der Rheinischen Missionsgesellschaft erklärt hiermit ihre Zustimmnng zu den von Herrn Prof. Lepsius in Berlin in seiner Schrift „das allgemeine lin-

guistische Alphabet" niedergelegten Grundsätzen der Orthographie und wird demgemäfs ihre Missionare für deren linguistische Arbeiten instruiren. Namens der Deputation:
Insp. WALLMANN.

[Barmen, 30th July 1855. The Committee of the Missionary Society of the Rhine declares hereby its assent to the principles of Orthography laid down by Professor Lepsius in his treatise on the Standard Alphabet, and will give directions accordingly to its Missionaries for their linguistic labours. For the Committee: Inspector Wallmann.]

Calw, Würtemberg, den 29. Oct. 1855.

Der Unterzeichnete mufs, auch abgesehen von dem umsichtigen Fleifs, womit dieses Standard Alphabet entworfen ist, schon um des harmonischen Zusammenwirkens willen, dringend wünschen, dafs wenigstens auf diesem Theile des Missionsgebietes Uniformität zu Stande komme, und schliefst sich darum demselben mit Freuden an.

Dr. CHR. G. BARTH,
Vorstand des Calwer Verlags-Vereins.

[Calw, Wurtemberg, 29th October 1855. The Undersigned, besides acknowledging the care and completeness of the views, upon which this Standard Alphabet is founded, cannot but earnestly desire for the sake of harmonious cooperation, that Uniformity may be attained at least in this part of the Missionary field, and therefore begs to give it his cordial assent. Dr. Chr. G. Barth, Director of the Calw Publishing Union.]

Evangelische Missions-Gesellschaft zu Basel.
Auszug aus dem Protokoll vom 9. Nov. 1855.

„Die Committee der evangelischen Missions-Gesellschaft hat „in Anerkennung der grofsen Wichtigkeit übereinstimmen- „der Grundsätze bei Feststellung des Alphabets bisher nicht „geschriebener Sprachen besonders auf dem Africanischen „Sprachgebiet beschlossen, das von Hrn. Prof. Dr. Lepsius in „Berlin aufgestellte System der Orthographie zu adoptiren und „den in ihrem Dienst stehenden Missionaren dasselbe zu all- „mähliger Einführung zu empfehlen.“

Namens der Committee:
JOSENHANS,
Inspector.

[Evangelical Missionary Society at Basle. Extract from protocol of 9. November 1855. „The Committee of the Evangelical Missionary Society, acknowledging the great importance of uniform principles in fixing the Alphabet of previously unwritten languages, particularly among the African races, has resolved to adopt the system of orthography proposed by Prof Dr. Lepsius of Berlin, and to recommend it to the Missionaries employed by this Society for gradual introduction.“ For the Committee: Josenhans, Inspector.]

American Board of Commissioners for Foreign Missions.

Missionary House, Boston,
June 20, 1856.

The Secretaries of the American Board of Commissioners for Foreign Missions have examined Dr. Lepsius's "Standard

Alphabet for reducing unwritten languages and foreign graphic systems to a uniform orthography in European letters," and regard it as an advance upon the practice of Missionaries of this Board heretofore in reducing languages to writing; and we will gladly do what we can to secure its general adoption.

R. ANDERSON,
S. B. TREAT,
S. L. POMROY, } *Secretaries.*

ADVERTISEMENT

TO THE SECOND EDITION.

A SECOND Edition of the English Version of the *General Linguistic or Standard Alphabet* is now offered to the public. It has undergone complete and careful revision; several minor points heretofore left undecided, have been settled by the light of experience and in accordance with the judgment of many distinguished scholars; and the Second Part, which exhibits synthetically its applicability to particular languages, has been much expanded and enriched.

The Church Missionary Society adopted the Standard Alphabet more than five years ago on conviction that it was theoretically the best. It appeared to be founded on clear scientific principles consistently carried out, and therefore simple—capable of easy comprehension and unlimited application. The interval has not disappointed their hopes. It has been applied successfully to at least fourteen African[1] and seven Asiatic[2] languages, and the test of experience enables the Society to commend it now, with far more confidence than when it first appeared, to all classes of students of languages, whether altogether unwritten, or rendered too often practically inaccessible by the cumbrous local alphabets in which their literature is embedded.

---

[1] *Aoṅgla, Bornu, Ewė, Fula, Gã, Hausa, Herero, Ibo, Masai, Nama, Nubian, Nupe, Oji, Zulu.*

[2] *Turkmenian, Kurd, Kafari, Pašto, Sindhi, Hakka-Chinese, Korean.*

This Alphabet is available for two very different classes of readers—the European student, and the uncritical Native. For the former, whether traveller, missionary, or philologist, the whole apparatus of diacritical marks will be needed, and more especially for such works as Grammars, Praxes, Dictionaries, &c., where the object is technical and linguistic. For the latter, many of the diacritical marks may be dispensed with, or will gradually drop off of themselves; and the Alphabet readily admits of such simplification, while preserving all its essential principles in their integrity.

The Standard Alphabet may be regarded as already lord of the domain of Africa, where it has had to compete with but few conflicting systems of any importance, either European or native. In Asia, the difficulties are greater, but here too its advance is encouraging. To refer more especially to India, not only is the possibility and expedience of "Romanizing" still far from conceded by many oriental scholars, who are naturally attached to Alphabets which they have mastered at the cost of so much labour, but ever since the opening of that great country to Europeans, attempts have been made, with more or less of system, to represent Hindu words and names in Roman letters. There is however only one scheme that can profess to compete with that of Prof. Lepsius. Considerable currency has been obtained in India for the system first propounded by Sir W. Jones, afterwards adopted with considerable modifications by Prof. Forbes and the late Prof. Wilson, and recently advocated with much earnestness by Sir C. Trevelyan and Prof. Monier Williams. The oriental student is much indebted to Sir C. Trevelyan for his weighty arguments in favour of the application of a Roman Alphabet to the languages of the East, which have never been met by a satisfactory answer; but the particular system, which he recommends, is far from perfect. This is not the place to enter into the objections which present themselves, but the many changes which this alphabet has successively undergone at the hands of Prof. Wilson and others, and the further changes still suggested by different patrons of this alphabet, show a want of complete confidence in it. The system of Prof. Lepsius is the result of many years' patient study as well as extensive practical experience; it is based on philological principles and a careful analysis of all the sounds possible to the organs of the human voice; full advantage has been taken of the researches of Sanskrit Grammarians; and, wherever available, the most widely received symbols have been adopted and incorporated into it. These are no slight claims to attention and cannot be overlooked by candid scholars.

It was under the conviction of the great services already performed by this Alphabet, and its capabilities for much further usefulness, that the Committee of the Church Missionary Society commissioned the writer of these lines to visit Berlin last autumn, and came to the following resolutions in consequence:—

Extract from Proceedings of Committee.

"The Rev. W. Knight reported his recent conference at Berlin, in company with the Rev. J. F. Schön, with Prof. Lepsius, respecting a final revision of the *Standard Alphabet,* and explained that the object had now been satisfactorily accomplished by the preparation of a second Edition of the work, and that it was now desirable to take steps for the promotion of its general adoption by circulating a large Edition among the Society's and other Missionaries, and also amongst learned men likely to take an interest in the question, and by furnishing Founts of Types to such of the Mission Printing Presses as may be ready to employ them.

Resolved—1. That an English Edition of 1500 copies of the Standard Alphabet be printed at Berlin under the direction of Prof. Lepsius, for circulation as suggested.

2. That the Secretary be authorized to urge upon the Missionaries of the Society the adoption of this system of orthography, and that as soon as there shall appear in any of the Society's Mission Presses in India or elsewhere a readiness to adopt and employ the system, the Committee will be ready to consider of the grant of a Fount of Types for such press."

Church Missionary House, London.
Aug. 26, 1861.

W. KNIGHT,
Sec. C. M. S.

CONTENTS.

Introduction

to

the Second Edition.

FIVE years have elapsed since the first edition of the Standard Alphabet was published. It has during that period enjoyed a wide circulation principally owing to the recommendation of the Committee of the Church Missionary Society, and the progress it has made leaves no doubt on our mind that it will ere long be universally adopted in all Missionary literature.

An intimate relation exists between linguistic science and Missionary labours. The latter, especially in new and hitherto unwritten languages, supply the former—chiefly by means of Translations, Vocabularies, Grammars, and Specimens—with rich, and in most cases the only, materials for further investigation and comparison. When we consider this close relation, we are led to expect that by degrees science also will employ our system more and more extensively, the fundamental principles of which have hitherto remained uncontroverted.

This Alphabet has as yet been more frequently applied to African languages than to any others. The reason for this is obvious. No attempts, or but very insignificant ones, have been made to reduce them to writing: at all events none such as could have stood in the way of the general introduction of an Alphabet otherwise acknowledged to be in every respect suitable.[1]

---

[1] The following works on *African* languages, in which the Standard Alphabet has been adopted, have come to the knowledge of the anthor:

1854.

S. W. Kölle (Church Miss. Soc.):

a) *African Native Literature, or Proverbs, Tales, Fables, and Historical Fragments in the Kánuri or Bórnu Language, and a Kánuri-English Vocabulary.* London. Chnrch Miss. Honse.

b) *Grammar of the Bórnu or Kánuri Lauguage.* London. Chnrch Miss. House.

1856.

J. B. Schlegel (North German Miss. Soc. at Bremen):

Agbalẹ ke me devio osrō̃ hlẹlẹ. Aoṅgla-Primer, printed for the German and Foreign School-book-Society at Calw. Stuttgart. Steinkopf.

1857.

J. F. Schön (Ch. Miss. Soc.):

a) *Fārawā letāfin māgāna Haúsa ko Mākōyi māgánan gaskia* etc. *[Haúsa Primer].* Berlin. Print. Unger.

b) *The Gospel according to St. Matthew, translated into Haúsa. Printed for the British and Foreign Bible Society.* London. Watts.

J. Erhardt (Ch. Miss. Soc.):

Vocabulary of the Enguduk Iloigob, as spoken by the Masai-tribes in East-Africa. Ludwigsburg (Würtemberg). F. Riehm.

H. Tindall (Wesl. Miss.):

A Grammar of the Namaqua-Hottentot Language. Cape-town. (Sold by Trübner.)

J. C. Wallmann (Inspector of the Berlin Miss. Soc.):

Die Formenlehre der Namaquasprache, ein Beitrag zur Südafrikanischen Linguistik. Berlin. (Published by W. Hertz.)

Hngo Hahn (Rhenish Miss. Soc. at Barmen):

Grundzüge einer Grammatik des Hereró im westlichen Africa, nebst einem Wörterbuche. Berlin. (Published by W. Hertz.)

J. B. Schlegel (North German Miss. Soc. at Bremen):

Schlüssel zur Ewe-Sprache mit Wörtersammlung, nebst einer Sammlung von Sprichwörtern und einigen Fabeln der Eingebornen. Stuttgart. Steinkopf.

J. Zimmermann (Basel Miss. Soc.):

a) *Genesi alo Mose kleṅkleṅ wolo lẹ; yẹ Gã wiemǫ lẹ mli. The first book of Moses in the Akra (Gã) Language.* (London. Watts.)

Far more difficult is the application of a new Orthography, even of the most perfect kind, to Asiatic languages, especially

---

b) *Daniel gbalo le, ye Gã wiemo le mli. The book of Daniel in the* *Akra (Gã) Language.* London. Watts.

c) *Johane ke Juda wodši le*, etc. *The Epistles of John and Jude, and the Revelation of St. John the Divine, in the Akra (Gã) Language.* (London. Watts.) 2d Ed. 1861. Basel.

d) *Spruchbuch des Calwer Verlagsvereins.* Stuttgart.

G. Christaller (Basel Miss. Soc.):

Kirchengebet und Katechismus (Anhang zu Barth's Biblischer Geschichte). Stuttgart.

1858.

J. F. Schön (Ch. Miss. Soc.):

Labári nāgari kámmāda anrūbútasi dagá Lukas. The Gospel according to St. Luke, translated into Haúsa. Printed for the British and Foreign Bible Society. London. Watts.

A. Steinhauser (Basel Miss. Soc.):

Kanemo-Wolo. Primer of the Gã Language. Stuttgart. Steinkopf.

A. Steinhauser & J. Zimmermann:

Gesangbuch, 168 Lieder in Akra. Stuttgart.

J. Zimmermann (Basel Miss. Soc.):

a) *A Grammatical Sketch of the Akra or Gã Language, and some Specimens of it from the mouth of the natives.* Stuttgart. Steinkopf.

b) *Bofoi le Asádši* etc. *The Acts of the Apostles translated into the Akra Language.* (London. Watts.) 2d Ed. 1861. Basel.

J. B. Schlegel (North German Miss. Soc. at Bremen):

a) *Jesu Kristo* etc. *History of Jesus, from the raising of Lazarus from the death to the day of Pentecost, with the Epistles and the Revelation of St. John the Divine, in the Ẇe Language.* Stuttgart. Steinkopf.

b) *Mawu-agbaba me nya veve tewe blaatõ vo eve. Dr. Barth's two times fifty two Bible Stories* etc., *translated into the Ewe Language as spoken in Añlo, Slave Coast, W. Afr.* Stuttgart. Steinkopf.

1859.

J. F. Schön (Ch. Miss. Soc.):

Letafin Musa Nabiu. The second book of Moses called Exodus, translated into Haúsa. London. Printed for the British and Foreign Bible Society.

J. C. Taylor (Native Clergyman, Ch. Miss. Soc.):

Isuama-Ibo Katekism, translated from Dr. Watts's first Catechism. (London). Watts.

to those which have possessed a settled native system of writing, and which, through either their literary or their practical

---

C. L. Reichardt (Ch. Miss. Soc.):
- a) *Primer in the Fulah Language.* Berlin. Unger.
- b) *Three original Fulah pieces in Arabic letters, in Latin transcription, and in English translation.* Berlin. Unger.

Lewis Grout (American Board):
The Isizulu. A Grammar of the Zulu Language, accomp. with a historical introduction, also with an appendix. Natal. J C. Buchanan. Pnblished by May & Davis, Pietermaritzburg; sold by Trübner. London..

J. Zimmermann (Basel Miss. Soc.):
- a) *Jesaya gbalo̩ le̩ ye̩ Gã wiemo̩ le̩ mli. The book of the Prophet Isaiah, in the Akra Language.* Printed for the British and Foreign Bible Society. Basel. C. Schnltze.
- b) *Bo̩fo kroṅkroṅ Paulo le̩ wolo ni enma eyamadše Romafoi le̩; ye̩ Gã wiemo̩ le̩ mli. The Epistle of St. Paul the Apostle to the Romans, in the Akra (Gã) Language.* (Londou. Watts.)
- c) *I. Kor. — II. Petri.*
- d) 8 *Wandtabellen.*

G. Christaller (Basel Miss. Soc.):
- a) *Otyi keṅkaṅ ṅhõma. Otji Primer, together with a Collection of Scripture Passages.* Basel. C. Schultze.
- b) *Ye̩ṅ awurade ne agyeṅkwã Yesu Kristo hõ ase̩mpa no, wo̩ Otyi kasa mu. The Gospel of our Lord and Saviour Jesus Christ, in the Otji Language, as spoken in Akuapem, Gold Coast, W. Afr.* (London). Watts.
- c) *Asomafo no nneye̩e̩ hõ ase̩m a Luka kyere̩w mae, wo̩ Otyi kasa mu. The Acts of the Apostles by St. Luke, in the Otji Language.* Printed for the British and Foreign Bible Society. Basel. C. Schultze.
- d) *Kristofo asafo a wo̩wo̩ Akuapem Tyi-dyom-ṅhoma. Hymnbook for the Christian Church in the Akuapem country in the Otji Language.* Stnttgart. Steinkopf.

L. Grout (American Board):
Imisebenzi Yabatunywa: i kumselwe ngabafandisi ba semerika ngokwa 'mazulu. (Acts of the Apostles translated by the Teachers of America among the Zulus.) Emsundnzi. J. Bnchanan.

H. Hahn and F. Rath (Rhen. Miss. Soc.):
Omahungi oa embo ra Yehova omukuru mu Otyihereró. (Tales of the word of Jehova in the Hereró Language.) Capetowu. S. Solomon.

importance, have long since afforded to Europeans occasion to express by Roman Letters the sounds which they contain.[1]

1860. 1861.

J. F. Schön (Ch. Miss. Soc.):
Oku Ibo. Grammatical Elements of the Ibo Language. London. Watts. (1861.)

J. Chr. Taylor (Native Clergyman, Ch. Miss. Soc.):
a) *Akukwọ ekpére Isuama-Ibo. A Selection from the Book of Common Prayer, translated into Ibo.* London. Watts.
b) *Isuama-Ibo Primer, by the Rev. Sam. Crowther, revised and enlarged by the Rev. J. Chr. Taylor.* London. Watts.
c) *Isuama-Ibo Sermon, preached at Trinity Church, Kissy road, Freetown, Febr. 17, 1859.* London. Watts.

Sam. Crowther (Native Clergyman, Ch. Miss. Soc.):
Nupe Primer. London. Watts.

G. Christaller (Basel Miss. Soc.):
a) *Ṅñyontobea ama Tyi-dyom-ñhoma ne Gã-lala-wolo no. Tune Book to the Otji and Akra Hymn-books.* Compiled by G. Auer. Basel. C. Schultze.
b) *Sechs Wandtabellen.* Basel.

J. Zimmermann (Basel Miss. Soc.):
a) *Exodus, in the Akra Language.*
b) *Sãdši kpakpai edẹ̆ ḷẹ. The four Gospels in the Akra Language.*

K. Rüdi (Basel Miss. Soc.):
Biblia mli sădši hă gbekebii fufobii. Bible Stories for little children in the Akra (Gã) Language. Basel. C. Schultze.

R. Lepsius:
Inǵil Yesū el Messīhnilin Markosin fāyisīn nagittā. The Gospel according to St. Mark, translated into the Nubian Language. Berlin. 1860. (W. Hertz.)

These and some other works, which we shall mention hereafter, have appeared under the auspices of no less than nine Missionary Societies or kindred Institutions of England, Germany, and America; and several of them have been printed and published at the cost of the British and Foreign Bible Society.

[1] With respect to the Asiatic languages the sanction of our system by the distinguished linguists of the Imper. Academy of Sciences at St. Petersburg, the natural centre for Asiatic Philology, is of decisive importance. We refer to the notice given in the Bullet. de la Classe Historico-philologique de l'Acad. Imp. des sciences de St. Pétersbourg, tome XIV. 1857. p. 238, Séance du 5. (17.) déc. 1856: *M. Dorn en présentant le glossaire Kourde de Mr. Lerch (Dialectes Kourmandji et Zasa) prêt à être mis*

Among these again the most difficult as well as the most important are the languages of India. Experience has convinced

---

sous presse, communique que lui et MM. ***Böthlingk, Kunik*** *et* ***Schiefner*** *se sont concertés avec* ***M. Lerch*** *quant au choix de l'alphabet le plus propre pour la publication des spécimens linguistiques Kourdes. On s'est décidé en faveur de l'Alphabet panlinguistique, proposé par Mr. Lepsius, auquel ont concourru les linguistes de Berlin et de Londres.* In consequence of this decision Mr. Peter Lerch has employed the Standard Alphabet in his work: "*Forschungen über die Kurden und die Iranischen Nordchaldäer*". First part: *Kurdische Texte mit Deutscher Uebersetzung.* St. Petersburg. 1857. Second part: *Kurdische Glossare, mit einer literarhistor. Einleitung.* 1858. The alphabet has since been likewise adopted by A. Schiefner, *Ueber die Sprache der Jukagiren* (Bull. de l'Acad. de St. Pétersb. tome XVI. 1859. p. 242 ff.); by J. Wiedemann, *Ueber die Livische Sprache und ihr Verhaltniss zu der Esthnischen* (Bull. t. XVI. 1859. p. 193 ff.); by Ahlquist, *Eine kurze Nachricht über das Wogulische* (Bull. Hist. philol. tom. XVI, 1. 2. 1859. p. 25 ff.); by the same, *Ueber das Mordvinische Verbum.* Helsingforth. 1859; by Ilminsky, *Ueber die Sprache der Turkmenen* (Bull. tom. I. 1860. p. 563-571); by Radloff, *Ueber das Tschuktische und Koreatische.* 1860.

With reference to the *Languages of Eastern Asia* we have principally to mention the application of the Alphabet to the *Chinese* langnage by the Rev. R. Lechler (Basel Miss.), in his translation of the Gospel according to St. Matthew into the dialect of the *Hakka Chinese (Evangelium des Matthaeus im Volksdialekte der Hakka-Chinesen)* Berlin. 1860. Unger. Prof. J. Hoffmann (Univ. of Leyden) has applied it to the *Japanese* language in his *Shopping-Dialogues* in Dutch, English and Japanese. London and The Hague. 1861. and the present writer to the *Tibetan* and the *Chinese* in two dissertations on the sonnds of some of the languages of Eastern Asia, in the transactions of the Berlin Academy, 1860.

It may here be added, that the author also introduced the new alphabet for the first time to a great extent for the transcription of *Arabic* names, in eight geographical maps of the North-eastern part of Africa and the adjacent countries of Asia, which form the first plates of the "Monuments from Egypt and Ethiopia after the Drawings of the Prussian Expedition to those Countries", published by him, Berlin; 1849-1859.

Dr. Trnmpp (Ch. Miss. Soc.) was the first who employed the Standard Alphabet for one of the *Indian* Langnages in his work: *A Sindhi Readingbook in the Sanskrit and Arabic character.* London. 1858 (publ. 1860). Careful observers will notice a slight deviation from our alphabet, as it at present appears, in the adoption of *c'* and *j́* instead of *č* and *ǰ*. The reason is that his "Reading book" had already passed through the press before the change, to the adoption of which he fully consents, was finally adjusted.

us that neither the internal consistency nor the physiological basis of our system of transcription has in the case of some of the sounds of these languages been sufficient to secure a ready acceptance for the symbols which we had proposed for their expression. No Alphabet can however force itself into universal adoption. It must make friends. These it will find partly by a clear organization, founded upon the actual nature of the subject under discussion—the laws of such organization being calculated to avoid the chaos of caprice which has hitherto prevailed—and partly by carefully considering the views and suggestions of all those concerned, whose approval we are anxious to purchase, when the concession would not overthrow the system itself.[1] The ancient Sanskrit is the basis of the modern Arian languages of India; its written character,

---

The greatest advantage however will result from a universal alphabet for such general linguistic works which have to deal with a great nnmber of different languages simnltaneonsly. In this respect we have the satisfaction to refer to the precedent of one of the most eminent linguists, viz. H. C. von der Gabelentz (not to confonnd with the Baron H. von Gablenz, the author of the fantastical Gavlensographic orthography), who in his researches on the Passive (*Ueber das Passivum*, Leipzig, 1860, and in the Transactions of the R. Saxon Society of Sciences, Vol. VIII.) has adopted the Standard Alphabet, and employs it for the langnages he treats. Likewise does Dr. Steinthal (Univ. of Berlin), who uses the Alphabet in his work on the characteristic features of the principal types of all languages (*Charakteristik der hauptsächlichsten Typen des Sprachbaues.* Berlin. 1860), and produces at the close (p. 332 sqq.) the whole *Standard Alphabet* in extenso, under the name of the *General Linguistic Alphabet*, the name which we used in onr first German Edition of the Standard Alphabet. (Hertz. 1855.) The same and Dr. M. Lazarus (Prof. on the Univ. of Bern) employ it throughont their valuable Journal for psychology of nations and lingnistic science (*Zeitschrift für Völkerpsychologie und Sprachwissenschaft.* Berlin. F. Dümmler.).

[1] In the pamphlet of Mr. J. T. Thomson, *an unpointed Phonetic Alphabet based upon Lepsius's Standard Alphabet, 1859*, many true views are expressed, bnt even if the theory were actnally faultless, he shows such disregard as to the prospect of the practical adoption of many of his proposals, that we can only regret the industry employed. The same may be applied to the pamphlet of Prof. H. A. Barb, *Die Transcription des Arabischen Alphabets.* Wien. 1860. (See below the remarks to the Arabic Alphabet.)

the Dēvanāgari, is with some modifications extended to all those languages. While however the ancient Indian language was perfectly expressed by the Dēvanāgari characters, the modern dialects have more or less departed from its pronunciation, but without transferring these changes into their written character. Of one fact indeed there is no doubt, and it is one that is recognized by all scientific judges of the Sanskrit; the ancient Sanskrit itself, as would naturally be anticipated, is not in various points pronounced by the Brahmans of the present day, as it was by those ancient Hindus to whom it was still a living language. Thus especially the palatals च, ज, which were originally pronounced as simple sounds *ḱ*, *ǵ* (to our ears very much like the Gutturals *k*, *g*), are now read without exception as compound sounds *tš*, *dž*, into which they have passed in course of time, a process which has taken place in many other languages besides these. In the same manner, the sounds ऐ and औ are described by ancient Grammarians as the diphthongs *ái*, *áu*, and are treated as such in speaking and writing; at present however they are pronounced as simple vowels *ē* and *ō*. The letters *ṛ* and *ṣ̌*, originally cerebrals, have lost their cerebral pronunciation and become dentals, so that now both ष and श are read *š* without any distinction. The vowel sign ˆ (*r̥*) written above the letters, which once formed a diphthong with the preceding vowel, seems to be now heard only as a consonant. The present pronunciation however of the Sanskrit forms the foundation of every attempt hitherto made to transcribe into Roman characters the actual languages of India. In the first edition of the Standard Alphabet only the ancient pronunciation of the Sanskrit was taken into consideration, which, if we treat the language in a strictly scientific manner, must indeed still be regarded as the Standard; but it cannot be denied that the present pronunciation of the Brahmans must also be taken into consideration. And this the more, because the same pronunciation very generally reappears in those cognate living languages which employ the Dēvanāgari character. For this reason, although we still recommend the adoption for strictly scientific use of the transcription of the ancient pronunciation, it has appeared convenient to exhibit by its side a transcription of the modern pronunciation also, and at the same time to adopt the latter for all living languages derived from the Sanskrit. This distinction at the same time facilitates the solution of a question which has been frequently mooted within the last few years, and which is of great importance as regards the universal adoption of the Standard Alphabet. In the first edition we have already intimated in several places (pp. 41, note 2; 44; 50), that the physiological principle of representing every simple sound by a single sign, and consequently every compound sound by several signs, may on Etymological grounds admit of certain appropriate exceptions. This is for instance the case, when an originally simple sound, although it may have been changed by assibilation into a double one, continues notwithstanding to be regarded in writing as a simple sound, and is so felt in the living language. With this view, for the double sounds *ty, dy, tš, dž, ts, dz*, which have resulted from simple palatals, we proposed (p. 42) the single signs *t́, d́, ť, d̆, ṭ, ḍ*. This actually happens in the case of the present pronunciation of the ancient Indian Palatals. The letters च, ज have not only preserved their simple form in all Indian Alphabets, although they have passed into the double sounds *tš* and *dž*, but the living language itself still treats these double sounds in more than one respect as simple ones. Yet notwithstanding all this there might still be a doubt whether we ought for these reasons to propose a single sign for the double sounds *tš* and *dž*. Considerable experience during the last five years has however convinced us that there would be great practical difficulties, both in India and Europe, in the way of bringing into universal adoption in Indian languages the written forms *tš* and *dž*, correct as these might be in themselves. Uniformity is always the main object of the Standard Alphabet, and this object in the case before us appears to be only attainable by the substitution of the simple bases *c* and *j*, to which the general suffrage seems to incline. We prefer therefore to make use of these two letters wherever the above mentioned reasons suggest an exception from the general rule. This will be chiefly the case in the Indian and in the Semitic languages, whilst for African or hitherto unwritten languages, as a general rule, we shall solve the difficulty by adhering to *tš* and *dž*.

We have indeed formerly shown the special disadvantage attached to the use of the letters *c* and *j*, since they have in different European orthographies very different pronunciations; viz.:

	English	German	French	Italian	Spanish
c =	*k* or *s*	*k* or *ts*	*k* or *s*	*k* or *tš*	*k* or *θ*
j =	*dž*	*y*	*ž*	*y*	*χ*

In order therefore to indicate the linguistic use of *c* and *j* for *tš* and *dž*, it is indispensable to add to them a diacritical sign, to distinguish them from the European letters *c* and *j*, and to indicate the especial linguistic power, which we wish them to possess. It will be seen on a subsequent page that we have already adopted the diacritical sign ˇ to distinguish the sounds *š* and *ž* from *s* and *z*, and it therefore appears most natural that we should employ the same diacritical sign over the new bases, *c* and *j*, to indicate the second part of the pronounced double sounds, viz. *tš* and *dž*. We consequently write *č* and *ǰ*.

It has also been before observed that the assibilation of originally simple palatal sounds has not unfrequently adopted other forms besides *tš* and *dž*, and that the following is a complete series of transitions of which some languages possess several together.

ḱ, *ǵ*
ky, *gy* (*ḱ*, *ǵ*)
ty, *dy* (*t'*, *d'*)
tš, *dž* (*č*, *ǰ*)
ts, *dz* (*ṭ*, *ḍ*)

Of these forms the first amplifications, *ky*, *gy*, happen to stand closely connected with their originals, the simple palatals, which can scarcely be pronounced without a distinctly audible *y*. Where then a simple basis is required, they need no special distinction, but may be denoted, like the simple palatals, by *ḱ* and *ǵ*. For the second and fourth amplifications the marks *t'*, *d'* and *ṭ*, *ḍ* have already been proposed in the first edition. For the third however, which we thought we had before most suitably expressed by *tš* and *dž*, we now employ *č* and *ǰ* for the reason which we have given. We write therefore the Turkish palatals *ḱ*, *ǵ* = *ky*, *gy*. In the Sindhi alphabet there appears by the side of *č*, *ǰ*, also a *d'* (= *dy*), and in the Pashto by the side of *č* and *ǰ* also *ṭ* and *ḍ* (= *ts*, *dz*), which have also descended from palatal sounds.

Another deviation from the first edition consists of the changing the aspirates (*t'*, *d'*, &c.) into their corresponding mutes with an *h* following (*th*, *dh*, &c.). That this change is not in contradiction to the fundamental laws of the Standard Alphabet is plain from the explanation of the aspirates we have already given (1st Ed. p. 44). Indeed, the aspiration is not absolutely one with the consonant, but partly follows it, and can therefore be expressed separately. Following the practice of Bopp and others, we previously marked the aspirates in the Sanskrit by an added *Spiritus asper*; we did so, because in the Dēvanāgari the aspirates are represented by single signs. But it has also been mentioned that in the Arabic transcription of the Hindustāni the Indian aspirates are already written separately. Still more decisive however is the practical ground that the notation of the aspirates as simple sounds, has not been favourably received, on account of the inconvenience attached to it in writing and printing. We believe therefore that we shall, in this point also, meet the views of the majority of those interested, if we free the Standard Alphabet of the inconvenient hooks of the aspirates, and substitute in their places the full *h*; except only in the more accurate transcript of the ancient pronunciation of the Dēvanāgari.

Lastly, in the first edition of the Standard Alphabet, the choice was left open between χ̓, θ̓, and the new bases γ, δ. We have found with great satisfaction, that the most intelligent voices have been raised in favour of the latter signs. We therefore do not hesitate to drop the reluctantly admitted signs χ̓, θ̓, and to substitute for them γ, δ. Of minor importance is the adoption in the present edition of the angular sign *š*, *ž* instead of the circular *s̆*, *z̆*, to denote the English sound *sh* and the French *j*. Whoever may prefer the latter form, may use it without hesitation. In favour of the former we find not only its use in several Slavonic languages, but also its greater clearness in writing and print, whilst the round form may easily be confounded with the *Spiritus asper* or *lenis*.

We have already in the first edition protested against the use of Italics to denote the deviating classes of sounds according to which we should, for instance, have to write: "da*n*d*a*" instead of in conformity with our system: *daṇda*. It gives us much satisfaction to perceive that Professor Max Müller has in his last publication, *The History of Sanskrit Literature*, relinquished this mode of transcription and substituted dots to express the Indian cerebrals. We must also repeat our decided protest against the use of *ch* and *sh*, according to the English pronunciation, instead of our *č* and *š*. We rejoice at the accession to our view of Dr. Caldwell, at least as far as the former sound is concerned, since in his last work[1] he has given up the use of *ch*, which he had previously adopted. Our Alphabet now agrees in most points with his, as far as regards the pronunciation of the present Indian languages. Still we consider the diacritical sign ˇ over *c* and *j* (*č*, *ǰ*) to be unavoidably necessary in order to distinguish them everywhere from *c* and *j* as used in European languages. As *ch* instead of *č*, so also *sh* instead of *š*, violates not only the fundamental laws of all correct transcription, but also the requirements of practical applicability. The combination *sh* can, according to the analogy of *kh*, *ph* etc., only indicate an aspirated *s*, as it actually occurs in the Chinese and other languages, and may also occur in any other, by the concurrence of a final *s* with *h* following, as in English *mishap*, in German *Grashalm.* Neither can we approve of the stroke *á*, *é*, *ó* in the Alphabet of Dr. Caldwell to denote long vowels, because this stroke is, as a general practice, never used in European languages to indicate the prosodic length of a vowel, but the accent of the word, as in the Greek.

These and some other imperfections in the proposals of Sir Charles Trevelyan adopted by Professor Monier Williams[2] and the Rev. G. U. Pope[3], should be avoided before

---

[1] *On the substitution of the Roman for the Indian Characters* (communicated to the Madras Literary Society by Sir Charles Trevelyan), 1859.

[2] A new collection of various essays referring to this subject has just been made by Prof. Monier Williams, entitled: *Original papers illustrating the history of the application of the Roman Alphabet to the languages of India.* London 1859.

[3] *One Alphabet for all India.* Madras 1859. This pamphlet, like that of Dr. Caldwell, was elicited by Sir Charles Trevelyan, when at Madras. While both essays contain strong arguments in favour of a Roman Alphabet for India, it would be incorrect to regard the authors, as advocating, in its integrity, the modification of Sir W. Jones's system, adopted by Sir Charles, and promoted by Professor Williams. Amongst other divergences, for example, Mr. Pope employs the circumflex to mark the ong vowels (*â*, *ê*, &c.), and the Spanish *ñ*. We have noticed one of the

we can either wish or expect that his long continued and laudable exertions for the introduction of the Roman Alphabet will meet with complete success. Just as little can the report of the Sub-Committee of the Madras Literary Society, and auxiliary of the R. Asiatic Society, on writing Indian words in Roman Characters (in the Madras Journal of Literature and Science, Vol. 3, New Series, Madras 1859), exert any decisive influence on the solution of the main question; since Messrs. Elliott, Bayley and Norman, the gentlemen composing the Committee, are not even agreed among themselves, but have conveyed in three appendices their own individual proposals, which deviate in some, and partly not unimportant, points from the main report composed by Mr. Elliott. Messrs. Elliott and Bayley have even gone so far as to return—in opposition however to Mr. Norman's protest—to the exploded method of denoting aspirates by *k'h, g'h, ch'h,* thus separating distinctly by means of a comma the mute from its aspirate, although the same is found to be so intimately connected that in the Dēvanāgari it is expressed by but one letter. These writers can, in this, as in some other points, plead the example of Sir William Jones, whose great services we have always acknowledged (see below), especially with reference to the vowel-system. It has however been already pointed out, that his transcription of the consonants was very defective, principally because the physiological laws of the system of sounds were not then fully recognized. The Sub-Committee appear unfortunately to have been unacquainted

---

most important of Dr. Caldwell's variations above—the abandonment of *ch* to express the first consonant of the palatal row. He has also misgivings as to the acute accent for denoting the long vowels, and even says, "For cursive writing, I suspect, it will be found that the simple horizontal line—the ordinary prosodial line of length—is the easiest" (p. 27). Even Mr. Williams hesitates not only as to *ch* but as to *sh*, and appears to propose *c* with a diacritical mark, while he thinks that "a similar modification of *sh* might perhaps be introduced with advantage." (See Williams's *Bág-o-bahar*, pp. XXVII–XXIX.) We welcome such approximations to our system.

with the proposals of the Standard Alphabet, which is especially based upon a critical choice, according to internal laws, amongst the different systems of notation hitherto used, and has the object not only to harmonize the wants and customs of Indian writers with European science, but also with the wants of Missionaries beyond India, embracing, as they do, all the rest of the world. They would otherwise have perhaps attempted to combine their Anglo-Indian standing-point with that of the Standard Alphabet.

Whilst referring to this subject we venture to call attention to the introduction to the Zulu Grammar by the Rev. Lewis Grout, in which the Standard Alphabet is thoroughly reviewed, both with regard to its intrinsic value, and its general applicability. Mr. Grout, Missionary of the American Board of Missions, has for some time (see p. 41) taken the lead in the diversified and fundamental discussions of the question of the Alphabet in American Missions, and especially at Natal. He therefore has a strong claim to be heard, and his example in applying the Standard Alphabet to his learned work on the Zulu language cannot fail to cause those who take a cordial interest in the question, to follow him with all the more confidence.

A few more observations on different points in relation to transcription into Roman Characters may now follow. We form the *Appellatives* of the letters in various ways. In naming the explosive Consonants we put the Vowel after, as: *ka, te, de, pe, qu;* in naming the fricatives and liquids we put the Vowel before, as: *es, ef, el, em, er.* Others again we call, as did the Greeks, by special names:—as in the English: *aitch, double-you, wy, zed;* the German *jod, vau, zet, ypsilon;* the French *ach, ygrec.* Lastly, we possess no common designation for sounds like *š*, *ž*, *χ* and others, or for such as do not exist in European languages; yet it is necessary to have such both in teaching, and in other cases. Under these circumstances it seems most advisable to follow the example of the

Sanskrit and other syllabic languages, adopting a uniform nomenclature throughout, and pronouncing every letter without difference, with an *a* following, thus: *ka*, *pa*, *la*, *ma*, *χa*, *šа*, *ža*, *va*, *ya*, and so on.

It is also necessary to come to a definite understanding, with regard to the *Order* of letters in Lexicons and similar works. It seems that a scientific arrangement can only be obtained, by keeping the Vowels and Consonants respectively by themselves, and by arranging the latter according to the different classes of the organs, i. e. gutturals, palatals, &c., or as aspirates, explosives (*fortes*, *lenes*), nasals, &c. In the first Edition (p. 47) we have (where an organic arrangement was necessary) given the preference to the classes of exspiration, because in them especially the bases of similar sounds are most closely kept together. For European use we have, however, recommended the European order of letters, and now consider it well to recommend the same to a still greater extent. It may in fact be introduced into all lexical arrangements, as a scientific order is only needed when one has to speak in a grammar or elsewhere of a scientific classification of sounds. Lexicons in foreign characters will necessarily follow the foreign arrangement; but, applied to Roman characters, either principle of arrangement deduced from sound would uselessly separate all the homogeneous roots and hard and soft letters, which belong to one another. Classified according to the organs, *ṅ*, *ń*, *ṇ*, *n*, and again *s*, *š*, *ṣ*, *ṣ̱* would be widely separated from each other; classified according to exspiration, *k* would be separated from *g*, *ṭ* from *ḍ*, *š* from *ž*, *θ* from *δ*, and so on. Within these classes of exspiration, it would also be necessary to place the bases with distinguishing marks before the simple bases, e. g. *ṭ* and *ṯ* before *t*, *ń* and *ṇ* before *n*, which seems not to be natural, and as to other letters such as *č*, *ǰ*, *š*, *ž*, *θ*, *δ*, it would be altogether doubtful what place should be assigned to them. Besides this, any arrangement of the letters according to the organs would present great difficulty to Europeans, who are accustomed only to the Latin mode, and this difficulty would be vastly increased, when we come to the order of the letters not only at the commencement, but in the body of each word. For foreigners however, who will have under any circumstances to relinquish their accustomed succession of letters, it is of little importance what new arrangement they may adopt, and a scientific one is of no advantage, where convenience and practical utility only are aimed at. The case would assume a different aspect, if the Alphabetical arrangements of European languages were as diversified as their orthographies. In this case a new and necessarily *organical* arrangement would be unavoidable. But inasmuch as all European nations use one and the same order of letters as handed down to them by the Romans, who received it from the Greeks, who again received it thousands of years ago from the Phoenicians, they possess also the right of communicating the historical arrangement, as well as the characters themselves, to foreign nations.

To enter into detail. We shall give the precedence to letters without diacritical marks; the rest, when there are several of them, will be arranged according to the organs of speech. As far as the signs ' and ʾ are concerned, the simple curve ' is not likely to be of much lexicographical use. Should it however be called for, it also would be treated as the distinguishing mark of a vowel, and would either be dealt with as not existing at all, or follow the simple vowel as *'a* after *a*, *'e* after *e*, and so on. For the Semitic sound ع two curves ʾ have been chosen in order that for European languages, we might not be obliged to take notice of this sound at all, more especially at the beginning of words. If we were to take any letter with a diacritical mark, for instance *q́*, some inconveniences would ensue. One would consent to write *'Abdallah*, *ʾAli*, but never *Q́abdallah*, *Q́ali*; we shall therefore treat ʾ like ' as not existing, and should take no notice of it in lexical arrangements, except where two words have no other mutual distinction, in which case we should place the word containing the ʿ immediately after the one that does not contain it, or which contains only one curve ʾ. Lastly, the four Greek marks may most easily be associated with those Roman ones, whose fricatives they are, consequently *δ* will come after *d*, *γ* after *g*, *χ* after *k*, *θ* after *t*. In conformity with this plan the Alphabet with the principal diacritical signs employed in the different languages could be arranged as follows: *a, ā, ă, ā̆, ā̃, â, ạ, ʾa, ʿa; b, b̄, b′, ḃ; č, č̄, č′, ċ; d, ď, d̄, ḍ, ḍ̌, ḍ, ḏ, ḍ, ḍ; δ, δ̱; e, ē, ĕ, ê, ē̃, ẹ, ẹ̄, ẹ̆, ẹ, ẹ̄, ẹ, ẹ, ẹ̃; f, f′; g, ǵ, ġ, g̃, ḡ, ġ; γ, γ́, γ̇; h, ħ; i, ī, ĭ, ĩ, ī̃, ị, ị̄, ị, ī; j, ǰ, ȷ̀, j̄; k, k̆, k̄, k̄, k′, k̄′, ḵ, k̄, k′; χ, χ́, χ̇; l, l̄, l′, ḷ, ł, ḷ, ḷ; m, ḿ, m′, ṃ; n, ń, ń, ṅ, n̈, ṅ′, ṇ, ṇ, n̈, ṇ; o, ō, ŏ, õ, ō̃, ọ, ọ̄, ọ̃, ọ, ọ̄, ọ, ọ̄; p, p̓, ṕ, p′; q, q′; r, ŕ, ŕ, ṙ, ṛ, ř, r̄, ṛ, ṝ; s, ś, ṣ, š, ṣ̌, š, ṡ; t, t̄, t′, ṭ, ṭ, ṭ, t′, ṭ, ṭ̄, ṭ′, ṭ′, ṭ; θ; u, ū, ŭ, û, ū̃, ụ, ụ, ů, ụ, ụ̄; v, v́, v′; w, ẃ, w̱; y, ỹ; z, ź, ẕ, ž, ž, ż,; x, ɛ; ǀ, ǁ, ǃ, ǂ; -ˊ, -⊥, -ˋ, -⊥, -ˊˊ, -⊥⊥, -ˋˋ, -⊤⊤, -ᵀ.*

The exposition of the scientific and practical principles according to which a suitable Alphabet for universal adoption in foreign languages might be constructed, has, with the few exceptions above mentioned, remained unaltered. These rules are founded in the nature of the subject, and therefore, though they may admit of certain carefully limited exceptions, they can undergo no change in themselves; they serve as a defence against arbitrary proposals which do not depend upon universal laws; they will explain and recommend the application which has been made of them already to a series of languages, and will serve as a guide in their application to new ones.

But we have not concealed, from the very beginning, that it is not in every person's power to apprehend with physiological and linguistic accuracy the sounds of a foreign language, or even those of his own, so as to apply with some degree of certainty the principles of our Alphabet to a new system of sounds containing its own peculiarities. A few only of our most distinguished Grammarians are possessed of a penetrating insight into the living organism of sounds in those very languages, which they have discussed. Much less can it be expected of Missionaries, who are often obliged without previous preparation to address themselves to the reduction and representation of a foreign language, that everything, which belongs to a correct adjudication of particular sounds (frequently apprehended only with great difficulty even by the ear), or to their connection with one another and with other systems of sounds, should present itself spontaneously to their minds.

We attach therefore, with reference to the practical utility of this book, special importance to its *Second Part*, which contains a collection of Standard Alphabets, carried out in conformity with the principles of our work. We have frequently observed that those, who have tried to make use of our Alphabet, have found the correct application less difficult by a comparison with a given and cognate Alphabet, than by the study of our preceding expositions. We believe that we have made the present edition still more useful by increasing the collection of Alphabets, as well as by a careful revision of those previously given. To facilitate the comprehension of the signs chosen for every Alphabet, we have added, in most cases, some short annotations, and a few connected lines of text. On the other hand we thought, that we might be permitted to pass over in silence, in this Edition, the Alphabets of other Grammarians, and only to add the indigenous signs, as far as they were at our disposal.

For the most essential advance, more especially in reference to *Indian* Alphabets, the present Edition is indebted to the learned and intelligent cooperation of the Rev. Dr. Trumpp. This gentleman has resided for several years in different parts of India, and has paid particular attention to the pronunciation of the most important Arian languages, with a special view to their practical application (see above p. 6). He returned in the spring of 1860 to Europe, and the author rejoiced to avail himself of the opportunity of his visit, which was particnlarly designed to bring all scientific and practical questions, which in the application of our Alphabet to the Indian languages would come into consideration, to a definite conclusion.

Finally, we have thankfully to state, that we are greatly indebted for a general revision of this second English Edition to the Secretary of the Church Missionary Society, Rev. W. Knight, and another member of its Committee, whom we have just mentioned, Rev. J. F. Schön, the author of the *Haúsa* and *Ibo* Grammars, who both visited Berlin for this purpose in the autumn of 1860.

Berlin, November 1861.

R. Lepsius.

FIRST PART.

HISTORICAL AND SYSTEMATICAL DEVELOPMENT.

The endeavour to establish a uniform orthography for writing foreign languages in European characters has both a *scientific* and a *practical* aim. The *scientific* aim is to bring these languages with their literature more completely within our reach, and to increase our knowledge of the nations to which they belong. The *practical* aim is to facilitate the propagation of the Christian faith and the introduction of Christian civilisation among heathen nations, especially such as have no written language, by furnishing them with a suitable alphabet.

The latter object is most intimately connected with the efficiency of all Christian missions. It is in this quarter that attention has been lately directed afresh to a want long felt in science, often suggested, but never yet satisfied, namely, the want of a *standard* alphabet universally current and applicable to all languages. In the Mission field, without doubt, the first decisive steps will be taken for the actual introduction of such a graphic system.

The Scientific Object of this Alphabet.

One of the grandest aims of modern science, and one which it has only lately been in a position to attempt, is the attainment of an accurate knowledge of all the languages of the earth. The knowledge of languages is the surest guide to a more intimate acquaintance with the nations themselves, and this not only because language is the medium of all intellectual intercommunication, but also because it is the most direct, the most copious and the most lasting expression of the whole national mind.

From the relations of separate languages, or groups of languages, to one another, we may discover the original and more or less intimate affinity of the nations themselves. We learn, for instance, by this means, that the Indians, Persians, Greeks, Romans, Slavonians, and Germans form a catenarian series whose parts are far more intimately connected with one another than with any link of the chain, which consists of the Babylonians, Hebrews, Phœnicians, Arabs, Abyssinians; and that the Egyptians, and the African tribes on their north-western and south-eastern boundaries, are much more intimately allied to both these groups, than to the rest of the African nations of which those who inhabit the continent to the south of the Equator form another such circle of nations, all closely related to each other.

In like manner will the chaos of the nations in Asia, America, and Polynesia, be gradually resolved into order, by the aid of linguistic science, the ultimate aim of which is the investigation and comparison of all the languages of mankind.

In order to learn any language, we must be able to read and write its primary elements — *the sounds*. This we can only do in so far as we are able to express them in our own alphabetical characters; and sounds which do not exist in our own language must be described by other methods. Every grammar of a foreign language must resolve these problems in its first pages. But since the orthographies of European nations vary considerably among themselves, grammarians of different nations represent the sounds of one and the same language by different letters.

For example, the same sounds will be expressed

by the	Germans	*u*,	*dsch*,	*sch*,	*ch*.
„	English	*oo*,	*j*,	*sh*,	—.
„	French	*ou*,	*dj*,	*ch*,	—.
„	Italians	*u*,	*g*,	*sc*,	—.
„	Spaniards	*u*,	—,	—,	*j* or *x*.
„	Dutch	*oe*,	—,	—,	*ch*.

The most difficult task, however, arises when we attempt to represent sounds which havo no corresponding signs in our own alphabet, and when me must therefore introduce new characters or apply diacritical marks to our own letters. The French and German languages distinguishing only 20 simple consonantal sounds, and the English 22, it is evident that these alphabets are not sufficiently extensive to represent the sonnds of the Asiatic languages, among which, the Arabic distinguishes and represents 28 consonants, the Turkish 33, the Sanskrit 34, the Hindustāni 35, or, including the aspirates, eveu 47. Still less is the European alphabet capable of furnishing a comprehensive system including all the essential differences of sound, which amount to more than 50 in number, in all these various languages.

But since, generally speaking, each grammarian has only occupied himself with one language, or with a small circle of languages, he has been satisfied with explaining the symbols he has employed, and the reasons of their selection, without reference to fellow labourers, or to predecessors in the same field; especially if belonging to different European nations, and therefore starting from different bases.

Hence the diversity of signs for one and the same sound in different languages, or even in the same languagc, is continually increasing; and has at length become so great, that the translator of Oriental works, the Tonrist, the Geographer and Chartographer, the Naturalist, the Ethuographer, the Historian, in short every one who has to do with the names and words of foreign languages, and above all others the *Linguist*, who studies and compares languages, find themselves entangled in an intolerable confusion of orthographic systems and signs, from which each individual finds it impossible to extricate himself.

It is therefore only in a comprehensive survey of the whole question that a solution of the problem will be found. We must start with that which is common to all systems, following their general direction, excluding arbitrary and isolated experiments, keeping in view all the theoretical and practical difficulties of the case, and directing all our endeavours to the construction of a complete and definite system founded on the nature of phonetic organism. This is the *scientific* problem of a universal alphabet.

It is scarcely necessary to state that we do not here advocate any change in the orthographies of European languages. Isolated attempts to alter established orthographies cannot produce any practical results nor render any aid to science.

The Practical Object of this Alphabet.

The aboriginal tribes of Africa, America, Australia, and Polynesia are almost intirely destitute of written language. This fact alone ccaracterises them as barbarous and uncivilised. And if there be no nobler calling for the civilised and Christian world than to impart to all mankind the treasures of religious knowledge and human culture so freely entrusted to their hands by Divine Providence, — and if the obligation of this calling, now more powerfully felt than ever, rests especially on those associations of high-minded Christian men, which have taken their name as *Missionary Societies* from this highest of all missions; — then it is their especial duty to furnish destitute nations, first of all, with that most important, most indispensable means of intellectual, moral, and religious culture, *a written language*. For universal experience has long taught that it is not sufficient for the missionaries to learn the language of the natives in order to introduce Christianity permanently into any country. Only where the word of God is read by the people themselves, and where a whole people are made susceptible of the spirit of Christianity by the distribution of the Bible and of Christian school-books, can a rapid, deep and lasting work be hoped for. *Bible Societies* must go hand in hand with *Missionary Societies*.

Hence for many years the Committees of the principal Missionary Societies have regarded it as an important object to reduce to writing the language of all the nations to which their missionaries have penetrated, and to prepare in all these languages translations of the sacred Scriptures, as well as Christian tracts. This presupposes an accurate and scientific study of those languages, and the preparation of grammars and dictionaries, which, in order to be clearly understood, must be founded upon a comparison of the foreign with the European languages, and upon the latest improvements of linguistic science.

It was a sense of the necessity of such linguistic studies which induced the Church Missionary Society to send the Rev. *S. W. Kölle* — a missionary especially adapted to the work — to Sierra Leone, mainly to study the languages of the thousands of manumitted slaves which are brought together from all parts of Africa at that point. The results of this exceedingly important linguistic mission are a comparative vocabulary, comprising more than one hundred distinct African languages, and carefully prepared grammars of two important languages — the *Vai (Vei)* and the *Bornu.* These works are now published by the same Missionary Society, in order to form the foundation for future translations into those languages of the Bible and other useful books.

The various Bible Societies have made efforts on the largest scale to effect the same object. The *British and Foreign Bible Society* of London had published, down to the middle of the past year (1854), 26 millions of Bibles, or parts of the same, in 177 different translations. These translations embraced 150 different languages, of which 108 belonged to countries beyond the bounds of Europe, viz. 70 to Asia, 17 to Polynesia, 8 to America, and 13 to Africa[1].

---

[1] See the last Report of the Bible Society, and more on the same subject in the most valuable and interesting work of *Samuel Bagster*: *The Bible of every Land, a History of the Sacred Scriptures in every language and dialect into which translations have been made; illustrated with specimen portions in*

It was natural that the European system of writing should be used for all those languages which had no system of their own. But here the same question arose as in linguistic science: Which orthography ought to be used? Was it advisable to force upon those nations to which the Bible was to be presented as their first reading-book, the English orthography, which is complicated, irregular, and singular even in Europe? Was it suitable that those nations should be compelled to learn to read and write for all future time after this fashion? And according to what principles should those sounds be expressed which are neither fonnd in the English alphabet nor in any other European system?

As, in these respects, there was no general law or authority, every missionary who had such a translation to prepare struck out a way for himself, and sought, according to his own fancy, or from a very confined view of the case, to solve the difficulty. If we examine the long catalogue of Bibles printed in Latin characters we shall find the most multifarious systems of letters employed, often in cognate languages, and even in one and the same language. Sometimes difficult and unintelligible groupings of consonants are employed as representations of simple sounds; at other times a multitude of new and unexplained diacritical signs are employed; and often a refuge has been sought in the complete rejection of all diacritical marks, and thus the correct expression of the language has been sacrificed. The great and increasing confusion resulting from this arbitrary mode of proceeding must be apparent.

When the publication of the New Testament and Psalms in the language of the African *Tšuana* (Betchuana, Betjuana, Sechuana) was lately completed by the London Missionary Society, the Secretary of the Church Missionary Society expressed to the Secretary of the Paris Society the joy which

---

native characters, series of alphabets, coloured ethnographical maps, tables, indexes, etc. London, Sam. Bagster and Sons. 1851. 4to. In this book 247 different languages are noticed in connexion with Bible translations.

he felt when he thought of the rich blessings which would thence accrue to that people, and to the labours of the French missionaries scattered among them. „But," replied his sympathising friend, "is it not sad, that these thousands of copies already published are entirely unavailable and sealed to our French missionaries who labour among the same people, and to all those who have received instruction from them, simply because they make use of another orthography?"

To avoid such palpable evils in future is the purpose of the proposed standard alphabet.

In Asia, the birthplace of alphabets, the chief nations already possess a written literature in their own native characters. This has afforded to European colonists and rulers, as well as to missionaries, the means of exercising an intellectual influence over those nations. The English Government in India therefore generally makes use of the alphabets most extensively employed in those regions, viz. the Persian and the Dēvanāgari letters, in order to govern and instruct the nations subject to their authority. The Bible Societies have also published more than 40 translations of the Sacred Scriptures in those foreign characters. But, nevertheless, it has been often and forcibly urged, that many important advantages would arise from the substitution of a European for all the native alphabets. For besides the superiority which the uniform division of the syllable into vowel and consonant gives to the European alphabet over the unwieldy Syllabic Alphabets of Asia, and still more over the Chinese Word-Alphabet, with its many thousands of symbols, every new alphabet constitutes a natural and almost impassable barrier between foreign and European civilisation by materially increasing the difficulty of acquiring such languages, and of becoming acquainted with their literature.

Hence the introduction of the European characters for the Indian languages has been recognised by the Government, and Bible Societies have already published a number of translations upon the same system. Commencements of the same kind have already been made in China by the Missionaries, and bid fair to succeed.

In every one of these instances the question recurred: Which European orthography is to be adopted? Which alphabetical system best harmonises the different European orthographies, and allows most easily of the application of diacritical signs to represent sounds not contained in the languages of Europe?

To this practical question, our proposal endeavours to furnish the answer.

What has been done by Science for the Solution of this Problem, up to the present Time?

The want of a uniform orthography was first seriously felt with regard to the Oriental languages in the British possessions in India, where the study of those languages became a practical necessity. At the same time no country could better suggest a comprehensive discussion of this question; for here the two most perfect, and, at the same time, most opposite phonio and graphic systems, the Sanskrit and the Arabic, have met, and have been actually blended together in the Hindustāni alphabet. This alphabet being essentially Arabic, and expressing the different Sanskrit sounds by diacritical signs, we find here the problem, which we propose to ourselves in respect of the European graphic system, already fully and historically solved in the Arabic.

The first person who took a comprehensive view of these difficulties, and undertook their solution as a problem worthy of his special attention, was *Sir William Jones*, a man of great learning and cultivated mind. He was President of the Asiatic Society in Bengal, and opened the first volume of its Transactions, published in Calcutta in 1788, with an Essay *On the Orthography of Asiatic Words in Roman Letters.*[1]

[1] *Asiatic Researches*, vol. I. 1788, p. 1—56. The Essai was republished in the edition of his works, London, 1799.

He points out the desideratum in simple words[1], and lays down, as the first principle, that the *orthography of any language should never use the same letter for different sounds, nor different letters for the same sound*[2]; he complains also of the great complication and perplexity of the present English orthography in this respect. He declares himself opposed to the doubling of a vowel in order to represent its length; and in reference to the *vowel*-system he adopts the Italian or German notation. This was one of the most important steps towards reducing the European alphabets, as applied to foreign languages, to a uniform orthography.

In reference to the *consonants,* he complains principally of the mixing up of *Roman* and *Italic* letters in the same words.[3]

He justly admits (p. 13.) that the Sanskrit and Arabic alphabets represent the sounds of their languages so perfectly, that no character can be taken away from, or added to them, without

---

[1] The treatise begins: "Every man, who has occasion to compose tracts on *Asiatic* literature, or to translate from the *Asiatic* languages, must always find it convenient, and sometimes necessary, to express *Arabian*, *Indian*, and *Persian* words, or sentences, in the characters generally used among Europeans; and almost every writer in those circumstances has a method of notation peculiar in himself: but none has yet appeared in the form of a complete system, so that each original sound may be rendered invariably by one appropriated symbol, conformably to the natural order of articulation, and with a due regard to the primitive power of the Roman alphabet, which modern Europe has in general adopted. A want of attention to this object has occasioned great confusion in history and geography," etc.

[2] P. 7.: "Mr. Halhed (in his Bengal Grammar), having *justly* remarked, that the two greatest *defects* in the orthography of any language are the *application of the same letter to several different sounds*, and *of different letters to the same sound*, truly pronounces them both so common in English, that he was exceedingly embarrassed in the choice of letters to express the sound of the Bengal vowels, and even to the last was by no means satisfied with his own selection."

[3] P. 8.: "If anything *dissatisfies* me in Mr. Halhed's clear and accurate system, it is the use of *double* letters for the long vowels (which might, however, be justified) and the frequent intermixture of *Italic* and *Roman* letters in the same word; which both in *writing* and *printing* must be very inconvenient."

manifest injury: and he unhesitatingly takes his stand not only against the vain endeavour to represent *foreign* sounds by English letters, but also against the introduction of entirely new characters.

He therefore recomments, as the only suitable and efficient method, the use of certain diacritical signs, especially such as had already been adopted by several savans of France and England.

These views are throughout so sound and so well founded on practical experience, that even at the present time they command our full assent. If, nevertheless, the alphabet proposed by him was imperfect, this was owing partly to his defective knowledge of the general organism of sounds and of the distinct sounds to be represented, and partly to the imperfect application of his own principles.[1]

It is much to be regretted, that the distinguished scholar *Gilchrist*, who had published many valuable works on the Hindustāni language, and had thereby gained great influence in India, did not become acquainted with the essay of Sir William Jones till too late to make use of the system in his own works[2], as he afterwards wished he had done. It is principally owing to this circumstance, that the unsuitable English vowel-system according to which Mr. Gilchrist writes *ee* for *ī*, *oo* for *ū*, *ŏŏ* for *ŭ*, *ou* for *au*, was almost universally adopted in India.

It is only since 1834 that the correct principles of Sir William Jones have obtained in India the consideration due to their im-

[1] He took, for instance, the Arabic *χet* for an aspirate like the indian *kh*, and the Arabic *γaïn* for a compound sound instead of a simple one. He considered the Arabic Lingnals as so similar to the Indian Cerebrals that he employed the same characters for both, although they differ materially, and in the Hindustāni are placed by the side of one another. He also gives to the letter *h* different significations accordingly as it stands alone or in connection with other letters, as *sh* (= *š*), *th* (= *θ*), *ch* (= *č*), *ch'h* (= *čh*). In the same manner he assigns various valnes to the letters *c*, *s*, and others.

[2] *Grammar of the Hindoostanee Language*, by *John Gilchrist*. Calcutta, 1796. p. 1. His *English and Hindoostanee Dictionary* had been published in 1787.

portance. This change was brought about by the critical investigations and influential exertions of *Sir Charles Trevelyan*, who was, for many years, connected with the administration of India. He contended successfully against the English *vowel*-system, supported by the works of Mr. Gilchrist, and secured the more general adoption of the German, Italian, or ancient Latin method, as proposed by Sir W. Jones. The former system may now be regarded as antiquated in India.

But though the exertions of Sir W. Jones and Sir C. Trevelyan have introduced a more correct *vowel*-system, it yet remains that the same principles be applied to the *consonant*-system, in which there has been no amendment since the time of Sir W. Jones[1], although it has been equally needed.

In the meantime an event occurred in France, which directed the attention of the learned to the necessity of establishing a consistent system of transcribing foreign alphabets into European letters.

The scientific results of the famous Egyptian Expedition were directed to be published by a commission of the most distinguished scholars, appointed for that purpose. The Geographical Atlas, consisting of 47 maps of the largest size, contained nearly 5000 Arabic words. These were to be written in Latin letters, and upon an accurate and intelligible system. For this purpose special conferences were instituted in the year 1803, in which Messrs. *Volney*, *Monge*, *Bertholet*, *Langlès*, *Sylvestre de Sacy*, *Caussin*, *Lacroix*, *Baudeuf*, *Marcel*, and *Michel Abeyd* took part.

The first of these, *C. T. Volney* (who on account of his political services at a later period was made a Count by Napoleon and a Peer by Louis XVIII.), had written in 1795 an Arabic

---

[1] Mr. *John Pickering* also adopted the *vowel*-system of Sir W. Jones in his *Essay on a uniform Orthography for the Indian Languages of North America*, but he retarded rather than advanced a correct system of *Consonants*. This Essay was first published by the Amer. Acad. of Arts and Sciences, of which he was a member; and also separately in Cambridge, U. S., 1820.

grammar, under the title, *Simplification des langues orientales, ou méthode nouvelle et facile d'apprendre les langues Arabe, Persane et Turque, avec des caractères Européens, Paris, an III.* He here speaks of the advantage which the use of European letters affords in learning the Arabic language; and proposes a method for representing the Arabic alphabet in the Latin characters. This transcription was founded on no definite principles, but yet was guided by the correct feeling, that every simple sound should he represented by a single sign or character, a rule, from which he only deviated in one case, hy writing *ai* for *e*. This led him to seek some single signs to represent the three simple sounds not found in the Latin alphabet, viz. German *ch*, English *th* and *sh*. For the two first he chose the Greek letters χ and ϑ, but for the third he invented the entirely new character φ. All other foreign sounds he sought to represent by graphic modifications of the letters most nearly expressing those sounds, not indeed hy the addition of disconnected marks of distinction, but by a change of the characters themselves, as for instance, ꞩ, ŧ, đ, ƶ.

The Commission of 1803 started upon this principle, and adopted the system for the geographical maps, yet with a change of nearly all the single characters. This change aimed at simplification, but only suhstituted one arbitrary system in the place of another, and even gave up some material advantages of the first plan. The characters χ and ϑ were set aside for ƙ and ŧ, whereby these letters were erroneously placed among the *explosive* letters; and the representation of the German *sch* by the single character φ, which, though inconvenient, was right in principle, was given up for the inaccurate compound *ch*; and instead of ŧ, đ, etc., *t*, đ, were written. But they did not stop here; they introduced for the *Description de l'Egypte* an orthography which dispensed entirely with all diacritical signs; which on this account was hoth materially incorrect and decidedly antagonistic to the principle of using always a single character for a simple sound.[1] Thus they wrote *ou*, *ey*, *kh*, *gh*, *ch*, for our *u*, *e*, *χ*, *γ*, *š*.

With this method Volney himself could not be satisfied. He therefore took up the same subject again at a later period, and published in 1818 his well-known treatise: *L'Alphabet Européen appliqé aux Langues Asiatiques.* This title expresses more than the book contains. The first half of the volume is taken up with the investigation of those sounds which belong to the European languages, and shows that the writer possessed but little native talent for investigations of this nature.[2] The second half treats exclusively of the *Arabic* Alphabet into the sounds of which he likewise does not penetrate very deeply. For the linguals he gives up the curves, and adds instead a short line under each letter, viz. *ṯ*, *ḏ*, *s̱*, *ẕ*. The characters *k* or *kh* he changes again to *χ*, and *t* (= *ϑ*) to *ṯ* or *s̱*, and the character for the corresponding soft sound to *ẕ*. For *sh* he proposes a lengthened or old-fashioned *s*, viz. ſ, or an inverted *j*, *ʃ*; while for *h*, *g*, *g*, (= *ḱ*, *ǵ*, *γ*), he retains the additions, although he changes their forms. The notations of the vowels also underwent changes. At the close, he makes an attempt to apply his system of notation to the Hebrew, and the first line of his Hebrew Lord's Prayer will give a good idea of the awkwardness of this third method of writing. It is the following (p. 209.):

abinω ſ^i b^e ſ^amim i^o q^add^aſ ſ^em-k^a.

---

[1] Both transcriptions are placed by the side of the Arabic names in the *Index Géographique*, which forms vol. XVIII. of Panckoucke's edition.

[2] He discovers a difference between French *ée* or *ez* (*donnée*, *donnez*) and the simple *é* (*armé*, *bonté*), and finds the former again in the German *eh* (*dehnen*), the latter in the German *besser*, or in the English *red*, *head*: s. p. 49 – 52. He pronounces the nasal in the German *Anker* as in the French *Ancre*, p. 59; the German *z* he resolves into *ds*, p. 83; and the Arabic *γain* he calls a *grasseyement dur*, in opposition to the *grasseyement doux* of the modern Greek *γ*, p. 100. The German *ch* in *ich* he places as a *soft* sound by the hard sound in *buch*, p. 103, etc., etc.

No one of the three editions of Volney's system met with any approbation or adoption, because his proposal was based neither upon scientific nor upon practical principles, because it embraced in its field of view only the *Arabic* alphabet, and because it admitted no direct application to other languages and especially not to those of India.

His exertions, however, were not forgotten, as by his will he founded an annual prize to be conferred by the Institute of France. This legacy was designated: *Pour le meilleur ouvrage relatif à l'étude philosophique des langues*, and at the same time the wish was expressed: *d'encourager tout travail tendant à donner suite et exécution à une méthode de transcrire les langues Asiatiques en lettres Européennes.* This endowment, which was recognised by an Ordonnance of 1820, has produced many good results for the advancement of linguistic science, but it has conduced so little to the solution of the problem in question, that the French Academy finally determined to omit this subject in their Programme, and only to propose exercises on comparative grammar.[1] The system of Sir W. Jones, which had

---

[1] Compare *Mémoires de l'Institut de France*, Académie des Inscr. et Belles Lettres, tome XIV., Paris, 1845, p. 7 seqq. In the year 1835 a book appeared by A. E. Schleiermacher: *De l'Influence de l'écriture sur le language, Mémoire qui en 1828 a partagé le prix fondé par M. le comte de Volney, suivi de Grammaires Barmane et Malaie, et d'un aperçu de l'alphabet harmonique pour les langues Asiatiques que l'Institut Royal de France a couronné en 1827.* The author gives in the preface p. IX seqq. a transcription of the Dēvanāgari, the Bengāli, and four Slavonic alphabets, with respect to an *Alphabet harmonique*, which he exhibits in the *Aperçu* mentioned on the title. But, as in neither place the reasons of this transcriptions are developed, and as the complete Memoir on the *Alphabet harmonique* has hitherto not been published, we must abstain from offering any opinion on it. The peculiar division, however, in 16 *gutturales*, 12 *palatales*, 15 *sifflantes*, 16 *linguales*, 9 *labiales*, 9 *nasales*, and 16 *mêlées*, and the 5 subdivisions of *lettres simples*, *variées*, *fortes*, *mouillées*, and *aspirées*, seem to indicate that the author starts from a physiological and linguistic basis different from that which we consider the correct one. At the same time, however, the principle of using single signs for simple sounds is constantly observed.

proceeded upon more correct principles and upon a broader basis, was, indeed, occasionally alluded to by Volney, but never followed.

No language has a system of sounds more rich and regularly developed than the *Sanskrit*, or expresses them so perfectly by its alphabets. The old grammarians of India did not, indeed, invent the Dēvanāgari characters, but they brought them to the state of perfection which they now possess. With an acumen worthy of all admiration, with physiological and linguistic views more accurate than those of any other people, these grammarians penetrated so deeply into the relations of sounds in their own language, that we at this day may gain instruction from them, for the better understanding of the sounds of our own languages. On this account no language and no alphabet are better suited to serve, not indeed as an absolute rule, but as a starting-point for the construction of a *universal linguistic alphabet*, than that of ancient India.

Hence it is that the late progress in the solution of the alphabet-problem has been associated in Europe, as formerly in India, with Sanskrit studies; especially since these studies were made the foundation of the new science of Comparative Philology. Here *Bopp* took the lead. In the earlier editions of his *Sanskrit Grammar* he had still employed the German compounds *tsch*, *tschh*, *dsch*, *dschh*, *sch*, *ng*, *kh*, &c.; but later, in his *Comparative Grammar*, published in 1833, he introduced single letters for all these sounds, and distinguished the various classes of sounds by certain uniform diacritical marks. This orthography was soon adopted by the very numerous school of German and other linguists, and may now be regarded as the historical basis upon which, on account of its intrinsic value as well as its extensive use in science, the future superstructure must be built. *H. Brockhaus*[1], *Benary*, *Gorresio*, *Roth*, *Benfey*,

[1] We mention particularly his Essay *Ueber den Druck Sanscritischer Werke mit lateinischen Buchstaben, Leipzig 1841*, in which he presents important considerations on the scientific advantage of printing large Sanskrit works in Latin letters.

Böthlingk, *Müller*, *Stenzler*, *Lassen*, *Weber*, and many others have adopted this principle, although, in particular instances, they have often differed among themselves as to the choice of the diacritical marks. But all these men had either the *Sanskrit* language alone in view, or at most those of the same family.

On the other hand, the *Semitic* scholars were equally exclusive, and generally retained the use of *sh*, *kh*, *gh*, *th*, *dh*, for our *š*, *χ*, *γ*, *θ*, *δ̑*. Yet some among them acknowledge the principle of *single characters for simple sounds*, of whom we mention especially *Caspari* and *Fleischer*. The latter, an eminent scholar in the Semitic languages, and formerly himself a follower of the old method of writing, adopted in his *Persian Grammar*, published in 1847, the signs *ǵ*, *ć*, *ḥ*, *ḫ*, *ǵ*, *ś*, *j̈*, instead of the double letters; as he had at an carlier period[1] chosen the Greek chracter *θ* for the English *th*.

After progress had thus been made by both parties acting independently of each other, it became necessary to discover a general system which might comprehend the two most important, but at the same time most widely separated, groups of the principal kuown languages. And it was evident that such a comprehensive system required a broader basis than any which had heretofore been proposed. That basis was to be discovered in the common ground from which both had started, namely, the *physiology of the human voice*, which is the common ground and standard, not only for the two above-mentioned groups of languages, but also for all the langnages of the globe.

The human voice has its natural bounds, beyond which no development of sounds is possible. Hence the apparent infinitude of articulate sounds does not consist in a boundless extent, but rather in an endless divisibility, within assignable limits.

---

[1] In his Catalogue of the Arabic, Persian, and Turkish Manuscripts, in the *Catalogus librorum manuscr. in bibl. senator. Lipsiensi*, by *R. E. Naumann*. Grimmæ. 1838. 4°.

They may all be classified upon a physiological basis, so that every sound may find its proper position in the general system.

Since the laws of the physical organism are unchangeable, it is only necessary to understand them correctly, and to observe their application to linguistic science.

In this department much has been effected, and most important steps have been taken towards a solution of the problem. We may here refer to the labours of *Kempelen, Liscovius, Dzondi, Willis, Brücke, Czermak*, and principally to the researches of *Joh. Müller.*[1]

The results also of physiological investigations have in several instances been applied to the science of language by *R. von Raumer, Rapp, Schleicher, Bindseil, Heyse*, and others.

Hence it appears that all previous conditions of the problem have been fulfilled. It has become possible to construct an alphabet, based on physiological principles, answering all the requirements of linguistic science, and embracing all the sounds contained in the two great alphabetical systems of Asia. This possibility alone justified, and indeed demanded, a new effort to reach the goal. Nevertheless, this attempt might perhaps have still been long deferred, or even given up entirely, on account of the great practical difficulties which oppose every attempt at union in the republic of letters, if another and more lively impulse had not been given to it, within the last few years, from *another quarter.*

What has been done by the MISSIONARY SOCIETIES *for the Solution of the Question?*

We have stated above, that the want of a uniform alphabet for those nations which are to be gained over to Christianity and civilisation, and which have no written language, is more and more strongly felt every day in missionary labours. The

---

[1] *Handbuch der Physiologie des Menschen*, Band 2. p. 180 sqq. 1840.

difficulty of introducing a convenient alphabet into practice is here much less than in the scientific world, as the Directors may recommend such an alphabet to the missionaries dispersed over the whole earth, which will usually be a sufficient motive for its reception.

The first recommendation from such a quarter was issued in the year 1848 by the Hon. Secretary of the *Church Missionary Society*, the Rev. *Henry Venn*, under the title, *Rules for reducing unwritten languages to alphabetical writing in Roman characters, with reference especially to the languages spoken in Africa.* We quote the first two paragraphs, which represent the missionary point of view in a clear and comprehensive manner: "The want of a standard system of orthography has been experienced by all persons engaged in the study of unwritten languages. Each translator having to choose his own system, it has not unfrequently happened that two or more persons engaged upon the same language have adopted different systems. This has prevented, in a great measure, the mutual assistance, which the parties might have rendered each other; and has retarded the formation of primers and educational works, and the translation of the Holy Scriptures."

"To obviate these difficulties, several of the Missionary Societies, whose missionaries are engaged in Vernacular Translations of African languages, have proposed the adoption of a common system of orthography, to be regarded as a standard system, and to be employed, as far as possible, in all works printed under their sanction. If in any particular case deviations from the system be thought necessary by the Translators, it is proposed that *such deviations should be referred home* before their adoption in printed works."

This proposal adopts and consistently maintains the true principle, that every simple sound is to be expressed by a single sign, and rectifies the English vowel-system.

In the year 1849, the attention of the *American Mission of*

Port Natal was drawn towards the difficulties of the orthography adopted for the Zulu language, and they submitted the subject to the examination of a committee.

About the same time the want of new signs for newly discovered African sounds, was felt in several other African Missions; and some such signs were introduced into various books, as in those published by the *Norwegian Society at Natal*, by the *English Church Mission among the Suahēli* on the eastern coast, and by the *American board on the Gaboon river* in the west, also in *Appleyard's Kaffir Grammar*, printed for the *Wesleyan Society*, at King William's Town. These circumstances led the Committee at *Port Natal*, in March, 1850, to address a general circular to the friends of Missions and African civilisation, proposing a plan for securing a uniform orthography for writing the South African dialects. In further pursuance of their plan, an essay was communicated in October, 1852, to the Conference of the *American Oriental Society*, at New York, and printed in vol. III. No. II. 1853, p. 421. sqq. of the Publications of this Society, under the title, *An Essay on the Phonology and Orthography of the Zulu and kindred dialects in Southern Africa*, by the Rev. *Lewis Grout*, Miss. of the Amer. Board in Southern Africa.

The general principles and requirements of an alphabet, adopted especially for African languages, are here developed with accuracy and acumen, and are applied in particular to the *Zulu* language, including the clicks peculiar to the most southern African languages. This alphabet, however, is not based on a sufficiently comprehensive system of phonology, and the single letters consequently are not arranged according to their natural affinities. The Sanskrit and other written languages were not taken into account, and the former use of compound consonants is supplied partly by altering the form of letters, partly by combining them with diacritical signs, as ŋ, ẏ, ħ, ṛ, ſ, or ., or *s*, or s̄, for our *ṅ*, *ń*, *χ*, *γ*, *š*.

In the Autumn of 1852, the author of the present paper, being in London, had the opportunity of discussing this subject (which had occupied his mind for several years) with some of the most influential members of Missionary Committees: and he was invited by the Rev. H. Venn to furnish him with a development of his alphabet, which appeared suitable for general adoption and conformable on the whole to the "*Rules*." Mr. Venn proposed to transmit such an explanation of the alphabet to the Missionaries. Prevented, at that time, from complying with this wish, he simply communicated a tableau of the alphabet, which was inserted by Mr. Venn in a second edition of the "*Rules*" in 1853.

Soon afterwards the author was again induced to direct his special attention to this subject, by a visit of the Rev. *S. W. Kölle*, in consequence of which he determined to bring forward his own long prepared project, after discussing it minutely with this gentleman, whose valuable contributions to African philology have been already mentioned. It was now judged proper to publish the proposed alphabet, which had hitherto only been communicated privately to several of the most distinguished linguistic scholars.

The author therefore resolved to explain the principles of his plan in an essay to be read in a general sitting of the *Academy of Berlin*, and to propose at the same time that the Academy should examine the alphabet in question, and, if approved, have types cut and cast for printing it. This proposal was laid before the historico-philological class, and a committee appointed, composed of Professors *Bopp*, *Jacob Grimm*, *Pertz*, *Gerhard*, *Buschmann*, with the assistance of Professor *J. Müller* from the physical class. This Committee approved the plan, with the exception of one member who denied in general the usefulness of all such endeavours; and on the 23rd of January *the Class ordered the cutting and casting of the proposed types*, which have consequently been used in the present pages.

About the same time, the interest on the subject having greatly increased, chiefly from the progress of Missions, a new step was taken in London for the furtherance of the object in view. Chevalier *Bunsen*, whose reputation as a statesman, a scholar, and a friend of every important Christian movement is universally acknowledged, called a meeting of distinguished men, more or less interested in the question, among whom we may name, Profs. *Wilson, M. Müller, Owen, Dietrich*, Sir *C. Trevelyan*, Sir *John Herschel*, Hon. Mr. *Stanley*, Messrs. *Norris, Pertz* from Berlin, *Babbage, Wheatstone*, and *Cull;* the Rev. Messrs. *Venn, Chapman*, Dr. *Trumpp*, and *Kölle*, and Mr. *Graham* of the Church Missionary Society, — the Rev. Mr. *Arthur* of the Wesleyan Missionary Society, — the Rev. Mr. *Trestrail* and Mr. *Underhill* of the Baptist Missionary Society. The author also had the honour of being invited to this meeting, and was happy to be present at the three last conferences. These were occupied principally with the physiological basis, which was generally acknowledged to be necessary, and was adopted without much dissent by the assembly.

With regard to the graphic system to be employed, *three* different proposals were examined.

The *first* was supported by Sir *Charles Trevelyan* (above, p. 31), who recommended the orthography which originated with Sir W. Jones, and which has been frequently applied in India. Its merits and soundness, in comparison with that of Gilchrist, were fully acknowledged; but at the same time its want of a physiological basis, and of a complete development in detail, could not be overlooked.

The *second*, by Prof. *M. Müller*, proposed to mark the deviations from known European sounds by printing the known letters in *Roman* characters, the foreign in *italics*. The principal objections against this intermixture of Roman and italic letters, of which Sir W. Jones had already decidedly disapproved (see above, p. 29), were the following: — This plan would exclude the ordinary significance of italics, which could hardly be supplied by any other means; neither is it applicable at all to writing. On these grounds it would prove most inconvenient for all missionary purposes. It would not meet the cases in which a European letter undergoes more than one modification, and would thus be incapable of expressing even whole classes of sounds. Finally, this theory, neglecting the continuity of historical development, introduces a novelty, which it can hardly be expected will be universally adopted.[1]

The *third* proposal was that of the author, and its object was only to bring the orthography hitherto used in science into more exact conformity with the laws of physiology, and to adapt it to practical purposes.

The object of the meetings was rather to prepare the question for further discussion and examination, than to adopt resolutions which should be considered as binding. The physiological system of phonology upon which the proposed alphabet had been based, was acknowledged to be substantially sound. And the author considers himself justified in stating that with respect also to the graphic system the views of the majority did not widely differ from his proposal.

The most important result of this conference, in the author's apprehension, was the determination announced at the last meeting in reference to *the practical object of this alphabet.* Mr. Venn expressed his "conviction that the interests of Missions would allow of no longer delay in the adoption of a *standard alphabet:* that the Church Missionary and other Societies had already substantially adopted, for this purpose, that of Professor Lepsius: and that as nothing had been concluded upon by this conference which held out any prospect of superseding or materially improving it, he and the parties with whom he acted must go forward in the course upon which they had

[1] [See Preface of this edition p. 12.]

entered; and without pledging their Missionaries to the adoption of every mark or sign, in every case, they must put forward Professor Lepsius's system as *the standard;* and all departures from it must be carefully canvassed, and marked as deviations, in works printed by the Societies."

The author was also requested to draw up the present sketch for the purpose of communication to missionaries. At the same time the Berlin Academy was requested to have two sets of their types struck off for the Church Missionary Society, that the forms of the characters might be identical; and orders were given for the execution in these types of two works on African languages, already prepared for the press.

It is hoped that this determination may be favourably regarded by all other Missionary Societies. We do not expect that everybody should agree in every detail of this alphabet; but it is not unreasonable to hope that it will be considered as a *standard*, and as affording a common basis by which other alphabets may be brought into the greatest possible agreement. Different languages may require different modifications. No language will require *all* the diacritical signs which must appear in the complete alphabet; while some languages may require still other marks of distinction peculiar to themselves. It is therefore necessary that the system should be elastic enough to admit of such reduction and enlargement without alteration in its essential principles. Cases may even arise in which material deviations from the proposed alphabet may appear unavoidable, and be advocated, on sufficient grounds, by scholars engaged in such researches. In all such cases, it is hoped that the Committees of Societies will require the reasons of such deviations to be laid before them and discussed, before the deviations are introduced into books printed by their authority. This principle is most important for the furtherance of the object in view, and was repeatedly insisted upon by Mr. Venn, as indeed it had been already laid down in the "*Rules*" (see above) issued by the Committee of his Society in the year 1848.

After these preliminaries we pass on to develop

The System proposed.

A comprehensive exposition of the *physiological basis* would here be out of place. We must limit ourselves to facilitating the understanding of the system. This will be best accomplished by not separating the phonic from the graphic system, but by presenting the former immediately in its application to the latter. We do not enlarge, therefore, on the definition of *Voice* and *Sound*, of *Vowel* and *Consonant*, and other physiological explanations, and shall only refer to them as necessity may demand.

A. The System of Vowels.

There are three primary vowels, as there are three primary colours. Like the latter, they can be best represented by the analogy of a triangle, at the top of which is to be placed *a*, at the basis *i* and *u* (pronounced as in the German and Italian languages).

The other vowels are formed between these three, as all colours between red, yellow, and blue. In the most ancient languages these three primary vowels only were sufficiently distinct to be marked in writing even when short. The Hieroglyphical, Indian, oldest Hebrew, and Gothic systems of writing admitted either of no other vowels at all, or at least of no other *short* vowels; in Arabic writing, even now, none but these three are distinguished.

Next after these were formed, the intermediate vowels *e* between *a* and *i*, *o* between *a* and *u*, and the sound of the German *ü* (French *u*) between *i* and *u*, also that of the German *ö* (French *eu*) between *e* and *o*. Thus arose the pyramid[1]

a

e *ö* *o*

i *ü* *u*

The distance between *a* and *i* and that between *a* and *u* is greater than that between *i* and *u*. The intermediate vowels *e* and *o* were, therefore, divided each into *two* vowels, of which one was nearer to *a*, the other nearer to *i* or *u*; and in the same manner two sounds were formed out of *ö*. All these vowels exist in European languages, and compose the following pyramid:

Germ. *a*

Fr. *è* Fr. *eu* (in *peur*) *ò* Ital.

Fr. *é* Fr. *eu* (in *peu*) *au* Fr.

Germ. *i* Germ. *ü* *u* Germ.

We might have wished to maintain for the middle series of vowels the two dots over the *u* and *o*, on account of the generally known precedent in the German orthography, the French double letter *eu* not answering the simple nature of the sound. A practical objection, however, to this mode is found in the circumstance, that occasionally over every vowel the sign of long ¯ and short ˘, and also that of the accent of the word ʹ will be necessary, for which the whole space over the letter is required. We have preferred, therefore, to preserve the two dots, and to place them under the vowel, as *o̤* and *ṳ*.

The distinction of the two modes of pronouncing *e* and *o* cannot be marked by the French accents, partly because the upper space is wanted for other signs too generally in use to be dispensed with, and partly because the acute accent would

[1] It may be compared with the following pyramid of primary and mixed colours:

red,

orange, *brown,* *violet,*

yellow, *green,* *blue.*

not be distinguished from the accent of the word. We add, therefore, as others have done before us, a line below to mark the broad open vowels e̱, o̱, and a dot below, to mark the pointed and closed vowels ẹ, ọ, the shape of these marks offering a certain analogy to the pronunciation itself.

From these combinations, the following system results.

a

e̱ ö̱ o̱

ẹ ọ̈ ọ

i ü u

We must mention, however, one other vowel, which exists in almost all languages, and ought not to be neglected by linguists. This is the *indistinct vowel-sound* from which, according to the opinion of some scholars, the other vowels, as it were, issued and grew into individuality, and to which the unaccented vowels of our non European languages in their old age often return, as in the English words nati*o*n, velv*e*t; the German lieb*e*n, V*e*rstand; the French sabr*e*, t*e*nir. This vovel comes among the clear sounding vowels next to ö, being itself a mixture of all the others, but it is capable of various shades, and sometimes approaches nearer to *a*, and sometimes to *i* or *u*. From all of these, however, as also from ö, it is distinguished by the absence of that clear resonance common to the others, which is lost by partially contracting the mouth or even closing it entirely: in the latter case it is heard through the nose.[1] This vowel is inherent in all soft *fricative* consonants, as well as in the first part of the *nasal explosive* sounds (see below); whence all these letters as r̥, n̥, m̥, appear sometimes as forming syllables.[2] It assumes the strongest resonance, as may be easily explained on physiological grounds,

[1] It may be compared to *grey*, which also does not belong to the series of individual colours.

[2] In the Chinese language, for instance, z̥ is used as a vovel in the roots *sz̥*, *tsz̥*.

in combination with *r* and *l*, which, as is well known, appear in Sanskrit as *r̥* and *l̥*, with all the qualities of the other vowels. We should feel inclined to represent this sound by the Greek letter *ε*, in order to distinguish it more fully from all the other vowels, and to fall in with the practice of Ludolf, Isenberg, Piccolomini, and others. However, there are strong objections to this: for it is not only very desirable to confine ourselves as much as possible to the use of Latin characters, but the ancient and modern pronunciation of the Greek *ε* is also as different from the sound we wish to represent as that of the Latin *ĕ*. Besides this, we represent the same sound in the vocalised consonants by a little circle (as *l̥*, *r̥*, *n̥*), and so it seems but natural to transfer this mark to the vowels. Accordingly we take the letter *e*, which, in most European orthographies, is used for an indefinite vowel [1], and subscribe the little circle to it (*e̥*). Hereby we gain the advantage that we can easily provide signs for those cases where the indefinite vowel approaches more closely to any of the common vowels, by subscribing the circle to them (as *ḁ*, *i̥*, *o̥*, *u̥*). Such a case occurs, e. g., in the Kanuri or Bornu language, where Mr. Kölle [2] finds it necessary to distinguish between *e̥* and *ḁ*.

[If we compare herewith the vowel-system of the English language and certain dialectic shades of vowels in other European languages, this pyramid of the vowels, it is true, is not sufficient for their complete notation. In the English language a new degree comes in between the top of the pyramid formed by the pure *a*, and the first row from it viz. *ė̱ o̱ o̱*. It will not be useless perhaps to add some observations on this point, although these sounds as far as we know are not developed in the foreign languages which form our special object, and it would therefore hardly seem necessary to settle their transcription.

[1] *Burnouf*, *Roger*, *Endlicher*, *Petermann*, *Edwards*, also *Bopp* and *Schön* and others write *ĕ*.

[2] In his *Grammar of the Bórnu or Kanuri Language*. London, 1854.

In the English language the pure full *a* has almost entirely disappeared, being divided into two sounds, one of which approaches to *e*, the other to *o*, both still bearing traces of their origin. This applies still more to the short than to the long sound. Although the *ā* in *father*, *master*, *past*, *half*, *demand*, *aunt*, *papa*, is not unfrequently pronounced pretty full and most resembling to the German and Italian *a*, yet according to others the most approved pronunciation softens its sound perceptibly towards *e*. We may write it for the present $\underset{e}{\bar{a}}$. Still more decidedly the short *a* of *hat*, *catch*, *have*, *wax*, *marry* takes the same direction. On the other side it is well known how nearly the *a* in *water*, *all*, *broad*, *fault*, approaches to *o*. It is more open i. e. it is nearer to the *a* than the French *o* is in *or*, *encore*, *sonne*. Let us indicate it now by $\underset{o}{\bar{a}}$. The corresponding short sound is heard in *what*, *wasp*, as well as in *hot*, *horrid*, and is more open than *o* in the French *vote*, the German *Gott*. On the same degree of the scale as the sounds $\underset{e}{a}$ and $\underset{o}{a}$ we find a short sound in the middle column which leads from *a* to $\underset{..}{o}$ and $\underset{..}{u}$, viz. the vowel in *but*, *cut*, *son*, *does*, *blood* a sound still more peculiar to the English language. We might, following the analogy of the two other sounds of this row, write it $\underset{\ddot{u}}{a}$, but we prefer the simpler notation $\underset{i}{o}$. Thus we get as a new row peculiar to the most approved English pronunciation the line of sounds $\underset{e}{a}$ $\underset{i}{\breve{o}}$ $\underset{o}{a}$.

Another peculiarity of the English language by which the vowel system is influenced, is the double pronunciation of *r*. When this letter is followed by a vowel, it is pronounced as a dental consonant with the top of the tongue as in other languages. When it closes a syllable or is followed by a consonant or a mute vowel, it changes its nature and becomes a vowel, exactly in the same sense in which the ancient Indians looked upon their $\underset{\circ}{r}$ as a vowel; to which it would correspond exactly if it were not pronounced on the guttural instead of the cerebral point of the mouth. The tongue and the soft palate are put, at the guttural point, into a slight sounding vibration without friction. The dental *r* thus becomes a guttural vocalic *r*, which in our system may be rendered very accurately by ṙ̥. This sound appears most unblended in words like *fur*, *her*, *Sir*, *word*, *waiter*, *steward*, *splendour* &c. The same sound becomes distinctly perceptible, like the second half of the diphthongs *iṙ̥ eṙ̥ uṙ̥ oṙ̥ aiṙ̥ auṙ̥* in words like *year*, *swear*, *moor*, *borne*, *hire*, *hour;* but it blends more closely with the vowels of the higher degrees, in *aṙ̥ aṙ̥ oṙ̥*, as in *far*, *war*, *born*, *curve*, because *a a o* are formed at a spot nearer to the place of its own. As a short sound it appears only in mute or quite unaccented syllables of the common conversation like *eṙ̥* or *ṙ̥*, as in *waiter*, *steward.* When such a diphthong is followed by a vowel, ṙ̥ is resolved into the consonant *r*, as is the Sanskrit *ṛ* in *r*, f. i. *star*, *starry; abhor*, *abhorrent; swear*, *swearing*, which are pronounced: *staṙ̥*, *stāri; ăbhaṙ̥*, *ăbhărent; sweṙ̥*, *swērin.* The *preceding* vowels in these combinations have no distinct qualification of long or short, but must be considered as ambiguous, in a similar manner as the nasalized vowels in the French language; yet together with ṙ̥ they always form a *long* sound, being a diphthong. Frequently ṙ̥ exercises an influence upon the quality of the vowels combined with it; and certain vocalic shades are pronounced only before ṙ̥; f. i. *o* in *oṙ̥* is more closed than *ọ*, *curtain* being pronounced more closed than *cut;* and even *eṙ̥* and *oṙ̥* in *swear*, *four* seem to be pronounced somewhat more open than *ẹ* and *ọ* in *way* and *no*, not distinctly enough, it is true, to take notice of.

In the French language also the pure *a* not unfrequently inclines towards an altered pronunciation. In *Paris*, *femme* it has clearly a sharper sound; and in common language *ḁ* is often heard instead of *ā* in *passer* and others, and *ḁ̆* instead of *ă* in *pas* and others. In Germany also: *ḁ̆* is a provincial pronunciation, as in Prussia proper *Fḁ̆nster* is spoken instead of *Fenster*, whilst *ḁ̄* and *ḁ̆* are frequently heard in the common Saxon dialect. In the south of Germany ę̆ is decidedly distinct from ĕ or ẹ̆, f. i. in *Bętt*, *Stęlle* by the side of *fętt*, *bęllen* &c. On the contrary people born in Berlin do not distinguish ē or ę̄ from ẹ̄, but pronounce *wẹr*, *bẹten* instead of *wę̄r*, *bē̦ten*.

These remarks will suffice to explain the following table, into the details of which it is not necessary to enter, though they may perhaps imply some slight deviation from what has been received hitherto; we add a few examples of pronunciation.

English.

	ā(ă)ar̥	
(ā)ă(ar)	- ọ̆ -	ā ă ar
- ę̆ -	- - or	- - -
ẹ̄ - ẹr	- - -	ọ̄ - ọr
ī ĭ ịr	- - -	ū ŭ ur

French.

	ā ă ã	
(ā)(ă) -	- - -	(ā)(ă) -
ę̄ ę̆ ę̃	ǭ ǫ̆ ǫ̃	ọ̄ ǫ̆ ǫ̃
ẹ̄ - -	ọ̄ - -	ọ̄ - -
ī ĭ -	ū ŭ -	ū ŭ -

German.

	ā ă	
(ā)(ă)	- -	(ā)(ă)
ę̄ ę̆	- ǫ̆	- ǫ̆
ẹ̄ (ẹ̆)	ọ̄ -	ọ̄ (ọ̆)
ī ĭ	ū ŭ	ū ŭ

English				French				German			
ā	*past*	ā	*naught*	ā	*mâle*	ǫ̆	*un*	ā	*That*	ǫ̆	*Sonde*
ar	*heart*	ŏ	*what, hot*	ă	*mal*	ọ̄	*peu*	ă	*hat*	ọ̄	*Mond*
ă	*hat*	ar	*war*	ã	*an*	ū	*sûr*	ę̄	*Bär*	ū	*gut*
ę̆	*head*	ọ̄	*note*	ę̄	*être*	ŭ	*sur*	ę̆	*fett*	ŭ	*Kutte*
ẹ̄	*hate*	ọr	*borne*	ę̆	*nette*	ọ̄	*cor*	ẹ̄	*Weh*		
ẹr	*swear*	ū	*hoot*	ę̃	*lin*	ǫ̆	*vote*	ī	*mir*		
ī	*heat*	ŭ	*hood*	ẹ̄	*épée*	ǫ̃	*on*	ĭ	*mit*		
ĭ	*hit*	ur	*moor*	ī	*cîme*	ọ̄	*cône*	ǫ̆	*Hörner*		
ịr	*year*			ĭ	*vite*	ū	*sourd*	ọ̄	*König*		
ọ̆	*hut*			ǭ	*peur*	ŭ	*sourde*	ū	*Thür*		
or	*fur*			ǫ̆	*heurter*			ŭ	*dürr*		

If we leave out of question the prosodial length, the complete pyramid of the European vowels may thus be traced:

a

a ọ a

ę ǫ ǫ

ẹ ọ ọ

i ụ u

But we have already observed that this accurate subdivision of vowels in our European languages needs not be applied to foreign languages. It would even be practically inconvenient to look for and to denote such subdivisions, instead of ranging them, where they may exist, under the more general heads — as far as it can be done without offence to the linguistic feeling. We should therefore not hesitate to reduce eventually the above pyramid to the simpler one without the second row, by the following parallelisms:

	English.	French.	German.
ā	*past, heart*	*mâle*	*That*
ă	*hat*	*mal*	*hat*
ã	—	*an*	—
ę̄	—	*être*	*Bär*
ę̆	*head*	*nette*	*fett*
ę̃	—	*lin*	—
ẹ̄	*hate, swear*	*épée*	*Weh*
ī	*heat, year*	*cîme*	*mir*
ĭ	*hit*	*vite*	*mit*
ō̤	—	*peur*	—
ŏ̤	*hut, fur*	*heurter*	*Hörner*
õ̤	—	*un*	—
ọ̤̄	—	*peu*	*König*
ṳ̄	—	*sûr*	*Thür*
ṳ̆	—	*sur*	*dürr*
ǭ	*naught, war*	*cor*	—
ǫ̆	*what, hot*	*vote*	*Sonde*
ǫ̃	—	*on*	—
ọ̄	*note, borne*	*cône*	*Mond*
ū	*hoot, moor*	*sourd*	*gut*
ŭ	*hood*	*sourde*	*Kutte*

We pass to another question respecting the vowels and ask: what is the position of the Russian "hard" *i* ы, the Polish *y*, in our system? We have to answer it so much the more as this vowel appears also in many other eastern languages.

The vowel *ų* takes the middle between *i* and *u*. The physiological reason is that in forming the *i*, the lips are broad, the tongue slightly elevated and stretched out, whilst, in forming the *u* the lips are round and put forwards, the tongue drawn back in itself, so that in the forepart of the mouth a cavity is formed, the diameter of which is greater than its entrance and issue; which is the reason of the hollow sound of this vowel. In forming the *ų*, the lips have the position of the *u*, the tongue the position of the *i*. So we are right in saying that *ų* takes the middle between *i* and *u*. But it is on the other hand evident, that there must exist still another middle which has the same right to be counted as a peculiar sound. For we may form a vowel in such a manner, that the lips take the broad position of the *i*, and the tongue is withdrawn as in the *u*. This is the vowel which is called in the Slavonic languages the hard *i*, the *yerį* ы of the Russians, which we write *į*.

The origin however of this sound is, according to my opinion, not in the Slavonic, but in the Tataric languages, where we find it in the Turkish, Turkmenic, Yakutic, and other cognate languages. Here this vowel is an essential part of the so called harmonic vowel system, whose peculiar arrangement demanded it as a necessary complement[1]. Vestiges of

[1] Without entering into the details of this question, we remark only, that the distinction of the lower and darker vowels *a o u* on the one side, and the sharper and clearer vowels *e ǫ ų i* on the other, exists in all languages and manifests itself in different ways. The same opposition however is of much greater influence in those languages, where it forms, as in the Mantschu, Mongolian, Kalmuki, Turkish, Jakutic, Hungrian, Finnic and others, the basis of the "vocalic harmony." There the three "hard" vowels *a o u*, which are pronounced in withdrawing the tongue, correspond to the opposite "soft" vowels *e ǫ ų*, which are pronounced in stretching out the tongue. The fourth "soft" vowel *i* would have no corresponding "hard" vowel, if it were not the vowel *į*, which is formed in drawing back the

it are even found in the Dravidic languages of India. Although there are intermediate vowels between *a* and *i̬*, as there are between *a* and *ṳ*, *a* and *i*, *a* and *u*, all these languages have taken up only the one vowel *i̬*, because this is the most distinct vowel of the column and the only one they wanted for their parallelism of vowels. There is however at least one language known to me, which makes use also of a second vowel of the *a—i̬* column, viz. the one which corresponds to *ọ*, as *i̬* corresponds to *ṳ*. The Rumanic or Wallachian language, as spoken north of the Danube, distinguishes a lower and a sharper vowel of the same kind, so as to fill up the place left open for it in our system.

We should like to keep for the sharper sound the Polish writing *y*. But this sign is already generally received for the semivowel of the palatals, and moreover would not be fit to form at the same time the basis for the deeper sound of the Rumanic language by taking a diacritical mark, because this mark ought to be added below where the space is occupied by the tail of the letter. No doubt, the basis of the sharper sound must be *i*, of the deeper sound *e*. They demand a common diacritical mark, different from those, which are already in use for other purposes (*i̥ e̥ ẹ ȩ*). We regret not to find any symbol already adopted and therefore propose as a clear and convenient sign for handwriting to put the angle below *i̬ e̬*.

The vowel-pyramid of our system takes in consequence the following form, where the new vowels *i̬ e̬* may be put with the same propriety on the *e—i* side or on the *o—u* side.

		a					*a*		
	e	*e̬*	*ọ*	*o*	or	*e*	*ọ*	*e̬*	*o*
	i	*i̬*	*ṳ*	*u*		*i*	*ṳ*	*i̬*	*u*
Lips:	broad	broad	round	round		broad	round	broad	round
Tongue:	forward	back	forward	back		forward	forward	back	back

---

tongue as far as the palatal point in the middle of the hard roof of the palate. Now there is a regular correspondence between *a o u i* and *e ọ ṳ i*.

In most of the European languages the "soft" vowels of the middle have supplanted the "hard" ones. In the Rumanic language the contrary has taken place, and in the Slavonic also no *o̤* or *ṳ* has been received, but only *ị*, as the following comparison shows.

German.	Rumanic.	Polish.	Russian.
a	*a*	*a*	*a*
e,ẹ o̤ o	*e ẹ o*	*e - o*	*e,ẹ - o*
i ṳ u	*i ị u*	*i ị u*	*i ị u*

In the languages however of the Turks and Jakuts the parallelism of the "vowel-harmony" has called forth the **two** forms between *i* and *u*, viz. *ị* and *ṳ*. The deeper sound *ẹ* has not been received; it would have been the most perfect corresponding "hard" vowel to the "soft" one *e*. But it has been in this respect supplanted by its nearest neighbour *a*, which in reality is neither "hard" nor „soft", or both together. The parallelism became

hard: *a o u ị* instead of *(a)* *ẹ o u ị*
soft: *e o̤ ṳ i*   *e o̤ ṳ i*

or according to our pyramidal arrangement the Turkish and Yakutic vowels are

a   *a*
e [ẹ] o̤ o instead of *e ẹ ö o*
i ị ṳ u   *i ị ṳ u*

It would be interesting to know, if there is no cognate language, where this last form of vowel harmony has been developed.

Similar, but not to be confounded, is another formation of vowels which one might call **Gutturalisation**. In no language, as far as I know, this formation has been independently organized as a peculiar part of the vowel system. But it has got a secondary influence in the Semitic languages, especially in the Arabic.

In forming the *ị*, the middle tongue is lifted up to the palatal point in the middle of the hard roof of the palate; from this point forward it slopes down almost perpendicularly so as to leave a cavity between this point and the teeth. We may however also pronounce an *i* in lifting up the tongue only to the deeper guttural point near the velum palati, and in pressing down the whole middle part of the tongue so as to form a cavity between the concave and lengthened tongue and the roof of the mouth. This position of the tongue is very different from the shortened shape of it in forming the *ị*. The tone of the vowel becomes generally somewhat deeper then the tone of the ordinary *i*. The change of formation and sounding is less in the other vowels and almost none in uttering the *ọ*, because also the ordinary pronunciation of this vowel is formed at the deeper guttural point. Again the vowel *a*, which is formed beyond the guttural point in the larynx itself, can not be pronounced purely with the same guttural motion of the tongue; it approaches perceptibly in its pronunciation to the *ọ*.

In the Arabic language this "gutturalisation" of the vowels is distinctly heard after and in conseqnence of, certain consonants. The Arabic Orthoëpists call this pronunciation the "thick" or "fat" one, the modern Grammarians use to call it the "emphatic" pronunciation. It is very naturally connected with the deep guttural consonants, which are with predilection developed in all the Semitic languages, and besides with the four linguals, viz. *k̔ ; q*, *χ γ*, *ḏ(ṯ) ḏ̂ ẕ ẕ*, sometimes also with *l* and *r*; it is not connected, and could not be, with ʾ and *h*, which are formed behind the deep guttural point in the larynx, nor with *k*, which, as well as *k̔ š̔ y* and all the rest, is pronounced before the same deep guttural point. But it strikes us as a peculiarity of the Semitic languages, that this gutturalisation of the vowels takes place after the four letters *ḏ(ṯ) ḏ̂ ṣ ẕ*, which are called by the Arabs, for this very reason, the "closed" letters, meaning the cavity-letters, and by the modern Linguists conventionally, though very improperly, the "lingual" letters. They are principally distinguished from the dental letters *d ð s z* by the circumstance that in pronouncing them with the forepart of the tongue, the throat is contemporaneously narrowed at the deep guttural point, as if one of these gutturals was to be uttered. This movement of the throat not only causes a somewhat different position of the forepart of the tongue from the dental position, but it imparts to them also the thick emphatic sound, which they transmit to the following vowels in gutturalising them. In the same way also *l* and *r* may be pronounced (as well as *n*, although it is not mentioned), if they are preceded by a lingual consonant without an intervening vowel. In the word اللّٰه *Allah* the *l* after *a* and *u* is always and by law of the orthoëpists pronounced emphatically. It is in this case no other letter then the Slavonic "hard" *l*, the Polish ł, (which in consequence is to be written in our system *l̦*.

It must be granted that the "thick" pronunciation of the vowels in the Semitic languages proceeds really from the consonants and has therefore no linguistic value in itself, because this vocalic tone appears exclusively after the said consonants which, on their part, keep their peculiar pronunciation even if they close a word or are followed immediately by another consonant. It is evident therefore that we have also in our transcription, as in the indigenous writing, not to express the gutturalisation, either in the vowels, or in the guttural consonants, but only in the lingual consonants *d̦(ț) ð̦ ș z̦* and in the Slavonic *l̦*.]

Finally, the clear vowels are further capable of a peculiar alteration, that of *nasalisation*. This is produced not by closing nor even by narrowing the canal of the mouth, but by simultaneously opening the canal of the nose. There is no consonantal element brought into play (although the nasalisation is mostly caused by the dropping of a nasal consonant), but it is an alteration entirely within the vowel. As such it has been rightly understood by the Indian Grammarians, who express the nasalisation (anusvāra) by a vowel-like sign, namely, by placing a dot over the letter. For the European alphabet, we choose the sign ˜ placed over the vowel[1], as the dot would be inconvenient in the case of the *i*, and write —

ã, *ẽ*, *ĩ*, *õ*, *ũ*, *õ̧*, *ṳ̃*; *ī̃*, *ē̃* etc.

The *length* of vowels is not expressed by the Greek sign ^, but by the line used in Latin prosody, which requires less space, and is more easily combined with the accent *ā*, *ā́*, *ḗ*, and so on. The shortness, if required to be specially expressed, is likewise, as in prosody, marked by ˘, *ă*, *ĕ*, *ĭ*, etc.

A complete and accurate theory of transcription would require a distinction of *diphthongs*, as such, since two vowels united by accent into *one* syllable are pronounced otherwise than when placed unconnectedly by the side of each other, and forming *two* syllables; the German word *Mai* having a differend sound from that of the Italian *mai.* Where it is necesary, the ordinary mark of diæresis may be imployed to indicate the separation, as *maï.* Practice, however, seems in most languages not to require any distinction.

B. The System of Consonants.

On the Division of Consonants.

The Consonants may be divided on different principles. Two principles of division, however, are prevalent, and will therefore be here adopted: although the exact place of every sound in the physiological system can result only from a minute inquiry into all its qualities.

---

[1] The same mark has occasionally been employed by *Burnouf* in his *Commentaire sur le Yaçna* (p. CXXIII, p. XL, tableau).

The first and most important division is that determined by the *place* in the mouth where the sounds are formed. The breath which forms the sounds issues from the larynx into the mouth, and is here modified in a manifold manner, until it passes the outward gate of the lips. Thus the breath on its way can be stopped in various places either by the lips or by the tongue. We are accustomed in our languages, like the Greeks and Romans, to distinguish *three* such stoppings, and thus to divide the consonants into three classes, *gutturals*, *dentals*, and *labials*, according as they are formed in the throat, at the teeth, or with the lips.

There is another essential difference in the pronunciation, in as far as either the mouth at the above-mentioned places is completely closed and reopened, or the passage of the breath is only narrowed without its stream being entirely interrupted by closing the organs. The consonants formed by the first process we call *explosive* or *divisible (dividuae)*, because the moment of contact divides the sound into two parts,[1] the others *fricative*, from their sound being determined by friction, or *continuous (continuae)* because this friction is not interrupted by any

---

[1] It will, on examination, soon appear that we often prononnce only half of a consonant, as, for instance, in all cases in which a nasal consonant meets another explosive letter of the same local class. The full pronunciation of an explosive letter requires the closing and opening of the organ. In *anda* we close the mouth with *n* and open it with *d*, the reverse in *adna*, pronouncing thus only half the *n* and half the *d*, whilst in *ana* and *ada* we prononnce the whole of *n* and the whole of *d* respectively; the same in *ampa* and *aṅka*, and so on. It is a decided mistake, to reckon *m* and *n* among the *consonantes continuae;* for in *m* and *n* it is only the vowel-element inherent in the first half, which may be continued at pleasure, whilst in all the continuous consonants it is the consonantal element (the friction) which must be continued, as in *f*, *v*, *s*, *z*. When in a final *m* we do not reopen the mouth, we prononnce only half an *m*, not a whole one. The complete consonant is best perceived when placed between two vowels. It is evident that in *ama* closing and opening are as necessary to the completeness of *m*, as in *aba* to that of *b*. This has been correctly understood by the Indian grammarians.

closing of the organs. The sounds *r* and *l* participate of both qualities, being *continuous*, and at the same time formed by a *contact*, which is vibrating in *r*, and partial in *l*.

We are thus enabled to give the following synopsis of the most generally known simple consonantal sounds.

The Simple Consonants in the European Alphabets.

	explosivae or dividuae.			fricativae or continnae.			ancipites.	
	fort.	len.	nasal.	fortis.	lenis.	semivoc.		
Gutturales	*k*	Ger. *g*	Ger. *ng*	Ger. *ch*, *h*	Mod. Gr. *γ*	Ger. *j*	gutt. *r*	
Dentales	*t*	*d*	*n*	Engl *sh*	Fr. *j*		dent. *r*	*l*
				sharp *s*	Fr. *z*			
				Engl. *th*(-in)	Engl. *th*(-ine)			
Labiales	*p*	*b*	*m*	*f*	Engl. *v*	Engl. *w*		

Upon what Principles are these Sounds to be rendered in a General Alphabet.

Of these sounds only 11, viz. *k*, *h*, *t*, *d*, *n*, *r*, *l*, *p*, *b*, *m*, *f*, have one and the same universally acknowledged value in the European alphabets, putting aside a few minor differences. The others require to be specially defined. Even among these the simple signs, *g*, *s*, *z*, *v*, and *w* are already so generally introduced into linguistic books in the value indicated above, that we may safely use them without further discussion.

We meet with some difficulty, however, with respect to the sounds of the German *ng*, *ch*, and *j*, the French *j* and *ch* (or English *sh*), the English sharp and soft *th*, the Modern Greek *γ*, and the guttural *r*. These nine sounds have been represented in linguistic books by various means.

The inconvenience of the common way of writing them will be evident, when we refer to the *principles* upon which every alphabet, aiming at general application, must be grounded, and which are essentially as follows: —

I. *Every simple sound ought to be represented by a single sign.* This excludes the combinations *ng*, *ch*, *th*.

II. *Different sounds are not to be expressed by one and the same sign;* contrary to which principle *ch*, *j*, *th* have been each used with a double value.

III. *Explosive letters are not to be used to express fricative sounds, and vice versâ.* On the contrary, the simple characters (bases) must form a separate series in each of the two great divisions; if not, inextricable confusion will inevitably arise.

If, then, we look for signs which can be applied to the sounds above indicated, so as not to violate these most important principles, we shall find the choice of letters more circumscribed than it would at first appear.

German ng.

In German and in English (as for instance, Germ. *enge*, Engl. *singing*) *ng* expresses the guttural *n* [1], for which linguistic use has very generally adopted *ṅ*, particularly in transcribing the Sanskrit. It is evident that *n* must remain the basis, and there is no reason for introducing any fresh diacritical sign.

Guttural r.

The guttural *r* differs from the usual dental *r*, in as much as the *velum palati* is put in vibration instead of the tip of the tongue. It is often thus pronounced in different dialects of the German, French, and other languages. The point over the letter marking already the guttural pronunciation of *ṅ*, no other diacritical sign will be chosen for the same purpose in *r*. We write it, therefore, *ṙ*.

---

[1] In most other languages, as in Sanskrit, it appears only before other gutturals; Indian scholars, therefore, do not generally distinguish it from the dental *n*.

German j.

The German *j* is the semi-vowel which, in English (*y*ear, *y*es), and somctimes also in French (Ma*y*ence, Ba*y*onne), is expressed by *y*. Following these precedents and the use generally adopted in linguistic books, we likewise express it by *y*.

German ch.

The German *ch* in *lachen* is known to be the *fricative* sound, which arises from the throat not being closed at the guttural point (which would give *k*), but only narrowed, so that the strong and continuous breath produces a friction, such as is heard at the teeth in *s*, and at the lips in *f*. The English, French, and Italians, do not know the sound at all; in the Spanish language it is marked by *j* or *x*. In the Semitic languages (Hebrew ח, Arabic خ) it is very frequent. Of European alphabets only the Spanish and the Greek have a single letter for this simple sound. The Latin language did not know the sound, and therefore did not express it. The signs hitherto used by linguistic scholars, *ch*, *kh*, *qh*, *k̃*, *x*, are in opposition to the inviolable principle that fricative sounds must not be represented by explosive bases, such as *c*, *k*, *q* (above No. III.), or are altogether improper, like *x*. The nearest applicable fricative basis would be *h*. But it will appear from the sequel that this sign would be used for six different sounds, if we do not confine it strictly to its proper meaning. The difficulty of finding an appropriate sign for this sound is therefore great, and has long been felt. We possess one, however, in a European alphabet, namely, the Greek, which is almost as generally known as the Latin. From this it has been adopted into the Russian alphabet; and the Spanish *x* owes its pronunciation, probably, rather to the Greek χ, than to the Latin *x*. The want of a new sign, which of course could not be supplied from an Oriental alphabet, had already caused Volney to propose the Greek χ in his alphabet of 1795, and, after the mistaken experiment of substituting ꝁ, to reproduce it in his last alphabet of 1818. The same sign is used by *Joh. Müller*[1], *Rapp*[2], *Bunsen*[3], and others.

We therefore consider it not only as an essential advantage, but even as the only means of solving all difficulties, to follow these precedents, and to receive the Greek *χ* as the representative of this sound in the general alphabet. Of the soft sound, which corresponds with the strong, we shall have to speak below.

English sh, French ch, German sch.

For the rushing sound of the English *sh* we should not hesitate to propose a new basis, and to borrow it, if necessary, from the Greek alphabet, if any such existed. But neither the Greeks nor the Romans had this sound; and we must avoid recurring to the Oriental, or even the Russian alphabet, as few persons could be expected to follow us so far. Our only resource, therefore, is to content ourselves with the nearest basis *s*, and to qualify this by a diacritical mark. This has been done, moreover, by all those that sought a single sign for this simple souud, except by Volney, who first proposed a newly invented sign Ψ, and afterwards preferred ʃ, viz. the inverted *j*. Some used *ś* or *s̄*. More generally *s̔* has been adopted, from the precedent of Bopp, who has used it since 1833. Others have preserved the combination *sh*, which not only offends against the simplicity of the sound, but has produced also the incorrect impression, that the rushing sound implied a stronger breath than the common *s*. We should adopt Bopp's *s̔*, on account of the authority of the precedent and its reception by his school, if it were not open to serious objections. The spiritus asper is, like *h*, a sign of aspiration, and from the analogy of *k̔*, *k̓*, *g̔* etc. (see below), one ought to

[1] Handbuch der Physiologie, vol. II. (1837), pp. 237, 238.
[2] Physiologie der Sprache, p. 65.
[3] Aegyptens Stelle in der Weltgeschichte, vol. I.

suppose an augmentation of the breathing of the *s*. This is not the case. It would be, therefore, introducing a new meaning of the spiritus asper, used only in this single case. Nor can we adopt *ś*, since the accent indicates the palatal series (see below), and the single precedent of *s̄* used by Schleiermacher has hitherto found no imitation.

We propose to write *š*, using a sign which we find already in constant and general use in the Serbian and modern Bohemian alphabets.

French j.

This letter is the soft and vocalised sound, which corresponds to the strong French *ch* (German *sch*), and stands exactly in the same relation to it as the French *z* to the strong *s*. Volney retained the French *j*, which we cannot use any more than *zh*, which has been introduced by others. There can be no doubt, however, that the parallelism with our *š* for French *ch* requires a soft *ž* for French *j*. Following the same analogy, the Serbians likewise write *ž*.

English strong th.

The English *th*[1] offers exactly the same difficulties as the German *ch*. It is a *littera fricativa* or *continua*, and must not, therefore, have the explosive letter *t*, for its basis. The only Latin character of the fricative division, which might be applied to it, is *s*, and, for the soft sound, *z*. Both, however, have been already applied each to two uses, and would besides have the disadvantage of favouring the tendency, common to most European nations, to substitute the usual dental *s* for the peculiar lisping sound. In this case, also, it will soon (when use shall have overcome the first-felt apprehension) be ac-

[1] The same lisping sound exists in the Arabic and many other languages, including several African tongues.

knowledged as an advantage, if, instead of *s* with a diacritical sign, we adopt the universally known Greek character θ as a new and original basis. Nor is it without precedent, θ having been used for this purpose by many, among whom we may again mention *Volney* (1795) and *Fleischer* (1831).

The soft English th, and the Modern Greek γ.

The sound of the soft English *th (thine, thou)* appears also in the Danish *d* and in the modern Greek δ; the soft guttural corresponding to the strong German *ch* presents itself in the modern Greek γ. It cannot be denied that it will be a real advantage if we find other bases for these soft sounds than χ and θ, as *z* differs from s, *ž* from *š*, *v* from *f*. Yielding to this conviction we mark the corresponding soft sounds similarly by the Greek letters γ and δ[1], the more so as we have already before us the weighty precedent of Fleischer (1831).

We do not undervalue the evident and serious difficulty, that by the reception of some Greek characters, the generally required confinement to the Roman alphabet suffers an exception; and we foresee that many who do not sufficiently appreciate the great importance of the organic laws of the alphabet, may be shocked at first. A further consideration will, however, soon make it evident, that the peculiar poverty of the Latin language in fricative sounds and letters, and the general tendency of all languages to transform the explosive into fricative sounds[2], have rendered the disproportion between the two great divisions of sounds, with respect to their graphic representation, already so great that an essential and lasting remedy is abso-

[1] There can be no doubt, that neither did χ and θ originally signify the fricative sounds substituted in a later time, but the aspirates *kh* and *th*. The epoch of the altered pronunciation of χ, ϑ, and φ, cannot be accurately defined, but was probably contemporaneous with the alteration of γ and δ, whilst β seems to have approached latin *v* in still earlier times.

[2] Instances of this tendency are generally known from the Romanic languages. See also below, where the Palatals are considered.

lutely required. There are, indeed, eight bases for the above stated nine explosive sounds, and only six for the twelve fricative sounds. An augmentation of the latter by introducing the Greek signs χ, γ, θ and δ, is consequently almost unavoidable; and their absolute necessity will soon be still more evident when we come to consider the Asiatic sounds in addition to the European.

We are thus enabled to give the following tableau of the European sounds:

Alphabet of the European Consonantal System.

	explosivæ or dividuæ.			*fricativæ or continuæ.*			*ancipites.*
	fortis.	lenis.	nasalis.	fortis.	lenis.	semivoc.	
Gutturales	*k*	*g*	*ṅ*	*χ h*	*γ*	*y*	*ṙ*
				š	*ž*		
Dentales	*t*	*d*	*n*	*s*	*z*		*r l*
				θ	*δ*		
Labiales	*p*	*b*	*m*	*f*	*v*	*w*	

Enlargement of the Alphabet by the Addition of the Foreign Sounds of Oriental Languages.

The Asiatic languages, especially the Indian and the Arabic, possess, besides the sounds hitherto considered, others, which hardly exist at all in European languages, or at least are only fully developed in Asiatic languages, and, therefore, can only find their proper position in a more comprehensive system. Instead of the three European classes, we must distinguish *seven*, which we shall now consider separately.

I. The Faucal Class.

h

We are accustomed to reckon *h* among the gutturals. It is

easily observed, however, that we pronounce this sound behind the guttural point, immediately at the larynx. When pronounced so softly as to be vocalised, *i. e.* so as to imply a vowel sound produced in the larynx (as with *z*, *v*, *ð*, *ž*) the friction ceases to be audible, and only the vowel element is heard. This vocalised consonantal breathing, is, therefore, not peculiarly marked in any language. *h* belongs, therefore, to the unvocalised strong fricatives.

Arabic أ, *Hebrew* א, *Sanskrit* अ, *Greek spiritus lenis.*

By closing the throat and then opening it to pronounce a vowel, we produce the slight explosive sound which in the Eastern languages is marked separately, but not in the European, except in the Greek. We perceive it distinctly between two vowels which following each other are pronounced separately, as in the Italian *sarà 'a casa*, the English *go 'over*, the German *See-'adler*,; or even after consonants when trying to distinguish, in German, *mein 'Eid* (my oath) from *Meineid* (perjury), or *Fisch-'art* (fish species) from *Fischart* (a name), &c. We indicate this sound, when necessary, by the mark ', like the Greeks.

Arabic ع, *ʿain.*

The slight sound just described can be pronounced hard by a stronger explosion almost at the same point of the throat. Thus arises the sound which the Arabs write ع.[1] We find it expressed by scholars generally by placing a diacritical sign over the following vowel, *ȧ*, *ȁ*, *á*, *ă*, *á*; sometimes below, *ạ*. This method would suppose, from the analogy of all systems of writing, that the ع were only an indication of a change in the vowel. It is, however, a full consonant, preceding the vowel. We indicate

---

[1] See on the accurate pronunciation of this and the other Arabic sounds my dissertation: *Ueber die Aussprache und die Umschrift der Arabischen Laute*, in the Transact. of the R. Acad. of Berlin. 1861.

it, therefore, with regard to its affinity to the soft sound, by doubling the spiritus lenis, ʾ̓.

Arabic ح, *ḱa.*

The fricative sound corresponding to ʾ̓ is not the common *h*, but a stronger aspiration, which requires a greater contraction of the faucal point, and is distinguished by the Arabs from the simple *h*. It has, therefore, been often indicated by *hh*. We write *ḱ* and have a precedent in the writings of Fleischer (1831), Ewald (1831), Vullers (1841).

The absence of any nasal sound in the faucal series is necessitated by the physiological position of the faucal point, the contraction of which closes at the same time the canal of the nose.

The faucal series is confined, therefore, to the four following sounds, thus represented: ʾ̓ ʾ *ḱ* *h*.

II. The Guttural Class.

As we have already excluded the *h* from this class, on account of its being pronounced *behind* the proper guttural point, we must, to be accurate, exclude the *y* also, and put it in the next following class, this sound being formed in the mouth *before* the guttural point.

Again we are obliged to comprise a sound peculiar to the Semitic languages, viz.

The Arabic ق *and Hebrew* ק, *qaf* or *qof*,

which is formed at the posterior soft part of the palate, although this class has its place of formation a little more forward, at the point where the *velum palati*, joins the hard palate. We indicate this sound by the sign which the Greeks and Romans substituted for it, although it cannot be proved that they pronounced it exactly in the same manner, viz. *q*.

We obtain by this addition the following complete guttural series: *k q g*; *ṅ*; *χ γ*; *ṙ*.

III. The Palatal Class.

In passing from the guttural to the dental point, another point may be distinguished, and has been fixed by several languages, namely, the *palatal* point which is situated almost in the middle or on the highest point of the hard palate, and occasionally extends to the gum of the upper teeth. We distinguish this class of letters from the Gutturals by a stroke put over them. A *ḱ* or *ǵ*, pronounced at this place by pressing the broad middle part of the tongue on the palate, will be easily distinguished from the deep gutturals *q*, *k*, or *g*.

In most languages *k* and *g*, before the vowels *e*, *i*, *ọ*, *ụ*, approach the palatal pronunciation, whilst before *a*, *o*, *u* they remain more guttural, owing to the formation of these vowels. A palatal *ḱ* is as different from the guttural *k* as the German *ch* in *ich*, which we write *χ́*, from the *ch* in *ach* or *Buch*, or as the common German *ch* in *Milch (Milχ́)* from the Swiss *ch* (our guttural *χ*) in the same word.

With regard to the Sibilants, no simple *s* can be pronounced at the *palatal* point The letter *s* is formed by the simple friction of the breath between the upper and lower teeth and is in consequence always dental. The rushing sound of the English *sh* or the German *sch* is formed in the hollow space left between the teeth and the palatal point, and may thus be regarded both as a *dental* and as a *palatal* sound.

Several languages distinguish two rushing sounds. If the tongue is drawn back in itself and a considerable hollow space is left between the middle of the palate and the teeth, a full rushing sound is heard, which may still be increased by putting forward the lips. This is the common English, German and French sound, which we write *š*. If the tongue in the contrary is stretched out as in pronouncing the other palatals, especially the *χ́* of the German *ich*, and only the tip of the tongue is withdrawn or turned down from the teeth so as to extend the cavity behind them only to the upper limit of the gum, the rushing sound becomes thinner and more like the *χ́* or the *s*. English and French often pronounce it when trying to utter the German palatal *ch* = *χ́*. We write it *š́* as a principally *palatal* variety of *š*. Both sounds, *š* and *š́*, are distinguished in the *Polish* language, where they are written *sz* (= *š*) and *ś* (= *š́*).

The latter sound *š́* is actually given in India to the Dēvanāgari श, according to the description of the most careful observers, and differs decidedly from the ष, which is a cerebral *ṣ̌* and now resembles more our full common *š*, as far as the original cerebral position of the tongue is no longer thoroughly retained.[1]

The palatal sounds have, as their physiological formation will explain, the peculiarity of easily assuming a shade of *y*, which appears most distinctly in the palatal *ń* and *ĺ*.[2] This slight shade which at first accompanies the palatal sound so closely that a fine ear perceives it as well before as after the moment

---

[1] There are learned Indian scholars who assert that the letters ष and श have actually quite the same pronunciation and I was induced by them for a moment, to change my opinion when I wrote the line in the Introduction p. 8. But I have since convinced myself that this was only a mistake of the English or German ear, which does not know the marked difference between *ṣ̌*, *š* and *š́*. Colebrooke, Wilkins, Carey and others were perfectly right in making the distinction.

[2] If, for instance, we pronounce the *n* and *l* in *ano*, *fule*, so as to press the broad middle of the tongue upon the high middle part of the hard palate, we shall no longer hear the French words *anneau*, and *foulé*, but something very like *agneau* and *fouillé*, with this difference only, that in the modern French pronunciation the tongue is not raised quite up to the palate, but only brought near it, so that the sound is more and more dissolved in *y*, *ayeau*, *fouyé*. To *t* and *d* also, in many languages, a slight sound of *y* is added, without producing the impression of a compound letter. If in certain languages it should appear convenient not to designate this secondary sound as a complete consonant, it would be very appropriate to introduce also for the sounds *ty dy* the palatal line, and to write *t́* and *d́*, as *y* is indeed of a palatal nature, and communicates the same to the *t* and *d*.

of closing the organ in uttering the explosive sounds, increases afterwards easily, só as to become independent, and to grow into a full subsequent *y*, next into a *χ́*, finally into a *š* or *ś*. Thus arises a series of compound sounds, which, from the palatal *k̆*, through *ky*, *ty*, *tš*, *tś*, frequently pass into *ts* and even into a simple *š*, *ś*, or *s*.

Such a transformation of former gutturals into sibilant dentals has occurred in many languages. The Greek *κοῖλον*, i. e. *koilon*, became in the Latin language *coelum*, i. e. *kǫlum*, and is sounded in the modern Italian *cielo*, i. e. *tšelo*; the Latin *caseus*, German *Käse*, has become, in English, *cheese*, i. e. *tšīz*; the Hebrew *gamal* (the camel), and the Arabic *gemel*, became *gyemel* or *dyemel*, afterwards *džemel*, at last even *žemel*. Such transitions in the history of languages never take place suddenly, but always gradually. It is a very common phenomenon that the explosive letters first produce the corresponding fricative sounds behind them, and afterwards pass entirely into them, and that at the same time the gutturals advance constantly towards the anterior part of the mouth.

The same transition of sounds has taken place in the Indian languages, compared with the old Sanskrit.

There the first two sounds of the Palatal class are pronounced by the natives, according to all descriptions, like the English *ch* and *j* in *choice* and *join*, or like the Italian *c* and *g* in *cima* and *giro*. These English and Italian sounds are, as no one that hears or pronounces them will doubt, compound sounds, beginning with the explosives *t* and *d*, and terminating with the fricatives *š* and *ž* or *ś* and *ź*. But in the sacred Dēvanāgari writing of the Indians, none but simple sounds were represented by single signs; and their language itself leaves not the least doubt that the sounds च and ज were really simple, not compound sounds. This is proved, for instance, by their not rendering the preceding syllable long, and by the possibility of doubling them.[1] These sounds were consequently pronounced originally in another manner than now, viz. as *simple* sounds. Even though we were not now able to define these sounds more accurately, we ought undoubtedly to indicate them in old Sanskrit by a peculiar sign. For this purpose, Bopp and his school have introduced the mark ′ over the letter, the same, which we have proposed in consequence of this important precedence. Of the peculiar case, when in a foreign alphabet these sounds are represented as simple from their being originally such, whilst they are now pronounced as compound, we have treated in the Introduction.

The series of *palatal* and *palato-dental* sounds will therefore be as follows:

ḱ ǵ ń; χ́ γ́; š́ ž́; ś̌ ź̌; y; ĺ.

It is to be observed only that *γ́* and the semivowel *y* are so near each other that the *γ́* will hardly appear in any language as a distinct sound by the side of *y*. It is self-evident that *y* needs not assume the palatal mark, as there is no corresponding guttural sound.

IV. The cerebral[2] Class.

This class, almost exclusively peculiar to the Indian, and amongst them originally to the Dravidian, languages, is formed by bringing the tip of the tongue backwards and upwards to the neighbourhood of the palatal point, so as to produce there the explosion or friction. To our ear, these sounds are

---

[1] It is evident that in no language a componnd sound can be donbled. If, resolving the English *riches* into its component sonnds *rits̆es*, one intended to double this sound, one could not write *richches*, i. e. *rits̆ts̆es* (for that would sound as in *which child*), but would only repeat the first element and write *ritches*, i. e. *ritts̆es*.

[2] *Cerebral* was the original English denomination, which arose indeed from a false translation of the Indian name *mūrdd́ańya*, i. e. letters of the *dome* of the palate, but has not yet been supplied by a more appropriate one.

nearest to the dentals. We retain for them also the diacritical sign introduced by Bopp and his school, viz. the dot under the letter, and write this Indian series

ṭ ḍ ṇ; ṣ̌; ṛ ḷ.

V. The Lingual or gutturo-dental Class

belongs as exclusively to the Arabic and cognate languages. In their formation, a dental and a guttural movement of the tongue are combined:[1] With respect to the former, the breadth of the tongue either touches or approaches the whole anterior space of the hard palate as far as the teeth, its tip being rather turned below. It is consequently entirely different from the Indian *cerebrals*, although these, too, are frequently called *linguals*. It appears, therefore, suitable to confine this latter denomination to the Arabic sounds, and to retain the former for the Indian, if it would not be preferable to substitute the name of *gutturo-dentals*.

The graphic representation hitherto adopted by Robinson, Caspari, Davids, and others, is a dot under the dentals, like that of the cerebrals. We have chosen instead of the dot, after the precedent of Volney, in contradistinction to the cerebral formation, a small line, which is little different from the dot hitherto used. The Arabs have developed only four letters of this class, namely: *ḏ(ṯ) δ̱ s̱ ẕ*.

VI. The Dental Class

exists complete in the European languages, and has been specified above.

The essential distinction of the two fricative formations *s* and *θ*, from the guttural and palatal *χ* and *χ́*, consists in the friction of the breath being formed and heard exclusively at the *teeth*.

[1] See above p. 57. and below the notes to the Arabic Alphabet.

When the tip of the tongue is placed at the very point of the friction, *θ* is pronounced; if it is laid against the lower teeth, whilst the upper side of the tongue is brought back behind the upper teeth, we have *s*. When the tongue recedes still farther, so that behind the upper and lower teeth a greater hollow space remains, the interior limit of which extents as far as the *palatal* point, this enlarged resounding space produces the palato-dental sounds *ś* and *š*, of which we have already spoken above. We might as well reckon the *š* and *ś*, *ž* and *ź* amongst the dentals as we hear their principal friction at the teeth. We will seen however in the second part several alphabets, where it seems more convenient to place these sounds with the palatals. The Indian cerebral *š* receives from the peculiar flexion of the tongue, which produces a double cavity in the mouth, a still different expression, indicated by the cerebral dot below.

The dental series remains, therefore,

t d n; s z; ϑ δ; r l.

VII. The Labial Class

is also known from European languages, and has been mentioned above, *p b m; f v; w.*

We ought perhaps to notice here the particular pronunciation of *w* in middle Germany, where this letter is no *labio-dental*, formed between the lower lip and the upper teeth, as *v* in England, France, Northern Germany, India, etc., nor the *semivowel w* of the English, Arabic and many other languages, but a pure *labial* sound, formed between the upper and lower lip without any *u*-position of the lips and tongue and without any concurrence of the teeth. This is however a sound which I never heard of in any language except the provincial German dialects, and for this reason it needs hardly a peculiar designation in our alphabet, where, if wanted, it might be written *w*.

If we now comprise the seven classes in a general tableau, we obtain the followiug synopsis:

The Consonants of the General Alphabet.

	explosivæ or *dividuæ.*			*fricativæ* or *continuæ.*			*ancipites.*	
	fortes.	lenes.	nasales.	fortes.	lenes.	semivoc.		
I. *Faucales.*	;	'		*ǩ h*				
II. *Gutturales.*	*k*	*q* *g*	*ṅ*	*χ*	*γ*		*ṙ*	
III. *Palatales.*	*ǩ*	*ǵ*	*ń*	*χ́, ś, š́*	*γ́, ź, ž́*	*y*		*ľ*
IV. *Cerebrales.* (Indicae)	*ṭ*	*ḍ*	*ṇ*	*ṣ̌*	*ẓ̌*		*ṛ*	*ḷ*
V. *Linguales.* (Arabicae)		*ḏ(ṯ)*		*s̱*	*ẕ, ḏ̱*			
VI. *Dentales.*	*t*	*d*	*n*	*s, ϑ*	*z, δ*		*r*	*l*
VII. *Labiales.*	*p*	*b*	*m*	*f*	*v*	*w*		

Examples of Pronunciation.

We follow here the vertical and not the horizontal order, because we thereby keep together all the letters, which in the different classes have the same bases.

Vowels.

ā engl. *father*, fr. *âme.*
ă ger. *Mann*, ital. *ballo.*
ḙ̄ fr. *mère*, ger. *Bär.*
ḙ̆ engl. *head*, ger. *fett.*
ẹ̄ engl. *cane*, *vein*, fr. *donné.*
ī engl. *see*, fr. *lit.*
ĭ engl. *sin*, fr. *fil.*
ō̰ engl. *all*, ital. *però.*
ŏ̰ engl. *hot*, *not.*
ọ̄ engl. *no*, fr. *faux.*
ū engl. *rule*, fr. *nous.*
ŭ engl. *foot*, fr. *ours.*
ọ̄ fr. *beurre*, *coeur.*
ọ̆ engl. *cunning*, *but.*
ọ̄ ger. *König*, fr. *feu.*
ṳ̄ fr. *fûmes*, ger. *Güte.*
ṳ̆ fr. *but*, ger. *Glück.*
ai engl. *mine*, ger. *Kaiser.*
au engl. *house*, ger. *Haus.*
aṳ ger. *Häuser*, *heute.*
ei span. *reina.*
oi engl. *join.*
ã fr. *an*, *en.*
ẽ fr. *examen*, *Inde.*
õ fr. *on.*
ọ̃ fr. *un.*
ẹ engl. *nation*, ger. *Verstand.*
ṛ̣ sanskr. ऋ.

l̥ sanskr. ऌ.
~~*s̥* chin. mandar. *tsz̥*.~~

Consonants.

A. Explosivae. *a.* Fortes.

ʾ arab. ع (*ʾaïn*).
k engl. *cool*, fr. *cause*.
k̐ old sanskr. च. [see above p. 72.]
č modern sanskr. च, engl. *ch*.
ṭ sanskr. ट.
t engl. *town*, fr. *ton*.
p engl. *pine*, fr. *peu*.

b. Lenes.

ʼ arab. ﺃ, hebr. א, gr. spir. len. ʼ.
q arab. ق (*qaf*).
g engl. *gold*, fr. *gauche*.
ǵ old sanskr. ज.
ǰ modern sanskr. ज, engl. *j*.
ḍ sanskr. ड.
ḏ(ṯ) arab. ط (see below).
d engl. *dear*.
b engl. *by*.

c. Nasales.

ṅ engl. *singing*, ger. *enge*.
ń sanskr. ञ, ital. *gnudo*, fr. *regner*.
ṇ sanskr. ण.
n engl. *no*.
m engl. *me*.

B. Fricativae. *a.* Fortes.

k̐ arab. ح (*k̐a*).
h engl. *hand*.
χ ger. *Buch*, *ach*; pol. *chata*.
š engl. *show*, fr. *chat*, ger. *schon*.
χ́ ger. *ich*, *recht*.
š̥ old sanskr. ष.
ś mod. ind. श, pol. *świt*.
ṣ arab. ص (*ṣād*).
s engl. *sense*, fr. *savoir*.
θ engl. *thin*, mod. gr. *θεός*.
f engl. *fine*.

b. Lenes.

γ arab. غ (*γaïn*). mod. greek γάλα
ž fr. *jeune*, pol. *bażant*.
γ́ mod. gr. *γέφυρα*.
ź pol. *poźno*.
z fr. *zèle*, engl. *zeal*.
ð engl. *thy*, mod. gr. *δίψα*.
ð̥ arab. ظ (*ð̥a*).
ẓ arab. ض (*ẓa*) (see below).

c. Semivocales.

y engl. *year*, fr. *Bayonne*, ger. *ja*.
w engl. *we*.

C. Liquidae.

ṙ germ. and fr. dialects.
ṛ sanskr. र.
r engl. *very*, ital. *rabbia*.
l' ital. *gli*, fr. *mouillé*.
ḷ sanskr. ळ.
l engl. *low*.

On the Aspirates and Consonantal Diphthongs.

Aspirates are those *explosive* sounds which are pronounced with a simple but audible breath. This class has been most fully developed in the Sanskrit, where the *fortes* as well as the *lenes* of all classes can be aspirated in this manner. In the ancient Greek only the *fortes* admitted of the aspiration, and these afterwards passed into the corresponding fricatives. The aspiration can only follow the explosion, not accompany it throughout, as it does the friction of the fricatives. Thus, a real composition takes place.[1] If, notwithstanding this, the aspirates are represented in the Sanskrit as single letters, this is to be explained by the circumstance, that the spiritus unites itself more closely with the explosive letters than any other consonant, and is of so little weight, that it does not make the preceding syllable long, being, properly speaking, no more than an increase of the breath necessarily inherent in every consonant. It is optional, therefore, either to regard the aspirates as single consonants, or as compositions with *h*. [We prefer now the latter. See above p. 11.]

In regard to the doubling of *consonants*, it will readily be granted, that they ought not to be employed merely to show that the preceding vowel is short and accentuated, but only where the duplication (from the prolongation of the friction or of the moment of touching) is distinctly heard, or the double letter is justified etymologically, as originating in the assimilation of different consonants, or wherever nothing is intended, but a transcription of a foreign orthography, which makes use of double letters.[2]

---

[1] The best linguistic proof is, that no aspirate can be doubled; when a duplication is intended, the unaspirated sound is placed before the aspirate. From *aḱa* arises by reduplication not *aḱḱa*, but *akḱa*. In Greek you write for the same reason *τίτθη*, *Βάκχος*, *Σάπφω*.

[2] Every double consonant is pronounced with but one closing or narrowing of the organ and with the intention to unite the first half of the double consonant to the preceding syllable, the second to the following.

On the Application of the General Alphabet to the Alphabet of particular Languages.

It has been remarked above, that the general alphabet, when applied to particular languages, must be capable of simplification as well as of enlargement. All particular diacritical marks are unnecessary in those languages where none of the bases have a double value. We then write the simple base without a diacritical mark *e*, *o*, *s*. Where two sounds belong to the same base, one only of the signs will often be wanted, especially in the case of long and short vowels.

If further essential differences should be shown, which are not yet represented in the general alphabet, and cannot be expressed by a modification of the bases already adopted, nothing prevents the selection, or, if necessary, invention of other new diacritical signs, without deviating from the principles above developed.

Among these latter cases we may reckon, for instance, the *clicks* of the southernmost African languages, which are formed, not by throwing out the breath, but by drawing it inward. We often produce the same clicks by the same movements of the tongue, but do not use them as articulate elements of speech. In the *Hottentot* language there are four clicks; in the *Zulu* and some other neighbouring languages to which they were transferred, only three.

The first, which had been written hitherto *q*, is made by pressing the tip of the tongue closely upon the middle palate and withdrawing it suddenly, and from the place of its formation is to be reckoned among the *cerebrals*. The second (found principally in the Hottentot, but, according to Boyce[1], also in some words of the Kafir language), arises, from placing the breadth

[1] Grammar of the Kaffir Language, p. 4. He writes it *qc*. I myself have heard it pronounced by Zulu Kaffirs.

of the tongue in the *palatal* position, and withdrawing it with a suction. The third, generally written *c*, is in the same manner *dental*, as only the tip of the tongue smacks against the upper teeth and the gum above. The fourth is formed at the side of the tongue, by drawing in the air towards the middle of the mouth from the right or left side. It has been called *lateral*, therefore, and generally rendered by *x*.

The pronunciation of these sounds becomes difficult only when they are connected with other sounds. Whilst the anterior part of the tongue is smacking, the throat can open itself for a *g* or *ṅ*, so that these latter sounds are pronounced almost at the same time with the click, or immediately after it.[1]

At the same time, the choice of *c*, *q*, and *x*, as signs of clicks, is inconvenient, since they are taken from the European alphabets, in which they express well known sounds, not bearing any relation to the clicks. Essential to the latter is the peculiarity of stopping in part, and even drawing back the breath, which appears to be most easily expressed by a simple bar /. If we connect with this our common marks for the cerebral or the palatal, a peculiar notation is wanted only for the *lateral*, which is the strongest sound. We propose to express it by two bars //. As the gutturals evidently do not unite with the clicks into one sound[2], but form a compound

---

[1] Boyce distinguishes only two accompanying gutturals, which he writes *g* and *n*; Appleyard and Grout mention three, *g* and two nasals, *n* and *ng* (*ṅ*). The author himself could only distinguish two gutturals, *g* and *ṅ*, as connected with clicks by the Zulu Kafirs just mentioned, who in the beginning of 1854, sojourned for some time in Berlin.

[2] We cannot, therefore, assent to Grout, who, instead of the former notation proposes the following:

$$\begin{array}{cccc} q & \dot{q} & \bar{q} & \ddot{q} \\ c & \dot{c} & \bar{c} & \ddot{c} \\ x & \dot{x} & \bar{x} & \ddot{x} \end{array}$$

Grout, in the above-mentioned work p. 34. accepts our mode of writing the clicks, but places the three sounds which appear in connection with

sound, we may make them simply to follow, as with the diphthongs. Thus we get the tableau: .

Palatals	´ (*qc*)	/	—	—
Cerebrals	(*q*)	!	!*g*	!*ṅ*
Dentals	(*c*)	ǀ	ǀ*g*	ǀ*ṅ*
Laterals	(*x*)	ǁ	ǁ*g*	ǁ*ṅ*

---

them, not *after* bnt *before* the click-letters and writes *nǀ*, *gǁ*, *ng!* etc. and the Rev. J. L. Döhne, Missionary to the American Board, C. J. M. in his Zulu Kafir Dictionary, Cape Town, 1857, p. XXXVIII, expresses himself distinctly against our proposal to write the clicks before their accompanying letters. On the other hand Wallmann and Vollmer have pnt the clicks after these lotters, in the before-mentioned works. All are agreed, we among the rest, that the two sounds, althongh perfectly different, are pronounced almost simultaneously; and Döhne states, even in reference to the Nama and Kafir: "In the former the guttural sound ***begins after the tongue has clicked*** and ***continues*** with a peculiar and distinct force; bnt this is little observable in the Kafir." I believe that I have remarked the same thing, with regard to the *g*, in the pronunciation of the Kafir. As far as I am aware, no one asserts that *g* is heard before the click. And neither does the etymological reason advanced by Döhne—"that it was impossible that from the ***in*** before the root ***iǀela*** ***iǀṅelo*** hnt (only) ***iṅǀelo*** can be made"—prove anything in favour of prononncing *ǀṅ* or *ṅǀ*, for eqnally little shonld we be justified in inferring from the fact that in the Sanskrit लेढि *lēṭ'i* "he licks" from लिह् *lih* and ति *ti*, *t'* mnst be pronounced not as *th*, bnt as *ht*. It appears to ns of little real importance whether one writes *ǀg* or *gǀ*, as both sounds are uttered, as nearly as possible, simnltaneonsly. It is however very desirahle, that a majority shonld declare itself in favonr of one or the other form, amongst linguists and Missionaries interested in the subject, to which majority the dissontient will then join themselves.

Dr. Bleek (The Library of Sir George Grey, vol. I, pp. 6 and 172) mentions a conference held in 1856 by the Rhenish Missionaries in Sonth Africa, by which 2 of our 4 click signs, viz. ǀ and ǁ were adopted, and the other two, viz. ! and / were exchanged for + and ǂ. There wonld he no great objection to the alterations, shonld a majority declare distinctly in favonr of them. Meanwhile, nothing advocating the Rhenish mode of writing, except Vollmer's book, has as yet come under my notice, while onr signs have already heen made nse of hy Wallmann and Gront. Here also it appears more essential that a choice shonld he made, than what the choice should be. The distinctive marks ! and / are made according to the organic

The difficulty of transcription is greatest in those systems of writing which, originating in an earlier period of the language, and fully developed, have been retained unaltered, whilst the pronunciation has undergone a change, as also in those in which several reformations have left their traces. An instance of this kind has already been mentioned in speaking of the Sanskrit palatals. The differences of European orthography have mostly arisen from similar circumstances. Some such difficulties, however, are presented by almost all existing alphabets which are not of modern formation. As the object of a standard transcription is to avoid, as much as possible, all such incongruity of sound and sign, no other course remains open in such cases than to fix upon a distinct period of the language in question, and to adapt its transcription to the different purposes of rendering, either the *actual* pronunciation, or the *ancient* one which had been expressed by the alphabet, and which may be deduced from it by linguistic researches. The difference is generally found to be greater in the vowels than in the consonants, the former being, in all languages, the more changeable element.

The *Arabs* write only three vowels, but pronounce these three letters differently in different localities, according to distinct rules: in like manner, a certain number of consonants have a different pronunciation in different dialects, although in literature they are expressed by means of one and the same written letter. Eli Smith and Robinson (in his work on Palestine) propose to represent the actual pronunciation in the country,

---

classes of the cerebral and palatal clicks, and if ǂ may perhaps appear more convenient than /, we may yet venture to say that + resembles too closely the letter *t*. On the other hand, we must appear ourselves as decidedly opposed to the use of *ng* instead of *ṅ*; and the more so, because in these languages both *n* and *g* are capable of being joined to clicks, and the reader is therefore led to believe, that *ng* before a click must be either a union of *n* and *g*, or of *ṅ* and *g*, which last frequently occur in connection in these languages.

and their endeavours are to be highly prized[1]; but the linguistic scholar will prefer to follow the written system fixed by literature, and to neglect the varying deviations and shades of modern pronunciation. Great difficulties are met with in transcribing the *Hebrew* system of punctation, which, having only in after times been grafted upon the alphabet inherited from former ages, appears to be inconsistent with itself.

In conclusion, we present the reader with a number of alphabets transcribed after our own system. We are aware that in many instances further researches must correct and complete our labours. We have followed the best and latest investigations to which we had access in each individual language. The attempt is intended to show the easy applicability of our alphabet to the most different languages; and to induce scholars to follow in the same way, and eventually to correct and improve the details.

---

[1] Compare also the excellent essay of *Lane* on the modern pronunciation of the Arabic vowels, inserted in the publications of the German Oriental Society.

SECOND PART.

COLLECTION OF ALPHABETS

REDUCED TO

THE STANDARD ALPHABET.

GENERAL DIVISION OF LANGUAGES.

LITERARY LANGUAGES.

A. Gender-languages.

- I. Japhetic (Indogermanic).
- II. Semitic.
- III. Hamitic.

B. No-gender languages.

- I. Asiatic.
  - I. Turanic or Tataric.
  - II. Monosyllabic.
  - III. Isolated.
- II. Polynesian or Malayan (Oceanic).

ILLITERATE LANGUAGES.

- III. Australian or Papuan.
- IV. African.
  - I. Primitive or South African.
  - II. Isolated or Middle African.
- V. American.

Our first division is in *Literary* and *Illiterate* languages. We call those languages literary, which for the most part have a system of writing and at least a beginning of literature. The illiterate languages have with few exceptions no writing. This makes of course a great difference with respect to the introduction of the Roman alphabet. It is far easier to introduce it among the latter nations than the former, where it has to overcome an indigenous alphabet with its characteristic features and historical claims, which it must respect even when not quite adequate to the physiological import of the respective letters. The illiterate languages offer only the difficulty of determining the true pronunciation of every sound without the important guide of an indigenous alphabet fixed by the speaking people themselves. The sounds once being known, the signs are easily applied. This is the reason why our explanatory remarks are more numerous in the first than in the second part. This division referring to the knowledge of writing is at the same time, generally speaking, a geographical one, since the European, Asiatic and in a great measure the Polynesian languages are *literary*, the Australian, African and American languages *illiterate*.

We combine with this first division a second, referring to the use of grammatical gender. It is not accidental but very significant, that, as far as I know without any essential exception, only the most highly civilised races — the leading nations in the history of mankind — distinguish throughout the genders, and that the *Gender-languages* are the same as those, which scientifically by linguistic reasons may be proved as descending from one original Asiatic stock. The development of peculiar forms for the grammatical genders proves a comparatively higher consciousness of the two sexes; and the distinction not only of the masculine and feminine, as in the *Semitic* and *Hamitic* languages, but also of the feminine and neuter gender, exclnsively expressed in the *Japhetic* branch, is only a further step in the same direction. The formation of genders has appeared to me so characteristic of the three principal branches, that I thought it (1844) a sufficient reason, to ascribe all the African nonsemitic languages, which distinguish the genders, to the Hamitic branch, viz.—besides the old Egyptian and the Coptic—the Beja language of the Bishari (whose ancestors were the Ethiopians of Meroë), the Dankali, Somali, Galla and other neighbouring languages, all those of the Libyan tribes between the Egyptian Oases and the Canarian Islands, including the Hausa farther on to the south, and even the widely distant languages of the miserably reduced Hottentots and Bushmen, whose immigration into their actual seats is still a curious problem, considering the absolute diversity of their language from all their northern neighbours and at the same time its traces of a certain affinity with the Egyptian language.

If we are not yet able to prove the affinity also of all no-gender languages to the former and to one another, although their original relationship is inseparable from the propagation of the one human race, it would certainly be too hasty an assertion, to say that we never should be able to do so. It seems however unquestionable, that the three great branches of gender-languages were not only in the past the depositaries and the organs of the historical progress of human civilisation, but that to them, and particularly to the youngest branch of them, the Japhetic, belong also the future hopes of the world. All the other languages are in decline and seem to have henceforth but a local existence. The *geographical* division seems therefore the most appropriate for them, and we prefer it for our purpose to the other, which might be based upon the different formations and features of language.

LITERARY LANGUAGES.

GENDER LANGUAGES.

SANSKRIT.

अ आ		ह		
इ ई उ ऊ	क ग ङ	≍		ख घ
ऋ ॠ ऌ ॡ अं इं etc.	च ज ञ	श	य	छ झ
ए ऐ ओ औ अँ आँ	ट ड ण	ष	र ळ	ठ ढ
	त द न	स	ल	थ ध
	प ब म	≍	व	फ भ
		ः		

The *Virāma* ्, indicates that no vowel is pronounced.

Ancient pronunciation.

a ā		*h*		
i ī u ū	*k g ṅ*	*x*	-	*k̕ g̕*
ṛ ṝ ḷ ḹ ã ĩ etc.	*k̆ ǵ ń*	*ś(χ́)*	*y*	*k̃ g̃*
ai āi au āu aṛ āṛ	*ṭ ḍ ṇ*	*ṣ̌*	*ṛ ḷ*	*ṭ̕ ḍ̕*
	t d n	*s*	*l*	*t̕ d̕*
	p b m	*x*	*v*	*p̕ b̕*
		ẕ		

Modern pronunciation.

a ā		*h*		
i ī u ū	*k g ṅ*	*x̌*		*kh gh*
ṛ ṝ ḷ ḹ ã ĩ etc.	*č ǰ ń*	*ś*	*y*	*čh ǰh*
ē ai ō au ar ār	*ṭ ḍ ṇ*	*š*	*r ḷ*	*ṭh ḍh*
	t d n	*s*	*l*	*th dh*
	p b m	*x̌*	*v*	*ph bh*
		ẕ		

Specimen.

अग्निमीळे पुरोहितं यज्ञस्य देवमृत्विजं । होतारं रत्नधातमं ॥
अग्निः पूर्वेभिर्ऋषिभिरीड्यो नूतनैरुत । स देवाँ एह वक्षति ॥
अग्निना रयिमश्नवत्पोषमेव दिवे दिवे । यशसं वीरवत्तमं ॥
अग्ने यं यज्ञमध्वरं विश्वतः परिभूरसि । स इद्देवेषु गच्छति ॥
अग्निर्होता कविक्रतुः सत्यश्चित्रश्रवस्तमः । देवो देवेभिरागमत् ॥ १ ॥
यदङ्ग दाशुषे त्वमग्ने भद्रं करिष्यसि । तवेत्तत्सत्यमङ्गिरः ॥

(Beginning of the Rigveda ed. Aufrecht.)

Old pronunciation.

Agním ī̥ḷai puṛáuhitã, yaǵńásya daivám ṛtviǵã,
háutāṛã ṛatnaďátamã.
agniz pū́ṛvaibiṛ ṛ̥šibiṛ ī́dyau nū́tanāiṛ utá,
sá daivā̃́ áihá vakšati.
agnínā rayím ašnavat, páušam aivá divái-divai,
yašásã vīṛávattamã.
ágnai! yã yaǵńám aďvaṛā̃́ višvátaz paṛibū́ṛ ási,
sá íd daiváišu gaǩati.
agníṛ háutā kavíkṛatuz satyáš ǩitṛášṛavastamaz
daiváu daiváibiṛ ā́ gamat.
yád aṅgá dāšū́šai tvám, ágnai, bádṛā̃́ kaṛišyási,
táváit tát satyám, aṅgiraz.

Modern pronunciation.

Agnim ī̥ḷēpurōhitã, yajńasya dēvam ṛtvijã,
hōtārã ratnadhātamã.
agniz pūrvēbhir ṛ̥šibhir ī̥dyō nūtanair uta,
sa dēvā̃ ēha vakšati.
agninā rayim ašnavat, pōšam ēva divē-divē,
yašasã vīravattamã.
agnē! yã yajńam adhvarã višvataz paribhūr asi,
sa id dēvēšu gaǩhati.

agnir hōtā kavikratuẕ satyaś čitraśravastamaẕ
dēvō dēvēbhir ā gamat.
yad aṅga dāśušē tvam, agnē, bhadrā karišyasi,
tavēt tat satyam, aṅgiraẕ.

Remarks.

We distinguish an **ancient** and a **modern** pronunciation of Sanskrit. Just as the Romanic nations pronounce the old Roman alphabet in a different way from the old Romans themselves, and the modern Greeks the old Greek alphabet differently from the ancient Greeks, by adapting to the written ancient language the gradually changed pronunciation of the living modern language: likewise the Brahmans of to day do not pronounce the Sanskrit in the same way as the old Brahmans of that time when the *Dēvanāgarī* writing was settled, but according to the sounds of the now living Indian lauguages. The linguistic rules of Pānini and his scholars are only adapted to the old pronunciation, which happily we are able, in following the instruction of the old Grammarians, to determine better than that of any other ancient language. A real intelligence of this language and its harmonic organism of sounds is not possible without knowing the true ancient pronunciation, and considering the eminent importance of the Sanskrit for the comparison of languages, it seems indispensable for scientific linguistic purposes to approach also in trauscribing the Devanāgari as near as possible to the ancient pronunciation. The euphonic rules respecting the letters च ज ए र्‍ etc. become absurd, if we suppose for them the modern pronunciation *č ǰ ē ar* etc. instead of *k̆ ǵ ai ar̥* etc. The case, however, is different, when the transcription aims at more practical purposes and must therefore have regard to the **actual** pronunciation of the Indians. With this view we have added the second scheme.

The ancient pronunciation of the Devanāgari letters has been discussed elsewhere by the author[1], and his views seem to have been appreciated for the most part. Some of them have been mentioned above. We repeat here the results in a few words. ऋ ṛ̥ and ऌ ḷ̥ are simple vowels and can therefore not be expressed by *ri* and *li*; their value is that of a cerebral ṛ or ḷ vocalized by the inherent sound of e̥. The *Anusvāra*, which enters instead of a nasal dropped at the end of words in *pausa* or before other consonants is a vocalic change of naʒalization, and is to be indicated as such by a diacritical sign over the vowel, not by adding any consonantal letter. ए ओ ऐ औ are diphthongs. The *Visarga* belongs not to one but to all local classes of consonants; it would therefore lead to mistakes, if we were to take *h* for its basis in our transcription. It was so weak a sound, that in the Devanāgari it was not represented by a full consonantic letter, but by two dots (:). Whe should retain the same indication if it had not already another European signification. A slight modification (ḥ) may suit our purpose. The sounds called *Gihvâmûlîya* and *Upadmānīya* would correspond to a very week χ and *f*, but, as they were of so fugitive and variable a nature, that in the Dēvanāgari they were, like the Visarga, only indicated, not substantially written by full letters, it seems advisable not to go farther in our transcription; we keep the Devanāgari indication by ẋ. With regard to the palatals च ज ञ *k̓ ǵ ń*, we have spoken above. The palatal fricative श has conserved in some regions its original sound χ́, but its transition into the actual sound ś seems to have soon taken place; we add the sign χ́ only in brackets. The letters ṣ̌ and ṛ better keep in lingnistic works the cerebral point, although there is no dental š and *r* in the Devanāgari. The solution of *k̓*, *ǵ* etc. into *kh*, *gh* etc. is against the apprehension of the ancient grammarians, who treat those letters as simple ones.

The *modern* pronunciation has not abandoned the simpleness of the vowels ṛ̥ and ḷ̥. The diphthongs ए and औ are turned

[1] *Paläographie als Mittel für die Sprachforschung, zunächst am Sanskrit nachgewiesen.* Berlin. 1834.

into simple vowels *ē* and *ō*. The palatals च and ज have been resolved into the compound sounds *tš* and *dž*, which, considering their etymology, we write *č* and *ǰ* (see the Introduction p. 9). श and ष sorrespond actually to the Polish letters *ś* and *sz*; we write them accordingly *ś* and *š* (see p. 71). ऋ has lost its cerebral nature, and we write it *r* without the dot so much the more as in other modern Indian languages there has been introduced a real cerebral *ṛ* by the side of *r*, this latter being still written with the Devanāgari sign ऋ. With respect to the Aspirates, we follow the Hindustāni writing, which resolves them into *kh, ph,* etc. We have already mentioned, that this solution into two letters is not against our physiological principles (see Introd. p. 11). We maintain the decided reprobation of the use of the letters *ch*, *chh*, *sh*, *ç* instead of our *č*, *čh*, *š*, *ś*, as incompatible with any sound principle of transcription. It is evident that we have to resolve the Devanāgari ligatures, including क्ष *kš*, into their component letters.

With respect to the separation of the single words, we have to follow, against the Devanāgari custom, the European principle, that every grammatically separated word is to be separately written in the latin transcription. This is effectuated without difficulty in the cases where consonants are to be separated from consonants or from vowels. With regard to the crasis of vowels between two words, we should resolve them simply into their component parts and leave it, as we do in latin poetry, to the reader to pronounce them according to the Sanskrit rules. We write therefore तथैवासीद् *tat́āivāsīd* with three words *tat́ā aiva āsīd* or, after the modern pronunciation, *tathā ēva āsīd*. We think it not necessary to indicate the crasis by an apostrophe, as it has been proposed, considering the frequency of the case, and the destination of the apostrophe in European writing to indicate the elision of a letter. We prefer to make use of the common sign of diæresis for the rare cases, where in Sanskrit the hiatus is demanded.

PĀLĪ.

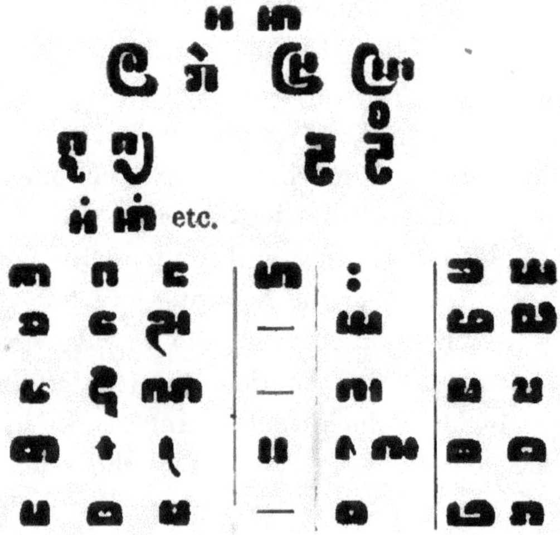

a ā

e ē o ō

i ī u ū

ã ā̃ etc.

k	g	ṅ	h	s	kh	gh
č	ǰ	ń	-	y	čh	ǰh
ṭ	ḍ	ṇ	-	ḷ	ṭh	ḍh
t	d	n	s	l r	th	dh
p	b	m	-	v	ph	bh

Specimen.

Namō Tassa, Bhagavatō, Arahatō, Sammā, Sambuddhassa!

1. *Namas sitvāna Sambuddhā, susuddhā, suddhavā sajā; Mahavansan pavakkhāmi, nānunānādhikārikā*
2. *Porāṇēhi katōpēsō, atīvitthāritō kvačī, ativakvačī sākhittō, anēka punaruttakō;*
3. *Vajjitā tēhi dōsēhi, sukhaggahaṇadhāraṇā, pasādasāvēgakarā, sutitōča upāgatā,*
4. *Pasādajanakē ṭhānē, tathā sāvēgakārakē, janayantā pasādanča, sāvēganča, sunātha tā.*

(Mahāvansō ed. Tournour, ch. I, 1—4.)

Remarks.

The *Pālī* is one of the older Prākrit languages, which, together with Buddhism, has been extended beyond India, principally to Ceylon, Birma and Siam. In these countries the Pāli is still used by the Buddhists for their religious books, where it is written in the different indigenous characters. The character which we have represented here is that of Siam. The palatal and cerebral sibilants, as well as the vowels *ṛ* and *ḷ* have disappeared; the cerebral *ṛ* has become a dental *r*. ञ and य have been dropped.

OLD PRĀKRIT.

अ आ	*a ā*
ए ओ	*ē ō*
इ ई उ ऊ	*i ī u ū*
अं इं etc.	*ã ĩ* etc.
ऐ औ	*ai au*

क ग ङ	ह		ख घ	*k g ṅ*	*h*		*kh gh*
च ज ञ	-	य	छ झ	*č ǰ ń*	-	*y*	*čh ǰh*
ट ड ण	-		ठ ढ	*ṭ ḍ ṇ*	-		*ṭh ḍh*
त द न	स	र ल	थ ध	*t d n*	*s*	*r l*	*th dh*
प ब म		व	फ भ	*p b m*		*v*	*ph bh*

Specimen.

मेत्री ॥ सुदं मए मुदिताए साअसादो जधा महाभैलवीगंसणसंब्भमा-दो भअवदीए विण्हुभत्तीए परित्तादा पिअसही सद्धेत्ति। ता उक्कण्ठि-देण हिअएण पिअसहीं कहिं पेक्खिस्सं.

(*Prabādha Čandrōdaya*, beginning of Act. IV.)

Maitrī: Sudā mē Muditāē sāasādō ǰadhā mahā Bhailavī gā-saṇasābbhamādō bhaavadīē Viṇhubhatrīē parittādā piasahī Saddhētti; tā ukkaṇṭhidēṇa hiaēṇa piasahī kahĩ pēkikhassā̃.

Remarks.

In the Indian literature the different dialects of the popular language are called *Prākrit* in contradistinction to the *Sanskrit* as the purer literary language of the higher classes. It appears in the dramatic works by the side of the Sanskrit and is written likewise with Devanāgari letters. It has lost the same sounds as the Pāli, and moreover the *ḷ*. The letters *ṅ* and *ń* only occur in conjunction with the letters of their own class.

HINDĪ.

अ आ		*a ā*	
ए	ओ	*ē*	*ō*
इ ई	उ ऊ	*i ī*	*u ū*
ऋ अं एं इं etc.		*ṛ ã ẽ ĩ* etc.	
ऐ औ		*ai au*	

क ग ङ	ह		ख घ	*k g ṅ*	*h*		*kh gh*
च ज ञ	श	य	छ झ	*č ǰ ń*	*ś*	*y*	*čh ǰh*
ट ड ण	ष	ड़	ठ ढ ढ़	*ṭ ḍ ṇ*	*ṣ̌*	*ṛ*	*ṭh ḍh ṛh*
त द न	स	र ल	थ ध	*t d n*	*s*	*r l*	*th dh*
प ब म	-	व	फ भ	*p b m*	-	*v*	*ph bh*

Specimen.

हेरोद राजा के समय में यिशू यहूदह देश के बेतलेहेम में जब जन्म हुआ, देखो पंडितों ने पूरब से यिरूशलेम में आके कहा॥ कि यहूदियों का राजा जो उत्पन्न हुआ, सो कहां है. क्योंकि हमने पूरब में उसके तारे को देखा है और उसके पूजा करने को आये हैं॥

(Matth. 2, 1. 2.)

Hērōd rāǰā kē samay mẽ Yiśū yahūdah dēś kē Bētlēhēm mẽ ǰab ǰanm huā, dēkhō panḍitō nē pūrab sē Yirūśalēm mẽ ākē kahā. Ki yahudiyõ kā rāǰā ǰō utpann huā, sō kahā̃ hai? kyõki hamnē pūrab mẽ uskē tārē kō dēkhā hai aur uskē pūǰā karnē kō āyē haĩ.

Remarks.

The *Hindī* is the language of the *Hindūs* in contradistinction to the Moslem population of India. It is spoken in the whole of North India, principally in the country of the upper Ganges and it is uuderstood almost in all India. It is written with Devanāgari letters, which to this purpose are but little altered.

The vowels ṝ ḷ ḹ, as well as the consonants ṅ, ṅ and visarga are no more in use; also the simple ṛ is very seldom used. ऋ and ष have lost their cerebral sound. Instead of ष, which is only used in Hindi prints, if the writer whishes to write a sanskrit word as closely as possible to the original Sanskrit, ख is very generally substituted with the pronuuciation of our common š. Provincially ष takes the pronunciation of χ, and the compound characters क्ष (kš) and ज्ञ (ǵṅ) that of čh and gy. The cerebral letters ड ḍ and ढ ḍh, when medial or final, take very frequently another pronunciation, which by European scholars uses to be indicated by a dot under the letter ड़, ढ़, and transcribed by ṛ and ṛh. This changement of sound seems to me to belong originally to the Dravidian languages where we find a similar occurrance, especially in the Tamil. ड़ and ढ़, are probably only slight assibilations of ड and ढ, as ǰ is an assibilation of ǵ. There is indeed physiologically very little difference between a c e r e b r a l ẓ and ṛ, ẓh and ṛh, the friction on the tip of the tongue, erected at the cerebral point, causing almost unavoidably a slight vibration of the tongue, and reminding by it of the letter r. A perfect analogy to it is the physiological proximity of γ and ṙ of the Arab. (cf. غزاة, γazāh, of which the French have made *razzia*), the slight friction of the γ at the guttural point causing likewise very easily a vibration of the soft palate. It would therefore be more consistent with the genius of the language, to write those two letters ẓ and ẓh; but it seems nevertheless advisable to prefer the hitherto usual transcription of ṛ and ṛh, so much the more as already in the Hindustāni writing the arabic characters ڑ and ڑھ have taken their basis from ر r, not from ڈ ḍ.

The traders and in general the lower class of natives, write and print the *Hindī* very frequently in a character called *Kaithī*, which is an imperfect imitation of the Devanāgari.

HINDŪSTĀNĪ.

							In Arabic or Persian words.
آ أ			ه			ع	ح
أو أي	ك گ	ن (ڱ)	-	-	كھ گھ	ق	خ غ
اَو اُ اِي اِ	ج چ	-	ش	ي	جھ چھ		ژ
	ٹ ڈ	-	-	ڑ	ٹھ ڈھ ڑھ		
اَنْ آنْ اِنْ etc.	- -	-	-	-	- - -	ط	ص ظ ض
اَوْ اَيْ	ت د	ن	س	ر ل	تھ دھ		ث ذ ز
	پ ب	م	-	و	پھ بھ		ف

a ā			*h*	.		*ʾ*	*ḱ*
ē ō	*k g*	*ṅ*	-		*kh gh*	*q*	*χ γ*
i ī u ū	*č ǰ*	-	*š*	*y*	*čh ǰh*		*ž*
â ā̃ ĭ etc.	*ṭ ḍ*	-	-	*ṛ*	*ṭh ḍh ṛh*		
ai au	- -	-	-	-	- -	*ṯ*	*s̱ ḏ ẕ*
	t d	*n*	*s*	*r l*	*th dh*		*θ δ z*
	p b	*m*	-	*w*	*ph bh*		*f*

Specimen.

جب هیرودیس بادشاه کي وقت یهودیه کي بیت لحم مین
عیسی پیدا هوا تو دیکهو کئي مجوسیون ني پورب سي اورشلیم
مین آئي ؞
کها که کهان هي وه جو یهودیون کا بادشاه پیدا هوا که هم
ني پورب مین اسکا ستاره دیکها اور اسي سجده کرني کو آئي هین ؞

Matth. 2, 1. 2.

J̆ab Hērōdīs bādšāh kē waqt yahūdiah kē Bait-laham mẽ ʿĪsā paidā hūā, tō dēkhō kaī majūsiō̃ nē pūrab sē Auršalīm mẽ ākē. Kahā kih kahā̃ hai wuh jō yahūdiō̃ kā bādšāh paidā hūā, kih hamnē pūrab mẽ uskā sitārah dēkhā aur ussē sijdah karnē kō āē haī.

Remarks.

The *Hindūstānī* or *Urdū* is still more generally understood through all India than the *Hindī*. It is a mixture of Hindu with Arabic and Persian. The Mohammedan conquerors, penetrating into India since the 11th century, carried with them their language and writing. The latter was received by the conquered population; but from the language only a number of words was inserted into the Indian language; the grammar, although mutilated, remained Indian, and likewise the system of sounds. It was therefore necessary to introduce for the Indian sounds new letters into the Arabic alphabet, principally for the cerebral sounds *ṭ ḍ ṛ*, which were expressed by the dental bases with the addition of four dots ٿ ڐ ڑ or other diacritical marks. The letters *ṅ ṅ ṇ* and *ṣ*, which already in the *Hindī* were of little use, dropped entirely. ष turned into ش *š*. ग and च were written گ or ڨ and چ. The anusvara was expressed by ں *n*. The merely Arabic letters *ʿ q χ γ ž ḍ(ṭ) ḏ ṣ ẓ θ ð z f* were still written in the Arabic and Persian words, but seldom preserved their original value. ء and ع are not pronounced at all; ح *ḥ* is not distinguished from ہ *h*; ص *ṣ* and ث *θ* sound like س *s*; ط *ḍ(ṭ)* like *t*. The letters *q χ γ ž z f* are pronounced by the Mohammedans often, but not generally, according to their arabic value, by the Hindus like *k*, *kh* or *k*, *g*, *j*, *j* or *s*, *ph* or *p*; *ḏ ẓ ð* are not distinguished from *z* by the Mohammedans, and pronounced *j* or *s* by the Hindu; *n* before *g* and *k* is mostly nasalized as *ṅ*. The anusvara is represented by ں, the dot of which in modern prints is commonly dropped at the end of words to indicate the nasalization of the vowel.

It is evident that we have to transcribe the Arabic letters according to their etymological value, not to their imperfect Indian pronunciation. On the other hand we are not authorized to replace the dropped Hindi sounds *ń ṇ ś* beyond the want of the Hindustāni writing itself. The sound ش *ś* is physiologically, as we have shown above, as well palatal as dental, and originates more frequently from palatal than from dental sounds. In most alphabets therefore we may range more conveniently this letter to the palatal row, where there exists one, than to the dental, to which *s* belongs. We may justly neglect the ءا in the beginning of words. The arabic و *w* is substituted to the Indian व which in Sanskrit was a dento-labial *v*. In Hindustāni the Arabic pronunciation *w* prevails almost entirely, even in Indian words. We transcribe it therefore *w*. Some times the Hindustāni is written and printed in Devanāgari letters, and in this case no notice is taken of the purely arabic letters, to which the Indian sounds and characters are substituted as stated above.

SINDHĪ.

(The Devanāgari and Arabic letters are given according to Dr. Trumpp's system.)

अ आ	क ग ङ	ग॒	ह		ख घ	-	ह़
ए ओ	च ज ञ	ज॒	श	य	छ झ	क़	ख़ ग़
इ ई उ ऊ	ट ड ण	ड॒		ड़	ठ ढ		
अं आं इं ईं etc.	. . .	.	.	. .	. . .	त़	स़ स़ स
ऐ औ	त द न	-	स	र ल	थ ध		स़ ज़ ज
	प ब म	ब॒		व	फ भ		फ़

آ اَ						ع	ح
اُو اِي	ک ڱ نڱ	ڳ	ھ		کھ گھ	ق	غ خ
	چ ج ڃ	ڄ	ش	ي	چھ جھ		
اُو اُ اِي اِ	ڻ ڏ ٽ	ڏ		ڙ	ڊھ ٽھ		
اَنْ آنْ اِنْ اِينْ etc.	. . . .	.	.	. .	. . .	ط	ض ظ ص
	ن د ت		س	ر ل	دھ تھ		ز ذ ث
اَوْ اَيْ	م ب پ	ٻ		و	ڀ پھ		ف

a ā						*ʾ*	*ḥ*
ē ō	*k g ṅ*	*ḡ*	*h*		*kh gh*	*q*	*χ γ*
i ī u ū	*č ǰ ń*	*ǰ̄*	*š*	*y*	*čh ǰh*		
ã ā̃ ĩ ī̃ etc.	*ṭ ḍ ṇ*	*ḍ̄*	-	*ṛ*	*ṭh ḍh*		
ai au ·	. . . .	.	.	. .	. . . .	*t̤*	*s̤ ḏ̤ z̤*
	t d n	-	*s*	*r l*	*th dh*	·	*θ ð z*
	p b m	*b̄*	-	*v*	*ph bh*		*f*

Specimen.

Hindū character.

जडुहीं ईसू यहूदा जे बेत्लहम में हेरोद जे पातिशाह जे डीहंनि में आयो त डिसु मजूसनि उभिरंदे खां यिरुशालेमि में अची चिआंउं त:

यहूद्यनि जो पातिशाहु जो आयो आहे सो किथे आहे छा काणि त उन जो तारो उभिरंदे में डिसी हुन खे पूजण आया आंह्यूं:

Matth. 2, 1. 2.

Musalmān character.

جَڎهِين عِيسَىٰ يَهُودَه جي بَيت لَحَم مِين هيرُوڎ جي پَتِشَاه
جي ڎِينهَن مِين جَايو تَ ڎِسُ مَجُوسَن اُبهِرَنْدي ڪهَان اَورْشَلِيم
مِين اَچِي چِيَائُون تَ ::
يَهُودِيَن جو پَاتِشَاه جو جَايو آهي سو ڪِتهِي آهي ڇهَا ڪَارَن
تَ اُنَ جو تارو اُبهِرَنْدي مِين ڎِسِي هُنَ کهي پُوجَن آيَا آنهِيُون ::

J̌aḍhī̃ Īsū (ʿĪsā) yahūdā (yahūdah) ǰē Bētlahama (Bait-laḣama) mē̃ Hērōda ǰē pātišāha ǰē ḍīhani mē̃ ǰāyō ta ḍisu maǰūsani ubhirandē khā̃ Yirušālēmi (Auršalīma) mē̃ acī čiā̃ũ ta.

Yahūdyani ǰō pātišāhu ǰō ǰāyō āhē, sō kithē āhē? čhā kāṇi ta una ǰō tārō ubhirandē mē̃ ḍisī huna khē pūǰaṇa āyā ā̃hyū̃.

Remarks.

The *Sindhī*, the language of the province of *Sindh* on the lower Indus, differs in essential points from the *Hindī* and is an old independant Prākrit language. There is a great number of different *Sindhī* alphabets, a survey of which

Capt. G. Stack gives in his "Grammar of the *Sindhī* language", Bombay. 1849. p. 3—8. They originate all from the Devanāgari, are none of them widely different, and are all incomplete inasmuch as they do not distinguish all the sounds in writing, which are distinguished in speaking. The European scholars have therefore preferred to make use of the most generally known and most complete alphabets, especially of the Devanāgari for the Hindus, and of the Arabic for the Muhammedans. Others, as the Missionaries A. Burn and A. Matchett have given the preference to the *Panǰābī* alphabet. Capt. Stack in his numerous writings uses the Devanāgari. Dr. Trumpp in his *Sindhī* Readingbook [1] uses besides the Devanāgari also the Arabic letters.

The four sounds, which we have written *ḡ j̄ ḍ̄ b̄* are peculiar to the *Sindhī*. Their pronunciation is that of the letters *g ǰ ḍ b* uttered with a certain stress in prolonging and somewhat strengthening the contact of the closed organ, as if one tried to double the sound in the beginning of a word *gga*, *dǰa* or *ǵǵa*, *ḍḍa*, *bba*. The letter ञ़ or ॻ is described as sounding like *ddy*; but I conceive that we have it to do here with the old pure palatal *ǵ*, which by our ear is not easily distinguished from *ď*, lying between our *g* and *d*. It belongs certainly by etymology to the palatal, not to the dental row, and the same apprehension is shown also by the figure of the corresponding *Hindustānī* characters, which are those of the palatal *ǵ* with the addition of a dot, not those of the dental *d*. For this reason we incline more to the expression by *j̄* or *ḡ′*, than to that by *ḍ̄′*. The cerebral *ṣ̌* has turned, as in the *Hindī*, to *š*; and besides the now dental र *r*, a new cerebral *ṛ* has been formed. With respect to the three letters *ḍ ḍ̄ ṛ*, there is a certain confusion in the book of Capt. Stack.

---

[1] A *Sindhī* Reading-book in the Sanskrit and Arabic character. London. 1858. 8.

There are only two characters ड and ढ distinguished by him, and the explanations given by him p. 6. *note* and p. 9, as to how to assign the two characters to the three sounds, are contradictory. As for ड *ḍ*, there is no reason to deviate from the Devanāgari; *ṛ* is distinguished as in the *Gujarātī* and *Bangālī* through the dot below ड़. The Arabic letters *ʾ ḱ q χ γ ḏ(ṯ) ḏ̣ ṡ ẓ θ δ z f* are generally expressed in modern prints by the Indian letters अ़ ह़ क़ ख़ ग़ त़ स़ स़ स़ स़ ज़ ज़ फ़ with dots below.

GUJARĀTĪ.

અ આ		*a ā*
એ ઓ		*ē ō*
ઇ (ई)	ઉ (ऊ)	*i ī u ū*
અં etc.		*ã ā̃ ī̃* etc.
(ऐ औ)		*ai au*

ક ગ (ङ	ઙ		ખ ઘ	*k g ṅ*	*h*			*kh gh*
ચ જ (ञ)	શ	य		છ ઝ	*č ǰ ń*	*ś*	*y*		*čh ǰh*
ટ ડ ણ	(ष)		ળ	ઠ ઢ	*ṭ ḍ ṇ*	(*ṣ*)		*ḷ*	*ṭh ḍh*
ત દ ન	સ	ર	લ	થ ધ	*t d n*	*s*	*r*	*l*	*th dh*
પ બ મ		વ		ફ ભ	*p b m*	-	*v*		*ph bh*

Specimen.

ने हेरोद राजाना दाहाडा ओमां इहूदमांना बेथलेहेम मां ईसूना जनमा पछी एम थउं के मागीओए पूरवथी इरूसालेम मां आवीने कहुं के.

इहूदीओनो जे राजा जनमो छे ते कांहां छे केम के हमे पूरवमां तेहेना ताराने जोओ ने हमे तेहेनुं भजन करवा आएवा छइए.

Matth. 2, 1. 2.

Nē Hērōd rāǰānā dāhāḍā ōmā̃ ihūdamā̃nā Bēthlēhēm mā̃ īsūnā ǰanmā pačhī ēm thaũ kē māgīōē pūravthī Irūsālēm mā̃ āvīnē kahũ kē.

Ihūdīōnō ǰē rāǰā ǰanmō čhē tē kā̃hā̃ čhē? Kēm kē hamē pūravmā̃ tēhēnā tārānē ǰōō nē hamē tēhēnũ bhaǰan karvā āēvā čhaiē.

Remarks.

Guǰarātī is the name of the dialect spoken in the province of *Guǰarāt* in the south of Sindh. It approaches very nearly to the Hindi, and is written in two characters, viz. in the *Dēvanāgarī* and in the peculiar *Guǰarātī* character, which is derived from the Devanāgari. In the Bālbodh all Sanskrit letters may occasionally be employed in Sanskrit words; but the sounds of *r̥ r̥̄ ḷ ḹ ṛ ḷ š ṡ* are not found in *Guǰarātī* words, and the nasal letters *ṅ* and *ń*, which occur in the language before the letters of their own classes, are represented by the anusvāra. The *Guǰarātī* letter *ś*, corresponding to the Sanskrit स is distinguished by the Brahmans from *ṡ*, but both are equally pronounced by the people as *s* and are therefore, confounded with one another. The cerebral ष is changed in *Guǰarātī* partly in *kh*, and partly in *ṡ*.

MARĀṬHĪ.

अ आ	*a ā*
ए ओ	*ē ō*
इ ई उ ऊ	*i ī u ū*
ऋ ऌ	*ṛ ḷ*
अं इं उं etc.	*ã ĩ ũ* etc.
ऐ औ	*ai au*

क ग ङ	ह	-	ख घ	*k g ṅ*	*h*	-	*kh gh*	
च ज ञ	श	य	छ झ	*č ǰ ń* / *ṭ ḍ*	*ś*	*y*	*čh ǰh* / *ṭh ḍh*	before *e, i* / before *a, o, u, ṛ, ḷ*
ट ड ण	ष	ळ	ठ ढ	*ṭ ḍ ṇ*	*ṣ̌*	*ḷ*	*ṭh ḍh*	
त द न	स	र ल	थ ध	*t d n*	*s*	*r l*	*th dh*	
प ब म	-	व	फ भ	*p b m*	-	*v*	*ph bh*	

Specimen.

आणि हेरोद राजाच्या दिवसांमध्यें येशू यहूदादेशांतील बेथलेहे-
मांत जन्मला असतां पाहा पूर्व प्रदेशापासून कोणी ज्ञानी यरूशालेमांत
येऊन बोलले कीं।

यहूद्यांचा जो राजा जन्मला तो कोठें आहे कां कीं आम्ही पूर्व प्र-
देशांत त्याचा तारा पाहिला आणि त्याला भजावयास आलों.

Matth. 2, 1. 2.

Āṇi Hērōd rāḍā čā divasā̃madhyē̃ Yēśū yahūdādēśā̃tīl Bēthlēhēmā̃t ǰanmalā asatā̃ pāhā pūrva pradēśāpāsūn kōṇī ǰnānī Yarūśālēmā̃t yēūn bōlalē kī̃.

Yahūdyā̃ṭā ḍō rāḍā ǰanmalā, tō kōṭhē̃ āhē? kā̃ kī̃ āhmī pūrva pradēśānt tyāṭā tārā pāhilā āṇi tyālā bhaǰāvayās ālō̃.

Remarks.

The *Marāṭhī* is spoken in a great part of Western Middle India. It has its own character, for which however the

Devanāgari may be substituted. The former character is called *Moḍ* and is generally used in common life. If the Devanāgari with few variations is employed to write the *Marāṭhī*, it is called *Bālbodh*.

The *Marāṭhī* and the *Bangālī* alone amongst the Prākrit languages use still the vowels *ṛ* and *ḷ*. It is a peculiarity of the *Marāṭhī*, that the letters च ज छ झ before the vowels *e*, *i* and *ī* are pronounced as in the other languages *č ǰ čh ǰh*, but before the deeper vowels *a*, *o*, *u*, *ṛ* and *ḷ* are changed into *ṭ ḍ* (and even *z*) *ṭh ḍh*. This reminds of the double pronunciation of the gutturals *c* and *g* in modern European languages according to the following vowel *a*, *o*, *u* or *e* and *i*. If exceptionally the pronunciation *č*, *ǰ* is kept before a deep vowel, य is inserted by some writers to indicate it without being pronounced separately, as in Italian the insertion of *i* in *ciò*, *già* indicates the pronunciation of *čo*, *ǰa*. Others mark the pronunciation of *č* and *ǰ* by putting a dot under the letter, च़, ज़, a system which seems to us preferable. It might be doubtful, if we ought to distinguish in the transcription those sounds or to follow the indigenous writing, in which the distinction is left, as in the Romanic languages, to the reader. But, as we have to represent in our transcription of foreign alphabets principally the actual state of pronunciation, and as those sounds are perfectly fixed in the consonantal system of the *Marāṭhī*, it seems evident, that we have to write these sounds separately. The analogy of *č* and *ǰ* seem to require the signs *ṭ* and *ḍ* instead of *ts* and *dz*.

PANǏĀBĪ or ŚIKH.

ਅ ਆ	*a ā*
ਏ ਓ	*ē ō*
ਇ ਈ ਉ ਊ	*i ī . u ū*
ਅਂ ਆਂ ਏਂ etc.	*ã ā̃ ē̃* etc.
ਐ ਔ	*ai au*

ਕ ਗ (*ṅ*)	ਹ		ਖ ਘ	*k g ṅ*	*h*		*kh gh*
ਚ ਜ (*ń*)	(*ś*)	ਯ	ਛ (*ǰh*)	*č ǰ ń*	*ś*	*y*	*čh ǰh*
ਟ ਡ ਣ	-	ੜ ਲ਼	ਠ (*ḍh*)(*ṛh*)	*ṭ ḍ ṇ*	-	*ṛ ḷ*	*ṭh ḍh* (*ṛh*)
ਤ ਦ ਨ	ਸ (*z*)	ਰ ਲ	ਥ ਧ	*t d n*	*s z*	*r l*	*th dh*
ਪ ਬ ਮ		ਵ	ਫ ਭ	*p b m*		*v*	*ph bh*

Specimen.

Yahūdākē Betlĕhĕm mẽ Hērōd rāǰākē kāl mẽ Yisū ǰamē hōē vēkhu paṇḍit pūrabtē Yirusalēm nū āē atē kahiyā sō kithē haigā ǰō yahūdiyā̃ kā rāǰā ǰanamyā kiūkē pūrab disāvič tiskā tārā asī vēkhdē hā̃gē aru tiskī pūǰā karṇēkō āē hā̃. Matth. 2, 1. 2.

Remarks.

The language of the *Sikh* in the *Panǰāb*, the country of the upper Indus, has received many Arabic and Persian words. It avails itself however only of a character derivated from the Devanāgari and called *Gurmūkhī*. The letters are the same as in the *Hindī* except that *ṣ* is dropped, and *ḷ* and *z* are added.

NIPĀLĪ.

Specimen.

हेरोद् राजाका उसी वक़्त में यिशु यिहूदाह मुलकका बेतलेहेम मा जन्मना वेला हेर पंडित पूरब दिशादेखि यिरुशलेममा आया और उनलाई कह्या जो यिहूदियां का राजा जन्मौ उ कहां छ क्याहा पूरब देशमा उसका तारालाई देखीकन हामि उस्को पूजा गरनकन आयों ॥ Matth. 2, 1. 2.

(N. T. Version by the Serampore Miss.)

Herōd rāǰākā usī waqt mẽ Yišū yihūdāh mulkkā Bētlēhēmmā ǰanmanā vēlā hēr paṇḍit pūrab dišādēkhi Yirušalēmmā āyā aur unlāī kahyā ǰō yihūdiyā̃ kā rāǰā ǰanmau u kahā̃ čha? Kyāhā pūrab dēšmā uskā tārālāī dēkhīkan hāmi uskō pūǰā garankan āyõ.

Remarks.

The *Nipālī* language, mixed with many Tibetan words, is spoken in a large tract on the southern slopes of the Himālaya, north west of Bangāl. The sounds are the same as in *Hindī*, and may be written with *Dēvanāgarī*, although in the country there are several peculiar characters derived from it, in use.

BAṄGĀLĪ.

অ আ	*a ā*
এ ও	*e ō*
ই ঈ উ ঊ	*i ī u ū*
ঋ ৠ ঌ ৡ	*ṛ ṝ ḷ ḹ*
অং আঁ এঁ ওঁ	*ȧ ā̃ ē̃ ō̃* etc.
ঐ ঔ	*ai au*

ক গ ঙ	হ		খ ঘ	*k g ṅ*	*h*	-	*kh gh*
চ জ ঞ	শ	য	ছ ঝ	*č ǰ ń*	*ś*	*y*	*čh ǰh*
ট ড ণ	ষ	ড়	ঠ ঢ ঢ়	*ṭ ḍ ṇ*	*ṣ*	*ṛ*	*ṭh ḍh ṛh*
ত দ ন	স	র ল	থ ধ	*t d n*	*s*	*r l*	*th dh*
প ব ম	-	(ব)	ফ ভ	*p b m*	-	*v*	*ph bh*

Remarks.

The language of *Baṅgal*, the most northeastern province of India, approaches more than any other of the modern Indian dialects to the *Sanskrit*. The character does not differ much from the Devanāgari. In the letter ব *b* the cross-line is dropped, so that there is actually no difference of sign between ব *b* and ব *v*. The language however continues to distinguish both letters, and so does our transcription.

URĪYA.

ଅ ଆ	*a â*
ଏ ଓ	*ê ô*
ଇ ଈ ଉ ଊ	*i ī u ū*
ଋ	*ṛ*
ଅଂ ଆଂ etc.	*ã ẫ* etc.
ଐ ଔ	*ai au*

କ ଗ ଙ	ହ		ଖ ଘ	*k g ṅ*	*h*		*kh gh*
ଚ ଜ ଞ	ଶ	ଯ	ଛ ଝ	*č ǰ ń*	*ś*	*y*	*čh ǰh*
ଟ ଡ ଣ	ଷ		ଠ ଢ	*ṭ ḍ ṇ*	*š*		*ṭh ḍh*
ତ ଦ ନ	ସ	ର ଲ	ଥ ଧ	*t d n*	*s*	*r l*	*th dh*
ପ ବ ମ	-	ଵ	ଫ ଭ	*p b m*	-	*v*	*ph bh*

Remarks.

The language of the province *Urīya*, the maritime country south of Bangal, approaches much to the *Baṅgālī*, but with a greater share of Arabic words. The sounds are almost the same, but the pronunciation is said to be in general somewhat harsher, and the cerebral *ṛ* is wanting entirely. The peculiar character of this country is often used there even in writing Sanskrit.

PAṢTŌ or AFΓĀN.

اَ or ۀ	ک	ګ	نګ	خ	غ			ق	ع	ح	ه	
اَ آ	ڇ	ج	-	ښ	ږ	ي						
اې اُو	څ	ځ	-	ش	ژ							
اِ اِي اُ اُو	ټ	ډ	ڼ			ړ						
اَيْ اَوْ	.	.	.	.	.	.	.	ط		ص	ظ	ض
	ت	د	ن	س	- .	ر	ل			ث	ذ	ز
	پ	ب	م			و				ف		

ạ	k	g	ṅ	χ	γ			q	ʒ	ḱ	h	
a ā	č	ǰ	-	š́(χ́)	ž́(γ́)	y						
ē ō	ṭ	ḍ	-	š	ž							
i ī u ū	ṭ	ḍ	ṇ			ṛ					.	.
ai au	.	.	.	.	.	.	.	d̠(t̠)		s̱	δ̱	ẕ
	t	d	n	s		r	l			θ	δ	z
	p	b	m			v				f		

Specimen.

پَه وَقت چِه عِيسىٰ دَ يَهُودِيَّه پَه بَيت لَحَم کښي پَه زَمَان دَ

هِيرُودِيس شَاه زُوولَيْ وَه نَاگَاه مَجُوسَان لَه مَشرِق نَه پَه اَورشَلِيم وَرَغلَه

وُښتَنَه ئي وَکړه چِه دَ يَهُودَانُ بَادشَاه چِه زُوولَيْ دَي دَا چَرتَه دَي

لَه دي سَبَب چِه ئي سَتُورَي پَه مَشرِق کښي مُو لِيدَلَي دَي اَو

مُوږ رَاغلِي يُو چِه سِجدَه ئي وَکړُو ۞

Matth. 2, 1. 2.

Pah waqt čih ʿĪsā da yahūdiyyah pah bait laħam kšē pah zamān da Hērōdis šāh zōwạlai wạh, nāgāh majūsān lah mašriqa nah pah Auršalīm wạraylạh, puštanah ē (yē) wạkṛah čih da yahūdānu bādšāh, čih zōwạlai dai, dā čạrtah dai? lah dē sababa, čih ē (yē) stōrai pah mašriq kšē mū līdalai dai au muž rāylī yū, čih sijdah ē (yē) wạkṛū.

Remarks.

The language of the Afghans is, in accordance with the geographical position of their country, a middle limb between the Sanskritic or Arian aud the Persiau or Eranian languages. They use the Persian characters with a few modifications. Besides the usual vowels this language has an obtuse vowel nearest approaching to *a*, which we write in consequence *ạ* (see above p. 49). It has in common with the Sanskritic languages the cerebral row; there is at least no difference of opinion with regard to the letters *ṭ* and *ḍ*, whilst, according to some writers, the letters *ṇ* and *ṛ* differ in sound from the Indian *ṇ* and *ṛ*. Slight deviations however appear sometimes to an ear not accustomed to physiological apprehension greater than they are, or result from unessential circumstances. Considering, therefore, that in most Indian languages the four cerebrals *ṭ ḍ ṇ ṛ* have been developed together, and that even in Afghan writing all the four characters have been likewise characterized by one and the same little circle added to the correspondiug dental letters, we do not hesitate to follow those who recognise the cerebral nature of the *Pạštō ṇ* and *ṛ*. Out of the original Palatals two new sounds have been formed besides *č* and *j*, viz. *ţ* and *ḑ*, as in the *Mahrāṭhī*, to which we refer (see above p. 109). This latter did not receive new signs for those sounds, the *Pạštō* on the contrary added one new sign ځ, expressing by it both *ţ* and *ḑ*. Only in modern times there has been introduced by the learned *Pạštō* scholar

Dr. Trumpp a second sign ځ for *ḍ* besides څ *ṭ*, remedying thus an obvious defect of the *Paṣ̌tō* Arabic alphabet.

There are two other sounds peculiar to this language which we must consider. They are represented by the characters ښ and ږ. Their pronunciation differs essentially in different parts of the country. In the western Afghanistan it approaches very near to the pronunciation of ش *š* and ژ *ž*; in the eastern portion, for instance in Peshawer, to that of خ *χ* and غ *γ*. According to Dr. Trumpp these letters are derived at least partly from Palatals — another part seem to proceed from original Cerebrals — and as the Afghans themselves have taken the bases of their signs from ش *š* and ژ *ž*, we propose to take the same bases *š* and *ž* in adding the palatal line *ṡ̌* and *ż̌*. Should it be desirable to indicate the eastern pronunciation specially we should take as bases *χ* and *γ* and add the palatal line *χ́*, *γ́*.

The Semitic letters which we have separated from the rest, are used only in Arabic or Persian words. We regret that the transcription of Capt. Raverty in his last Afghanic publication (1860) has deviated so far both from any sound principle and from practical suitableness.

OLD BAKTRIAN (ZEND).

Vowels. Consonants.

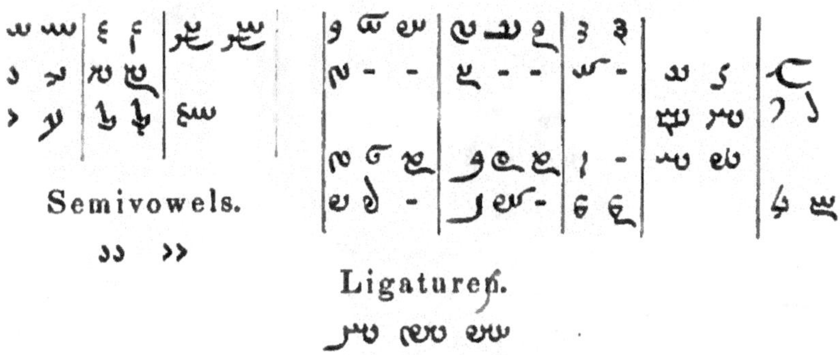

Semivowels.

Ligaturen.

Original pronnnciation.

a ā	*ę ę̄*	*ą̃ ą̄̃*	*k ḱ h*	*g ǵ γ*	*ṅ ń*	- -	- -
i ī	*ẹ ẹ̄*		*ḱ* - -	*ǵ* - -	*ń* -	*ś ź*	*ý* -
u ū	*o ō*	*å*				*š ž*	
			t t́ θ	*d d́ δ*	*n* -	*s z*	*r ŕ*
y(ii) w(uu)			*p ṕ* -	*b b́* -	*m ḿ*	- -	*v v́*

sk st ah

Later (Persian) pronunciation.

a ā	*ę ę̄*	*ą̃ n̄*	*k χ h*	*g* - *γ*	*ṅ (ń)*	- -	- -
i ī	*ẹ ẹ̄*		*č* - -	*ǰ* - -	*ń* -	*ś ź*	*ý* -
u ū	*o ō*	*å*				*š y̌*	
			t θ (θ)	*d d́ δ*	*n* -	*s ż*	*r (ŕ)*
y w			*p f* -	*b ṿ* -	*m (ḿ)*	- -	*v χ̬*

sk(š) st ah

Specimen.

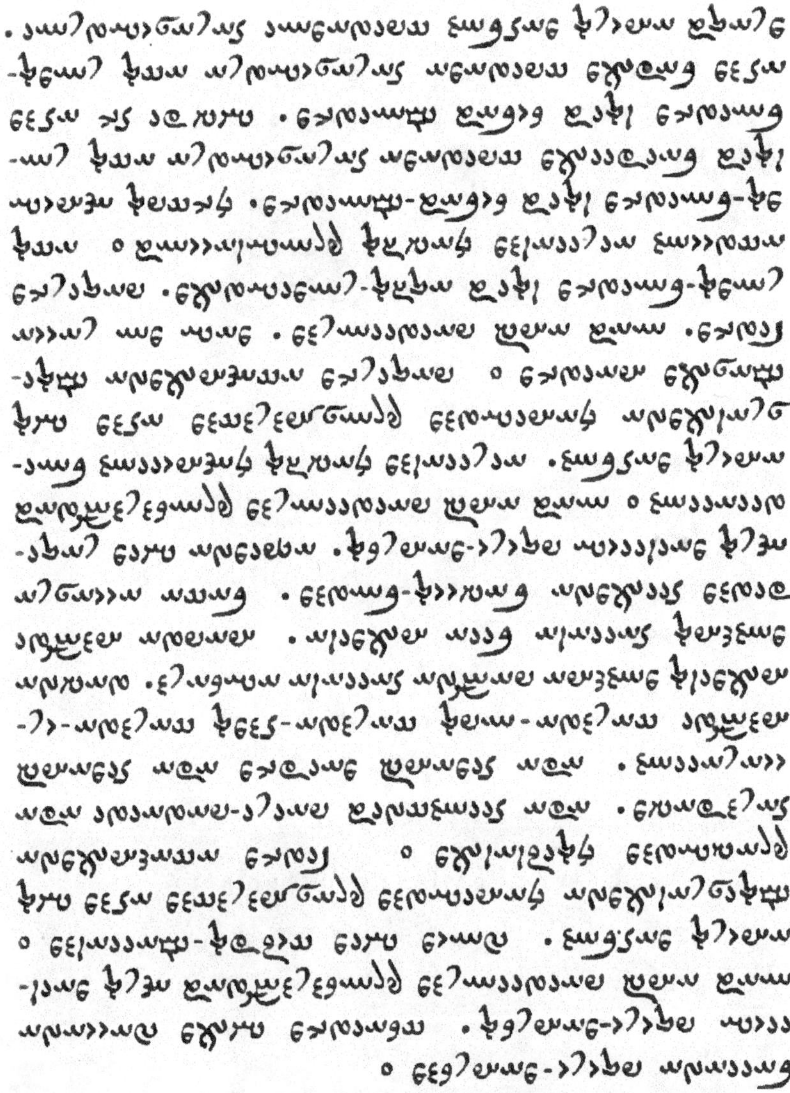

Vendidād, first fargard.

Mraoδ Ahurō maźdâ śpitamāi Źaraθustrāi: Aźem dadăm, śpitama Źaraθustra, aśō rāmō-dāitīm nōiδ kudaδ šāitīm; ўẹdi źī aźem nōiḍ daiďyãm, śpitama Źaraθustra, aśō rāmō-dāitīm nōiδ kudaδ-šāitīm, vīśpō aṅhus aśtwâ airyanem vaẹjō frāsnawāδ. [Aśō rāmō-dāitīm nōiδ aojō rāmistãm, paoirīm bitīm, āaδ ahẹ̄ paityārem, mas mā rawa šaθãm haitīm.] Paoirīm aśaṅhāmča šōiθranãmča vahistem frāθẹreśem, aźem ўō Ahurō maźdâ: Airyanem vaẹjō vaṅhuyâ dāityayâ. Āaδ ahẹ̄ paityārem frākereñtaδ Aṅrō mainyus pouru-mahrkō, aźimča ўim raoiďitem źyãmča daẹwō-dātem. Daśa awaθra mâṅhō źayana, dya hãmina, [hapta heñti hãminō mâṅha, pañča źayana askare;] taẹča heñti śareta-āpō, śareta-źemō, śareta-urwarayâ; aďa źimahẹ̄ maiďīm, aďa źimahẹ̄ źareďaẹm, aďa źyâśčiδ pairi-pataiti, aďa fraẹstem vōiyna-nãm. Bitīm aśaṅhãmča šōiθranãmča vahistem frāθẹreśem aźem ўō Ahurō maźdâ: Gāum ўim Śuγďō-šayanem. Āaδ ahẹ̄ paityārem frākereñtaδ Aṅrō mainyus pouru-mahrkō, śkaitīm ўãm gawača dayača pouru-mahrkem.

Remarks.

We call **Old Baktrian**, as others before us, the language of the Avesta (Zendavesta), the sacred books of the Eranian nations, especially the Baktrians and the Persians. These books of the Zoroastrian religion first originated in Baktria, in the vicinity of northern India, and are the principal witness of an old Baktrian civilisation, of which we know but little beyond. It was probably not before the time of the empire of the Achaemenides that they were introduced from the east to the west of Eran, and particularly amongst the Persians. The language still approaches so nearly to the Indian Sanskrit, that it was principally by the comparison with this language that Burnouf and Bopp were first enabled to decipher the Zend language. The Zend writing has the same origin as all the other phonetic writings, including even the Devanāgari, with the exception of the Persian cuneiform characters. We are of the opinion, that the Zend alphabet existed already in the original country of the Avesta in the same perfection and completeness as we know it actually, or even higher, but that it may have undergone several changes when introduced into Persia and brought in contact with other cognate alphabets of the western countries. It approaches most nearly to the Pehlevi writing. We take this character of the Persian inscriptions and of the Persian handwriting, of the time of the Sassanides, not as the origin, but as the reduction of the Zend character, answering to the poor and partly *semitized* system of sonnds, which at that time prevailed in the Persian language. Both writings underwent apparently the same alterations in their common signs for several centuries till about A. D. 600 and then attained essentially that same state which we still find in our Zend, Parsi and Huzvāresh manuscripts.

In the mean time also the original pronunciation of the old Baktrian alphabet was altered, since its migration into Persia, in conformance to the altered sounds of the Persian language, as they prevailed already in the time of the Achaemenides and still more in subsequent centuries,—just as the pronunciation of the Devanāgari letters approached more and more nearly to that of the modern Indian languages. The right apprehension of the old Baktrian sounds is traditionally preserved only in the alphabetical lists, which were faithfully, but, owing to the ignorance of the writers, incorrectly, copied from one manuscript into the other and thus handed down to us in a tolerably comprehensible state. The arrangement of the original sounds as above stated, is principally the result of the comparison of those ancient alphabets. It ought, according to our opinion, to be followed in every linguistic publication on the Zend language and might even do good services in a critical revision of our actual text.

The vowel system is the most developed of all the ancient languages we know, not excepting even the Devanāgari.

There are two characters for each of the vowels *a i u ẹ ẹ o ā*, one for the short and another for the long ones. The semivowels ננ and ›› , *y* and *w*, were, conformably with their signs, reckoned not as consonants, but as vowels. All the explosive consonants, *r* included, had both a simple and an aspirated form. Two nasal sounds are lost even in the alphabetical lists, where they are represented by the repeated sign of the simple *n* ʃ. The pairs of corresponding sibilants are given as stated above. The letter ⊂, *ý* was, as a palatal consonant, different from the semivowel ננ, *y*, in the same way as ‍ *v* from ›› *w*. The letter *r* had two signs, the latter of which was formed by adding to the simple ʔ *r* the upper stroke ˒ (‍)to indicate the aspiration (as in *k̓*, *t̓*, *p̓*). ‍ was an aspirated *v*. The later pronunciation changed the aspirates *k̓ t̓ p̓ g̓ b̓* into the corresponding fricatives *χ θ(s) f γ v̤*. In consequence of this change the sign ‍ *g̓* disappeared entirely from the manuscripts, and ‍ became an almost arbitrary variation of ‍. We retain the writing *ð*, although the actual pronunciation seems to be not quite clear. The letter ‍ *d̓* escaped the assibilation; but it lost the aspiration and was pronounced like *d*; we keep however the hook to distinguish it from ‍ *d* etymologically. The aspirate ‍ *b̓* was softened to *v* (perhaps to the German *w* see p. 75); we write it *v̤* in putting a dot beneath, only to distinguish it from the afterwards identical initial *v* ‍. The aspiration of *ń* was lost, as that of *ṅ* already previously; *ḿ* is mostly dissolved into *hm*. The palatal sibilants ‍, *ś* and ‍ *ź* took almost entirely the pronunciation of *s* and *z*; we write them *ś* and *ź* to indicate their palatal origin. On the contrary ‍ *s* assumes very often, in the mouth of the Parsis, the pronunciation ‍ *š*, and still more particularly ‍ *z* that of *ž*. There are linguistical reasons why we should not, in this case, follow them, but adhere, in our transcription, to the old sounding, although the usage of European scholars would be in favour of *ž* for ‍. The pronunciation of ‍ *s* as *š* caused its confusion with , and , originally *ž*, is softened to *y* and used almost as identical with . This latter circumstance will perhaps justify our transcription of by *ỹ*, with the basis of *y*, according to the actual pronunciation, and with the addition of our diacritical sign of assibilation ˇ, to denote its former sound. The letter *ý* is (like *v*) always used in the beginning of words, *y* (like *w*) in the middle; it is nevertheless necessary, in our transcription, to distinguish them both, one being considered as a consonant, the other as a vowel. We therefore write *ý* with the palatal line. The aspiration of *ṙ* dropped, and then *ṙ* became identical with *r*. On the contrary the aspiration of *ẇ* increased and gave rise to the later pronunciation *χw*, and ultimately to *χ* alone, thus producing a confusion with *χ*. We write the in virtue of its etymology *χ̬*. There is no indication of its ever having been pronounced explosively as *q* or *kh*. The first of the three ligatures , *sk*, was in later times pronounced *š*, and therefore occasionally confounded with .

A glance at these alterations shows, that the principal difference between the old and the later pronunciation consists in the disappearance of the aspirations, which were peculiar to the Baktrian throat, and which either dropped without any compensation, or changed the explosive sounds into fricative.

With respect to the vowels there is a general influence of the western languages to be observed in the less decided distinction between the long and short vowels. This is the reason of many confusions, and explains, how the letter *ẹ́* had been hitherto taken for *ē* and as almost identical with *ẹ̄*, and why moreover and , and , or even and , and are frequently used in the MSS. for one another. The most striking change however took place in the letter , which originally and still in the alphabetical lists, represented the anusvara of *ā*, viz *ā̃*, corresponding to 𐬄, *ą̃*, but which afterwards was used as a separate c o n s o n a n t a l nasal after the vowels and before certain consonants. The fact is, that the difference between *ą̃* and *ā̃* was obliterated; the sign 𐬅 became therefore disposable and was employed to express to a certain extent what is called (though not rightly) by Sanskrit scholars the „substituted" anusvāra, whilst 𐬄 was reserved for the „necessary" anusvāra. This, now almost constant, use of 𐬅 obliges us in spite of the evident misunderstanding which gave rise to this use, to look in our transcription for a corresponding c o n s o n a n t a l sign, and there could hardly be a more convenient one than *ñ*, the more so as it is already employed by Burnouf. Simultaneously with this corruption, the entire designation of the anusvāra sound, which existed in the Baktrian, but not in the Persian language, fell into confusion, and the peculiar expressions, which, according to the alphabetical lists, must have originally existed, were either exchanged for 𐬅 *ñ* or 𐬨 *m*, or they disappeared altogether lengthening only the remaining simple vowel. The vowel sign 𐬃 seems to us composed not of 𐬁 and 𐬊, but of 𐬁 and 𐬎, and to have been originally the diphthong *āŭ*, which was afterwards changed into *â*.

We do not state at length the reasons for the assertions as given above; they will be found discussed in a special dissertation read before the Berlin Academy.

In the specimen, we have made use only of the later pronunciation, because our manuscripts contain it to so large an extent, that we cannot substitute the original sounds without altering the actual state of the text.

OLD PERSIAN (CUNEIFORM).

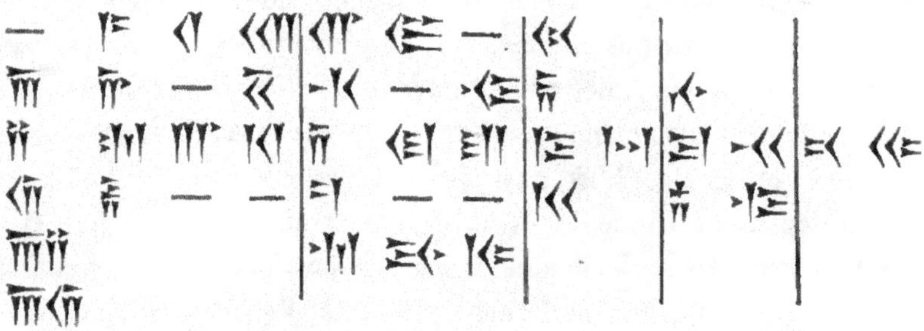

Foreign characters of doubtful meaning: 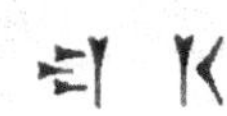

ḁ	ka,i	ḱu	χa,(i),u	ga,i ?	ǵu	-	ha,i,u		ya,i,u			
a	ča,i,(u)	-	ša,i,u	ǰa,(u)	-	ži	śa,i,(u)		ra,i	ŕa,(u)		
i, ē	ta,i	t́u	θa,i,u	da,i	d́u	δi	sa,i,(u)	za,i,(u)	w,i	ẃu,a	na,i	ńu
u, ō	pa,i,u	-	-	ba,i,u	-	-	fr,a					
ai				ma	ḿu	vi						
au												

Specimen.

Detached inscription A. at Behistun (Rawlinson).

Adạm Darỵạwuš, χšayạθiyạ wạzạrkạ, χšayạθiyạ χšayạθiyanam, χšayạθiyạ Parsiyạ; χšayạθiyạ dạhyunam, Vištaspạhya puṡạ, Aršamạhya nạpa, Hạχamạnišiyạ. θatiyạ Darỵạwuš χšayạθiyạ: Mạna pita Vištaspạ, Vištaspạhya pita Aršamạ; Aršamạhya pita Ariyarạmnạ, Ariyarạmnạhya pita Čišpiš; Čišpišhya pita Hạχamạniš. θatiyạ Darỵạwuš χšayạθiyạ: Awạhyạraδiyạ wạyạm Hạχamạnišiya θạhyamạhyạ, hạča pạṙuviyạt amata amạhyạ; hạča pạṙuviyạt hya amaχạm tōma χšayạθiya ahạ ~~θātiyạ~~ Darỵạwuš χšayạθiyạ: 8 mạna tōmaya tyiyạ pạṙuwạm χšayạθiya ahạ adạm nạwạmạ 9; ďuvitatạrnạm wạyạm χšayạθiya amạhyạ.

Remarks.

The cuneiform rock-inscriptions of the time of the Achaemenides usually contain three identical texts, each of which is written in a different language and in a different writing. The last of them is the Assyrian text, in a Semitic language, the writing of which is, as system, the oldest of the three, consisting, like the hieroglyphical, partly of ideographic and partly of phonetic signs. The second or middle text, usually called Median and by Rawlinson and Norris Scythic, contains a language which, although it is not yet sufficiently explored, seems to be essentially Turanian. It is written with a syllabarium of nearly 100 characters, which for the greater part are taken, both as to figure and to sound, from the Assyrian stock. Whilst therefore, we must regard this alphabet as a later one with respect to the Assyrian, it is, on its part, older than the third writing, the first according to its place on the tablets, viz. the Persian alphabet, which we have here to consider.

This Persian cuneiform writing is purely alphabetical and contains vowels as well as consonants. Some of its characters are very similar to some of the second writing, but entirely different in sound. There are scholars (Oppert, Rawlinson), who would claim also for this writing a certain syllabical nature, inasmuch as they contend that part of the consonants change their graphic signs according to the following vowel without altering their pronunciation. This opinion, however, unplausible as it is in itself, is disproved moreover by the circumstance that not all the classes of consonants are liable to this law of changing the figure, but only such classes where a simultaneous change of sound may be accounted for by linguistical reasons. We may therefore be certain that every different sign belongs to a different sound.

The vowel *u* possessed the most general influence on the

preceding consonant. This vowel was apparently in all positions pronounced with a strong breathing, which in Greek was often expressed by χ or even by *k* (*Uwrązwiyą*, *Uwakšatąrą* = Χωρασμία, Κυαξάρης). This breathing was transmitted to every preceding explosive letter, except the labials *p* and *b*. The letters *k*, *t*, *g*, *d*, *m*, *n*, *r* became accordingly aspirates and were expressed by peculiar signs.

The Palatals *č* and *ǰ* seem to have no aspirate, owing to their assibilation which ranged them in this respect amongst the fricative letters. We distinguish the aspirates from the corresponding non-aspirates by placing the spiritus asper over them, and we prefer this writing so much the more, instead of separating the aspiration by the addition of *h*, because the formation of the aspiration *m̔*, *n̔*, *r̔*, *w̔* is almost peculiar to the old Persian language and would hardly be rightly appreciated, if we write *mh*, *nh*, *rh*, *wh*. We follow in this case only the precedent of Rawlinson and others, who write however *m̓*, *n̓*, etc. instead of indicating an aspiration.

The second vocalic influence is that of the vowel *i*, the softening and assibilating power of which is well known from other languages, especially from the Romanic. In the old Persian language this influence was confined to the explosive sonant letters *ǰ*, *d*, *m*. It consisted in loosening their explosion into the corresponding soft friction, changing therefore *ǰ* into *ž*, *d* into *δ*. The labial *b* is neither affected by *u* nor by *i*, for we find *ba*, *bu*, *bi* with the same consonantal sign. But the softer labial explosive *m* took its place and was altered before *u* and *i* into *m̔* and *v* (which however was perhaps pronounced not as dentolabial *v*, but as pure labial *w̱*, see above p. 75). The semivowel *w* was no doubt regularly pronounced with the same strong guttural breathing as the vowel *u*, and the same sign was used before *a* and before *u*; we write it therefore *w̔*; yet the vowel *i*, when following, was not consistent with this guttural nature of the *w̔*; the aspiration was dropped, and the letter was changed into our common *w*: *ẃa*, *ẃu*, *wi*.

The letter 𐏂 corresponds always to the sanskrit *tr*, the zendic *θr*, and was therefore hitherto transcribed in roman letters by *tr*. But it cannot be doubted, that this single letter expressed, as all the other letters, only one simple sound, not two sounds, which moreover, if they ever were intended, ought to be written, according to the laws of the language, *θr* not *tr*. The combination *θr* however exists besides (*Miθra*, *Xšaθrita*) and must therefore have been different in pronunciation. In the Turanian text we find instead of the letter 𐏂 two *š* or (as Rawlinson reads them) two *s*, and in other cases one *š* (or *s*), as in *Aššina* or *Ašina*, *čišša*, etc. To the latter word, in Persian *čiśa* corresponds the first part of the name of *Τισσαφέρνης*, and in the Pehlevi (*Huzvāreš*) and Pārsi the same original *tr* reappears as the simple sibilant س *ś* (*ś*), as in سه, سه, سه, *three*. It seems therefore advisable to follow this obvious hint in transcribing the letter 𐏂 by *ś*. We write the letters 𐎧 and 𐎰 *χ* and *θ*, instead of *k'h* and *th* of Rawlinson, or *k* and *t* of Bopp, having found the aspirates *k*, *t* already before *u*. They are not seldom produced by a following *r*, analogous to the frequent combination of *fr*; and in Greek they are expressed by *χ* and *θ*, as in *Ἀχαιμένης*, *Μίθρας*. To *ǰ* and *d* before the vowel *a* correspond evidently the sounds *ž* and *δ* before *i*.

With regard to the vowels, there is no distinction made between the short and the long, and the shortest and most obtuse vowel, which was not identical with, but only approaching to our *ă*, was not written at all, although it formed syllables. We are thus very often at a loss to know where this indistinct vowel was pronounced and where not. It seems therefore important, to mark clearly in our transcription this interposed vowel, wherever it may seem expedient to write it. It will be more consistent with the genius of the language and in the same time more approaching the true pronunciation, if we write the vowel 𐎠 in all positions *a*, and the supplementary vowel *ą*. There is still another point, where the original writing is defective regarding the vowels. It has been proved that the characters *i* and *u* express not only these simple vowels, but also their respective guna-vowels. The preceding consonants indicate sometimes this guna-pronunciation; in other cases grammatical reasons alone can decide upon our writing. But at all events we prefer to render the guna-vowels by *ē* and *ō* instead of *ai* and *au* as others do. Here is not the right place to discuss this and other points, which are developed by the author in a special treatise. It remains only to state that there are still two unknown signs to account for, the first of which is only found in two foreign proper names, the second in a peculiar term for the word „king", which does not occur in the earlicr inscriptions, but only in later ones, where it seems to be introduced from a foreign language. Thus we take the Persian alphabet stated above as complete, and regard the letters  and  as undeciphered foreign characters.

MODERN PERSIAN.

	Persian sounds.							Arabic letters.
ـَ ـَا	—	أ	—	ه	—			ع ح
ـِ ـُ	ک	گ	—	خ	غ			ق
ـِ ـِي ـُ ـُو	چ	ج	—	ش	ژ	ی		
ـَی ـَو ـَای ـُوی	—	—	—	—	—	—		ظ ض ص ط
	ت	د	ن	س	ز	ر	ل	ث ذ
	پ	ب	م	ف	—	و		

	Persian sounds.							Arabic letters with their Persian pronunciation.
a ā	-	ʼ	-	*h*				ʿ(ʼ) ḥ(*h*)
e o	*k*	*g*	-	*χ*	*γ*			*q*(*g*)
i ī u ū	*č*	*ǰ*	-	*š*	*ž*	*y*		
ai au āi ūi	-	-	-	-	-	-		*ḏ*(*t*) *ṣ*(*s*) *ẓ*(*z*) *ḏ̣*(*z*)
	t	*d*	*n*	*s*	*z*	*r*	*l*	*θ*(*s*) *ḏ*(*z*)
	p	*b*	*m*	*f*		*w*		

Specimen.

زموبد بدین گونه داریم یاد
هم از گفت آن پیر دهقان نژاد
کز آنپس چنان کرد کاوس رای
که در پادشاهی بجنبد ز جای
از ایران بشد تا بتوران و چین
گذر کرد از آنپس بمکران زمین
ز مکران شد آراسته چون عروس
برآمد دم نای و بوق و کوس
بپذرفت هر مهتری باژ و ساو

نَكَرْد آزمون گَاو بَا شِير تَاو
چُنَان هَم گُرَازَان بِبَربَر شُدَنْد
جَهَانْجُوى بَا تَاج وُافْسَر شُدَنْد

Firdusi, Book of the kings (ed. J. Mohl, t. II, p. 4.).

Zi-mōbed bed-īn gūne dārīm yād,
hem ez goft i ān pīr ı dihqān-nižad:
k-ez ān-pes čunān kerd Kā'ūs rāi,
ki der pādišāhī bi-jumbed zi-jāi,
ez Īrān bi-šud tā be-Tūrān u-Čīn.
guδer kerd ez ān-pes be-Mekrān-zemīn,
zi-Mekrān šud ārāste čūn ʿarūs:
ber-āmed dem ī nāi ū-būq u-kūs.
bi-peδireft her mihterī bāž u-sāw,
nekerd āzmūn gāw bā šīr i tāw.
čunān hem gurāzān be-Berber šudend,
jihānjūi bā tāj u-efser šudend.

Remarks.

It is well known that the modern Persian language has admitted a great many Arabic words as well as the Arabic character. It uses consequently all the Arabic letters in the Semitic part of the language, but only in writing. In the language spoken the purely Semitic letters ض ص ظ ط ح ق ع are prononnced like the Persian sounds ز س ز ت ه ک أ, and even the letters ث and ذ, which once had their peculiar pronunciation as θ and δ, are actnally pronounced like س *s* and ز *z*. We keep nevertheless the old value in our transcription, as Persian writing does, for the sake of etymology.

The vowels *e* and *o* are not distinguished in writing from *a* and *u*, and the *i* or *ī* „of junction“ is not written at all. These and some minor deviations from the regular pronunciation are not received in our transcription.

ARMENIAN.

Vowels.				
			հ (յ)	
ը	կ գ ք	—	խ ղ	
ա	ճ ջ չ	—	շ ժ	յ
ե է ո օ	ծ ձ ց	—	— —	
յ, ի ւ, ու	տ դ թ	ն	ս զ	ր ռ լ
	պ բ փ	մ	(ֆ) ւ	վ

Modern pronunciation in Armenia.

ẹ			h (h̓)	
a	k g k̓	-	χ γ (γ̂)	
e ĕ o ŏ	č ǰ č̓	-	š ž	y
i u	ṭ ḍ ṭ̓	-	- -	
	t d t̓	n	s z	r r̄ l
	p b p̓	m	(f) v	w

Specimen.

ՄԻՆՉ չեւ բնաւ էր ինչ, ասեն, ոչ երկինք եւ ոչ երկիր եւ ոչ այլ ինչ արարածք՝ որ յերկինս կամ յերկրի, Զրուան ոմն անուն էր, որ թարգմանի բախտ կամ փառք։ Զհազար ամ յաշտ արար՝ զի թերեւս որդի մի լինիցի նմա, որում անուն Որմիզդ, որ զերկինս եւ զերկիր եւ զամենայն որ 'ի նոսա՝ առնիցէ. եւ յետ հազար ամի յաշտ առնելոյ՝ սկսաւ ածել զմտաւ, ասէ. օգո՞ւտ ինչ իցէ յաշտս զոր առնեմ, եւ լինիցի՞ ինձ որդի Որմիզդ, եթէ 'ի զուր ինչ ջանայցեմ։ Եւ մինչ դեռ նա զայս խորհէր, Որմիզդ, եւ Արհմն յղացան յարգանդի մօր իւրեանց.

Eznik, Refutatio haeres. (Petermann, Gramm. Armen. p. 44.)

Minǰ ǰyev pnau ēr inǰ, asyen, woǰ yerkinḱ yeṿ woǰ yerkir yev woǰ ail inǰ araraṭḱ wor ḱyerkins kam ḱyerkri, Zruan womn anun ēr, wor ťargmani baχt kam ṕařḱ. Ẹzhazar am ḱašt arar zi ťyeryevs wordi mi liniṭi nẹma, worum anun Ormizd, wor zyerkins yev zyerkir yev zamyenain wor i nosa ařniṭē. Yev hyet hazar ami ḱašt ařnyeloḱ ẹsksau aṭyel ẹzmtau, asē: Ōgut inǰ iṭē ḱašṭẹs zor ařnyem, yev liniṭi inḍ wordi Ormizd, yeťē i zur inǰ čanaiṭyem? Yev minǰ dyeř na zais χorhēr, Ormizd yev Arhmẹn ḱγyeṭan ľargandi mōr iureanṭ.

Remarks.

We are told that the actual Armenian alphabet was made up in the 5th century by the learned grammarian Mesrob. The figures of the letters are taken from the Greek figures of that time, as their uncial forms show; the alphabetical order fixed by the numerical value of the letters, is likewise that of the Greek, but occasionally interrupted by those purely Armenian letters which were unknown to the Greek. The accordance of the letters common to both alphabets, as well as the orthography of the ancient proper names, and to a certain extent even the etymological comparison of the cognate Indian and Eranian languages, with which the Armenian is closely connected, prove that the actual pronunciation of a large part of this people differs in some points widely from the ancient pronunciation. We speak of the Turkish Armenians, better known than others in Europe by their countrymen in the Mechitarist convents of Venice and Vienna. The principal alteration of the old pronunciation consists in their pronouncing the ancient *tenues* as *mediae* and vice versa. In Armenia proper, however, and the surrounding provinces this change has not taken place. This has been carefully verified by the author examining personally the pronunciation of a learned

Armenian from Tiflis.[1] We can not, in consequence, hesitate to abandon the usual system taught, according to the Turkish pronunciation, hy Enropean Grammarians, and to follow that of the indigenous Armenians. There we find the letters կ տ պ, *k t p* distinctly pronounced without any aspiration as real dry *tenues*[2] like those of the Hungarian, of several German dialects, of the Sanskrit and other languages; գ դ բ, *g d b*, are our common mediae and ք թ փ, *ḱ t ṕ*, the true aspirates, pronounced as the so called tenues of northern Germany, France, England and others, with a sensible breathing from the lungs. The pronunciation of the two palatal classes is more difficult. There is no aspiration heard in չ and ց, although they correspond evidently to the aspirates of the other classes. Only the stronger closing of the organ is the same as in the aspirates, whilst, in opening the organ, the aspiration turns into a slight breathing *ž* or *z*, as if one would pronounce *ttž* and *ttz*. We write therefore *c̄* and *ṭ* to indicate the double value of the first element. The *č* and *ǰ* are pronounced nearly as in *church* and in *join*; but ձ *ḍ* and ծ *ṭ* are hardly discernible, the one being pronounced as *dz*, the other as *tz*. The tongue takes in hoth palatal classes its full palatal position, in the first more behind, near the soft palate, in the second more foreward above the teeth. The letter ղ is now pronounced every where as the arabic غ *γ*, although it is proved, that it was in many cases formerly, and still in the 5th Ct., a kind of soft and more palatal *l*, distinguished from the stronger and more guttural *l*, the value of which is now that of our common *l*. The ղ originated from *l* was therefore in former

---

[1] Cf. the Armenian Grammar published in Armenian by Bogratuni (Venice 1852), and Petermann, who states the same in the Memoirs of the Berlin Academy 1860. p. 82.

[2] See my exposition about the true character of the *tenues*, *mediae* and *aspiratae* in my treatise on the Arabic sounds and their transcription in the Memoirs of the Berlin Academy 1861. p. 105 sqq.

times written ղ̓ or Լ̓, and took its name ղ̓իւն *yiun*, not from the ղատ *yat*, but from the լիւն *liun*. Hence the mistake, that in several Armenian grammars the letter ղ *γ*, is reckoned amongst the liquids. It would perhaps be recommendable to linguists to distinguish the ղ̓ even in the transcription from the original ղ by adding the original hook (ղ = *γ*, ղ̓ = *γ̓*). The letter յ was originally *y* or a short *i*. It is still pronounced as *ĭ* in the diphthongs *ai* and *oi*. In the beginning and at the end of words it changes commonly into *h*, which we write for the sake of etymology *h̓*. The sound of ր is that of our common *r*, whilst ռ is pronounced as a strong double *r*, which we write *r̄*. The figure and value of Փ *f* is of later origin and is found almost entirely in foreign words. Վ is the dento-lābial *v*, not the english *w*, to which the consonantal ւ between vowels nearer approaches, although it resembles more the *w* of middle Germany. The vowel *u* is represented by its simple form ւ only as the second part of a diphthong, otherwise it is written ու. The letter ե (called եչ *yeǰ*) is almost regularly pronounced *ye*; this is always the case in the beginning of words, and ո *o* in the same position is pronounced *wo*. The vague vowel ը *e̥* is seldom expressed in writing, but always pronounced in certain combinations of consonants. We follow in our specimen the actual pronunciation without entering farther into the interesting etymological questions.

KURD (*Zazá* dialect).

i̥
a ā
ę ę̄
e ē o̤ o ō
i ī ṳ u̇ ū
au eu ai ei

a	*ā*	*ę*	*ę̄*	*ȫ*
i	*ī*	*e*	*ē*	*ṳ*
u	*ū*	*o*	*ō*	*i̥*

au ai eu ei

–	ʼ	–	[*ḱ*]*h*			
	q					
k	*g*	*ṅ*	*χ*	*γ*		
ḱ	*ǵ*	*ń*			*y*	
č	*ǰ*	–	*š*	*ž*		
t	*d*	*n*	*s*	*z*	*r*	*l*
	ď		·			
p	*b*	*m*	*f*	*v*	*w*	

Specimen.

J̌áiki bī či ńébī, yau Aláh bę̄, yau ārewāṅčī bę̄. Āriš tęḱnáini. Rōǰ yéke béri āri qáfelnā šę̄ kéiye, šáʾue kéiye rā kaut, sebáh węríšt, āmę̄ āréye, auńáike árdi mesáhi̥di čįńi; áya šáuʾe nęwete paʾúte, auńái ke myáne šáʾue yau lúʾe āméi zęre, šíe mesáhe, árdi węrdī. Ārewāṅčī węríšt, yau čúa geráute, dai lúʾeru; ęrzía lúʾe tępíšte, lúʾe bęrmái. Lúʾe vā ke ārewāṅčīra: te me verá de, ęz túeri kéinai pašáde Mįsri wazénʾa. Ārewāṅčī vā ke: ęz yau męrdṳmu ārewāṅčia, ti̥ méri čitáu kéinai pašáde Mįsri wazénʾi? Lúʾe vā ke: ti̥ me męḱše, ęz túeri wazénʾa, ę̄ke me ńéwaište kéinai pašáde Mįsri, ti̥ me verá de. Ārewāṅčī vā ke: ti̥ méri suáṅd buáne. Lúʾe ārewāṅčīri suáṅd węnd, ārewāṅčī lúʾe verá dai.

P. Lerch, Forschnngen über die Kurden. I, p. 88.

Remarks.

The language of the Kurds in the mountanous countries of Kurdistan and Laristau seems to be divided into 5 chief dialects, these of *Zazá*, *Kurmáṅǰi*, *Kelhúri*, *Gurâni* and *Lūri*.

The alphabet given above is that of the *Zazá* dialect, as fixed by P. Lerch in his Researches on the Kurds. The *Kurmáňji* has no ň nor ď. The Kurds have no peculiar writing nor any literature. There exist only some modern specimens of their language written in Persian letters. Mr. Lerch therefore employed in his work the Standard alphabet (see above, p. 6). The vowel ị is not our ị, but our vague vowel ẹ approaching to i. Instead of Mr. Lerch's ṭ and ḍ we have now proposed to write č and ǰ. There are in the Kurd language many Arabic words, which, if written in Arabic or Persian writing, keep all their Arabic letters. But, as the people have no written literature, we think, that Mr. Lerch was right in transcribing only the sounds that they really pronounce, amongst which we see also the semitic letters *q* and *ḱ*.

OSSETIAN.

Georgian characters.

ჷ				
ა				
ე			ო	
(ე)	(ჷ)	—		
ი				უ

ყ	-	-	-	ჰ	-		
კ	გ	ქ	-	ხ	ღ		
ქ́	გ́	კ́	-	-	-	ჲ	
ჭ	ჯ	ჩ	-	შ	ჟ		
წ	ძ	ც	-	-	-		
ტ	დ	თ	ნ	ს	ზ	რ	ლ
პ	ბ	ფ	მ	ჶ	-	ვ	

	ị ī̤			
	a ā			
e ē			o ō	
ẹ ẹ̄		ọ	ọ̄ -	
i ī				u ū

q'	-	-	-	h	-		
k'	g	k	ṅ	χ	γ		
ḱ'	ǵ	ḱ	-	-	-	y	
č'	ǰ	č	-	š	ž		
ṭ'	ḍ	ṭ	-	-	-		
t'	d	t	n	s	z	r	l
p'	b	p	m	f	-	w	

Specimen.

Dialect of Jalgusidse.

Maχ fịd keṭị de arwịtị mideg; siγdeg went de nom; erṭewent de meligad; went bar dew, kwịd arwịtị mideg, afteder bast'ịl; ǰul ne bonṭị radt' maχen abon; eme nịwaǰ maχen ne χeste, kwịd maχ nịwaǰịst'em ne χesǵịnten; eme ne ma baftaw maχ fịlewzerenị, fele fẹrwezịnken maχ fịdbịlịzey; emeneme dew u meligad, tịχ eme ịsdịrad mịkk'agme. Amin.

Digorian dialect.

Maχ fidẹ keči dē arwitiy mịedẹg; qeḍōz uodẹ de nōn; arṭauodẹ de p'aṭ'aχǰinādẹ; uodẹ dē barẹ, arwiy mịedẹg kud, zaṅχay bọl uoteḍeṛ; maχ ḍol ṭaruniy tuχey rädt'e maχan āboniy; ama χalārkane nie χaste maχan, maχt'er kud χalārkanān nie χaskinten; ama ne ma farāduyunkane; falfayerwāzunkane maχ fudbuluzey; oy tuχey dawon ey paṭ'aχjināde, tuχe ama st'urjināde mukk'āgey mukk'āgma; fauod.

Tagaurian dialect.

Maχ fịd keṭị dē arwịṭịy mideg; siydeg uod de nōm; erṭauod de paṭ'aχḍinād; uod de bar, arwịy mideg kud, zaχịl auteder; maχ ḍul onịnen rādt' maχen ābon; eme χalārken ne χaste maχen, maχt'er kud χalārkenem ne χastinten; eme ne ma ferāduinken; fele ferwēzịnken maχ fịdbịlịzey; ay tịχey key is dewon paṭ'aχḍinād, tịχ eme st'ịrḍinād mịkk'āgey mịkk'āgme; fauod.

The Lords prayer. Sjögren, Osset. Sprachl. p. 32.

Remarks.

The Ossetes have no alphabet of their own; but their system of sounds approaches so much to the Georgian or Grusinian, that the Ossete Jalgusidse, as well as afterwards Dr. Rosen, both found it convenient to employ the Georgian alphabet to represent the Ossetian language, for which it was necessary to add but a few consonantal signs. It was by far more difficult for Sjögren to adapt to the same language the Russian alphabet. This eminent scholar distinguishes three dialects, two northern, the Digorian and the Tagaurian, and one southern, which he met with in the writings of Jalgusidse. We use above the Georgian alphabet, to connect our transcription with former labours. The letters ჭ́ გ́ კ́ (*ḱ' ǵ ḱ*) have been added by Jalgusidse, to denote the softened sounds rising from the gutturals *k' g k* before *ẹ i ị*. Sjögren doubts without reason about the letter *ḱ'*, which is even demanded to complete the system and which may exist too in the two other dialects without having been remarked. He explains erroneously the letter ღ as *ǵ* or *gh*, since it corresponds, as Rosen rightly states, to the sound of our *y*. The special designation of *ṅ* by Sjögren seems to be less essential, since neither Jalgusidse nor Rosen have made this distinction. We keep however the letter *y*, though not distinguished by Rosen from *i*. The Digorian dialect, according to Sjögren has *t́ d́* instead of *ḱ ǵ*. As they are all apparently real palatals, the dialectical difference can only be very slight, so as to make it advisable to write also in the Digorian dialect *ḱ ǵ*. The Ossetian *tenues* of our first column of consonants approach perceptibly to the peculiar pronunciation of the Georgians and other Caucasian nations. The true *tenuis* (cf. above p. 134) is pronounced with its full explosion, but with closing the glottis and in consequence without any pectoral aspiration (*h*), after which follows the new opening of the glottis (ʾ) in order to utter the appertaining vowel. Hence our transcription *kʾ*, *tʾ*, *pʾ* etc. The aspirates of the third column have but a slight aspiration, and we write them so much the more without the spiritus asper (*ḱ t* etc.), as their opposition to the first column is already indicated there. As to the vowels Sjögren makes very nice distinctions, especially of the different *e* sounds, of which he states three gradations, observing, that the most open *e* (his *æ*) approaches very nearly to the English *a* in *hat*, *fat*. It will certainly be found convenient to reckon his second gradation, the short *e*, and his third gradation, the long *é*, both being nearer to *i* than *æ*, as one class in our transcription. We get therefore two classes, *e̱ ē̱* and *ẹ ẹ̄*, the former being pronounced very open; and as this class is more frequent in the language than *ẹ ẹ̄*, we leave the line underneath and write *e ē* and *ẹ ẹ̄*. Likewise we write *o ō* for the open *o*, and *ọ* for the closed *o*, which Sjögren writes *ω*. The indistinct *i̥* sound, the *ü* of Sjögren, approaches nearest to *i*, but it has nothing to do with the hard *i̯*, as is shown clearly by the fact, that it softens a preceding *k* or *g* into *ḱ* and *ǵ*. In the Tagaurian dialect the letters *ẹ̄*, *ọ*; *ḱ*, *ǵ*, *ḱʾ*, *č*, *ǰ*, *čʾ*, *š*, *ž* are wanting.

LITUANIAN.

	a ā		k	g	(ṅ)	-	-				
ẹ ẹ̄			k̃	ǵ	-	-	-	y			
(e) ē		ō	č	ǰ	-	š	ž				
i ī		u ū	t	d	n	s	z	r	l	ł
			p	b	m	-	-	v			

aĭ aŭ eĭ uĭ
eă iă oă
ăi ău ĕi

p' b' m' n' r' l' š' ž' s'

Specimen.

Ménů Saulìżę védė, pìrmą pavasarëlį.
Saulìżė ankstì këlės, Mėnìżis atsiskýrė.
Ménů vëns vaikszting̃jo, Auszrìnę pamylëjo.
Perkúns didei supýkęs jį kárdu pérdalyjo.
Ko Saulìżės atsiskýrei, Auszrìnę pamylëjei,
Vëns naktý vaikszting̃jei? szirdìs pilnà smutnýbės.

(Dainos. Schleicher, Litau. Lesebuch p. 3)

Transcription.

Mḗnoă Săulúžẹ vẹ̄dē, pírma pavasarḗli.
Săulúžē anksti kḗlēs, Mēnúžis atsiskírē.
Mḗnoă viăns văikštinḗyo, Ăušrínẹ pamīlḗyo.
Pẹrkū́ns didĕĭ supíkẹs yi kárdu pẹ̄rdalīyo
Kō Săulúžēs atsiskírĕi, Ăušrínẹ pamīlḗyĕi,
Viăns naktí văikštinḗyĕi? širdís pilná smutníbēs.

Remarks.

The standard work on the Lituanian language is the Grammar of A. Schleicher (Litauische Grammatik. Prag 1856.). He there treats extensively the phonic part of the language.

We refer, therefore, to his work in the following remarks. The Lituanians have no peculiar writing; they use generally the German or Latin letters with several diacritical marks. Schleicher follows in general their common orthography, adding only some nicer distinctions and moreover the accentuation of the single words, and the quantity of the vowels. The vowels not accentuated are represented as long by adding the stroke above (*ā ū* etc.), and as short by adding occasionally the sign ˘ or by leaving them without any mark; but the quantity of the accentuated vowels is expressed by the accent itself, which is the acute (*á*) for the long, and the grave (*à*) for the short vowels. The dropping of an original *n* behind a vowel is indicated by a little hook under the vowel. As this mark is of no phonetic value, but only an etymological hint, it may be entirely omitted as in most other languages. If, in linguistic books, it seems convenient to express the nasalisation, with which these vowels once were pronounced, our sign ˜ is to be added over them. There are two classes of *e*, one open *ę*, and the other closed *ę*. The former bears no diacritical mark, the latter is marked by Schleicher by a dot over it (*ė*). But as the latter is by far the most frequent, as even our short specimen may show, we prefer to mark the open *ę*, and to leave without dot the closed *e* (*ẹ*). As this closed *e* (*ẹ*) is found to be only long, as well as *o*, which neither occurs short, it might seem convenient not to indicate at all the length of *ē* and *ō* by the stroke. But we think that it would in the contrary offend the reader, and still more the linguist, to find that amongst the other vowels *a ę i u*, *e o*, *ā ę̄ ī ū* the two unmarked *e* and *o* belong exclusively to the long and not to the short vowels. We write therefore *ē* and *ō*, as in modern Sanskrit. There are three other vowels, written by Schleicher *ę*, *ë* and *ů*, which designe three diphthongs formed by *ę i* (or *ẹ*) and *o* preceding a very short *a*. Schleicher describes them as sounding like *ä*[a] *i*[a] (or *ė*[a]) and *ô*ᵃ, and remarkes, that *ę* in old prints was expressed by *ea*, and *ė* by *ie*. The diphthongic nature is certainly to be expressed in our transcription. We indicate therefore the fugitive *a* by writing those three diphthongs *eă*, *iă* and *oă*. There are besides two other kinds of diphthongs, of which the one, written *ái áu éi ùi* by Schleicher, has the accent on the first vowel, the other, written by the same *ai au ei* or with the accent of the word *aí aú eí*, on the second vowel. It is of course necessary to distinguish both, but, as the accent ′ on vowels is destined, in the Standard alphabet, to indicate only the accent of the word, we prefer to mark rather the accentless part of the diphthong by the sign of brevity ˘, in writing *aĭ aŭ eĭ uĭ* similar to *eă iă oă* and in contradistinction to *ăi ău ĕi*, by which we distinguish the second kind of diphthongs. According to Schleicher the *a* in his diphthongs *ái áu éi* is pronounced long. This distinction, however, which might be expressed by writing *āĭ āŭ ēĭ* seems to us not essential enough as to be marked in the common writing. We should even prefer to write only *ai au ei*, as the combination of these vowels seems always to be diphthongic, not dissylable, if it was not for the analogous writing of the diphthongs *eă iă oă*. We refer moreover to the similar formation of diphthongs in the Rumanian language.

The guttural consonants are often changed into the palatals *ḱ ǵ* and the dentals *t d* into *č ǰ*. This change originates in a peculiar propensity of the language, prevailing still more in the Slavonic languages, to insert between the consonant and the following vowel a shade of *i* or *y* especially before one of the palatal vowels *i* or *e*. In the Lituanian orthography this half *y* is commonly expressed by *i* or *j*, and on the end of words by an apostrophe or (as in the work of Schleicher) by our palatal line. We prefer, according to our principles, to put the stroke also in the middle of the words: *loб́o*, *kurḿu*, as in *verṕ*, *vēḿ*. The guttural *ł*, written already in Žemaitic books like the Polish *ł*, is to be distinguished from the common *l*; but the guttural *ṅ*, as being used only and always before *k* and *g*, may remain without mark. The letter *c* occurs only in foreign words and is to be written *ts* (or *ţ*) according to its pronunciation.

We add for the convenience of the reader the alphabet of Schleicher:

Vowels.

(Stand. A.)	(Schleicher.)				(Stand. A.)	(Schleicher.)			
a =	*a*	*à*	*ą*		*eă* =	*ẹ*	*ẹ̇*	*ẹ̈*	*ẹ̈́*
ā =	*ā*	*á*	*ą̇*	*ą*	*iă* =	*ë̆*	*ë̂*		
ȩ =	*e*	*è*	*ę*	*ę̀* (*ė̀*)	*oă* =	*u*	*ü̋*		
ȩ̄ =	*ē*	*ė*	*ę̄*	*ę́*	*aĭ* =	*ái*			
ē =	*ė*	*ë́*			*aŭ* =	*áu*			
i =	*i*	*ì*			*eĭ* =	*éi*			
ī =	*y*	*í*	*į*	*į́*	*uĭ* =	*ùi*			
ō =	*o*	*ó*			*ăi* =	*ai*	*aí*		
u =	*u*	*ù*	*ų*		*ău* =	*au*	*aú*		
ū =	*ū*	*ú*	*ų̄*	*ų*	*ĕi* =	*ei*	*eí*		

Consonants.

(Schleicher.)

k	*g*	(*n*)	-	-			
ki, k̓	*gi, ǵ*	-	-	-	*j*		
cz	*dż*	-	*sz*	*ż*			
t	*d*	*n*	*s*	*z*	*r*	*l*	*ł*
p	*b*	*m*	-	-	*v*		

OLD SLOVENIAN.

(Church Slavonic, old Slavonic.)

Glagolitic.

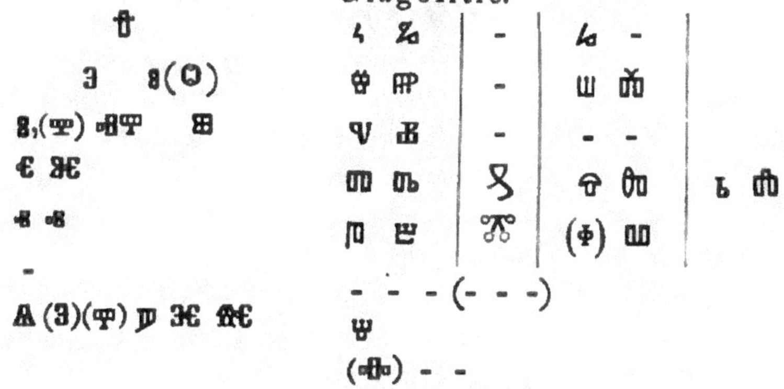

Cyrillian.

а

е о (ѡ)

ї ꙑ оу, ȣ

ѧ ѫ

ь(й) ъ

ѣ

ꙗ ѥ и ю ѩ ѭ

ай ей ий ой ꙑй

к	г	-	х	-			
ч	-	-	ш	ж			
ц	ѕ	-	-	-			
т	д	н	с	з		р	л
п	б	м	(ф)	в			

н̓ р̓ л̓ (к̓ г̓ х̓)

щ

(ѳ ѯ ѱ)

a

e o(ŏ)

ï į u

ẽ õ

ĭ(j) ŭ

ě(aĭ)

ja je i(ji) ju jẽ jõ

aj ej ïj oj įj

k	*g*	-	*χ*	-			
č	*ǯ*	-	*š*	*ž*			
ț	*ḑ*	-	-	-			
t	*d*	*n*	*s*	*z*		*r*	*l*
p	*b*	*m*	*(f)*	*v*			

ń ŕ ľ (ḱ ǵ χ́)

št

(θ ks ps)

Hard vowels: *a u į o õ ŭ*   Soft vowels: *e ï i ě ẽ ĭ*

Specimen.

Kij člověkŭ otŭ vasŭ imį sŭto ovĭţĭ i pogublĭ jedinõ otŭ ńiχŭ ne ostavitĭ devêtĭ desêtŭ i devêti vŭ pustįńi, i idetĭ vŭ slędŭ pogįbŭšêjẽ, dońĭdeže obrêštetĭ jõ? I obrętŭ vŭzlagajetĭ na ramja svoi radujẽ sẽ, i prišĭdŭ vŭ domŭ sŭzįvajetĭ drugį i sõsędį glagolẽ imŭ: radujte sẽ sŭ mŭnojõ, jako obrętoχŭ ovĭţõ svojõ pogįbŭšôjõ. Glagolõ vamŭ, jako tako radostĭ bõdetĭ na nebesi o jedi nomĭ grěšĭnitę kajõštijimĭ sẽ neže o devêti desêtŭ i devêti pravĭdĭ nikŭ, iže ne trębujõtĭ pokajanija. Li kaja žena imõšti desêtĭ dragŭmŭ, ašte pogubitĭ dragŭmõ jedinõ, ne vŭžizajetĭ svętilĭnika, i pometetĭ χramŭ, i ištetĭ priležĭno, dońĭdeže obrêštetĭ? I obrętŭši sŭzįvajetĭ drugį i sõsędį glagolôšti: radujte sẽ sŭ mŭnojõ, jako obrętoχŭ dragŭmõ, jõže pagubiχŭ. Tako, glagolõ vamŭ, radostĭ bįvajetĭ prędŭ anŭgelį božiji o jedinomĭ grěšĭnitę kajõštijimĭ sẽ.

Ev. Luc. 15, 4—10.

Remarks.

The Old Slovenian, the language spoken in the 9th century by the Slovenians in Pannonia, is no longer a spoken language. It is now only used for liturgical purposes by the Slavonic nations belonging to the Greek church, as the Russians, Bulgarians, Servians. It is the most ancient of all the Slavonic languages known and therefore of high linguistic interest. This is also the reason, why we must adapt our transcription as closely as possible to the old signs, rendering every one by a distinct and exclusive character, even in those cases, where the actual pronunciation does not distinguish them. The monuments of the old Slavonian literature are preserved in two kinds of writing, the Glagolitic and the Cyrillian. It is now proved by Miklosich beyond any doubt, that the more ancient of the two, the Glagolitic, is based on an old national alphabet, which originally was taken from the Greek, but was remodelled in the 9th century and adapted to Christian literature by the two Slavonic apostles, Cyrillus and Methodius, brothers.

The so called Cyrillian alphabet was introduced by St. Clemens soon after, about 900, simultaneously with the introduction of christianity amongst the Slovenians in the countries of the Haemus. It was soon preferred to the former both on account of its greater facility of design and its similarity with the Greek uncial alphabet from which it only differs by a few signs expressing letters unknown to the Greek.

The Glagolitic alphabet, as we read it now in the manuscripts, is not indeed the original, but has evidently undergone several modifications, owing partly, as we may suppose, to the arranging hands of Cyrillus, partly to the contact of the later Clementine (Cyrillian) alphabet and the eastern dialect, to which the latter was specially adapted. We have in our mode of transcribing it only consulted this modified form, being almost identical, as regards the single letters, with the Clementine or Cyrillian.

The vowels *a e o* in both alphabets offer no difficulty. There is a secondary form of *o*, which in the original Glagolitic alphabet may have referred to a distinct mode of pronunciation, *(ǫ?)*, but which is now only used for the interjection *ω̑*, and may, therefore, be transcribed by *ō*.

The Glagolitic Ⰻ may have been destined originally for the guttural *į* in *ŭį*, instead of which we find also *ŭi*, the gutturalisation of *į* being indicated by the prefixion of *ŭ*. Afterwards the same sign was also employed for *i*, though not in all manuscripts. *e* and *je*, *i* and *ji* were first distinguished in the Cyrillian alphabet, not yet in the Glagolitic, where we find only *ja* and *ju*. The Cyrillian и, although it takes in the alphabetical order the place of the Greek Η, expressed originally, we believe, the diphthong *ji* (и = й), as ї or і the simple *i*. But и was afterwards also employed for ї, and identified with Glagolitic Ⰻ. We therefore are now only able to make a convential distinction in our transcription between *ī* (= Gl. Ⰺ, Cyr. ї), *i* or *ji* (= Gl. Ⰻ, Cyr. и), and *į* (= Gl. ⰟⰊ, Cyr. ꙑ). The character й which occurs in the later Cyrillian manuscripts after vowels indicates the abridgement of *ji* or *i* into *j*, by which letter we transcribe it.

The compound character in the Glagolitic alphabet for *u* and the corresponding double character iu the Cyrillian is derivated from the Greek *ου*. The Glagolitic letters, which we transcribe by *ê õ jẽ jõ*, perhaps also *ja* and *ju*, may have had originally — as we are led to believe from their paleographic forms — a pronunciation somewhat different from the Cyrillian, to which our transcription is adapted.

A peculiarity of the Slavonic languages, which probably proceeds from the presence of certain Tataric elements, consists in the systematic distinction of guttural and palatal vowels, generally called hard and soft vowels. The guttural or hard vowels are *a u i̯ o õ ŭ*; the palatal or soft are *e ï i ę̄ ẽ ĭ*. The palatal tendency, however, is so predominant, that not only the soft vowels, but also the hard are very often pronounced with a slight preceding *i* or *j*. The merely phonetic origin of this *j* is testified by etymology as well as by the compound form of the letters which represent it as adherent to the respective vowels. This is the origin of the diphthongs *ja*, *je*, *ji*, *ju*, *jẽ* and *jõ*. It might be desirable and would certainly be more consistent with the genius of Slavonic language to write these compound vowels by single caracters as it is done in the native writing. The division into two signs, however, is preferable by more than one reason, and is not against the rules of our standard alphabet. We have thought it convenient to write this slight *i*-sound not by a full consonantic *y*, but by *j*, representing as if it was half a *y*, although this sign *j* does not occur in our general alphabet. This designation offers besides the advantage of being in concordance with the almost general mode of writing adopted by most Slavonic nations writing with Roman letters, as well as by most of the respective linguists. We have therefore preferred it to any other designation, which we might have invented. In a similar way also the shortened and indefinite vowel *ḙ* of other languages, behind or between consonants, has taken in Slovenian either the palatal or guttural form and has become a surd yet perceptible *ĭ* or *ŭ* (*i, u mutescens*). These two sounds ь *ĭ* and ъ *ŭ* are in most cases remains of corresponding fuller vowels and were no doubt formerly more distinctly pronounced than they are actually. There can be no doubt that we must follow the original writing in transcribing them by separate characters. We have chosen for that purpose the two signs *ĭ* and *ŭ*, adopted already in the Rumanian alphabet, as well as by several linguists. The sign of brevity ˘ is the less objectionable, as the distinction of long and short simple vowels is little known to the Slavonic languages. The later pronunciation of the Old Slovenian dropped the *ŭ* more completely than the *ĭ*; yet, for etymological reasons, *ŭ* most also be written even in cases, when it seems it was not any more pronounced.

The distinction between guttural and palatal pronunciation applies also to many of the Slovenian consonants, according to their combinations with either a hard or soft vowel. The palatal modification, however, as in the case of the vowels, is also in this case the predominant, and the only expressed in writing. The dental consonants, by this modification, are generally assibilated; the liquids *n l r* and in foreign words also the gutturals *k g χ* become palatalised or softened, in which case they are marked by some diacritic sign. The character ь however is not by itself a sign of this palatal modification, but represents still a real vowel, which only bestowes on those of the preceding consonants, which are capable of it, the palatalised form. It would be, therefore, inexact to replace in our transcription the *ĭ* by the palatal line added to the preceding consonant.

The vowel ѣ is unknown to the Glagolitic alphabet. It is evidently formed by a combination of the Glagolitic ⰰ *a* with the Cyrillian ь *ĭ* and represents therefore the diphthong *ĭa* or *aĭ*. But since the diphthong *ĭa* or *ja* had been expressed from the beginning by the sign ꙗ (analogous to the combinations *je ji ju jẽ jõ)* and since Miklosich has proved that the character ѣ could not in many cases where it is employed represent a combination beginning with *j*, we do not doubt, even without referring to other reasons, that the value of ѣ was originally *aĭ*, afterwards *ę*, which on account of its diphthongic origin we transcribe by *ȩ́*. The frequent interchanges which take place in the manuscripts between the two signs ѣ and ꙗ, are, in this respect, of no import.

The diphthongs *rŭ lŭ rĭ lĭ* are considered by Miklosich (p. 34 sqq.) as the vowels *r̥ l̥*, an opinion which is supported by the New Slovenian. But historically founded as this explanation seems to be, it could not justify our adopting it against the Cyrillian mode of writing, by which these sounds are written as double characters, and even in this combined form do not figure in the alphabet. Only in those rare cases where *r* and *l* without the addition of *ŭ* and *ĭ* represent a syllable, we might be justified in transcribing them respectively by *r̥* and *l̥*.

With regard to the consonants we have still to mention that we have preferred the single transcription *ţ* and *ḑ* to the combined *ts* and *ds*, as being, especially together with *č* (and *ǰ*), more adequate to the Slavonic phonetic system, which opinion is also supported by the general adoption in the latin Slavonic alphabets of the corresponding single signs *c* and *z*. The contracted form for щ we transcribe by *št* as it is done already in the Glagolitic codex Clozianus. A real softening of the consonants takes place in the Old Slovenian language only with regard to the liquids *n r l*, which in this softened state we transcribe by *ń ŕ ľ*. The consonants *θ f ks ps* are only used in Greek words. ȣ and щ are only compendia for оу and шт.

SERBIAN (Illirian).

Cyrillian writing.

Vowels							
а	к	г	-	х	-	ј	
е о	ч	џ	-	ш	ж		
и у	ц	-	-	-	-	р	л
р	т	д	н	с	з		
ја је ји јо ју	ћ	ђ	-	-	-		
ај еј иј ој уј	п	б	м	(ф)	в		
	љ	њ					

Latin writing.

Vowels							
a	*k*	*g*	-	*h*			
e o	*č*	*dž*	-	*š*	*ž*	*j*	
i u	*c*	-	-	-	-		
r	*t*	*d*	*n*	*s*	*z*	*r*	*l*
ja je ji jo ju	*ć*	*dj*	-	-	-		
aj ej ij oj uj	*p*	*b*	*m*	(*f*)	*v*		
	lj	*nj*					

Standard alphabet.

Vowels							
a	*k*	*g*	-	*h*	-		
e o	*č*	*ǰ*	-	*š*	*ž*	*j*	
i u	*ṭ*	-	-	-	-		
r̥	*t*	*d*	*n*	*s*	*z*	*r*	*l*
ja je ji jo ju	*c̀*	*j̀*	-	-	-		
aj ej ij oj uj	*p*	*b*	*m*	(*f*)	*v*		
	ľ	*ń*					

Hard vowels: *a o u r̥*
Soft vowels: *e i*

Specimen.

Мили боже! чуда великога!
Или грми, ил' се земльа тресе,
Ил' удара море у брегове?
Нити грми, нит' се земльа тресе,
Нит' удара море у брегове,
Већ дијеле благо светительи:
Свети Петар и свети Никола,
Свети Іован и свети Илија
И са ньима свети Пантелија;
Ньим' долази блажена Марија,
Рони сузе низ бијело лице.

National songs of the Serbians ed. by *Vuk Stefanović Karajić.*

Mili bože! čuda velikoga!
Ili gr̥mi, iľ se zemľa trese
Iľ udara more u bregove?
Niti gr̥mi, niť se żemľa trese,
Niť udara more u bregove,
Već dijele blago svetiteľi:
Sveti Petar i sveti Nikola,
Sveti Jovan i sveti Ilija,
I sa ńima sveti Pantelija;
Ńim' dolazi blažena Marija,
Roni suze niz bijelo litse.

Remarks.

The Serbians, as far as they belong to the Greek church, write their language in the Cyrillian character, the Roman Catholics in Roman letters. This language, to which the Khorvatian (Croatian) is nearly allied, has neither the vowel *i̧*, nor the two Old Slavonian surd vowels ь ĭ and ъ ŭ, of which the former appears only in combination with the characters *n* and *l*, indicating their soft pronunciation, which we render by the palatal line, *ń ĺ*, as in all the other Slavonic languages. About the palatal modification of the vowels we refer to the Old Slovenian. In Serbian the letter р is often used as vowel and forms syllables, although it is not distinguished in writing from the consonant р. We think it the more necessary to mark the vowel *r̥* by the little circle underneath, as it even occurs before other vowels, for instance *gr̥oțe umr̥o* in three syllables. In writing *č š ž* for ч ш ж we have the advantage to be in concordance with the latin alphabet used already in the country. The letters ћ and ђ express very nearly the same sounds as *ć* and *dź* in the Polish alphabet, where we refer to for our transcription by *ċ* and *ј̇*. The signs џ (= дж, *ǰ*) and ђ (*ј̇*) have been added by Vuk Stefanoviċ. The pronunciation of х comes nearest to *h*, as it is written in the latin alphabet; but in many words of Serbian dialects it is either omitted or replaced by other consonants.

RUSSIAN.

а
э о
ѣ
і ы у
я е и ё ю
ай ей ой уй яй ѣй
(ѵ)
(ь ъ)

к	г	-	х	г(ђ)	
ч	-	-	ш	ж	
ц	-	-	-	-	
т(ѳ)	д	н	с	з	р л
п	б	м	(ф)	в	

щ (ѳ)
ть дь нь сь зь ль
(пь бь мь рь вь)

a
e *o*
ẹ
i *ị* *u*
Palatalised vowels:
ja je ji jo ju
aj ej oj uj jaj jẹj
(*i*, *v*)
(— —)
Hard vowels: *a o u ị*
Soft vowels: *e ẹ i*

k	*g*	-	*χ*	*γ*	
č	-	-	*š*	*ž*	
ṭ	-	-	-	-	
t	*d*	*n*	*s*	*z*	*r ł*
p	*b*	*m*	(*f*)	*v*	

šč (*θ*)
Palatalised consonants:
t' d' n' s' z' l'
(*p' b' m' v' r'*)

Specimen.

Во дни тѣ вышло отъ Кесаря Августа повелѣніе, сдѣлать перепись по всей землѣ. Сія перепись была первая въ правленіе Квиринія Сиріею. И пошли всѣ вписываться, каждый въ свой городъ. Пошелъ также и Іосиѳъ изъ Галилеи, изъ Города Назарета, въ Іудею, въ городъ Давидовъ, называемый Виѳлеемъ, потому что онъ былъ изъ дома и рода Давидова, вписаться съ Маріею, обрученною ему женою, которая была беременна. Въ бытность ихъ тамъ, наступило время родить ей. И родила сына своего первенца, и спеленала его, и положила его въ ясли; потому что не было имъ мѣста въ гостинницѣ.

Ev. Luc. 2, 1—7.

Vo dni tje vi̯šlo ot Kesarja Avgusta poveleṅije, sdełat' perepis' po vsẹj zemle. Sija perepis' bi̯ła pervaja v pravleṅije Kviriṅija Sirijẹju. I pošli vsje vpisi̯vatsja, každi̯j v svoj gorod. Pošoł takže i Josif iz Galileji, iz goroda Nazareta, v Judjẹju, v gorod Davidov, nazi̯vajemi̯j Viflejem, potomu čto on bi̯ł iz doma i roda Davidova, vpisatsja s Marijẹju, obručonnoju jemu ženoju, katoraja bi̯ła beremenna. V bi̯tnost' jiχ tam, nastupiło vremja rodit' jẹj. I rodiła si̯na svojeyo perventa, i speleṅała jeyo, i położiła jeyo v jasli; potomu čto nje bi̯ło jim mesta v gostinnitẹ.

Remarks.[1]

The pronunciation of the Russian has gradually deviated very much from the Russian orthography. It would therefore be useless to transcribe Russian words literally. The Russian vowels especially are subject to varying pronunciation, f. i. я = *a*, *ẹ*; э = *e̱*, *ẹ*; ѣ or е = *e̱*, *ẹ*, *o*, *je̱*, *jẹ*, *jo*; і = *i*, *ji*; о = *o*, *a*; ій or ый = *i̯j*, *i̯j*, *oj*, and thus the Russian alphabet as we have given it above, only refers to the regular and original value of the letters, not to their many later modifications. We agree with the best Slavonic scholars in transcribing the Russian letters according to their pronunciation and not to their character. The two characters *e* = э and ѣ were no doubt originally the same as the Old Slovenian е (э) and ѣ, i. e. *e̱* or *e* and *ẹ*. But since the pronunciation of ѣ had in certain combinations passed into *e̱*, both signs were frequently interchanged. In order to economise our diacritical signs we write *e* instead of *e̱*, keeping the diacritical point merely for *ẹ*, which is of much less frequent occurrence. It might even be doubted, if the distinction of *e* aud *ẹ* would be at all indispensable and practically convenient. The original value of и = *ji* is mostly preserved

[1] Miklosich, Vergleichende Lautlehre d. Slav. Spr. 1852. Böhtlingk, Bull. hist. philol. de l'Acad. de St. Petersbourg. tom. IX, p. 37 ff.

in the beginning of words and after vowels; і = *i* occurs only before vowels. As in the Old Slovenian we transcribe the palatalised vowels by prefixing the letter *j*, and employ the same sign for the affixed й. We follow in this respect only the general use of those Slavonic nations which employ Latin characters. It has appeared convenient not to transcribe at all the two signs ь and ъ, which in Russian do not form any more a distinct articulation, but only indicate the preceding consonant to be either palatalised or not. As we transcribe the palatalised consonants by adding the palatal line, we do not require any other sign for ь. After gutturals the sign ь does not occur and their pronunciation before the soft vowels is hardly more different from that before hard vowels than in any other language; we, therefore, do not express any palatalisation of gutturals. The consonants of the palatal row are not capable at all of a second palatalisation, or it is here at least so week, that its existence is denied by several scholars. We may, therefore, conveniently omit it in our transcription. It has also been doubted, whether the labials and *r* are ever palatalised, and this palatalisation, if it ever exists, is at all events, as far as I can perceive, much wecker than after the dentals. It may, however, be indicated where according to the Russian orthography the sign ь is still written behind them. The guttural or hard л *ł* of several Slavonic languages, which is pronounced with an energetic depression of the middle tongue and a simultaneous raising of the behind part of the tongue at the guttural point, differs so perceptibly from our common *l*, as to claim a special sign, and as the character *ł* for this letter is already generally used in the Polish and Sorbian writing, we can not hesitate to adopt it also in our transcription. The palatal line of *l̕* may be dropped. The letter г between vowels ceases to be explosive and becomes the soft fricative which we write *γ*. The letters ѵ ѳ о only occur in Greek words, ѵ with the double pronunciation either of *i* or *v*, which we render by these two respective signs.

CHESKIAN (BOHEMIAN).

		a á			*k*	*(g)*	-	*ch*	*h*			
	e é		o ů(ó)		*č*	-	-	*š*	*ž*		*j*	
i í		y ý		u ou(ú)	*c*	-	-	-	-			
l r					*t*	*d*	*n*	*s*	*z*		*l*	*r*
					p	*b*	*m*	*(f)*	*v*			

ja já je ji jí

aj áj ej ij íj oj ůj uj yj ýj

ň ř ť ď

		a ā			*k*	*(g)*	-	*χ*	*h*			
	e ē		o ů		*č*	-	-	*š*	*ž*		*j*	
i ī		i̦ ī̦		u ū	*ṭ*	-	-	-	-			
l̥ r̥					*t*	*d*	*n*	*s*	*z*		*l*	*r*
					p	*b*	*m*	*(f)*	*v*			

ja jā je ji jī

aj āj ej ij īj oj ōj uj i̦j ī̦j

ń ř ť ď.

Hard vowels: *a o u y*
Soft vowels: *e i*

Specimen.

	Transcription.
Těšme se blahou naději,	*Ťešme se blahou naďejī,*
Že se vrátí zlaté časy,	*Že se vrāťi zlatē časi̦,*
Že se nám zas vyjasněji	*Že se nām zas vi̦jasńejī*
České hory, české hlasy.	*Českē hori̦, českē hlasi̦.*
Ať jen český šat se nese,	*Ať jen českī̦ šat se nese,*
Mužně hájí mravy dávné,	*Mužńe hājī mravi̦ dāvnē,*
Nade všecko ono slavné,	*Nade všeṭko ono slavnē,*
Pravočeské:	*Pravočeskē:*

Milujme se, nedejme se,
Vybíme se, napíme se,
Milujme, napíme se,
A pak vybíme se. —
Amen, rač to Bože dáti!
Oroduj za nás, svatý Václave,
Vejvodo České země!
Milujme se etc. — *vybíme se.*

Dokuď v nás krev otců plyne,
Hruď zahřívá, ruce sílí:
Sláva česká nezahyne,
Hlavu ztýči lev náš bílý.
Tak jako medvědům v lese,
Nepřátelům budem hráti,
Oni budou tancovati,
Až zapějem:
Milujme se etc. — *vybíme se.*

Milujme se, nedejme se,
Vi̯bīme se, napīme se,
Milujme, napīme se,
A pak vi̯bīme se. —
Amen, rač to Bože dāt́i!
Oroduj za nās: svati̯ Vāṭlave,
Vejvodo Českē zeḿe!
Milujme se etc. — *vi̯bīme se.*

Dokuď v nās krev otṭů pli̯ne,
Hruď zahřīvā, ruṭe sīlī:
Slāva českā nezahi̯ne,
Hlavu zti̯čī lev nāš bīli̯.
Tak jako medv́edům v lese,
Nepřātelům budem hrāt́i,
Ońi budou tanṭovat́i,
Až zaṕejem:
Milujme etc. — *vi̯bīme se.*

Hussite song.

Remarks.

Although the vowels *y* and *ý* are in modern pronunciation scarcely distinguished from *i* and *ī*, yet we have not conceived ourselves authorised to give up in our transcription this distinction, which, besides being historical, is moreover still preserved in several phonic combinations as well as in the general pronunciation of certain dialects. The single *i* is frequently, especially in the beginning of words, pronounced like *ji*, by which signs we transcribe it in this case. The long *ō* has changed into *ū* and is now written *ů*, which writing we have preserved as both concordant with pronunciation and etymology. The vowels *r̥* and *l̥* are in the Cheskian alphabet not distinguished from the corresponding consonants. We distinguish them, however, by our usual diacritic sign.

The letter *g* has been regularly (except in foreign words) replaced by *h* both in pronunciation and writing, which change we must adopt in our transcription. Also the letter *f* is of foreign origin but has been introduced in a few native words. The palatalised consonants *ň ť ď* we mark by the palatal line *ń t́ d́*. The palatalisation of *r* has in Cheskian as well as in several other Slavonic languages, passed into a slight assibilation, coming up to a combination of *r* and *ž*, for which we have preserved the national transcription by *ř*. The palatalisation of consonants is in Bohemian sometimes marked above the following vowel (*těšme*, *naději*, *mužně*, instead of *t́ešme, nad́eji*, *mužńe)* or even sometimes not marked at all (*vráti, oni* instead of *vrát́i*, *ońi)*. We do not follow this irregularity.

POLISH.

a
e o
é ó
i y u
ę ą
ja, ia je, ie ji, i jo, io ju, iu ję, ię ją, ią
jaj, iaj jej, iej
aj ej ij oj ój uj yj

k	*g*	-	*ch*	*(h)*	
cz	*dż*	-	*sz*	*ż*	*j*
c	*dz*	-	-	-	
t	*d*	*n*	*s*	*z*	*r ł*
ć	*dź*	-	*ś*	*ź*	
p	*b*	*m*	*(f)*	*w*	

ń rz l ṕ b́ ẃ ḿ f′
szcz ść (x)

a
e o
ẹ ọ
i ị u
ẽ õ
ja je ji jo jọ ju jẽ jõ
jaj jej
aj ej ij oj ọj uj ịj

k	*g*	-	*χ*	*(h)*	
č	*ǰ*	-	*š*	*ž*	*j*
ṭ	*ḍ*	-	-	-	
t	*d*	*n*	*s*	*z*	*r ł*
c̀	*ȷ̀*	-	*s̀*	*z̀*	
p	*b*	*m*	*(f)*	*v*	

ń ř ľ ṕ b́ v́ ḿ f′
šč s̀c̀ (ks)

Specimen.

I stało się, w oneż dni wyszedł dekret od Cesarza Augusta, aby popisano wszystek świat. Ten popis pierwszy, był od starosty Syryjskiego Cyryna. I szli wszyscy, aby się popisali, każdy do miasta swego. Szedł też i Józef od Galilei z miasta Nazarethu, do Judskiej ziemie, do miasta Dawidowego, które zowią Bethlehem: przeto iż był z domu i pokolenia Dawidowego, aby był popisan z Maryą poślubioną sobie małżonką, która była brzemienną. Ev. Luc. 2, 1—5.

I stało s̀ẽ, v onež dńi vịšedł dekret od Ṭesařa Augusta, abị popisano všịstek s̀vjat. Ten popis pjervšị, bịł od starostị Sịrij-

skjego Ṭịrịna. I šli všịsṭị, abị sě popisali, každị do mjasta svego. Šedł też i Josef od Galileji z mjasta Nazaretu, do Judskjej zjemje, do mjasta Davidovego, ktore zovjõ Betlehem: přeto iż bịł z domu i pokolenja Davidovego, abị bịł popisan z Marịjõ pośłubjonõ sobje małżonkõ, ktora bịła břemjennõ.

Remarks.

About $y = ị$ see above p. 54. The distinction in the Polish orthography between *ja*, *je* etc. in the beginning and *ia*, *ie* etc. in the middle of words has neither an etymological nor phonetic reason, and we write therefore indistinctly as in all the other Slavonic languages *ja*, *je* etc. In the middle of words the Poles use to write *i* instead of *ji*; we write *ji* according to the pronunciation. As for the palatal affixe *j* see above. The *h* only occurs in words taken from the „*Small-Russian*". The *f* likewise is of foreign origin. The consonants *ć dź ś ź* are palatalised dentals, the palatal affix of which has been assibilated and the principal consonant assimilated to this assibilation. We are of opinion that the Polish *ś* resembles the palatal *s* (*ś*) of several ancient languages; but as identity of both cannot be proved, and as moreover the Polish sibilants are of a dental and not, like the other, of a guttural origin, we have preferred to adhere in our transcription to the native orthography as closely as possible: and as the palatal line in our alphabet has another meaning, we have written *c̀ s̀ z̀* and accordingly also *j̀* for the Polish *ć ś ź* and *dź*. In doing so we are the more justified as the diacritic sign ` has been employed in Sorbian already by native scholars for the same purpose.

On the other hand it would be a great simplification of Polish orthography and at least a great orthographic improvement for scientific purposes, if the irrational, complicated and erroneous compound signs *cz sz szcz*, as well as the more rational writings, but which are against other rules of our transcription, *dż c dz*, might be given up and replaced by the simple and rational signs *č š šč ǰ ṭ ḍ*. The transcription of *ŕ* and the other palatalised consonants has been discussed above, as well as that of the guttural *ł*. The palatal line of *l̓* may also here be dropped (see above p. 156), *l* being always palatalised where it is not guttural (*ł*). The vowel *ó* has a very closed pronunciation approaching almost *u*; we write it *ọ*, which in our general alphabet comes nearest to it. Again the vowel *e* sometimes approaches very closely *i*, and is written in these cases by careful writers *ė*; we have to render this pronunciation by our *ẹ*.

SORBIAN (High-Lusatian, Wendic)

according to different Sorbian writers.

			a				*k*	*(g)*	-	*ch*	*h*		
		e		*o*			*č,tž,cž, tsch*	*dž,dż*	-	*š,sch*	*ž,ż*		
	é,ė				*ó*		*c,cz,z*	*dz,ds*	-	-	-		
i			*y,ė*			*u*	*t*	*d*	*n*	*s*	*z*	*r*	*ł,w*
ja	*je*	*jé*	*ji*	*jo*	*jó*	*ju*	*è,ć,cž,cż*	*ds,tz,ts*	-	-	-		
aj	*ej*	*éj*	*ij*	*oj*	*ój*	*uj*	*p*	*b*	*m*	*(f)*	*v,w*		

ń ŕ lj,l̓,l̓,l ṕ b́ v́ ḿ f́

			a				*k*	*(g)*	-	*χ*	*k*		
		e		*o*			*č*	*ǰ*	-	*š*	*ž*		
	ẹ				*ọ*		*ṭ*	*(ḍ)*	-	-	-		
i			*ị*			*u*	*t*	*d*	*n*	*s*	*z*	*r*	*ł*
ia	*je*	*jẹ*	*ji*	*jo*	*jọ*	*ju*	*è*	*(ǰ̀)*	-	-	-		
aj	*ej*	*ẹj*	*ij*	*oj*	*ọj*	*uj*	*p*	*b*	*m*	*(f)*	*v*		

ń ŕ l̓ ṕ b́ v́ ḿ f́

Remarks.

The pronunciation of the vowels written by the native Sorbians *é* and *ó* approaches very near that of *i* and *u*, although it seems not to be identical with it. We distinguish them, therefore, also in our transcription in writing them *ẹ* and *ọ*, the acute ´ being against the principles of the Standard alphabet (see above p. 47). For the same reason, we must replace the signs *ch* and *y* by our *χ* and *i̦*; but we keep the character *ł*, although it is mostly pronounced as *w* and has preserved its original value only dialectically. About *c̀* see above our remarks on the Polish alphabet. The letters which we have renderd by *d̦* and *j̀* are distinguished as peculiar sounds by Tecelin, Seiler, Jordan and others. Miklosich, however, does not mention them at all. The letters *g* and *f* appear only in foreign words.

RUMANIAN (Walachian).

Cyrillian letters.

a
е ъ о
і ѫ у, ȣ
(ꙟ)
ĭ ȣ̆
аĭ еĭ іĭ оĭ ȣĭ ѫĭ ъĭ
аȣ̆ еȣ̆ іȣ̆ оȣ̆ ѫȣ̆ ъȣ̆
іа іе іо іȣ еа оа
еаȣ̆ еіȣ̆ оіȣ̆

к	г	-	х	-		
ч	џ	-	ш	ж		
т, ꙥ	д	н	с	ꙁ, з	р	л
ц	-	-	-	-		
п	б	м	ф	в		
щ	(ѳ)					

Mixed letters.

a
е ъ о
і î ȣ
(î)
ĭ ȣ̆
аĭ еĭ etc.

к	г, g	-	х	-		
ч	џ, g	-	ш	j, ɉ		
t	d	n	s	z	р	л
ц	-	-	-	-		
п	б, b	m	ф	в		
щ						

Etymological alphabet.

a
e *o*
i *u*
ѫ = *â ê î ô û* } *ả ẻ ỉ ỏ u*
ъ = *ă ĕ ĭ ŏ ŭ* }
ĭ ŭ
aĭ eĭ etc.

c, ch	*g, gh*	-	*h, ch*	-		
c, ci	*g, gi*	-	*ș, s*	*j*		
t	*d*	*n*	*s*	*z, ḑ, di*	*r*	*l*
ț, ti	-	-	-	-		
p	*b*	*m*	*f*	*v*		
st, sc						

Standard alphabet.

a
e e̯ o
i i̯ u
(ĭ)
ĭ ŭ
aĭ eĭ iĭ oĭ uĭ i̯ĭ e̯i
{ *aŭ eŭ iŭ oŭ (i̯ŭ) e̯ŭ*
{ *ĭa ĭe ĭo ĭu ĕa ŏa*
ĕaŭ eĭŭ oĭŭ

k	*g*	-	*h(χ)*	-	
č	*ǰ*	-	*š*	*ž*	
t	*d*	-	-	-	
ṭ	-	*n*	*s*	*z*	*r l*
p	*b*	*m*	*f*	*v*	

št šč

Specimen.

Cyrillian letters.

Ші а фост ꙟн зілеле ачелеа, ешіт-а порȣнка дела Кесар Аȣгȣст, съ се скріе тоатъ лȣмеа. Ачеастъ скрісоаре ꙟнтѫї с'а фъкȣт, домнінд ꙟн Сіріеа Кірінеȣ̆. Ші мерџеа тоцї съ се скріе, фіе-каре ꙟн четатеа са. Ev. Luc. 2, 1—3.

Mixed letters.

Ші a фost în ziлеле ачелеа, ешіt'a порȣnka de ла Kesap Aȣgȣst, sъ se skpie toatъ лȣmea. Ачеastъ skpisoape întîiȣ s'a фъkȣt domnind în Sipiea kipineȣ̆. Ші mepgea toцї sъ se skpie, фie-kape în четatea sa.

Etymological writing.

Și a fost în ḑilele acelea, eșit'a porunca de la Cesar August, să se scrie tótĕ lumea. Acéstă scrisóre ântîiŭ s'a făcut, domnind în Siriea Cirineŭ. Și mergé toţĭ să se scrie, fie-care în cetatea sa.

Transcription.

Ši a fost įn zilele ačelĕa, ešit'a porunka de la Kesar Aŭgust, sę se skrie tŏatę lumĕa. Ačĕastę skrisŏare įntįĭŭ s'a fękut, domnind įn Sirĭĕa Kirineŭ. Ši merĵĕa toțĭ sę se skrie, fiekare įn četatĕa sa.

With accents.

Ši a fost įn zílele ačĕlĕa, ešít'a porúnka de la Késar Aŭgúst, sę se skrie tŏátę lúmĕa. Ačĕástę skrisŏáre įntįĭŭ s'a fękút, domnínd įn Síriĕa Kirinéŭ. Ši merĵĕá tóțĭ sę se skríe, fiekáre įn četátĕa sa.

Remarks.

The Rumanian language which is principally spoken in the Principalities of Moldavia and Wallachia and also in Transylvania and some isolated neighbouring districts, originated in the Roman colonies of ancient Dacia, and has preserved, notwithstanding many foreign admixtures, an essential Romanic character. It was written formerly with Cyrillian letters, which, however, in modern times have been replaced by the Roman, being less heavy and more convenient for European literary commerce. The introduction of the Roman letters is owing to the endeavours of a number of native scholars and extends already even to the newspapers. We may predict that it soon will be generally adopted. It is the more to be regretted, that it is just the most learned of these reformers of the Rumanian alphabet, who have encumbered this reform with unnecessary difficulties by following, instead of the phonetic principle — which prevailed in the Russian-Romanic alphabet — an etymological. Whilst most other nations justly endeavour to render their orthography as much as possible accordant with the successive changes of pronunciation and to avoid thereby such inconveniences as are most conspicuous in the English orthography, the Rumanian scholars have generally attempted to bring back the modern language to the old Roman orthography given up long since so far as regards pronunciation. They write e. g. the vowel *į* (in their Russian alphabet ѫ) by five different signs, viz. *â ê î ô û* and the vowel *ę* (ъ) by *ȧ ė i̇ ȯ u̇* according to the supposed, yet often problematic, origin of these respective vowels from a latin *a e i o u*.

Trying to introduce a doctrinal orthography of this kind into common writing, would soon cause general confusion. Wherever a rich and widely diffused literature does not protect an orthography differing from the pronunciation, a nation has no other corrective for its orthography than its innate feeling and its living pronunciation; you cannot force upon the people the result of learned researches, which they can neither appreciate nor understand. Others indeed go not so far; they follow the simpler principle of preserving for those sounds, for which the Latin alphabet has no particular letter, the Russian signs; but thereby they surrender the homogeneity of writing and its evident advantages. We have above registered the Russian Alphabet, a mixed and an etymological Alphabet, and have selected the specimens accordingly. For linguistic works the notation of the accents of words would be valuable; we have noted them in a second specimen to show how easily they combine with our transcription.

A remarkable peculiarity of the Rumanian language, especially of the northern Daco-Rumanian dialect, is the formation (mentioned above p. 55) of an *ę* vowel by the side of the *į*, which we find in the Slavonic languages. We know of no native Latin notation of these sounds, which could come under consideration; our transcription we have tried to justify at another place.[1]

[1] Transactions of the Berlin Akademy. 1861. p. 151.

The Rumanian language is distinguished by a multiplicity of vocalic combinations; it is therefore necessary to mark, systematically and for the eye, the difference of the numerous monosyllabic diphthongs from the dissyllabic combinations, containing the same elements as the former. The vowels *i* and *u*, when following upon consonants at the end of words, almost lose the very body of sound, without disappearing entirely in pronunciation, being as it were only whispered. We consider these sounds as identical with the Old-Slovenian ь and ъ, to which we refer, holding the transcription there proposed *ĭ* and *ŭ*, which moreover is already in general use in the country itself. We retain also the analogous Rumanian notation of the short unaccented *i* and *u* in the second place of diphthongs *aĭ*, *eĭ*, *iĭ*, *oĭ*, *uĭ*, *ĭ̦ĭ*, *aŭ*, *eŭ* etc. (as in *haĭde, voĭnik, suĭ, daŭ*), in order to distinguish these diphthongs from the dissyllabic combination of vowels *ai, oi, ui* (as in *tain, voire, suit, audŭ*). From the same reason we note the semivocalic short and unaccented *i*, *e* and *o* in the first place of the diphthongs *ĭa ĭe ĭo ĭu*, *ĕa ŏa* with the same mark of brevity (as in *ĭarna, kĭeĭe*, *kĭorŭ*, *lúmĕa*, *tŏatẹ*), to distinguish them from the dissyllabic *ia*, *ie*, *ea*, *oa* (as in *scrie*, *Galilea*, *ploa*).

The notation *č ǰ š* and *ž* results from our general alphabet as well as *ţ* which latter has the advantage of being is use already in the country; the softened *d* is rendered *ḍ* by some authors, and is said to exist in dialects with the pronunciation *dz*; but the common pronunciation no longer distinguishing *ḍ* from *z*, we prefer to omit in transcription the difference.

OLD ICELANDIC.

a á	*k g*	—	*h*	*(j)*
e é ö o ó	*t d*	*n*	*s z*	*r l*
i í y ý u ú			*þ ð*	
æ œ	*p b*	*m*	*f v*	
au ei ey	*x*			
ja jö jo				
ja ju				

a ā	*k g*	—	*h*	*(i)*
e ē ọ o ō	*t d*	*n*	*s z*	*r l*
i ī ṳ ṳ̄ u ū			*θ ð*	
ē̤ (or *ai*) *ō̤* (or *oi*)	*p b*	*m*	*f v*	
au ei eṳ	*ks*			
iă iọ̆ iŏ				
ia iu				

Specimen.

	(Transcription.)
Hljóðs bið ek allar	*Hliōðs bið ek allar*
helgar kindir,	*helgar kindir,*
meiri ok minni	*meiri ok minni*
mögu Heimdallar:	*mọgu Heimdallar:*
vildu at ek Valföðrs	*vildu at ek Valfọðrs*
vél framtelja,	*vēl frāmtelia,*
fornspjöll fíra	*fornspiọ̆ll fīra*
þau er ek fremst um man.	*θau er ek fremst um man.*

Beginning of the *Vǫluspa* (*Edda* ed. Munch).

Remarks.

The old manuscripts differ from each other in their orthography, which has been reduced to fixed rules only by modern scholars. We have given above the alphabet, almost as it is written by Rask. Scandinavian editors usually write *ja*, *jö*, *jo*, instead of the *ia*, *iö*, *io*, of the manuscripts, even where these diphthongs have grown out of the vowel *i* by the influence of a following *a* or *u* (nom. pl. *skildir* the shields, acc. pl. *skiöldu*, nom. sg. *skiöldr* for *skiöldur*, gen. sg. *skialdar*). Premising that in all such cases the vowel *i* remained the predominant, we propose to write these diphthongs respectively *iă*, *iǫ̆*, *iŏ*, in order to distinguish them from *ia* = *ja*, as in *telia* (to tell), *telium* (we tell), which might be written also *telja*, *teljum*. It seems to us not improbable, that the letters *æ* and *œ*, which proceed from *ā* and *ō* before an *i* of the next syllable, ought to be considered as real diphthongs, *āi* and *ōi* (like the Latin *ae* for *ai*), although their actual pronunciation is that of *ę̄* and *ǭ*. With regard to the double *ĕ* (*ę̆* and *ė̆*), pointed out by J. Grimm as having existed in the old language, we prefer to follow the manuscripts, which give only one *e*. The characters *þ* and *đ* represent the hard and the soft pronunciation of the English *th*.

WELSH (KI̥MRI).

y		*c*	*g*			*ch*	*h*	-		
a		*t*	*d*	*n*	*nh*	*s*	(*z*)		*r*	*rh*
e *o*						*th*	*dd,d,dh*		*l*	*ll*
i *u* *w*		*p*	*b*	*m*	*mh*	*ff,ph*	*f,v*		*w*	

ai ae aw au oi oe ei ew eu

ia ie io iw

i̥		*k*	*g*	-	-	*χ*	*h*	-		
a		*t*	*d*	*n*	*ń*	*s*	(*z*)		*r*	*ŕ*
e *o*						*θ*	*δ*		*l*	*l̄*
i *ṳ* *u*		*p*	*b*	*m*	*ḿ*	*f*	*v*		*w*	

ai aẹ au aṳ oi oẹ ei eu eṳ

ĭa ĭe ĭo ĭu

Specimen.

1. *Bu hefyd yn y dyddiau hynny, fyned gorchymyn allan oddi wrth Augustus Cesar, i drethu yr holl fyd.* 2. *Y trethiad yma a wnaethpwyd gyntaf pan oedd Cyrenius yn rhaglaw ar Syria.* 3. *A phawb a aethant i'w trethu, bob un i'w ddinas ei hun.* 4. *A Ioseph hefyd a aeth i fynu o Galilea, o ddinas Nazareth, i Iudea, i ddinas Dafydd, yr hon a elwir Bethlehem am ei fod o dŷ a thylwyth Dafydd.* 5. *I'w drethu gyd â Mair, yr hon a ddyweddïasid yn wraig iddo, yr hon oedd yn feichiog.*

Ev. Luc. 2, 1—5.

Transcription.

1. *Bṳ hevi̥d i̥n i̥ di̥δĭaṳ hi̥nni̥, vi̥ned gorχi̥mi̥n alan oδi urθ Aṳgṳstṳs Kesar, i dreθṳ i̥r hol̄ vi̥d.* 2. *I̥ treθĭad i̥ma a unaẹθpwi̥d gi̥ntav pan oẹδ Ki̥reniṳs i̥n ŕaglau ar Si̥rĭa.* 3. *A*

faub a aęθant i'u treθy̤, bob y̤n i'u δinas ei hy̤n. 4. *A Ĭosef hevi̥d a aęθ i vi̥ny̤ o Galilea, o δinas Nazareθ, i Ĭudea, i δinas Davi̥δ, i̥r hon a elwir Beθlehem am ei vod o dī̥ a θi̥lwi̥θ Davi̥δ.*
5. *I'u dreθy̤ gi̥d ā Mair, i̥r hon a δi̥weδiasid i̥n uraig iδo, i̥r hon oęδ i̥n veiχĭog.*

Remarks.

The vowel *y* is not the Slovenian hard or guttural vowel *į*; it is the obtuse and indistinct vowel which we have found in other languages as *e̥*, and which we write here *i̥*, because it comes nearest to *i*, and takes its rise in most cases, though not always, in *i*. In modern writing every short *i* is usually written *y*. We write the diphthongs *ĭa, ĭe, ĭo, ĭu,* with the mark of brevity ˘, in order to distinguish them from the dissyllabic combinations of the same vowels. The diphthongs *ae* and *oe*, though often confounded with *ai* and *oi*, yet in pronunciation differ from them slightly; we therefore write them *aę* and *oę*. The aspirated liquids *ń, ḿ, ŕ*, are peculiar to the Welsh, and we prefer to put the sign of aspiration over the letter instead of placing the full *h* after it, the aspiration being more closely connected with the liquid letter than the composition with *h* would indicate. The fourth liquid letter, viz. *l*, has likewise, besides its simple pronunciation, an aspirated one, expressed by doubling it, *ll*. As in this case the *l* becomes at the same time a palatal pronunciation, the middle of the tongue touching the palatal point on the palate, and the aspiration passing on both sides of the tongue over the eye-teeth, it might be still more exact to render this letter by *l̄*; we omit, however, the palatal line, to spare a diacritical sign which is not absolutely necessary, there being only one aspirated *l*. The letter *w* is the vowel *u* before consonants, and the consonant *w* before vowels. The letter *z* occurs only in foreign words.

HEBREW.

Former pronunciation.

-		ע	א	-	ה	-			;	'	-	h	-		
י	ו	-	ק	-	ח	-			-	q	-	χ	-		
		כ	ג	-	שׁ	-			k	g	-	š	-		
a̤,i̤,ṳ,ā̤		ט	-	-	צ	-			ṯ	-	-	ṣ	-		
i,a̤i	u,a̤u	ת	ד	נ	ס	ז	ר	ל	t	d	n	s	z	r	l
		פ	ב	מ	-	-			p	b	m	-	-		

Later pronunciation.

e̤

e   á a â   o

ì ī i ē ê   ă   ô ó u ū û

ĕ   ŏ

ע	א	-	ה		-			;	'	-	h		-		
-	ק	-	ח		ג			-	q	-	χ		γ		
כ	ג	-	כ		-	י		k	g	-	χ́		-	y	
ט	-	-	צ		-			ṯ	-	-	ṣ		-		
-	-	-	שׁ	שׂ	-			-	-	-	š	ś	-		
ת	ד	נ	ס		ז	ר	ל	t	d	n	s		z	r	l
-	-	-	ת		ד			-	-	-	θ		δ		
פ	פ	מ	פ		ב	ו		p	b	m	f		v	w	

Specimen.

1. בְּרֵאשִׁית בָּרָא אֱלֹהִים אֵת הַשָּׁמַיִם וְאֵת הָאָרֶץ׃ 2. וְהָאָרֶץ הָיְתָה
תֹהוּ וָבֹהוּ וְחֹשֶׁךְ עַל־פְּנֵי תְהוֹם וְרוּחַ אֱלֹהִים מְרַחֶפֶת עַל־פְּנֵי הַמָּיִם׃
3. וַיֹּאמֶר אֱלֹהִים יְהִי אוֹר וַיְהִי־אוֹר׃ 4. וַיַּרְא אֱלֹהִים אֶת־הָאוֹר כִּי־טוֹב

וַיַּבְדֵּל אֱלֹהִים בֵּין הָאוֹר וּבֵין הַחֹשֶׁךְ׃ 5. וַיִּקְרָא אֱלֹהִים לָאוֹר יוֹם
וְלַחֹשֶׁךְ קָרָא לָיְלָה וַיְהִי־עֶרֶב וַיְהִי־בֹקֶר יוֹם אֶחָד׃ 6. וַיֹּאמֶר אֱלֹהִים
יְהִי רָקִיעַ בְּתוֹךְ הַמָּיִם וִיהִי מַבְדִּיל בֵּין מַיִם לָמָיִם׃ 7. וַיַּעַשׂ אֱלֹהִים
אֶת־הָרָקִיעַ וַיַּבְדֵּל בֵּין הַמַּיִם אֲשֶׁר מִתַּחַת לָרָקִיעַ וּבֵין הַמַּיִם אֲשֶׁר מֵעַל
לָרָקִיעַ וַיְהִי־כֵן׃

Genes. 1, 1—7.

Former pronunciation.

1. *Bị raʾạšit bạrạʾạ ʾịlạ̄him ʾịt hạ šạmạim uạ ʾịt hạ ʾạrṣ.*
2. *Uạ hạ ʾạrṣ hạiạtạh tụhu uạ bụhu, uạ χụšk ʿạl pạnại tạhum*
uạ ruχ ʾịlạ̄him mạrạχạpt ʿạl pạnại hạ mạim. 3. *Uạ iạʾạmạr*
ʾịlạ̄him: iạhi ʾạur, uạ iạhi ʾạur. 4. *Uạ iạrʾạ ʾịlạ̄him ʾịt hạ*
ʾạur ki ṭạub; uạ iạbdil ʾịlạ̄him bạin hạ ʾạur uạ bạin hạ χụšk.
5. *Uạ iạqrạʾạ ʾịlạ̄him lạ ʾạur iạum, uạ lạ χụšk qạrạʾạ lạilạh;*
uạ iạhi ʿạrb uạ iạhi bụqr iạum ʾạχạd. 6. *Uạ iạʾạmạr ʾịlạ̄him:*
iạhi rạqiʿ bị tạuk hạ mạim, uihi mạbdil bạin mạim lạ mạim.
7. *Uạ iạʿạš ʾịlạ̄him ʾịt hạ rạqiʿ, uạ iạbdịl bạin hạ mạim ʾạšạr*
mị-tạχt lạ rạqiʿ uạ bạin hạ mạim ʾạšạr mị-ʿạl lạ rạqiʿ; uạ
iạhi kịn.

Later pronunciation.

1. *Bẹrēʾšiθ bârâʾ ʾĕlōhîm ʾēθ haššâmayim wẹʾēθ hâʾâreṣ.*
2. *Wẹhʾâareṣ hâyẹθâh θōhû wâvōhu, wẹχōšeχ́ ʿal pẹnê θẹhôm*
wẹrûχ ʾĕlōhîm mẹraχâfeθ ʿal penê hammâyim. 3. *Wayyōʾmer*
ʾĕlōhîm: yẹhî ʾôr wayẹhî ʾôr. 4. *Wayyarʾ ʾĕlōhîm ʾeθhâʾôr kî*
ṯôv; wayyavdēl ʾĕlōhîm bên hâʾôr ûvên haχōšeχ́. 5. *Wayyiqrâʾ*
ʾĕlōhîm lâʾôr yôm, wẹlaχōšeχ́ qârâʾ lâilâh; wayẹhî ʿerev wayẹhî
vōqer yôm ʾeχâδ. 6. *Wayyōʾmer ʾĕlōhîm: yẹhî râqîʿ bẹθôχ́*
hammâyim, wịhî mavdîl bên mayim lâmâyim. 7. *Wayyaʿaś*
ʾĕlōhîm ʾeθhârâqîʿ, wayyavdēl bên hammayim ʾăšer mittaχaθ
lârâqîʿ ûvên hammayim ʾăšer mēʿal lârâqîʿ; wayẹhî χ́ēn.

Remarks.

The Hebrew writing of our books and manuscripts is remarkable as being composed out of two apparently heterogeneous elements of a very different date and origin. The one element contains real characters, which, although their form was slightly altered after the exile, yet, as to their figure and alphabetic composition, belong no doubt to the oldest epochs of Hebrew, or perhaps even Semitic civilisation. The other element, the pointing, was added only about seven hundred years after Christ. By this addition no character of the old sacred text was altered; it only served to fix the traditional pronunciation. According to the opinion now generally received, the old pronunciation did not differ from the modern one. The ancients, it is supposed, wrote only the consonants, and left all the vowels to be supplied by the reader. Our opinion is, that a mere consonantal alphabet would presuppose by far too abstract a phonic doctrine on the part of its inventors, and, even if such a systematic separation of the consonants had been possible, there would have been no reason for not inventing corresponding signs for the other separated element, viz. the vowels. Moreover the first and most necessary requisite of every writing is its intelligibility, which could not be attained without written signs for the principal and most expressive vowels. We therefore consider the Hebrew alphabet to have been, like all the other old Asiatic alphabets, essentially syllabic, i. e. representing by each character a full vocal syllable. With this syllabic character of the Hebrew letters it is not incompatible, that the inherent vowel is occasionally replaced by another pure vowel following, or eclipsed by the influence of the accent of another vowel in the same word. The two characters י and ו represented in the old Hebrew, as in the other Semitic alphabets, the two vowels *i* and *u*, being the two most remote from the vowel *a*, and therefore the most important in writing. They were primitive vowels in many words, in which they are still pronounced as such, as in the roots דִּין *din*, שׁוּר *šur*, or in the proper names צִידוֹן *Ṣidun (Ṣidôn)* Σιδών, צִיּוֹן *Ṣiun (Ṣiyyôn)* Σιών.

Placed, however, before other vowels in the beginning of a syllable they represented also the semivowels *y* and *w*, into which, according to their nature, they usually pass in the Greek and Latin, and almost all languages. Yet, this semivocalic power is only a derivative and secondary one, the primary being always and even in the pointed writing its vocalic power. One might be inclined to attribute also to the letter א a mere vocalic power in the primitive writing, considering the frequent use of the א quiescens in the pointed writing, and comparing the letter 𐎠 *a* in the analogous old Persian writing. But a further consideration disproves this opinion. It is as easy to prove that the letter 𐎠 in the name of 𐎭𐎠𐎼𐎹𐎺𐎢𐏁 *Dariawuš* (דָּרְיָוֶשׁ, *Darius*) has no consonantic element, as to prove that the letter א in שָׁאוּל *Šaʾul* Σαούλ (part. of שָׁאַל *šaʾal*) has no vocalic element. The Semitic א never takes a semivocalic power, nor is it an aspiration, but a slightly explosive consonant. The condition of the א quiescens is therefore totaly different from that of the י or ו quiescens.

If the assertion is selfevident, that each system of phonetic writing must represent the most essential and prominent elements of that language, for which it was originally intended, we must presume, that in the language which was first written with this Semitic alphabet, only three vowels were necessary to make it intelligible, *a*, *i* and *u*, as in the old Egyptian, old Persian, Assyrian, and likewise, though with a separation of long and short vowels, in the Sanskrit, the Arabic and other languages. We may be almost sure, that also the Hebrew language of the time of Moses and David did not yet distinguish all the vocal shades, represented in the pointed system of the 7th century after Christ, but only the three principal vowels *a*, *i* and *u*. But the language of our oldest Hebrew texts supposes already the separation of long and short vowels, which was indispensable for certain grammatical distinctions. Yet the old writing knows only one *i* and one *u* and no separate *a*. We must therefore suppose either that this writing was invented for a condition of the Hebrew language before the time, to which our historical knowledge of it reaches, or that it was taken from another people and therefore, from the beginning, was defective in expressing the Hebrew vowels. This discrepancy between pronunciation and writing necessarily increased in the space of perhaps 2000 years, the former always advancing, the latter being stationary, till the invention of the vowel-points brought them both again together. The question now is, whether and how far our way of transcribing may be applied even to the oldest Hebrew text and its primitive pronunciation. We still have a certain number of unpointed texts of several other Semitic languages, the writing of which we may likewise suppose to be defective. The usefulness of a general and regular way of transcribing these texts as well as the oldest Hebrew, in a linguistical point of view, can scarcely be contested; for a transcription offering to the reader only unreadable consonants is certainly as inconvenient as a transcription with more or less arbitrary vowels, of which the genuine are not discernible from the hypothetical. We may therefore be justified in proposing a transcription according to our views especially in application to the oldest Hebrew, for the interpretation of which we possess more ample means.

The principal thing to be done in this respect is, to separate in the language the ancient phonic elements from the later.

A later origin and introduction we attribute to all the fricative modifications of consonants (indicated by the non insertion of the *dagesh lene*), which are of mere phonic import without any grammatical signification. The age of the pronunciation indicated by the *dagesh forte*, which also serves to distinguish grammatical modifications, is more doubtful. Whilst in reference to the pointed writing we propose transcribing the *dagesh forte* (as the Arabic *tešdid*) by duplication of the consonant, we should, as regards the old writing, prefer the transcription with the usual line of duplication above the consonant.

As to the vowels, the difficulty of a regular transcription is greater, owing to the defectiveness of the old writing. The gradual increase of vowels may be considered a general rule in most languages. The later origin and secondary value of the pointed vowels in Hebrew cannot be contested; this results also from the fact, that they no-where, like the old vowels י and ו, distinguish different roots. The *e* and *o* vowels of the pointed system may still be traced back to their respective primary vowels, and replaced by them without altering or obscuring the language itself. But it has already been observed, that the Hebrew language in all parts of the Old Testament supposes the distinction of a short *i* and *u* as well as of a long *ā*, although they are not separately expressed. We must in consequence supply these vowels, where they are wanted. It is another imperfection of the old writing, that it does not indicate, whether the inherent vowel *ạ* or no vowel at all is to be pronounced. We find the same defect in the Old Egyptian and Habessynian writing, as well as in several modern Indian writing systems in which no (Sanskritic) *virāma* is used, and the nearest analogy occurs in the old Persian. We are thus at a loss to know, except by inference from the pointed writing, or from grammatical laws, or from foreign transcription, whether we have to read י as *i*, or as *ại*, or as the semivowel *ĭ (y)*, and ו as *u*, or as *ạu*, or as the semivowel *ŭ (w)*. In fact י was pronounced as *i* in אֱלִישָׁה *'Ạlišạh ('Ĕlîšâh)* Ἐλισά, צִיּוֹן *Ṣiun (Ṣiyyôn)* Σιών; as *ại* in קֵינָן *Qạinạn (Qēnân)* Καινᾶν, מִצְרַיִם *Mạṣrạim (Miṣrayim)* Μεσραΐμ; as *ĭ (y)* in יַרְדֵּן *Ĭạrdạn (Yardēn)* Ἰόρδανος, מִדְיָן *Mạdĭạn (Midyân)* Μαδιάμ; and ו as *u* in אַשּׁוּר *'Ạšur ('Aššûr)* Ἀσσούρ; לוּד *Lud (Lûd)* Λούδ; as *ạu* in עֵשָׂו *ʿẠšạu (ʿĒśâu)* Ἡσαῦ, רְעוּ *Rạʿạu (Rẹʿû)* Ῥαγαῦ; as *ŭ (w)* in נִינְוֵה *Ninạŭịh (Nînẹwēh)* Νινευί, יָוָן *Ĭạŭạn (Yâwân)* Ἰωυάν, לֵוִי *Lịŭi (Lēwî)* Λευί.

It is evident, therefore, that to make from any unpointed Semitic writing a proper and readable transcription, a previous knowledge of the language is indispensable. Modern researches have taught, that, among the pointed vowels, long ◌ָ (*å*) takes its rise mostly in *a*, short ◌ָ (*o*) in *u*, long ◌ַ (*á*) always in *a*, short ◌ֶ (*e*) mostly in *i*, ◌ֵ (*ē*) in *i* or *ai*, ◌ֹ (*ō*) in *u* or *au*, or in a degenerated *ā*; ◌ִי and וּ answer to the old heavy vowels *i* and *u*, ◌ֵי and וֹ to old *ai* and *au*; ◌ִ (*ı*) and ◌ֻ (*u*), as well as ◌ְ *šẹwâ mobile* take their rise often in old *a*. These general facts afford a general rule for transcription, without however superseding the special consideration of each particular case. Our specimen will best show, what is here meant. But it is important, that the reader should always be able to distinguish immediately the vowels added by the learned transcriber from those written in the original text. The former are to be indicated for this purpose by the little circle placed underneath.

In transcribing the pointed writing, it is not less desirable to facilitate to the reader as much as possible the distinction between the old and the later writing. Apparently this might be attained by treating, in harmony with the received view, all old characters, including י and ו, as pure consonants, and the new points as the only vowels, e. g. כִּי *kiy*, רָקִיעַ *roqiyʿ*, הָאוֹר *hâ·owr*, טוֹב *ṭowv*, וּבֵין *uwvēyn*. The reader, then, would in the transcription have simply to regard all consonants as representing the old writing, all vowels as representing the points. This mode of transcription, however, would not only offer to the eye a form of writing incapable of being read (nobody being able to pronounce combinations such as *-iyʿ*, *-owv*) and therefore offensive in itself, but it would not even correspond to the intentions of the authors of the pointed system, who, according to our view, did not mean—as little indeed as the old writers themselves—to consider the י and ו as consonants, which they never could have been.

The notation ִי, וּ, ֵי and וֹ, differed from long ִ, ֻ, ֵ and ֹ, no longer in sound but only in origin. In transcription, however, the distinction is necessary; we, therefore, represent the combination of the ancient character and the points by *î*, *û*, *ê*, *ô*, the simple vowels if long by *ī*, *ū*, *ē*, *ō*, if short by *i*, *u*, *e*, *o*. The distinction between long and short vowels, although the authors of the pointed system neglected it, is the more necessary, as the difference of quantity, at least in ָ and ֶ, coincides usually with a difference of origin. The long ָ, being pronounced by those who used the points, and still by the Spanish and other Jews, as a very broad *ǭ*, was indicated by the same sign as the short *o*, although the former originated in *ā*, the latter in *u*; and the long ֶ (*ę̄*) taking its rise in *a* was not distinguished from the short ֶ (*e*) which took its rise in *i*. We prefer, following other authorities, the transcription of long ָ and ֶ by *â* and *ê* instead of *ǭ* and *ę̄*; and for the sake of etymology we represent וֹ and ֵ by *ō* and *ē* instead of *ǭ* and *ę̄*, the diacritical point not being indispensable. The shortest pronunciation of the vowels ַ, ֶ and ָ, by which they lose—not indeed in reality, but in the laws of the Hebrew rhythmic system—their syllabic value, is indicated by the addition of a *šęwâ*. We have already in other cases expressed this extreme shortness, which amounts almost to a total absence of vocalic sound, by putting the sign of brevity above the letter; we therefore write *ă*, *ĕ*, *ŏ*, for ֲ, ֱ, ֳ. The same mark might be placed above the *šęwâ mobile ĕ̥*, if this were not already sufficiently marked by the little circle.

The vocalic organism of the Hebrew language at the time of the introduction of the points will in its remarkable regularity best appear in the schema given above. There we see, starting from the central vowels *a*, *i*, *u*, in a vertical direction the weakened, in an horizontal direction the gradually strengthened vowels on each side in their regular position; and those signs, which have a double pronunciation (ֶ, ָ, ֻ, ֹ), are found by the side of each other, as are also on the other hand those different signs, which have the same pronunciation (ִ and ִי, ֵ and ֵי, ֹ and וֹ, ֻ and וּ).

There is no distinction in the Hebrew writing between the *šewâ mobile*, which we write *ẹ*, and the *šewâ quiescens*, which we omit altogether, because it was not pronounced at all.

In our specimen we have, for the sake of comparison with the old writing, retained the sign of א ʼ in the beginning of words; being, however, there necessarily understood, it may be omitted as in the Arabic writing. The *paθaχ furtivum*, as indicating only the natural phonic transition from the vowels *ī*, *ē*, *ū*, *ō* to one of the deep gutturals הּ, ע, ח, does not want any transcription. The letter כ, when it becomes fricative, we transcribe *χ́*, since it was doubtless spoken nearer to the palatal point than ח *χ*. The guttural (emphatic) pronunciation of ט (arabic ط) and צ (arabic ص) is undoubted; we therefore write *ṭ* and *ṣ*; to regard the former as a medial—on account of the Arabic ط = *ḍ* (see below)—there is no reason. The ancient sound שׁ *š* was later split up into a deeper sound שׁ and a clearer one שׂ, which latter approached very near to ס *s*, and therefore must have been spoken much like the Polish *ś* (see above p. 161). The signs *χ*, *γ*, *θ*, *δ*, require no farther explanation. The accents of words, where it appears useful to mark them, may easily be added.

SYRIAN.

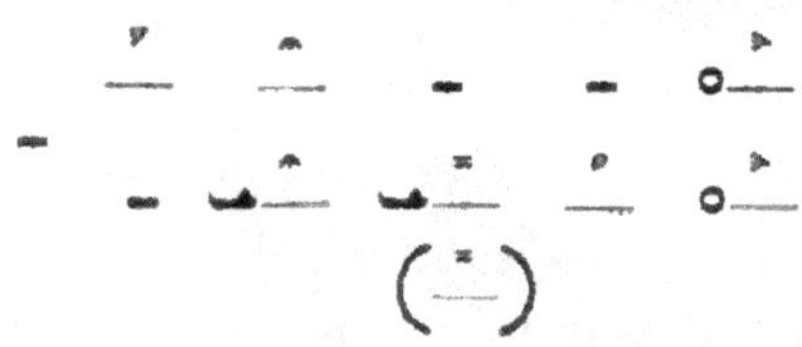

a	e	-	-	u
	e̤			
-	ē	ī	ō	ū

ʿ	ʾ	-	h	-		
-	q	-	χ	-		
k,χ́	g,γ	-	š	-	y	
ṭ	-	-	ṣ	-		
t,θ	d,δ	n	s	z	r	l
p,f	b,v	m	-	-	w	

Specimen.

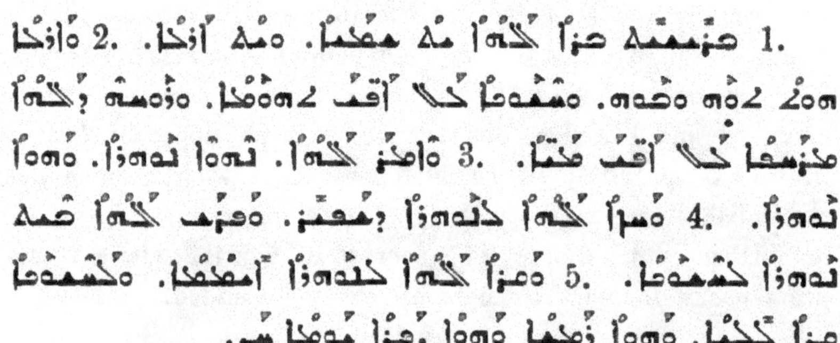

Gen. 1, 1 –5.

1. Be̤rīšīθ be̤rōʾ ʾalōhōʾ yōθ še̤mayōʾ we̤yōθ ʾarʿōʾ. 2. Wàrʿōʾ he̤wōθ tūh we̤būh we̤χe̤šūχ́ōʾ ʿal ʾapai te̤hūmōʾ, we̤rūχeh dàlōhōʾ me̤raχe̤fōʾ ʿal ʾapai mayōʾ. 3. Wèmar ʾalōhōʾ: nehwēʾ nūhrōʾ wahe̤wōʾ nūhrōʾ. 4. Waχe̤zōʾ ʾalōhōʾ le̤nūhrōʾ de̤šapīr wafe̤raš ʾalōhōʾ bēθ nūhrōʾ le̤χe̤šūχ́ōʾ. 5. Waqe̤rōʾ ʾalōhōʾ le̤nūhrōʾ ʾīmōmōʾ wale̤χe̤šūχ́ōʾ qe̤rōʾ līlyōʾ wahe̤wōʾ ramšōʾ wahe̤wōʾ ṣafrōʾ yaumōʾ χad.

Remarks.

Besides the old points of the Syrian writing, we find in the manuscripts, since the 7th century, also the Greek vowels added to the Syrian letters in small figures, as we have exhibited them above. They represent the five vowels *a*, *e*, *i*, *o*, *u*, of which *a* is always short, *o* (= *ō̧*, replacing an older long *ā*) and *i* are always long, *e* is long, when united with ܝ (as vowel-sign) or ܐ quiescens, short, when placed without either, and *u*, always united with ܘ (as vowel-sign), is sometimes long and sometimes short. The short ܶ *e* represents in the language at the same time the short *i*; we follow, however, in this respect the indigenous writing, transcribing it by *e*. The want of an indication where an audible *šewā̧* is to be pronounced and where the consonant alone without any vowel is spoken, exists also in the Syrian writing. Tradition alone supplies this imperfection. In the modern pronunciation the feeble consonantal sound of ܐ ʾ is often dropped entirely, although the letter is still written, and the appertaining vowel is then immediately connected with the consonant preceding the ܐ: e. g. *dalōhōʾ*, is pronounced instead of *dḙʾalōhōʾ*. In such cases we propose to keep, for the sake of etymology, the sign ʾ, but to place it over the vowel connected with it, writing e. g. *dảlohoʾ*. The same letters represent in Syrian writing the explosive and their corresponding fricative letters. Sometimes the former are indicated by a dot over them, the latter by a dot beneath; but usually those dots are omitted. In every case the transcription has to follow the pronunciation.

ARABIC.

ـَ	ـَا ,ـٰ	—	ع	أ	—	ح	ه	—	—	—		
ـِ	ـِي	ك	ق		—	خ		غ	—	—		
ـُ	ـُو	—	ج		—	ش		—	—	—	ى	
ـَيْ	ـَوْ	—	ط		—	ص		ض	—	ظ		
		ت	د		ن	س		ز	ث	ذ	ر	ل
		—	ب		م	ف		—	—	—	و	

a	*ā*	-	*;*	*'*	-	*ḥ*	*h*	-	-	-		
i	*ī*	*k*	*q*		-	*χ*		*γ*	-	-		
u	*ū*	-	*ǰ(ģ)*		-	*š*		-	-	-	*y*	
ai	*au*	-	*ḍ*		-	*ṣ*		*ẓ*	-	*ð̣*		
		t	*d*		*n*	*s*		*z*	*θ*	*ð*	*r*	*l*
		-	*b*		*m*	*f*		-	-	-	*w*	

Specimen.

سُورَةُ ٱلْبَقَرَةِ بِسْمِ ٱللّٰهِ ٱلرَّحْمٰنِ ٱلرَّحِيمِ 1. ذٰلِكَ ٱلْكِتَابُ لَا
رَيْبَ فِيهِ هُدًى لِلْمُتَّقِينَ 2. ٱلَّذِينَ يُؤْمِنُونَ بِٱلْغَيْبِ وَيُقِيمُونَ
ٱلصَّلٰوةَ وَمِمَّا رَزَقْنَاهُمْ يُنْفِقُونَ 3. وَٱلَّذِينَ يُؤْمِنُونَ بِمَا أُنْزِلَ إِلَيْكَ
وَمَا أُنْزِلَ مِنْ قَبْلِكَ وَبِٱلْآخِرَةِ هُمْ يُوقِنُونَ 4. أُولٰٓئِكَ عَلَى هُدًى مِنْ
رَبِّهِمْ وَأُولٰٓئِكَ هُمُ ٱلْمُفْلِحُونَ 5. إِنَّ ٱلَّذِينَ كَفَرُوا سَوَآءٌ عَلَيْهِمْ
ءَأَنْذَرْتَهُمْ أَمْ لَمْ تُنْذِرْهُمْ لَا يُؤْمِنُونَ 6. خَتَمَ ٱللّٰهُ عَلَى قُلُوبِهِمْ

وَعَلَى سَمْعِهِمْ وَعَلَى أَبْصَارِهِمْ غِشَاوَةٌ وَلَهُمْ عَذَابٌ عَظِيمٌ 7. وَمِنَ
ٱلنَّاسِ مَنْ يَقُولُ آمَنَّا بِٱللَّهِ وَبِٱلْيَوْمِ ٱلْآخِرِ وَمَا هُمْ بِمُؤْمِنِينَ
8. يُخَادِعُونَ ٱللَّهَ وَٱلَّذِينَ آمَنُوا وَمَا يَخْدَعُونَ إِلَّا أَنْفُسَهُمْ وَمَا
يَشْعُرُونَ

Sūratu ʼl baqarati. Bismi ʼllāhi ʼl-raħmāni ʼl-raħīmi. 1. *Δālika ʼl kitābu, lā raiba fīhi hudạn lil muttaqīna,* 2. *allaδīna yuʼminūna bi ʼl γaibi, wa yuqīmūna ʼl-ṣalā̤ta, wa mimmā razaqnāhum yunfiqūna,* 3. *wa ʼllaδīna yuʼminūna bimā unzila ilaika wamā unzila min qablika, wa bi ʼl āχirati hum yūqinūna.* 4. *Ulāʼika ɜalạ hudạn min rabbihim, wa ulāʼika humu ʼl mufliħūna.* 5. *Inna ʼllaδīna kafarū sawāʼun ɜalaihim aʼanδartahum am lam tunδirhum; lā yuʼminūna.* 6. *Χatama ʼllāhu ɜalā̩ qulūbihim, wa ɜalā̩ samɜihim, wa ɜalā̩ absārihim γišāwatun, wa lahum ɜaδābun ɜaḏ̣īmun.* 7. *Wa mina ʼl-nāsi man yaqūlu: āmannā bi ʼllāhi wa bi ʼl yaumi ʼl āχiri, wa mā hum bimuʼminīna,* 8. *yuχādiɜūna ʼllāha wa ʼllaδīna āmanū, wa mā yaχdaɜūna illā anfusahum, wa mā yašɜurūna.*

Remarks.

Our only object here is the written language and its pronunciation, as it has been fixed very accurately for the Koran and faithfully handed down. This pronunciation is still followed by the Readers of the Koran, and is in use in a number of Bedouin tribes. The manifold deviations of the modern dialects have never beeu admitted in writing; and the pronunciation of the Koran is still everywhere understood and regarded as the best. When, however, in particular cases it is desirable to render a different dialectic pronunciation by Roman characters, then it is necessary to determine first the individual pronunciation — as is done by Eli Smith in his appendix to Robinson's Palestine — and to transcribe it accordingly.

Arabic writing, like that pronunciation which the Orthoepists teach, distinguishes only three vowels, *a*, *i*, *u*, — which may be long or short — and two diphthongs, *ai* and *au*. The latter have sometimes lost their second element in pronunciation, though in writing it is retained; f. i. عَلَى, صَلَوةً *ʒalai*, *ṣalauta*, are pronounced *ʒala*, *ṣalāta*. It is the same as with the *ι subscriptum* in the Greek, which is still written but not pronounced. This analogy will justify our writing in such cases even in Arabic — for etymological reasons — an *i* or *u subscriptum*: *ʒala*, *ṣalāta*. In the Article *al*, the vowel, when following upon a vowel, is passed over, which, like other elisions, we note in the European manner by an apostrophe. The sign *Madda* ~ is either a mark of the length of the vowel, and then to be rendered accordingly; or it represents at the same time ء *Hamza*, in which case this will have to be added: شَنَآنُ *šanaʾānu*. The perpendicular *Fatḱa*, also, is mostly only the sign of a long vowel.

Hamza (see above p. 68) must necessarily be transcribed only in the middle of words; in the beginning its omission produces no ambiguity; we write therefore *yuʾminūna*, but *allaδīna* instead of *ʾallaδīna*. Our sign of ʒ for ع shows its phonetic relation to the weaker ء ʾ, and has moreover the practical advantage of being convenient before a capital letter in the beginning of names: *ʒAlī*, *ʒAkka*. Of ح = *ḱ* and ق = *q* we have spoken above (p. 69), as also of the linguals or gutturo-dentals ط, ظ, ص, ض, *ḍ*, *δ̣*, *ṣ*, *ẓ*. With respect to the accurate pronunciation of the latter sounds, especially the medial ط *ḍ*, which hitherto by European scholars has been taken for a tenuis and therefore connected with the basis *t* (*th*, *t*, *ʻt*, *ṭ*), we refer our readers to a special treatise by the author, in which these questions are discussed at length.[1] It may be doubted whether ج is to be rendered by *ǵ* or *ǰ*, the former representing the older and purer, the latter the more general modern pronunciation; we prefer the latter, for which we find an additional reason in the fact, that the foreign languages which have adopted this letter with the whole Arabic alphabet or in Arabic words, almost universally pronounce it *ǰ*. The *Tešdīd* ّ is a sign of reduplication of the consonant over which it is placed; in transcribing, the consonant itself is to be repeated instead. The *J̌asm* ْ is of importance only in syllabic writing, showing the absence of a vowel; in transcription it requires no distinctive mark. In all cases of assimilation of consonants, the etymological point of view must prevail in transcription as it does in the native writing, the assimilation being generally self evident even for us. We write therefore *radadtu, aχaδti*, not *radattu, aχatti*. The article *al* ought to be always kept separate, according to the custom in all European languages; only, before the *solar* letters its assimilation, producing a closer connexion in sound with the following noun, may be marked by a line of connection. We therefore write *al kitābu*, but *al-raḣīm*, *al-nāsu*, to show the pronunciation *arraḣīm*, *annāsu*. The almost general extinction of the sound of ه *h* at the end of words is no reason why it should not be noted there, as in the midst of words, by *h*. In the same manner, ة at the end is to be transcribed *h*, when pronounced so; but when spoken as *t*, is to be written *t*. There is no difficulty in making this distinction, as the different pronunciation of ة is determined by a definite rule.

[1] On the sounds of the Arabic language and their transcription. Publications of the Berlin Academy 1861.

GE̥ʿE̥Z (ETHIOPIC).

ዐ አ	-	-	ሐ ሀ		ʿa ʾa		-	ḱa ha	
ኰ ጐ	ቈ	-	ኈ		ḱa ġa	k̇ʾa	-	χ̇a	
ከ ገ	ቀ	-	ኀ		ka ga	kʾa	-	χa	
ፀ ዘ	ጸ	-	ሠ	የ	ṭa ḍa	ṭʾa	-	ša	ya
ተ ደ	ጠ	ነ	ሰ	ረ ለ	ta da	tʾa	na	sa	ra la
ፐ በ	ጰ	መ	ፈ	ወ	pa ba	pʾa	ma	fa	wa

Classes

1	2	3	4	5	6	7.
ከ	ኩ	ኪ	ካ	ኬ	ክ	ኮ
ka	*kū*	*kī*	*kā*	*kē*	*ke̥*	*kō*

etc.

a e̥
ā
ē ō
ī ū
aĭ aŭ

Specimen.

በቀዳሚ ፡ ገብረ ፡ እግዚአብሔር ፡ ሰማየ ፡ ወምድረ ። ወምድርሰ ፡ ኢታስተርኢ ፡
ወኢኮነት ፡ ድሉተ ፡ ወጽልመት ፡ መልዕልተ ፡ ቀላይ ፡ ወመንፈሰ ፡ እግዚአብሔር ፡
ይጼልል ፡ መልዕልተ ፡ ማይ ። ወይቤ ፡ እግዚአብሔር ፡ ለይኩን ፡ ብርሃን ፡ ወኮነ ፡
ብርሃን ። ወርእዮ ፡ እግዚአብሔር ፡ ለብርሃን ፡ ከመ ፡ ሠናይ ፡ ወፈለጠ ፡ እግዚአብ
ሔር ፡ ማእከለ ፡ ብርሃን ፡ ወማእከለ ፡ ጽልመት ። ወሰመዮ ፡ እግዚአብሔር ፡ ለብር
ሃን ፡ ዕለተ ፡ ወለጽልመት ፡ ሌሊተ ፡ ወኮነ ፡ ሌሊተ ፡ ወጸብሐ ፡ ወኮነ ፡ መዓልተ ፡ ፩ ።

Gen. 1, 1—5.

1. *Bakʾadâmī gabe̥ra ʾe̥gzīʾabe̥ḱēr samāya wa me̥dra.* 2. *Wa me̥drsa ʾītāstarʾī waʾīkōnat de̥lūta waṭʾe̥lmat malʿe̥lta kʾalāĭ wa manfasa ʾe̥gzīʾabe̥ḱēr ye̥ṭʾēle̥l malʿe̥lta māĭ.* 3. *Wa ye̥bē ʾe̥gzīʾabe̥ḱēr laye̥kūn be̥rhān wa kōna be̥rhān.* 4. *Waʾre̥ʾe̥yō ʾe̥gzīʾabe̥ḱēr labe̥rhān kama šanāĭ wa falatʾa ʾe̥gzīʾabe̥ḱēr māʾkala be̥rḱān wa māʾkala ṭʾe̥lmat.* 5. *Wa samayō ʾe̥gzīʾabe̥ḱēr labe̥rḱān ʿe̥lata wa laṭʾe̥lmat lēlīta wa kōna lēlīta wa ṭʾabḱa wa kōna maʿālta ʾaḱada.*

Remarks.

The Abyssinians have transformed the old Himiaritic writing into a complete syllabarium, divided into seven rows according to the different inherent vowels. Five of them are pronounced with the long vowels *ā*, *ē*, *ī*, *ō*, *ū*; the first row, which alone we have exhibited above, with a short *a* approaching in pronunciation to *e*, and the sixth either with the obtuse vowel *ẹ* or without any vowel. This latter uncertainty has been observed already in several other languages (see above p. 178). To show the true character of the language, it is important to mark all the long vowels with the sign of length over them, although the first of them alone *(ā)* has a short one *(a)* corresponding to it. The sixth form of *y* and *w* (ይ *yẹ* and ው *wẹ*) is also employed to express the short diphthongic *i* and *u* after vowels. The consonantal value of *y* and *w*, in fact, disappears in this position, and it seems therefore justifiable to deviate in such cases from the indigenous custom, which is only a consequence of the syllabic writing, and to write in our transcription *aĭ* and *aŭ* according to the pronunciation instead of *ay* and *aw*.

Amongst the consonants, the Semitic letters *ẕ*, *ṯ*, are wanting. The sound of ሠ and of ሰ is at present the same. But the Amharic palatal row, the forms of which are all taken from those of the dental row, shows plainly that ሰ belonged to the dentals and was formerly pronounced *s*, and that ሠ in consequence corresponded to *š*. The same conclusion is arrived at from the palaeographical form of ሠ, as well as from etymological reasons. Two classes of sounds are not found in any other Semitic alphabet. One of them is the same as the Ossetian class of *tenues* (see above p. 140). Our transcription by *k'*, *t'*, etc. renders exactly the pronunciation. The other is a new local class, which may be regarded as a peculiar developement of the Semitic *q*. It is of a deep guttural nature, and palaeographically derived from the next guttural class *k*, *g*, *χ*, *k'*, which latter is pronounced somewhat nearer to the palatal point. Some scholars call the letters of the former class diphthongs, regarding the characteristic phonic element of the class as a vocalic *u* belonging to the following vowel. If we had here to deal with an augmentation of the inherent vowel, we should find the same augmentation as well after other consonants as after the gutturals. But it is only a peculiar deep gutturalisation of the consonantal element, approaching in some respect to the sound of *kw*, *gw*, etc.—in a similar way as the palatals *ḱ*, *ǵ* etc. in other languages approach to the combination of *ky*, *gy*, etc.—without being identical, however, with the combination of the two letters *k* and *w*, or *g* and *w*, etc., which would have been written ክው, ግው, etc. The transcription by *k̃*, *g̃* etc. would give a right hint to the reader, but appears too artificial and unusual. We prefer therefore to write *k̇*, *ġ*, *χ̇*, *k̇'*, adding the guttural point over them. With regard to the letters ፀ, ጸ, ጰ, it results from the whole system of sounds in this language, that they form a peculiar class of explosive letters, corresponding to the other classes. Their original pronunciation was probably *t'*, *d'*, *t'*, and afterwards *ṭ*, *ḍ*, *ṭ'*, the medial of which (*ḍ*) passed finally into the pure fricative *z*, as we find it pronounced in Amharic.

AMHARIC.

ዐ	አ	-	-	ሐ	ኀ	ሀ			
ኰ	ጐ	ቈ	-	ኈ		-			
ከ	ገ	ቀ	-	ኸ		-			
ቸ	ጀ	ጨ	ኘ	ሸ		ዠ			
ፀ	-	ጸ	-	ሠ		-		የ	
ተ	ደ	ጠ	ነ	ሰ		ዘ		ረ	ለ
ፐ	በ	ጰ	መ	ፈ		-		ወ	

a	*e̥*			*̓*	*̕*	-	-	*k̋*	*ḳ̋*	*h*		
	ā			*k̇*	*ġ*	*k̇'*	-	*χ̇*		-		
ē	*ō*			*k*	*g*	*k'*	-	*χ*		-		
ī		*ū*		*č*	*ǰ*	*č'*	*ń*	*š*		*ž*		
aĭ	*aŭ*	*āĭ*	*āŭ*	*ṭ*	-	*ṭ'*	-	*ṡ̌*		-	*y,ĭ*	
				t	*d*	*t'*	*n*	*s*		*z*	*r*	*l*
				p	*b*	*p'*	*m*	*f*		-	*w,ŭ*	

Specimen.

በሐዋርያት ፡ ዘመን ፡ በቤተ ፡ ክርስቲያን ፡ እንዴህ ፡ ያለች ፡ አንድነት ፡ ነበረችባት ፡
ሁላቸው ፡ አንድ ፡ ሥጋ ፡ አንዲት ፡ ነፍስም ፡ እስኪሆኑ ፡ ድረስ ። ክርስቲያናትም ፡
ሁሉ ፡ ሀክርስቶስ ፡ ከቶ ፡ አልተለዩም ። ሁላቸው ፡ የአዳም ፡ ልጆች ፡ እንደ ፡
ነበሩ ፡ በሥጋ ፡ ሁላቸውም ፡ ለራሳቸው ፡ ያለ ፡ ክርስቶስ ፡ የጠፉ ፡ ኃጥአን ፡
እንደ ፡ ነበሩ ፡ እንዴሁም ፡ በሃይማኖት ፡ ሁላቸው ፡ ባንድ ፡ ክርስቶስ ፡ ዳኑ ።

Isenberg, Amharic Gramm. p. 14.

Bak̋awāryāt zaman babēta Kre̥stīyān e̥ndēh yālač ande̥nat nabarače̥bāt hūlāčaŭ ande̥ še̥gā andīt nafse̥m ʾe̥skīhōnū de̥ras Kre̥stīyānāte̥m hūlū ba Kre̥stōs katō altalayūm hūlāčaŭ ya ʾAdam le̥ǰōč e̥nda nabarū baše̥gā, hūlāčaŭm larāsāčaŭ yāla Kre̥stōs yat'afū χāt'e̥ʾān e̥nda nabarū ʾe̥ndēhūm bahāimānōt hūlāčaŭ bānde̥ Kre̥stōs dānū.

Remarks.

The Amharic alphabet differs from the *Ge̥ʾe̥z* only by the accession of several new sounds, which by the inhabitants are called „Islamitic", being indeed for the most part Arabic sounds. To these belong especially the palatal letters *č*, *ǰ*, *ń*, *š*, *ž*, *č'*, all derived as to form, from the corresponding dentals. The sibilant ሠ, which originally, as we have observed in reference to the *Ge̥ʾe̥z*, seems to have been sounded as *š*, has been divided, as in Hebrew, into two sounds; the letter ሠ being confined to the sharper sound *ś*, which must have approached the Polish *ś*, and ሸ being added to represent the deeper sound *š*. The letter ሐ, corresponding in *Ge̥ʾe̥z* with the Arabic ح *ḣ*, had lost in Amharic its strong breath, being almost weakened to the sound of the simple ሀ, *h*. In a subsequent time, therefore, when Arabic words, containing the letter ح, *ḣ*, were introduced into Amharic, a new Amharic letter was wanted to express this strong spirans, and ኀ was added for this purpose. We distinguish in consequence this new letter from the older one only by a diacritical point, placed under it, *ḥ̇*. The vocalisation is the same as in the *Ge̥ʾe̥z*.

OLD EGYPTIAN.

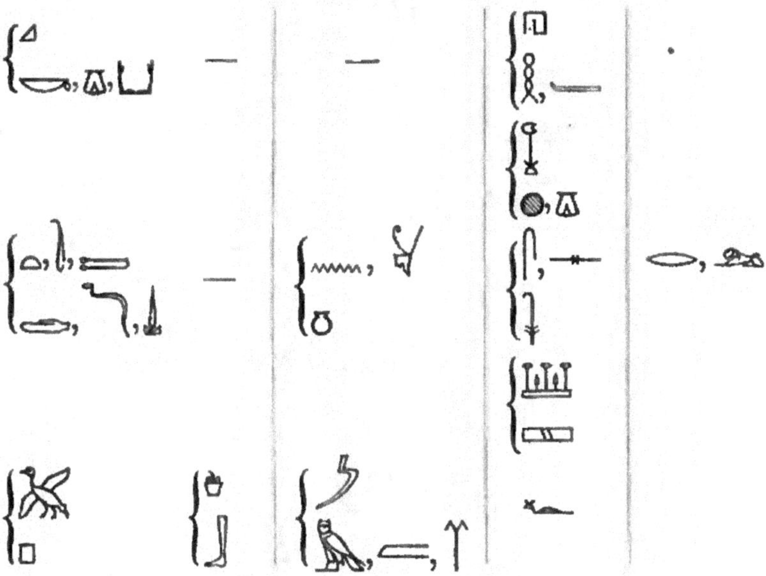

—	a̤, i̤, ṳ, e̤
	a
	a (ȧ)
	a (ā)
	i
	i (ī, ē)
	u
	u (u, ō?)

k (ḳ)	-	-	h (ḥ)	
			χ (χ̣)	
t (ṭ)	-	n (ṇ)	s (ṣ)	r (l)
			š (ṣ̌)	
p (p̣)	b (ḅ)	m (ṃ)	f	

Specimen.

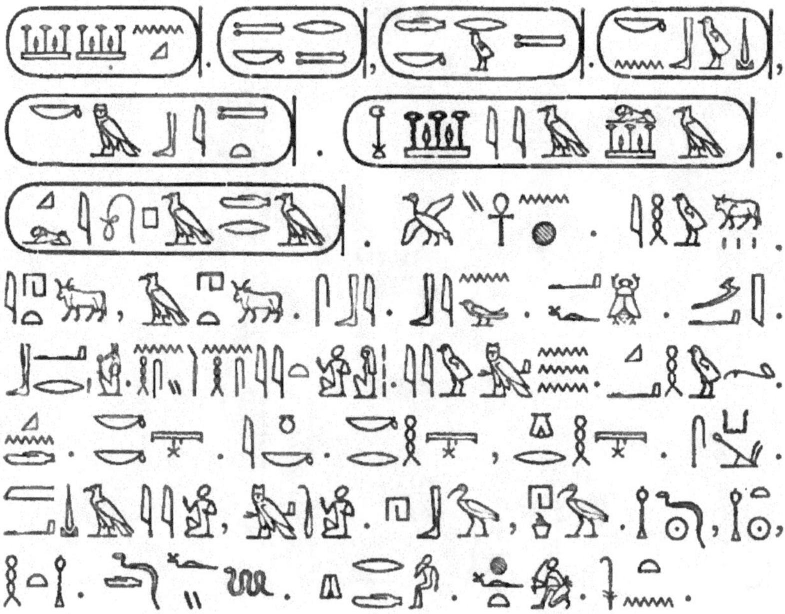

Šišạnk (שִׁישַׁק, Σέσωγχις). *Tạkrut* (תִּכְלֹת, Τακέλωθις). *Kạnbut*, *Kạmbatt* (Καμβύσης). *χšiarša* (cuneif. *χšạyarša*, אֲחַשְׁוֵרוֹשׁ, Ξέρξης). *Klaupatra*. *Pianχ* (Φινάχης). *ahu* (ⲉϩⲟⲟⲩ). *ahẹt* (ⲉϩⲉ,ⲧ). *seba* (ⲥⲉⲃⲓ). *banị* (ⲃⲟⲛⲓ). *af* (ⲁϥ, ⲁⲁϥ). *ma* (ⲙⲏⲓ, ⲙⲉ). *Bar* (בַּעַר). *nẹhẹsi* (negros and) *nẹhẹsitu* (negresses). *iuma* (ⲉⲓⲟⲙ, ⲓⲟⲙ). *kahu* (ⲕⲱϩ). *kẹnt* (ϭⲟⲛⲧ), *kạkẹ* (ⲕⲁⲕⲉ). *anụk* (ⲁⲛⲟⲕ). *kụrh* (ϭⲱⲣϩ). *skạ* (ⲥⲕⲁⲓ). *matai* (ⲙⲁⲧⲟⲓ). *hịbụ* (ϩⲓⲃⲟⲩⲓ, ϩⲁⲃⲓⲟⲩⲓ). *hạt* (ϩⲁⲧ). *tạtfi* (ϫⲁⲧϥⲓ). *χrụtị* (ϧⲣⲟⲩⲓ). *χeft* (ϣⲁϥⲧ). *sutẹn* (ⲥⲟⲩⲧⲛ̀).

Remarks.

The hieroglyphic writing was at all times essentially an ideographic writing, in which every sign expresses a whole idea and its corresponding words. It is true that we find from the oldest times a certain number of pure phonetic signs intermingled with them, but of secondary nature. Those are not intended to supplant the ideographic signs, but to suggest the proper words for them, to supply them with grammatical forms, and to write foreign names. Besides those two classes of signs, there are others of an intermediate nature. It is evident that our transcription could not reproduce in any way this complicated system of writing; we have only to deal with its phonetic part and to determine the different sounds of the ancient language. This task has been accomplished once already by the Egyptians themselves, viz. by the Christian Egyptians, when they changed their indigenous writing for the Greek alphabet, adding to it six new characters for the same number of sounds peculiar to the Egyptian and unknown to the Greek language. The comparison of the old Egyptian with the Demotic and Coptic writing, and the examination of proper names transcribed anciently from hieroglyphics into foreign languages and vice versa, are the principal means to determiue the old Egyptian pronunciation. They are perhaps not quite sufficient to remove all the doubts which are still entertained amongst Egyptian scholars, yet I may refer to what I have said on this point in another place.[1]

The pronunciation of the Egyptian sounds, as given above in our transcription, is what the later Egyptians themselves gave to the hieroglyphic signs. They may have erred in some points, but those points are doubtful also for us, and it would therefore be advisable not to decide any thing in advance of this later pronunciation, before those donbts have been thoroughly removed. We add here only a few remarks on special points.

The short vowels rarely were written, but were regarded as conveyed in the respective consonants. The three vowel

---

[1] Königsbuch p. 163 sqq.

signs 𓇋, 𓄿, 𓂝, which are imperfectly distinguished in the corresponding Demotic, are not distinguished at all in the Coptic words, and in the transcription of Greek and Roman names. All three are rendered in the Coptic and in these transcriptions by the vowel *a*, with which *e* and *o* are regarded as identical. In the hieroglyphic writing, however, they very rarely interchange with one another. There 𓇋 is mostly found in the beginnig of words, 𓄿 mostly in the middle or on the end of words. The sign 𓂝 seems to have expressed originally long *ā*, which not seldom passed into *o*, as from the Demotic sign = *o*, representing the hieroglyphic 𓂝, as well as from the Coptic, might be inferred. To the same sign we find in Hebrew ע often corresponding, and this letter might then also indicate rather the lengthening of the preceding vowel, not the consonantal sound ʿ, which seems to have been always unknown, as well as the sound of א ʾ, in the Egyptian language. The sign \\ appears first in the end of the Old reign, and in the perpendicular form ||. This may have been an abbreviation of 𓇌, but seems to be used rather for the short *i*, in contradistinction to 𓇌, which represents long *ī* or *ē*. Between 𓅱 and the later introduced sign 𓏲, both standing for *u*, there is no difference to be observed. More seldom is 𓍯, which perhaps was meant for long *ū* or *ō*.

Almost all the consonants seem to contain originally a certain implied vowel, or at least to unite more easily with certain vowels then with others. We observe principally two classes of consonants in this respect, the one of which prefers to be followed by the vowel *a*, the other by *u* or *i*. In this, too, we find the reason, why in later times the consonantal value of certain signs has changed through the influence of the following vowel. Especially the closed vowels *u* and *i* caused not seldom, as we know also from other languages, an assibilation or softening of the preceding consonant. Accordingly, we find 𓈎 mostly united with *a*, 𓂝 more often with *u* or *i*. To both corresponds *k* in Coptic and in Greek names, and כ in Hebrew names. It is true that we find not seldom Hebrew ק *q* for hieroglyphic △; but this is as little able to prove, that the Egyptians had the merely Semitic sound of ק, as the regular Arabic writing قَلُوبَطْرَه *Qleobatrah* is to decide anything about the pronunciation of the Greek κ or τ. In the Demotic writing, the signs corresponding to the hieroglyphic △ and 𓎡 express indifferently the sound *k*, and the union of either of them, with the demotic substitute for the hieroglyphic 𓉔, expresses the Greek χ, which was pronounced *kh*. The demotic sign for 𓎡, however, had in other cases also the sound of the Coptic letter ϭ, which itself took its form from that sign and was pronounced *k̄* or *č*. This proves clearly enough, that the hieroglyphic language did not know the sound of the Coptic ϭ. Instead of △ we find sometimes the sign 𓎼, and instead of 𓎡 we find also 𓐍, which letter, however, by the present hieroglyphic scholars is generally confounded with 𓐍 (= 𓐍). There is no single character in the Hieroglyphic nor in the Demotic writing for the sound of the medial *g*, which in demotic is sometimes written 𓈖 i. e. 𓈖△ = *nk* (cf. also the hieroglyphic 𓈖△ for Hebrew ק in the originally Semitic name of the Bubastide king *Šišaq* = *Šišank*). The characters 𓏏, 𓍿, 𓂧 for *t* replace one another often, though not in all cases. The following characters 𓍿, 𓆓, 𓍘, which occasionally change with one another and sometimes also with the preceding characters, show a tendency to duplication, *tt*. Afterwards, they are inclined to pass into the sound of the Coptic ϫ = *č*, which Coptic sign indeed seems to come from the demotic form of hieroglyphic 𓍘. The original hieroglyphic pronunciation *t* was however known even as late as in Roman times. The same character is found sometimes as substitute for the Hebrew צ, as in 𓍘𓅄𓂋𓈉 *Taro*, which has been compared with the Hebrew צוֹר or צֹר *Sōr*, Tyrus; but in these cases we must remember that by the side of the Hebrew צ there is commonly found, as an older sound, the Aramaic ט, as in טוּרָא, *Ṭûrâ*, from which also the Greek form *Τύριος* is taken. The choise of the hieroglyphic was due perhaps rather to the decided emphatic pronunciation of ט in such cases then to the assibilitated pronunciation of צ. The medial sound of *d* in foreign names was sometimes indicated in hieroglyphics by , and in Demotic by i. e. *nt*; this proves sufficiently that the Egyptian language did not use the simple sound of *d*. *p* connects itself readily with *a*, □ with *u* or *i*. The identity of the consonantal value in both results from the fact, that originally □ was added to the less frequent in order to indicate its phonetic value. There is no doubt about the sound of *b*, which before *u* and *i* is mostly written , before *a*, often . The sounds of *m* and *n* have never changed by the influence of the following vowel; = *nu* dropps its inherent *u* only in later times. The characters and , although they rarely interchange, seem to be distinguished chiefly by the subjoined or inherent vowel, the former preferring *a*, the latter *u* or *i*. The closed pronunciation of *u* and *i* caused naturally a strengthening of the breath in . The same case happens with and , the former of which was originally explained by the latter (as by □, and by or , by or), but differed afterwards from it by inclining rather to *a*, wilst inclined to *u* or *i*. It is for this reason that in later times passed more frequently from the pronunciation of *χ* into that of *š*. Amongst the characters representing *s*, unites constantly with *u*. and represent both *š*, but the former prefers *a*, the latter *u* or *i*. There was no distinction between the two sounds *r* and *l* in the old sacred language; it belongs rather to the later popular dialects. The lion as *r*, and more frequently as *l* occurs principally in foreign names since the time of the later dynasties.

If, now, any one wishes to denote in the transcription this

system of vocalisation, which might be compared with similar facts in the Old Persian and Old Slovenian languages and which was more in use at certain times then at others, he ought to chose one and the same diacritical sign, as, for instance, a point underneath, so as to distinguish from the others those consonantal characters which unite preferably with *u* or *i*, aud at the same time to signalize their frequent change in later pronunciation through the influence of these vowels. The sound of 𓇋 might also be provisionally denoted by *ȧ* with a point above. But, if we consider, that this distinction of the two classes of signs did not indicate originally a phonetic difference of consonantal value, that there was never a systematic uniformity in regard to their use, and that in auy case several points of this question remaiu still unexplained, we cannot attach a great value to the introduction of this diacritical point in our transcription. Scientific exactness, however, demands, that all the vowels, added by the transcriber conjecturally, are to be signalized as such to the reader. We write therefore, as in other languages, for supposed vowels *ạ*, *ị*, *ụ* and if the vowel is quite uncertain, *ẹ*.

COPTIC.

		⸗̣			
		ⲁ			
	ⲉ ⲏ		ⲟ ⲱ		
ⲓ (ⲩ)					ⲟⲩ
ⲁⲓ	ⲉⲓ	ⲟⲓ	ⲁⲩ	ⲉⲩ	ⲟⲟⲩ

			ϩ			
ⲕ	(ⲅ)	-	ϧ			(ⲭ)
ϭ	-	-	ϣ			
ⲧ	ⲇ	ⲛ	ⲥ	ⲣ	ⲗ	(ⲑ)
ϫ	-	-	-			
ⲡ	ⲃ	ⲙ	ϥ			(ⲫ)
(ⲝ)	(ⲯ)	(ⲍ)				
(ϯ)						

		e̥			
		a			
	e ē		*o ō*		
i (*u̥*)					*u*
ai	*ei*	*oi*	*au*	*eu*	*ou*

			h			
k	*g*	-	*χ*			*kh*
č	-	-	*š*			
t	*d*	*n*	*s*	*r*	*l*	*th*
ċ	-	-	-			
p	*b*	*m*	*f*			*ph*
ks	*ps*	*ζ*				
ti						

Specimen.

Ⲓⲏ̅ⲥ̅ ⲇⲉ ⲉ̀ⲧ ⲁⲩⲙⲁⲥϥ ϧⲉⲛ Ⲃⲏⲑⲗⲉⲉⲙ ⲛ̀ⲧⲉ ϯ ⲓⲟⲩⲇⲉⲁ̀ ϧⲉⲛ ⲛⲓ ⲉ̀ϩⲟⲟⲩ ⲛ̀ⲧⲉ ⲏ̀ⲣⲱⲇⲏⲥ ⲡⲟⲩⲣⲟ ϩⲏⲡⲡⲉ ⲓⲥ ϩⲁⲛ ⲙⲁⲅⲟⲥ ⲁⲩⲓ̀ ⲉ̀ⲃⲟⲗ ⲥⲁ ⲡⲉⲓⲉⲃⲧ ⲉ̀ ⲓ̀ⲗⲏ̅ⲙ̅ ⲉⲩϫⲱ ⲙ̀ⲙⲟⲥ.
2. ϫⲉ ⲁϥ ⲑⲱⲛ ⲫⲏ ⲉ̀ⲧ ⲁⲩⲙⲁⲥϥ ⲡⲟⲩⲣⲟ ⲛ̀ⲧⲉ ⲛⲓ ⲓⲟⲩⲇⲁⲓ ⲁⲛⲛⲁⲩ ⲅⲁⲣ ⲉ̀ ⲡⲉϥⲥⲓⲟⲩ ⲥⲁ ⲡⲉⲓⲉⲃⲧ ⲟⲩⲟϩ ⲁⲛⲓ̀ ϫⲉ ⲛ̀ⲧⲉⲛⲟⲩⲱϣⲧ ⲙ̀ⲙⲟϥ.

Iēsus de et aumasf χen Bēthleem ẹnte ti Iudea χen ni ehou ẹnte Ērōdēs puro hēppe is han magos aui ebol peiebt e Ierusalēm eučō ẹmmos. 2. *Če af thōn phē et aumasf puro ẹnte ni Iudai annau gar e pefsiu sa peiebt uoh ani če ẹntenuōšt ẹmmof.*

Remarks.

The vowel Ⲏ corresponds, like the hieroglyphic 𓇌, to our long *ī* or *ē*, and Ⲱ to *ū* or *ō*. The compound ⲞⲨ for the simple vowel *u* is taken from the Greek; and when this vowel forms the second part of a diphthong, it is, as in the Greek, rendered only by Ⲩ; we have therefore to pronounce ⲀⲨ and ⲈⲨ as *au* and *eu;* but the diphthong *ou*, which in the common Greek is not in use, was therefore written ⲞⲞⲨ, in order to distinguish it from the simple ⲞⲨ = *u*. There are on the other hand three diphthongic combinations with Ⲓ, viz. ⲀⲒ, ⲈⲒ, ⲞⲒ = *ai*, *ei*, *oi*. It is probable that we have also to regard the combinations ⲎⲒ, ⲰⲒ and ⲎⲨ (ⲎⲞⲨ), ⲰⲨ (ⲰⲞⲨ) as diphthongs: *ēi*, *ōi*, *ēu*, *ōu;* and that even *āi* and *āu*, as well as the single *ā*, existed in the language, without being distinguished in writing, as *a* and *ā* were not distinguished in the Greek alphabet. The single Ⲩ occurs in a few Egyptian words, changing with Ⲓ, Ⲉ or Ⲏ; it may then be expressed by *y*. The marks ̇, ̄, ̀ over consonants indicate usually the indistinct vowel, which we write *ẹ*. The peculiar Egyptian sounds Ϭ and Ϫ show even by their form that the former springs from *k*, the latter from *t* (see above). It seems therefore that their pronunciation approached to the Polish sounds, written in our transcription by *č* and *č*. They were most frequently confounded with one another and passed afterwards into the softer sounds *ǰ* and *ǰ*, as Ⲕ, Ⲧ, Ⲡ were pronounced in later times *g*, *d*, *b*. The letters Ⲅ and Ⲇ occur only exceptionally in Egyptian words for Ⲕ and Ⲧ; but they were usually preserved where they occur in Greek words. The Greek letters ⲭ, ⲑ, ⲫ had by no means in the Coptic alphabet the pronunciation of our *χ*, *θ*, *f*, but represented the aspirated sounds *kh*, *th*, *ph*; they were almost peculiar to the Memphitic dialect and are often resolved into ⲕϩ, ⲧϩ, ⲡϩ; while the Theban dialect usually keeps the tenues ⲕ, ⲧ, ⲡ instead. The letter ϧ, our *χ*, belongs only to the Memphitic dialect and is replaced in the Theban dialect by ϩ *h*. The letters ⲯ and ⲍ occur regularly only in Greek words; the two former are sometimes met with in Egyptian words instead of the ordinary combinations ⲕⲥ and ⲡⲥ; and ⲍ seems to have been pronounced like ⲥ. The sign ϯ represents the syllable ⲧⲓ, which latter is often written instead.

BEǏA (BIŠARI, ETHIOPIAN).

a	-	’	-	*h*		
e o	*k̇*	*ġ*	-	-		
i ĭ u ŭ	*k*	*g*	*ṅ*	-		
	-	*ǰ*	-	*š*	*y*	
		ḍ	-	-		
	t	*d*	*n*	*s*	*r*	*l*
	-	*b*	*m*	*f*	*w*	

Specimen.

Bábu iyáne hob, anĭ ogauíb gébhe. Anĭ asogimék hok, barúk iṅkertinía heb. Batúk ótu dáitui; nauatrít kítkai; nauatrít tiketiék, aréyi hóki. Anĭ kákan, barúh áiṇe. Úra ótak tu šágal uhat’áit tákat ehé, shúle ǰilláida.

Remarks.

The name of the *Beja* is well known to the Arabic writers of the middle age, and designates still the different tribes of the Bishari, Hadenduwa and other descendants of the *Blemmyes* of Roman times and of those *Ethiopians*, whose chief town Herodotus calls Meroë. They dwell in the country between Egypt and Habesh, east of the Nile. The distinction between long and short vowels in their language is not well developed; they are all rather long; which is more perceptible, when the accent of the word falls upon them. It is even doubtful, if the combinations *ai*, *ei*, *oi*, *au*, are to be taken as diphthongs or as two syllables. We prefer therefore to leave all the vowels without indication of length except where sometimes a decidedly short *i* or *u* appears, written by us *ĭ* and *ŭ*, and to use more frequently the accent, which falls for the most part on the last or on the penultimate syllable. It is remarkable, that we meet also in the *Beja* the peculiar class of deep gutturals, which we found in the Abyssinian language approaching to the compound sounds of *kw*, *gw*, and which we write also here *k̇* and *ġ*. On the other hand, we observe the cerebrals *ṭ* and *ḍ*, specially found in India, and resembling in the *Beja* sometimes a combination of *tr* and *dr*. There is no *p*, as in the Arabic, and the letter *ǰ* is very rare, and seems to be taken from the Arabic, as it mostly appears in words taken originally from that language.

GALLA.

Tutschek, Grammar 1845.

a	*a*	*â,ã,ȧ*	ʼ	-	-	-	*h*	-		
e	*ê*		*k*	*g*	*c,q*	-	*ch*	-		
	e		*tch(tż,t̕ź)*	*dj(dż,d̕ź)*	*tsh*	-	*ź*	-		
i	*i*		*t̕*	*dy*	-	*ñ*	-	-	*y*	
o	*o*		-	*d̕*	-	-	-	-	-	*l*
u	*u*		*t*	*d*	*t*	*n,ṅ*	*ç*	*z*	*r*	*l*
			(p)	*b*	*p*	*m*	*f*	*(b)*	*w*	

Standard Alphabet.

ă	*a*	*ā*	ʼ	-	-	-	*h*	-		
ĕ	*ẹ*		*k*	*g*	*k'*	-	*χ*	-		
	e		*č*	*ǰ*	*č'*	-	*š*	-		
ĭ	*i*		*t́*	*d́*	-	*ń*	-	-	*y*	
ŏ	*o*		-	*ḍ*	-	-	-	[illegible]	-	*ḷ*
ŭ	*u*		*t*	*d*	*t'*	*n*	*s*	*z*	*r*	*l*
			-	*b*	*p'*	*m*	*f*	-	*w*	

Specimen.

Wak'ayo laftana, goftako: ati na guba teza, ani zi d́alan taa. Ilo haman nati ḍufe, aka mukni adu narra k'abu, ati hama nati k'abi, goftako, gadiza na tai. Zi wamaḍetanĭ ola, zi wamaḍetanĭ bula; batinana batte, nan ḍabin, bae zin ḍabu, zababi na olč'i. (Tutschek, Gramm. p. 84.)

Remarks.

The difference of long and short vowels is not clearly developed, except in *a* and *ā*; the latter of which Tutschek writes also *ã* or *ȧ* according as it is contracted from *awa* or *aya*. The tone of all the vowels at the end of words is sometimes almost entirely lost, in which case he writes them in a smaller form. We prefer the same indication which we have already employed in other languages for the same purpose, viz. the sign of brevity. The consonants in the third column are exactly the same as the corresponding consonants of the Abyssinian language, according to the pronunciation of a Galla man, whom I met in the *Sudān*; and it is, therefore, questionable, whether this particular kind of tennes belongs originally to the one or to the other of these languages. The letter *t̃* of Tutschek seems to be our letter *t́*, inclining to the Polish *ć*. We prefer the transcription by *t́*, corresponding to the soft sound *d́*, Tutschek's *dy*. The sound of his *ñ* comes nearest to our *ń*. I should not wonder, if also the sound *t'* existed in the *Galla*, although it has not yet been noticed. The letter, which Tutschek writes *d'* is almost the same as the *ḍ* of the *Beǰa*, except that it is perhaps still softer and seems to contain more of *n* than of *r* in its pronunciation. If there exists any corresponding *ṭ*, it is at least very rare; but the second *l*, which approaches very near to the Polish *ł*, belongs to the same class; we write it therefore *ḷ*.

TAMAŠEQ.

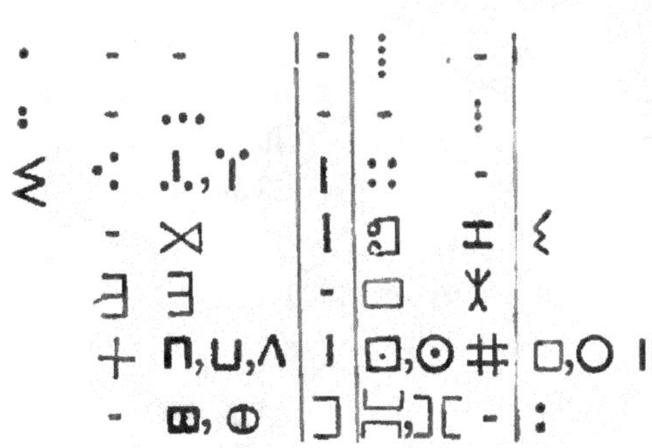

ā	-	-	-	*h*	-	
ū	-	*q*	-	-	*γ*	
ī	*k*	*g*	*ṅ*	*χ*	-	
	-	*ǵ*	*ń*	*š*	*ž*	*y*
	ṯ	*ḏ*	-	(*s̱*)	*ẕ*	
	t	*d*	*n*	*s*	*z*	*r l*
	-	*b*	*m*	*f*	-	*w*

Specimen.

As kelad sawalen aχχuten, ahulaγ iyen deγ emir en tafsit kelad isbelbel; itkar akal s takat. Isela s azībarā; yusa d γur es, inna s: éwod, kaī ahulaγ, ma full teǵed takat tareγ? Inna s ahulaγ: elkameγ ūllī, tarūnet s takat.

(Hanoteau, Gramm. Tam. p. 135.)

Remarks.

The Libyc branch of the Hamitic nations is still spread over a large part of northern Africa. We know best at present the languages of the Kabyles and of the *Imušaγ* or *Tuareg* by the two respective grammars of Hanoteau. The latter language, called *Támāšeq* or *Tamašeγt* (with the addition of the feminine *t* to the gentile name) is more free from Arabic influence than the former. A peculiar alphabet of old Libyc origin is very generally in use, though without any literary application in books. These letters, which are first printed in the grammar of Hanoteau, are called *Tifinaγ* (plur. of *Tafineq* or *Tafineγt*). The three vowel signs, the first of which might rather correspond to the Arabic أ than to the Latin *a*, and the two latter of which are used also for the semivowels *w* and *y*, are of so rare and indefinite use—owing probably to the influence of the Arabic writing system—that our transcription can only render the living pronunciation, not the *Tifinaγ* writing. We write instead of Hanoteau's *k̄*, *kh*, *ch*, *j*, *ñ*, *ou*, according to our system *q*, *χ*, *š*, *ž*, *ṅ*, *w*. The letter *ṅ*, being used only before gutturals, may give up its diacritical point. The letter *ṣ* and, according to Hanoteau, perhaps also the letter *χ*, occur only in Arabic words. The letter *ṭ* is often replaced by or confounded with *ḍ*. The description of the letter, which we write *ẓ*, is not sufficient to remove all doubts about its pronunciation. The sound of the letter ⁝ being that of the Arabic غ should be rendered by *γ*, and we must protest expressly against the transcription *r'* of Hanoteau, *rh* of

Dr. H. Barth, and any other which takes *r* as its basis. It would cause a great confusion, if the very common blunder of European travellers, to whom the sound and etymological value of the Semitic غ is unknown, and who invented the new French word *razzia* i. e. غزوة, *γazzwah* (impetus, incursio), found its way into linguistic science. In *Tamašeq* (contracted from *Tamašeyt*), where *γ* and *q* constantly interchange, it is even easier than in other languages, to see that *γ* has nothing whatever to do with *r*.

HAǗSA.

	ẹ			*k*	*g*	*ṅ*	*h*	-		
	a ā			*tš(č)*	*dž(ǰ)*	-	*š*	*ž*	*y*	
e ē		*ọ̄*		*t*	*d*	*n*	*s*	*z*	*r*	*l*
		o ó		*ts*	*dz*	-				
i ī			*u ū*	*p*	*b*	*m*	*f*	-	*w*	

Specimen.

Yāo muka taffi faraúta, mu uku. Yaro da obansa suna da bindiga, ni ina da dusi tšikin alšifu. Da muka taffi tšikin dāši babu karre tare da mu; amma oban yaro ya sanni enda nāma ši ke.

(Schön, Hausa Gramm. p. 165.)

Remarks.

We give the alphabet as it has been reduced to our principles already by Schön in his „Grammar of the Hausa language. 1862.“ It seems that in the Hausa no monosyllabic diphthongs are used, all vowels being pronounced separately. The combination *tš* originates partly in the contraction of *t* and *š* (cf. *itaši* or *itši*, tree). In such cases at least the transcription of *tš*, *dž*, seems preferable to that of *č* and *ǰ*. In the specimen, not all the existing distinctions of letters are exhibited.

NAMA (NAMAQUA).

a ā		*q*	-	-	*h*		
e ē	*o ō* (*o̩*)	*k*	*g*	*ṅ*	*χ*	-	-
i ī	*u ū*	*t*	*d*	*n*	*s*	*z*	*r*
ă ĕ ĭ etc.		-	*b*	*m*	-	-	*w*

au ou ai ei oi ui Clicks: pal. /, cer. ǃ, dent. ǀ, lat. ǁ

Specimen.

/Guro mĩs. Tita ge ǃqūta sa Zūi-ǁgoata; ǀkara Zūi-ǁgoaz ge ti ei-ǃā u-hã tite. Taree? Ama Zūi-ǁgoabada ge nĩ hoa χūn /amei ǃau, ǀnam zĩ nĩ /go̩m. ǀGam-ǁẽi mĩs. ǃQub sa Zūi-ǁgoab ǀonsaz ge ǁause /gei ǀkuru tite. Taree? Zūi-ǁgoabada ge nĩ ǃau zĩ nĩ ǀnam ēda ǁẽib ǀons dawa tā ǀaχare, ṅū, ǃgai-dī, /ho̩mi zĩ gaχa-ǃna; êda ǁêisa hoa /hãgu ǃna /gei, ǀgore, gare zĩ gan-gan.

(Wallmann, Nama Grammar p. 83.)

Remarks.

Wallmann in his „Formenlehre der Namaquasprache. 1857.“ has already introduced the Standard alphabet. He attributes to the five vowels a pure and an imperfect pronunciation, which latter he writes consequently *ḁ*, *e̥*, *i̥*, *o̥*, *u̥*. The existence of one aspirate *k̔* = *kh* would be very strange. Tindall in his „Grammar and Vocabulary of the Namaqua-Hottentot language“ p. 15. compares this sound expressly with the *q* of our Standard Alphabet. We prefer therefore this writing, whilst we take his *gh* for our *χ*. The characters *f*, *l*, *y* are introduced by him for foreign names. On the click-sounds see above p. 81. We find in the Korana dialect of the Hottentot language, according to Appleyard (The Kafir language p. 17, sqq.), the same clicks as in the Nama dialect, and besides the letters *č*, *t̥*, and *y*. With regard to the gutturals, Appleyard gives three fricatives, without a sufficient description however. He says: „*ch* resembles the Dutch *g*; *kh* is a deeper sound; and *x* still deeper, and very harsh.“ We shall, therefore, not venture at present to render those sounds.

MANǰU.

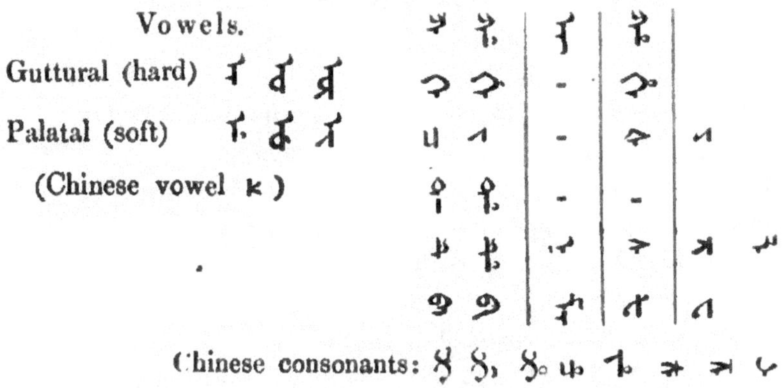

a	*o*	*u*	*ka,o,u*	*ga,o,u*	*ṅ*	*χa,o,u*		
e	*ụ*	*i*	*ḱe,ụ,i*	*ǵe,ụ,i*	-	*χ́e,ụ,i*		
(*ụ*)			*č(či)*	*ǰ(ǰi)*	-	*š*	*y*	
			ṭa,o	*ḍa,o*	-	-		
			te,ụ	*de,ụ*	*n*	*s(si)*	*r*	*l*
			p	*b*	*m*	*f*	*v*	

ḱh ǵh χh čh ǰh ṭ ḍ ž

Specimen.

Jụse ama eme-i saiin eχ́e babe kemụni soṅkolome yabụmbi. Saχaku bitχ́e-be χulači saiin gụčụ-be baχa ǵese, χulaχa bitχ́e-be sabụči fe gụčụ-be ačaχa ǵese. Χančikiṅǵe-be ụrgụǰebụ Kụṅṭe-i χ́endụχ́eṅǵe. Siṅagan-de ḍakilara aṅgala gosiχolo. Manǰụ bitχ́e-be ụrụnaku ụrebụ akuči Nikan bitχ́e-be χafụkiyame ǵedụkeleme mụtembio.

Remarks.

The *Manǰu* is the only Tungusian language well known to us. It uses, as almost all the Tataric languages, the so called vowel-harmony, according to which the guttural vowels *a*, *o*, *u* are wont to combine with one another in the same word, and likewise the palatal vowels *e*, *ụ*, *i*. European scholars are accustomed to transcribe by *ô* and by *ou* or *u*. It is important to avoid henceforth this transcription, which necessarily gives a false idea of the *Manǰu* vocalism. The quantity of vowels is in this, as in most of the cognate languages, of no consequence, and the vowel *ô* is not longer then any other; its pronunciation is that of *u*, and in Chinese it is always rendered by a close *ọ* in contradistinction to , which is pronounced *ọ*. We write them consequently respectively *o* and *u*. Both belong, as in all languages, to the guttural or hard vowels. The vowel , on the contrary, is decidedly a palatal or soft vowel, and can, therefore, not be pronounced as our common *u*. It approaches indeed rather to the very close Swedish *u*, with which Castrén compares the same palatal vowel in the Buryetic and Samoyedic languages, and which sounds to our ears almost as *ụ*. Castrén and Schiefner have already chosen for this sound the most convenient transcription *ụ*, wherein we follow them also for the *Manǰu*. The vowel *e* is pronounced in most of the Tataric languages broad as *ẹ*. There is still a seventh vowel , which, however, is used only for the indistinct *u* vowel of the Chinese words *su̥* and *tu̥* when they are written in *Manǰu*. We write it, as in Chinese, *u̥*.

The *Manǰu* consonants were transcribed by Amyot, Langlès and others according to the Chinese pronunciation. Rémusat and his followers have rightly substituted the genuine pronunciation. The general opinion is, that the letters and , and , and , as well as the letters and , and , differed only in form not in sound, and were consequently also in transcription not distinguished from one another. But the circumstance that the first letters *k*, *g*, *χ*, *ṭ*, *ḍ*, occur exclusively before the guttural vowels *a*, *o*, *u*, and the second letters *ḱ*, *ǵ*, *χ́*, *t*, *d*, exclusively before the palatal vowels *e*, *ụ*, *i* (*t* and *d* only before *e*, *ụ*), shows clearly, that the first were likewise pronounced as guttural and gutturo-dental, the second as palatal and dental consonants. It is therefore as essential for our transcription, as for the genuine writing, to distinguish both classes by their respective diacritical signs. The only doubt which could be raised against this view, would spring from the combinations *ṯi* and *ḏi*, which occur in the indigenous syllabarium and in a few words in the dictionary, whilst there is no mention of the combinations *ti* or *di*. But the same dictionary proves, that the combinations *ṯi*, *ḏi* are as little used in any original *Manǰu* word as *ti*, *di*; only in a few Chinese words received into the *Manǰu* the syllables *ṯi* and *ḏi* are found. The *Manǰu* at present pronounce the letters *č*, *ǰ*, *s*, before *i* very like the Polish *ć*, *j́*, *ś*, which latter transcription might be used in consequence; it seems, however, scarcely necessary to go farther in our distinction of sounds than the *Manǰu* themselves. The nasal *ṅ*, whose form is a composition of *n* and *k̄*, only occurs at the end of words, or, if in the body of a word, before *k* or *g*, *k̄* or *ġ*. The letter *r* also is never found at the beginning of a word. The pronunciation of the letter ᠸ, which occurs only before *a* and *e*, is not *w*, as European scholars write it, but *v*. The letters *č*, *ǰ*, *š*, *y*, *s*, *ṯ*, *ḏ* are, like the palatal or dento-palatal letters, not combined with *u*, nor *š*, *y*, *t*, *d*, like the gutturals, with *i*. The letters *k̄h*, *ġh*, *χh*, *čh*, *ǰh*, *ţ*, *ḑ*, *ž* are employed only in Chinese words.

The forms of the *Manǰu* letters show, that only five vowels and thirteen consonants were originally distinguished, the others, which have only a secondary form, having as we may presume, arisen as sounds only later. The letters *u̥*, *g* and *χ*, *ġ* and *χ̂*, *ḏ*, *d* are distinguished by diacritical signs from *o*, *k*, *k̄*, *ṯ*, *t*; and *ǰ*, *p*, *š*, *f* are modifications of *y*, *b*, *s*, *v*, and *ṅ* is a composition of *n* and *k̄*. The original alphabet was therefore very simple, viz. *a*, *o*, *u*, *e*, *i*; *k*, *k̄*, *č*, *ṯ*, *t*, *b* (or *p*); *n*, *m*; *s*; *y*, *r*, *l*, *v* (or *f*). The letters are written in vertical columns, which run from left to right.

SHARRA-MONGOLIAN.

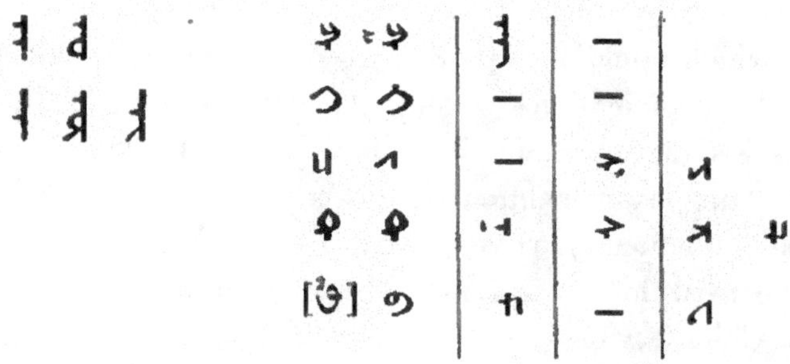

a	*o(u)*		*k(χ)a,o*	*g(γ)a,o*	*ṅ*	-		
e	*o̤(ṳ)*	*i*	*ke,ṳ,i*	*ġe,ṳ,i*	-	-		
			č(ṭ)	*ǰ(ḍ,z)*	-	*š*	*y*	
			t	*d*	*n*	*s(ši)*	*r*	*l*
			[*p*]	*b*	*m*	-	*v*	

Remarks.

The *Mongolian* alphabet is essentially the same as the *Manǰu*; it wants only several letters, whose developement has not taken place, as *ṭ*, *ḍ*, *f*. The fricative *χ* is not distinguished from *k*, one dialect using *k*, the other *χ*, in the same words. The letters *č* and *ǰ* are pronounced in other dialects *ṭ* and *ḍ* (or *z*); *ǰ* and *y* have the same form in writing except in the middle of words. The peculiar sign for *p* occurs only in foreign words; but *b* sounds almost as *p* at the end of words.

The *Western Mongols* (*O̤lo̤t*, *Kalmṳks*) distinguish seven vowels, three guttural *a*, *o*, *u*, and four palatal *e*, *o̤*, *ṳ*, *i*; and, besides, the following consonants: *k*, *g*, *χ*, *γ*; *ṭ* (pronounced *č* before *i*), *š*, *y*; *t*, *d*, *n*, *s*, *z*, *r*, *l*; *p*, *b*, *m*, *v*.

BURYETIC.

Castrén.

a o u

ä ö ü e i

Castrén.

			h				
k	*g*	*ŋ*	*x*	-			
ć	*ʒ́*	-	-	-			
c	*ʒ*	-	*ś*	*ź*	*j*		
t	*d*	*n*	*s*	*z*	*r*	*l*	
p	*b*	*m*	-	-			

Palatalised consonants: *k̃ x̃ t̃ d̃ ñ r̃ l̃*

Standard Alphabet.

Guttural (hard) vowels: *a o u*

Palatal (soft) vowels: **ẹ ọ ụ e i*

			h			
k(*ḵ*)	*g*	*ṅ*	*χ*	-		
**č*	**ǰ*	-	-	-	*y*	
ṭ	*ḍ*	-	*š*	*ž*		
t(*ṯ*)	*d*	*n*	**s*(*ṣ*)	*z*	*r*	*l*
p	*b*	*m*	-	-		

Palatalised consonants: **k′* **χ′* **t′* **d′* **n′* *r′ l′*

Specimen.

Urdo zaχēn terme dēne ọpči ulan χuyibe,
eǰe tọ̄ne bariči, kọgọ cine mordonai;
bar′on talaṅ χobdone ḍer ḍebe belēle;
abe tọ̄ne gargaiǰe, kọgọ čine mordonai.

Castrén, Burjätische Sprachlehre, p. 241.

Remarks.

The palatal vowels *e* and *i* combine also with guttural vowels in the same word. The vowel *ụ* sounds, according to Castrén, like the Swedish *u*, somewhat different from *ü*, with which it corresponds however in other Tataric languages. The consonants *k*, *t*, *s*, are said to sound emphatically before guttural vowels, that means, *t* and *s* are pronounced as gutturo-dentals, and *k* as a deep guttural in contradistinction to its palatal pronunciation before the palatal vowels. The letters *g*, *l*, *r*, *n*, *t*, *d* before *i* pass in several dialects into *y*, *l'*, *r'*, *n'*, *s*, *d'*. The fricative *χ* passes in most dialects before the guttural vowels into *k*, which before palatal vowels sounds like *kh*, as *t* like *th*. Those letters, to which we have added an asterisk, are not found in all the dialects.

YAKUTIC.

Guttural (hard) vowels:	*a o u į*				*h*	
Palatal (soft) vowels:	*e o̤ ṳ i*	*k*	*g*	*ṅ*	*χ γ*	
		č	*ǰ*	*ń*	-	*y ỹ*
		t	*d*	*n*	*s*	*r l ł*
		p	*b*	*m*	-	

Specimen.

Saχa uṅuoγun ṳrdṳgṳnen orto, ōl da gįnnar tọmuruon ǰonunan āttanįaχ tustāχ. Sįraidarįn bįsīta χaptaγaįdįṅi, munnulara seb ulaχan, χaraχtara sasarχai bieter χara, astara χara kọnọ̤ χoyū, bįtįk χasan da ṳmmet.

Böhtlingk, Ueber die Sprache der Jakuten, p. 61.

Remarks.

Böhtlingk in his Yakutic Grammar writes this language with the following Russian letters: а, о, у, ы, ä, ö, ӱ, і; һ, к, г, ҥ, х, ҕ, ч, џ, н', ј, ј, т, д, н, с, р, л, l, п, в, м.

The letter which we write $\tilde{y}$ with our diacritical sign of nasalisation is, according to Böhtlingk, a nasal *y*, and resembled in this respect perhaps to the old Baktrian کد, which we have rendered, however, by *ṅ* as an explosive letter.

TURKISH.

ـَ	ـُو	و	ى	(ع)	ا	—	(ح)	ه		
ـَ	و	ـُ	ىِ	ـ	ق	—	—	—		
				ك	گ	ڭ	خ	غ		
				چ	ج	—	ش	(ژ)	ى	
				ط	(ظ)	—	ص	(ض)		
				ت	د	ن	س	ز	ل	ر
							(ث)	(ذ)		
				پ	ب	م	ف	و	—	

a	*o*	*u*	*ị*	(ʿ)	-	-	(*ḱ*)	*h*		
e	*ọ*	*ụ*	*i*	*q*	-	-	*χ*	*g*		
				ḱ	*ǵ*	*ṅ*	-	-		
				č	*ǰ*	-	*š*	(*ž*)	*y*	
				ṯ	(*ḏ*)	-	*s̱*	(*ẕ*)		
				t	*d*	*n*	*s*	*z*	*l*	*r*
							(*θ*)	(*δ*)		
				p	*b*	*m*	*f*	*v*	-	

Specimen.

ای اوغل شویله بلمش اول که حق سبحانه و تعالی آشکار و نهانده
و یرده و کوکده و بو جهانده و اول جهانده عقل ایله ادراک اولنور ؞
اما کندونک ذات شریفی تصور عقلدن منزهدر ؞ اما اکر دیلرسن که
الله تعالینی بلهسن اول کندو کندوکنی بیل و کندو حالکدن
خبردار اول ؞ زیرا هر کم کندونی بلدی حق سبحانه و تعالینی بلدی
بو سوزدن مقصود که سن بلنمشسن و اول بلیجیدر یعنی سن
نقشسن اول نقاشدر ؞

Kasembeg, Turkish Gramm., transl. by Zenker p. 17.

Ei ogụl šọile bilmiš ol ḱi ḱaq sobḱānahu ve taʿāla āšikār ve nihānde ve yerde ve kọḱde ve bu ǰehānda ve ol ǰehānda ʿaqlile idrāḱ olunur; amma ḱendiniṅ ðātĭ šerīfi tasavvurĭ ʿaqịldan munezzehdir. Amma eǵer dilersin-ḱi allah taʿālani bilėsin, evvel ḱendi ḱendiṅi-bil, ve ḱendi ḱalịṅdan χaberdar ol; zirā her ḱim ḱendini bildi ḱaq sobḱānahu ve taʿālani bildi: bu sọzden maqṣūd ki sen bilinmišsin ve ol biliǰi-dir, yaʿni sen naqịšsin, ol naqqāš-dir.

Remarks.

The notation of the vowels is so variable and imperfect, that the transcription can only be regulated by the living pronunciation. Long and short vowels are generally not distinguished in genuine Turkish words. The connective *i*, however, called *ḱesrĭ iðāfe*, is shorter then the common *i*; we write it therefore *ĭ*. In foreign words the long vowels are usually pronounced as such and may be so written. The accent of the words is not very distinct, but floating as in the French language, and depending upon the whole sentence; we indicate it therefore only in exceptional cases. The ا is but a *fulcrum* for various vowels and must not be rendered by our consonantal sign ʾ, the sound of the Arabic *hamza* ء not being used in the Turkish language. The letter ه *h* at the end of a syllable is pronounced only after a long vowel (ا, و, ی); after a consonantal letter it indicates only the presence of one of the short vowels *e* or *a*, which we write then in our transcription instead of *h*. According to the vowel-harmony the four guttural-vowels *a*, *o*, *u*, *ḭ* combine together, and the four palatal vowels *e*, *ǫ*, *y*, *i* likewise. As in other cognate languages, the guttural consonants *ʿ*, *q*, *k̑*, *χ*, *γ*, *ṯ*, *ḏ̂*, *ṣ*, *ẓ*, combine with the guttural vowels, although the latter four (*ṯ*, *ḏ̂*, *ṣ*, *ẓ*) have almost lost their emphatic or guttural pronunciation. The consonants *h*, *ḱ*, *ǵ*, *t*, *s*, *z* are on the other hand only used with palatal vowels; the other consonants are *anceps*. The letter *ʿ* has lost its peculiar Semitic pronunciation, and ق is pronounced as a common guttural *k*, whilst *ḱ* and *ǵ*, both written ک, are uttered nearly at the palatal point and generally followed by a slight *y*; we write them consequently *ḱ* and *ǵ*. The *ṣaγḭr nun*, which springs always from *nk* or *ng* is dialectically still pronounced *ṅ* or *ṅk*, in Constantinople as *n*. The letters ظ *ḏ̂* and ذ *δ* are pronounced as *z*, and ث *θ* as *s*; و has not the Arabic sound of *w*, but that of *v*. The letters ع *ʿ*, ح *k̑*, ژ *ž*, ظ *ḏ̂*, ض *ẓ*, ث *θ*, ذ *δ* are not found in original Turkish words, but only in words received from the Arabs or Persians. The specimen is taken from the Turkish-Tataric Grammar of Mirza A. Kasem-beg, translated by Zenker (1848), p. 17, and shows at the same time several essential deviations in our representation of the Turkish sounds from that of the author. We had the great advantage to consult personally one of the most competent scholars in this matter, the consul Dr. Rosen, who is both practically and scientifically perfectly acquainted with the pronunciation of the Turkish language, as well in Constantinople as in the chief provinces of the Turkish empire.

TURKMENIAN.

					q			*h*			
a	*o*	*u*	*ı̢*		*k*	*g*	*ṅ*	*χ*(?)	*γ*		
ẹ̄	*e*	*o̤*	*ṳ*	*i*	*č*	*ǰ*	-	*š*	-	*y*	
					t	*d*	*n*	*s*	*z*	*r*	*l*
					p	*b*	*m*	*f*	-	*w*	

Cf. Ilminsky, in the Bulletin de l'Acad. Impér. des sciences de St. Pétersbourg, t. I, 1860. p. 563 sqq.

KAZAK (WESTERN KIRGHIZ, small horde).

Guttural (hard) vowels: *a ā o u ı̢*	*k*	*g*	*ṅ*	(*χ*)	*γ*	*y*		
Palatal (soft) vowels: *ẹ e ẹ i o̤ ṳ*				*š*	*ž*			
	t	*d*	*n*	*s*	*z*	*r*	*l*	*l̠*
	p	*b*	*m*	-	-	*w*		

Specimen.

Ası̢ṅ āsı̢ṅ āsı̢ṅa — bíreket bersén bāsı̢ṅa,
bo̤denedeí žoryaláp — kı̢ryá'uldaí kuryaláp
Kı̢dı̢r kelsín kāsı̢ṅá — nosé turyán boz ṳigé
Kı̢dı̢r atá dāresín — bei bišesé bul̠ ṳidṳ́n
uniké kursák ko̤teríb — u͜yá ko̤zé žaresín, etc.

(Speech of thanks after a feast.)

Remarks.

The *Kı̢ryı̢z* (*Kirghiz*) are divided into the eastern tribes (the black or mountain *Kirghiz* or *Burut*), who alone call themselves *Kı̢ryı̢z*, and the western tribes (*Kirghiz-Kaissaks*) who call thẹmselves *Kazak*, and are subdivided into four hordes, the great, the middle or Sibirian, the small, and the inner or Bukeyew horde. The alphabet, as well as the specimen, belong to the small horde and have been communicated to the author by Dr. Lerch. He has observed that some *Kazak* individuals pronounce the letter *ž* as *ǰ*, and others sometimes *χ* instead of the common pronunciation *k*. Ilminsky writes *q* instead of *k* before the palatal vowels.

SAMOYEDIC DIALECTS.

Castrén.

Vowels										
a o u y	-	'	-	*h*	-			
ä ö ü i e ụ	*k*	*g*	*r*	*x*	-			
	ć	*ʒ́*	-	*ś*	*ź*	*j*		
	c	*ʒ*	-	-	*ẓ*			
	t	*d*	*n*	*s*	*z*	*r*	*ƀ*	*l*
	p	*b*	*m*	*f*	-	*w*		

Palatalised consonants: *t̃ d̃ c̃ ñ s̃ z̃ r̃ l̃*

Standard Alphabet.

Vowels										
Guttural (hard) vowels: *a o u į*	-	'	-	*h*	-			
Palatal (soft) vowels: *e̤ o̤ ṳ i e ụ*	*k*	*g*	*ṅ*	*χ*	-			
	č	*ǰ*	-	*š*	*ž*	*y*		
	ṭ	*ḍ*	-	-	-			
	t	*d*	*n*	*s*	*z*	*r*	*ṛ*	*l*
	p	*b*	*m*	*f*	-	*w*		

Palatalised consonants: *t́ d́ ṭ́ ń ś ź ŕ ĺ*

Remarks.

The sounds represented above belong to five different dialects, of which none possesses all of them. The *Yurak* wants the letters: *e̤, χ, ṛ, š, ž, č, ǰ, ḍ, f*; the *Taugį*: *į, e̤, o̤, ṳ, χ, h, ṛ, ŕ, š, ž, č, ǰ, z, ź, ṭ, ṭ́, ḍ, p, w*; the *Yenissei*: *į, e̤, o̤, ṳ, χ, ŕ, š, ž, č, ǰ, z, ź, ṭ, ṭ́, ḍ, p, w*; the *Ostyak*: *', ṛ, ŕ, ž, ś, ź, ṭ́*; the *Kamassin*: *į, ṛ, ŕ, č, ǰ, ś, ź, ṭ́, ḍ, f*. About the vowel *ụ* see above p. 210, and about *į* p. 54. The letter ' is principally heard at the end of words, when another consonant is dropped. The peculiar letter, which Castrén writes *ƀ*, but in which, as he observes, the sound of *r* predominates, seems to be a cerebral *ṛ*. (Castrén, Gramm. der Samojed. Sprache, herausg. v. Schiefner. 1854.)

MAD'ARIC (HUNGARIAN).

a á o ó u ú	*k*	*g*	-	*h*	-		
e é ö ő(ö̋) ü ű(ü̋) i í	*cs(ch,ts)*	*ds*	-	*s*	*zs(ż)*		
	ty	*gy(dj,dy)*	*ny*	-	-	*j(y)*	*ly*
	cz(c,tz)	*(dz)*	-	-	-		
	t	*d*	*n*	*sz*	*z*	*r*	*l*
	p	*b*	*m*	*f*	*v*		

Standard.

a ā o ō u ū	*k*	*g*	-	*h*	-		
e ē ọ ọ̄ ụ ụ̄ i ī	*č*	*ǰ*	-	*š*	*ž*		
	ť(ty)	*ď(dy)*	*ń(ny)*	-	-	*y*	*ľ(ly)*
	ṭ	*(ḍ)*	-	-	-		
	t	*d*	*n*	*s*	*z*	*r*	*l*
	p	*b*	*m*	*f*	*v*		

Specimen.

1. *És lőn az napokban, Augusztus császártól parancsolat adaték ki, hogy mind az egész föld beirattatnék.* 2. *(E beiratás lett e őször, mikor Sziriában Czirénius tiszttartó volna.).* 3. *Mennek vala azért mindenek, hogy beirattatnának, kiki az ő városába.* 4. *Felméne pedig József is Galileából, Názáretnek városából Júdea tartományába, a Dávid városába, mely Bethlehemnek neveztetik, mivelhogy Dávidnak házából és háznépe közűl való vala;* 5. *Hogy beirattatnék Máriával, ki neki jegyeztetett vala feleségűl, és vala várandós.*

Ev. Luc. 2, 1—5.

1. *Ēš lọ̄n az napokban, Augustuš čāsārtōl parančolat adatēk ki, hoď mind az egēs fọld beirattatnēk.* 2. *(E beiratāš lett elọ̄sọr, mikor Siriāban Ṭirēniuš tisttartō volna.).* 3. *Mennek vala azērt mindenek, hoď beirattatnānak, kiki az ọ̄ varošāba.* 4. *Felmēne pedig Yōžef is Galileābōl, Nāzāretnek vārošābōl, Yūdea tartomā-*

ńāba, a Dāvid vārošāba, meľ Bethlehemnek neveztetik, mivelhoď Dāvidnak hāzābōl ēš hāznēpe ko̧zū̯l valō vala; 5. *Hoď beirattatnēk Māriāval, ki neki yeďeztetett vala felešēgū̯l, ēš vala vārandōš.*

Remarks.

Besides the fully assibilated palatals *č* and *ǰ*, there exists in the Maďaric language another class of slightly assibilated palatals, corresponding to the Polish and Serbian *ć*, *ȷ́*, and still more to the Cheskian *t'*, *ď*, *ń*. They are now inconsistently written *ty*, *gy*, *ny*, *ly*, the two former being uttered at exactly the same point of the palate. Undoubtedly they ought to be written either *ḱ*(*ky*) and *ǵ*(*gy*), or *t'*(*ty*) and *ď*(*dy*). As, in fact, they approach more to the dentals than to the gutturals, and are pronounced even nearer to the teeth, than *č* and *ǰ*, and as moreover *ty* and *gy* (*dy*) not seldom are derived from the dentals *t* and *d* (*Dorotya* = Dorothea, *gyemant* = diamant) and instead of *gy* in former times *di* or *dj*, and sometimes even *dy*, were also written, we naturally prefer to write *t'* and *ď*, as well as *ń* and *ľ*. The explosives of the first column are the real dry *tenues* (see p. 134).

MORDVINIAN (*Mokša* dialect).

Hard:	*a*	*o*	*u*	*i̯*		*k*	*g*	*ṅ*	*h*	-		
Soft:	*e̯*	*e*	*i*			*č*	*ǰ*	-	*š*	*ž*	*y*	
					ṭ	*t*	*d*	*n*	*s*	*z*	*r*	*l*
						p	*b*	*m*	*f*	*v*	-	

Palatalised consonants: *ľ*, *n'*, *s'*, *ď*, etc.

Specimen.

Aľa i traks.

Aľat ašil̯ alašats, tak son traksints lańks kambras sots. Son'ts se̯n ašize̯ arśa, što kambrasis' traksti af laďai, ozas' trakst lańks, sęńksa što ičkezi yalga molems ez yorśa. Son ozaś, karmaś trakst aiďamįnza; traksįś ańtsak, ozadįt ala askiľai. Aľaś trakst pańtsisį; traksįś kolai savįr moli. Aľat kętsa mandįl, trakst košarizę, sońdiinza arai, son mant̨-ezda ardįz tui. Traksįś kolai savįr moli, livskidį i lęksi; a ardįmats aš soń, kuť i šavik. Traksįś melę aľat alu praś; af madręna: traksįś asįz śas šača arnemā. A śavįk eręvi sodams: kona savįr yakamā šačs, sęndi af lindemā.

(The peasant and the cow, a Mordvinian fable. Gramm. of Ahlquist, p. 120.)

Remarks.

The Mordvinians live with few exceptions on the upper and middle banks of the Sura, a tributary of the Wolga. Their language is divided into two dialects, the *Mokša* and the *Ersę*, the former of which is treated in the lately published Moksha-Mordvinian Grammar of Dr. Ahlquist[1]), whose personal experience of the spoken language we had the advantage to consult. His Grammar is printed in the Standard alphabet with a few unimportant deviations. We should prefer to write *ę* instead of *ä*, although the sound is the deep English sound (*a̤*), of which we have spoken above p. 50 sqq. His hard *ị* (ы) is our *į*. As to the peculiar *t̨*, which is pronounced with a more lengthened pressure of the tongue against the upper teeth, the description seems to indicate the same emphasis, which we have met with already in several other Tataric languages. For this reason we prefer to write *t̨*. The Mordvinian language participates in the vowel-harmony which is found in the cognate languages, and its consonants are subjected to the influence of the following palatal vowels by assuming a shade of *y*, expressed by the palatal line: *ŕ ľ* etc.

---

[1] Forschungen auf dem Gebiete der Ural-Altaischen Sprachen. I. Theil 1861.

LIVONIAN.

			a			
		ę		*ǫ*		
	e		*o̤*		*o*	
i			*ṳ*			*u*
			e̯			
			i̯			

k	*g*	*ṅ*	*(h)*		
			š	*ž*	*y*
t	*d*	*n*			
			s	*z*	*r*
p	*b*	*m*	*(f)*	*v*	-

Specimen of the Kolken dialect.

Un se púoga kītis temmi̯n: o iza, ma um patti̯ tiend vasti̯ tōvast un vasti̯ sīnda, un ęb uo emīn vẹ̄rt, ku sa mīnda ėntš púogaks nutād. Bet iza kītis ėntš puōšidi̯n: túogid nẹnt ama yuvād ǫrnd un ēdigid tẹ̄nda, un āndagid tẹmmi̯n suormi̯ks kẹddi̯ un kēṅgad yalgi̯. Un túogid u̇d, liebiz vāškiz un tapāgid sie, las mēg si̯ǫmi̯ un luštīgil vẹlmi̯. Siest ku min púoga vẹl' yera kuoli̯n, un ni ta um taggiš yels sǫnd, ta vẹl' kaddi̯n, un um lievti̯d. Un ne u̇rgist luštīgi̯l vẹlda.

Ev. Luc. 15, 21—24. (Sjögren-Wiedemann, Liv. Gramm. vol. I, p. 354.)

Remarks.

The Livonian language is at present spoken in Livonia by only eight persons in the village of Salis, in Courland by several thousands. Of the two Courland dialects of Kolken and Pisen, the former has one vowel more than the latter, viz. *e̯*. Since it has besides the two palatal vowels *o̤* and *ṳ*, also the two guttural vowels *e̯* and *i̯*, the vowel-system is very complete. The vowel-harmony however has left only a few traces. The sound of *h* is almost entirely dropped, and *f* occurs only in foreign words. The standard work upon the Livonian language is that of Sjögren, edited by Wiedemann, St. Petersbourg. 1861. in 2 vols. 4°, and the alphabet used in this work is our Standard alphabet. Only, *j* is employed instead of our *y*, and *a̤* instead of *ẹ*. There is a difference made between the *ą* of the Pisen dialect, and *o̥* of the Kolken dialect: the first is an *o* still more open than *o̥*. We should prefer to write both *o̥*, as they do not occur in the same dialect. The vowels *o̥* and *ǫ* are essentially the same as our *ę* and *į*. Our proposition, however, to write them so was at the time of publication not yet known to the learned editor of Sjögren's work.

TAMIḶ (TAMULIAN).

Vowels						Sanskrit sounds
அ ஆ	க	க	ங	-		h
எ ஏ ஒ ஓ	ச	ச	ஞ	ய		ǰ
இ ஈ ஐ உ ஊ	ட	ட	ண	ள		š
	ற	ற	ன	ழ		-
	த	த	ந	ர	ல	s
	ப	ப	ம	வ		-

Vowels						Sanskrit sounds
a ā	*k*	*γ,g*	*ṅ*	-		*h*
e ē o ō	*č*	*ž,ǰ*	*ń*	*y*		*ǰ*
i ī į u ū	*ṭ*	*ḍ*	*ṇ*	*ḷ*		*š*
	ṯ	*ḏ*	*ṇ̀*	*ṛ*		-
	t	*δ,d*	*n*	*r*	*l*	*s*
	p	*b*	*m*	*v*		-

Specimen.

Yennattinālyenil Parābaran tammuḍịya orē pēḍāna kumāranị vižuvāžikkaḍavaṅ yavanō avan kaḍḍupōyāmal nittiya žīvanị aḍị-yumpaḍikku averịyē koḍuttu ivvaḷavāi ulayattāriḍattil anbāi irunðār. Ev. Joh. 3, 16.

Kumāran avanị nōki, tayappanē tēvanukum umakum virōtamāi pavam žịtēn itumutal umuḍịya kumāḍaṅ yaṅḍu arịkapaḍuvaterku nāṅ pātiraṅ allaveṅḍu sonān. Ev. Luc. 15, 21.

Remarks.

We follow principally Caldwell in his "Comparative Grammar of the Dravidian languages." London 1856. The vowel *ị* is mostly weakened from final *ă* and *ā*, but "every trace of the sound of *a* has disappeared", says Caldwell. It is mostly long, but sometimes also short. It is evident, therefore, that we have to do with a simple vowel, not with a diphthong, as it is represented by Caldwell and others (*ei* or *ai*), and that the Tamils were right in giving to it a simple sign. It "accords in sound very nearly with the sound of *ê* or *ey* in *Turkey*", according to Caldwell. We have no doubt, that it is the same as that *Tuḷu* vowel, which has been compared by a good observer to "a short and indistinct *ụ*." These different descriptions lead us to believe, that it is the vowel peculiar to most of the Tataric and several Slavonic languages, which we write *ị* (see above). The diphthong *au* occurs only in Sanskrit words. The slight change of sound which all the vowels, except *ū*, undergo after the cerebral consonants, including partly also the common *r* and *l*, is, in connection with certain traces of the vowel-harmony (Caldwell p. 101. 136.), most interesting for the linguist, but cannot be represented in transcription. With regard to the consonants, the letter *ṭ*, *ḍ* is erroneously taken for a semivowel by Caldwell (p. 108) who writes it R. The Tamil Grammarians themselves divide their consonants (C. p. 102) into six surds or explosives (*vallinam*): *k*, *č*, *ṭ*, *t*, *p*, *ṯ*(R), six nasals (*mellinam*): *ṅ*, *ń*, *ṇ*, *n*, *m*, *ṉ*, and six semivowels: *y*, *r*, *l*, *v*, *ṛ*, *ḷ*. The pronunciation of the letter *ṯ*(R) is generally described as a peculiar combination of *t* and *r*, or, if sonant, of *d* and *r*, which again shows its explosive nature, and prevents any transcription with the basis of *r* or R, instead of *t* (or *d*). The Tamulians would certainly have arranged their *varga's*, as we have done it, according to the Sanskrit principle, if they had not followed too closely the Sanskrit alphabet, in rejecting at the end the four letters *ṛ*, *ḷ*, *ṯ*, *ṉ*, which the Tamulians have added to the Sanskrit alphabet. For the old Vedic ळ *ḷ* had disappeared in Sanskrit, and ड़ *ṛ* corresponds in the Tamil, as in the Hindi, Hindustani, Sindhi etc. to the dental *r*. The Dravidian and Hindi *ṛ* was derived from *ḍ* and was probably slightly different from the Sanskrit *ṛ*; we should even prefer to write the Dravidian sound *ṛ̌*, if two diacritical signs were not too heavy, and if the transcription *ṛ* were not already too generally received. It is indeed our opinion (see above p. 99. upon the Hindi letters ड़ *ṛ* and ढ़ *ṛh*) that the Tamulian letters *ṯ*, *ḏ* have a similar relation to the cerebrals *ṭ*, *ḍ*, as the palatals *č*, *ǰ*, have to the gutturals *k*, *g*; and we take *ṯ*, *ḏ*, *ṛ*(*ṛ̌*) as peculiar slight assibilations or vibrations of the cerebrals *ṭ*, *ḍ*, *ṛ*, approaching to the combinations *ṭš*, *ḍž*, *ṛž*; for there is physiologically a very slight difference between *ř* and *š*, *ṛ* and *ž*. At all events we must choose single characters for the single Dravidian letters. This assibilation of *ḷ*, *ḍ*, *ṛ* pushes the tip of the tongue a little forward and nearer to the dental point. Hence the letter ண, our *ṉ*, which occurs only before *ḏ* and at the end of words, and which originally belongs certainly more to the cerebrals than to the dentals, as even its figure shows. By a Tamulian euphonic law, the surd letters *k*, *č*, *ṭ*, *ṯ*, *t*, *p*, are pronouneed as sonants, wherever they occur singly in the middle of a word, and three of them, *k*, *č*, *t*, lose in this position even their explosive nature and become sonant fricatives. No sonant letter, on the contrary, begins a word. This law explains the fact, that in Tamil and partly in Malayālam the same characters serve to express the surds and the sonants. Our transcription must of course follow in this respect the pronunciation. If in the middle of a word the surd letter is to be pronounced, its charaoter is repeated. The sonant க (*k*) is pronounced *γ*; the sound of *g* is sometimes retained in Sanskrit words. The sonant ச (*č*) is pronounced *ž*, "as a very soft *sh*"; the sound of *ǰ* is sometimes heard "in vulgar Tamil", and "in the use of those Sanskrit derivatives in which the letter ज *ǰ* is found in Sanskrit." The sonant letter த (*t*) is pronounced "with the sound of the soft English *th*"; the sound of *d* occurs only, "when it is combined with a nasal, as in *andam.*" The Tamil வ has not the English sound *w*; it is generally rendered by *v*, and we keep this transcription, although the description of this sound might raise the doubt, whether it were not rather pronounced like the *w* of middle Germany (see above p. 75). The Tamil is destitute of sibilants and aspirates, as well as of the simple spirans *h*. The letters *ś*, *š*, *s*, *h*, if occurring in Sanskrit words, are represented by the corresponding Grantham characters; *ś* in Sanskrit derivatives of earlier date is replaced by the Tamil *č* or *ž*, the Sanskrit *š* by the Tamil *ṭ* or *ḍ*, sometimes by *ṛ*, or even by *t* or *d*; the Sanskrit *s* sometimes by *t*, *č* or *ž*, and sometimes it is omitted altogether. The Sanskrit *h* is omitted in the Tamil. The connection of consonants and vowels is analogous to that in the Sanskrit, the above given vowel characters being used only in the beginning of words.

MALAYĀLAM.

Vowels					
അ ആ	ക ഗ	ങ	ഹ ഃ	-	ഖ ഘ
എ ഏ ഒ ഓ	ച ജ	ഞ	ശ	യ	ഛ ഝ
ഇ ഈ ഉ ഊ	ട ഡ	ണ	ഷ	ള	ഠ ഢ
ഋ ൠ ഌ ൡ	റ ൦	-	-	ഴ	- -
ഐ ഔ	ത ദ	ന	സ	ര ല	ഥ ധ
	പ ബ	മ	-	വ	ഫ ഭ

Vowels					
a ā	*k g*	*ṅ*	*h ḥ*	-	*kh gh*
e ē o ō	*č ǰ*	*ń*	*ś*	*y*	*čh ǰh*
i ī u ū	*ṭ ḍ*	*ṇ*	*ṣ*	*ḷ*	*ṭh ḍh*
ṛ ṝ ḷ ḹ	*ṯ ḏ*	-	-	*ṛ*	- -
ai au	*t d*	*n*	*s*	*r l*	*th dh*
	p b	*m*	-	*w*	*ph bh*

Specimen.

Entakondennāl Dēiwam tande ēgaǰātanāiya puṭane, awenil wiśwasikkunawen orutenum naśiččapōkāte, nittyaǰīwan uṇṭākēṇṭunnatina, taruwān takkawaṇṇam eṭeyum lōkatte snēhičču.

Ev. Joh. 3, 16.

Appōḷ makan awanōṭa, appanē, ńan swerggattina nēreyum, ninde munbākeyum pāpam čeytirikannu inimēl ninde makan enna čollappeṭuwān yōgyanalla enna parańu. Ev. Luc. 15, 21.

Remarks.

In *Malayālam* *e* and *ē*, *o* and *ō* are represented only by one character; in our transcription, however, they ought to be marked according to their quantity. We have excluded the compound letter *kš*, which is generally exhibited in Grammars. There is a peculiar nasal in *Malayālam*, *Telugu* and *Kanarese*, which is pronounced *m* at the end of a word; but it may also euphonically be substituted for any other nasal and will then be pronounced accordingly. In our system it need not be marked. The letter വ is pronounced *w*, not *v*, as in the other dialects. Cf. the Grammar of the Malayalim language by the Rev. Joseph Peet (Ch. Miss. Soc.). 2[d] ed. Cottayam. 1860.

TUḶU.

a ā	*k g*	*ṅ*	*h z*		*kh gh*
e ē o ō	*č ǰ*	*ń*	*ś*	*y*	*čh ǰh*
i ī ị u ū	*ṭ ḍ*	*ṇ*	*š*	*ṛ ḷ*	*ṭh ḍh*
r̥ r̥̄	*t d*	*n*	*s*	*r l*	*th dh*
ai au	*p b*	*m*	-	*v*	*ph bh*

Specimen.

Yēsu, Yehūdada Bethlehēmuḍu arasāi Herōda dinoleḍị puṭṭi bokka indā ǰōtiserị mūḷayiḍịdị Yerūsalēmagu battịdị Yehūdyeregị arasu ādị puṭṭināye vōḷu uḷḷe dāyeg anduṇḍa yeṅkuḷu āya boḷḷinị mūḍayiḍị tūdu āyagị ārādhane malpere battā andịdị paṇḍerị. Ev. Matth. 2, 1. 2.

Remarks.

The *Tuḷu* is ordinarily written in the *Malayālam* character. The vowel, which we write *ị*, has been compared to a short and indistinct *ṳ* (see above p. 225).

KARNĀṬAKA (KANARESE).

ಅ ಆ		ಕ ಗ	ಙ	ಹ ಃ	-	ಖ ಘ
ಎ ಏ	ಒ ಓ	ಚ ಜ	ಞ	ಶ	ಯ	ಛ ಝ
ಇ ಈ	ಉ ಊ	ಟ ಡ	ಣ	ಷ	ಳ	ಠ ಢ
ಋ ೠ		ತ ದ	ನ	ಸ	ರ ಲ	ಥ ಧ
ಐ ಔ		ಪ ಬ	ಮ	-	ವ	ಫ ಭ
		(ಱ)				

a ā		*k g*	*ṅ*	*h ḥ*	-	*kh gh*
e ē	*o ō*	*č ǰ*	*ń*	*ś*	*y*	*čh ǰh*
i ī	*u ū*	*ṭ ḍ*	*ṇ*	*š*	*ḷ*	*ṭh ḍh*
ṛ ṝ		*t d*	*n*	*s*	*r l*	*th dh*
ai au		*p b*	*m*	-	*v*	*ph bh*
		(*ṭ*)				

Specimen.

Yātakkendere ātanalli viśvāsa riḍuvavarellaru naśavāgade nitya ǰīvavannu honḍuva nimitta Dēvaru tanna vobbanē maganannu koṭṭa hāge ǰagatanna aṣṭu prīti paḍisidanu. Ev. Joh. 3, 16.

Adare maganu avanige tandeyē paralōkakke virōdhavāgiyū ninna mundeyū pāpa maḍiddhēne nānu innu ninna magarendu kareyalpaḍa yogyanalla annalu. Ev. Luc. 15, 21.

Remarks.

In *Kanarese* the letter *ṭ* is confined to the poets.

TELUGU (TELIṄGU).

అ ఆ	క గ	ఙ	హ ః	-	ఖ ఘ
ఎ ఏ ఒ ఓ	చ జ	ఞ	శ	య	ఛ ఝ
ఇ ఈ ఉ ఊ	ట డ	ణ	ష	ళ	ఠ ఢ
ఋ ౠ etc.	త ద	న	స	ర ల	థ ధ
ఐ ఔ	ప బ	మ	-	వ	ఫ భ
	(ఱ)				

a ā	*k g*	*ṅ*	*h ḥ*	-	*kh gh*
e ē o ō	*č,ṭ ǰ,ḍ*	*ń*	*ś*	*y*	*čh ǰh*
i ī u ū	*ṭ ḍ*	*ṇ*	*š*	*ḷ*	*ṭh ḍh*
ṛ ṝ ḷ ḹ ă â etc.	*t d*	*n*	*s*	*r l*	*th dh*
ai au	*p b*	*m*	*s*	*v*	*ph bh*
	(*ṭ*)				

Specimen.

Yendu vallananṭe ayanayandu viśvāsamunśēvāḍevvadō vaḍu naśamu pondaka nitya ǰivamunu ponde nimittamu Dēvuḍu tana yoka kumāruniččinattugā ḍagattunu prītipallačenu. Ev. Joh. 3, 16.

Appuḍu kumāruḍu āyana tō tandrī paralōkamunakunnu nīkunnu virōdhamugā pāpamu čēsi yunnānu yikamīdaṭa nī kumāruḍani piluvabaḍa nēnu yogyuḍanu gānanenu. Ev. Luc. 15, 21.

Remarks.

The two first letters of the second class have two sounds; they are pronounced *č* and *ǰ* in all Sanskrit derivatives, and in *Telugu* words before *i*, *ī*, *e*, *ē*, *ai*; before the other vowels they are pronounced *ṭ* and *ḍ*, as in *Marāṭhi* (see above p. 109). "The letter *ṭ* is found in Telugu (as in Kanarese) poetry, but in the modern dialect of the Telugu it has fallen into disuse."

KWAN-HWA (MANDARINIC)

dialect of *Nan-kiṅ.*

Vowels.

a

e *o*

i *ị* *u(ụ)*

ṛ

au(ao) ai ei eu

Vowels with end-consonants.

aṅ eṅ iṅ uṅ

an en in

Consonants preceding a vowel.

$k_{y,w,yw}$	$kh_{y,w,yw}$	*ṅ*	$h_{y,w,yw}$	-
$tš_{w}$	$tšh_{w}$	-	$š_{w}$	y_{w}
$ts_{y,w,yw}$	$tsh_{y,w,yw}$	-	-	$ž(ř)_{w}$
$t_{y,w}$	$th_{y,w}$	$n_{y,w}$	$s_{y,w,yw}$	$l_{y,w,yw}$
p_{y}	ph_{y}	m_{y}	*f*	*w*

Tones.

phiṅ͵, the floating; *šaṅ'*, the ascending; *khyu`*, the descending; *ži͵*, the returning.

High	*phiṅ*	*pa͵*
Low	*phiṅ*	*pa͵*
	Šaṅ	*pa'*
	Khyu	*pa`*
	Ži	*pa͵*

Specimen.

希律王時耶穌既生於
猶太伯利恆有博士數
人自東方至耶路撒冷
曰生而爲猶太人王者
安在我在東方見其星
故來拜之

Ev. Matth. 2, 1. 2.

1. *Hiˏ-lyuˎ waṅˌ šiˌ, Yeˌ-suˏ kiˋ seṅˏ yuˏ Yeuˌ thaiˋ Peˎ-liˋ-heṅˌ, yeuˊ poˎ sịˋ suˎ žinˌ, tsiˋ tuṅˏ faṅˌ tšiˋ Yeˌ-luˋ-saˎ-liṅ.*
2. *Yweˎ: seṅˏ ṛˌ weiˌ Yeuˌ-thaiˋ žinˌ, waṅˌ tšeˋ, ṅanˏ tsaiˋ? Ṅoˊ tsaiˋ tuṅˏ faṅˌ kyanˋ khiˌ sinˏ, kuˋ laiˌ paiˋ tšiˏ.*

Remarks.

The *Kwan-hwa* or Mandarin dialect is spoken by the people of the middle provinces of China and likewise by the higher officers and cultivated classes throughout the whole country. In this dialect, which is better known in Europe than any other, the monosyllabism is developed to the highest degree, every syllable being a whole word ending with a vowel or one of the two nasals *n* and *ṅ*. In former times the *Kwan-hwa* distinguished surd, sonant and aspirate consonants, as we have shown elsewhere[1]; at present the sonants have disappeared. The letters *f* and *w* are always followed by a vowel; all the others may have inserted between them and the following vowel one of the semivowels *y* or *w*, or both of them, as our alphabet shows. European scholars use mostly instead of these semivowels the full vowels *i* and *u* (or dialectically *e* and *o*). We do not repeat here the reasons, why this custom is scientifically and practically inconvenient. We have spoken in the same place upon the letter *ž*, as to which we are not sure, whether its actual pronunciation is not rather *ṛ*, as its place in the sound-system as well as the description of the sound by some scholars, seem to suggest. The vowel *u* is often dialectically pronounced *ụ*, which may be written wherever it seems suitable. The sound of *ṛ* occurs only in one word, formed by this single letter, but with different tones. It is commonly written by the grammarians *eul*, or *ulh*, or

[1] Ueber Chines. und Tibet. Lautverhältnisse. Schriften der Berlin. Akad. 1861.

urh etc., but it is nothing else than a vocalised, probably cerebral, *ṛ* (or *ḷ*) which we write consequently *r̥*. The vowel, which we had formerly proposed to write *z̤*, according to the pronunciation of Mr. Guzlaff, whom we consulted about it, seems to be derived in the Chinese system of sounds from the vowel *u*; but it is pronounced entirely like the Tatarian and Slavonic "hard" *i*. The Russian missionaries represent it therefore by their ы, and we have to render it consequently by *į*. It occurs only in the words *sį* and *tsį*. The tones which, in Chinese, are an essential element of speech for the distinction of words, were hitherto represented by European accents of quite a different meaning, or not expressed at all, and some scholars used the same accent for one tone and others for another; for ex. Morrison and Rémusat represent the *šań*-tone by *pà*, the *khyu*-tone by *pá*, the high as well as the low *phiń*-tone by *pâ*; Marshman and Medhurst, the *šań*-tone by *pá*, the *khyu*-tone by *pà*, the two *phiń*-tones by *pa*; Medhurst in the *Fu-kyen* dialect, the high *šań*-tone by *pá*, the low *šań*-tone by *pà*, the two *phiń*-tones by *pā* and *pâ*, others the *šań*-tone by *'pa*, the *khyu*-tone by *pa'*. A new system was under these circumstances indispensable. The system, which we formerly proposed and have repeated above, follows as closely as possible the indigenous writing, completed by the missionaries of the southern provinces. The Mandarin dialect has only five tones, the *phiń*-tone alone being divided into a higher and a lower; we omit therefore the little horizontal line which distinguishes the lower i. e. deeper pronunciation of the other tones.

HOK-LO.

Vowels									Tones
a	*k*	*g*	*kh*	*ṅ*	*h*	-		high *phiṅ*	*pa,*
ọ	*tš*	*dž*	*tšh*	-	-	*y*		low „	*pa˪*
e *ọ*	*ts*	*dz*	*tsh*	-	-	-		high *šoṅ*	*pa'*
i *ị* *u*	*t*	*d*	*th*	*n*	*s*	*l*		low „	*paᵀ*
ã *ẽ* *ĩ* *õ* *ũ* *ị̃*	*p*	*b*	*ph*	*m*	-	*w*		high *khi*	*pa\`*
ai *au* *oi* *eu*								low „	*pa˸*
								high *nyip*	*pa*
								low „	*pa˳*

Remarks.

The *Hok-lo* dialect is spoken in the north-eastern part of the province of Canton, in the department of *Tšau-tšyu.* The alphabet, as stated above, has been furnished to the author by the Rev. Lechler who lived several years in this country. The nasalisation of the vowels is less open and more squeezed than in the french vowels. The *Fu-kyen,* to which the *Hok-lo* dialect belongs, distinguishes all eight tones, but the low *šoṅ*-tone is pronounced with a peculiar modification, which might be expressed by *paᵀ*.

HAKKA.

Vowels.	Consonants.					Tones.
a	*k*	*kh*	*ṅ*	*h*	-	high *phiṅ* : *pa,*
e *o*	*tš*	*tšh*	-	*š*	*y*	low *phiṅ* : *pa˪*
i *ị* *u*	*ts*	*tsh*	-	-	-	*šoṅ* : *pa'*
m̥	*t*	*th*	*n*	*s*	*l*	*khi* : *pa\`*
au *ai* *oi* *ui* *eu*	*p*	*ph*	*m*	*f*	*w*	high *nyip* : *pa*
						low *nyip* : *pa*

Specimen.

1. *Hiˏ-lutˎ woṅˌ kaiˋ šiˌ, Yaˌ-s̥iˏ kiˋ yenˌ tšhutˎ šeˋ, tshaiˋ Yuˌ-thaiˋ kokˎ paˎ-liˋ-henˌ yipˎ, yuˏ kiˊ tšakˎ yuˏ tshoiˌ leṅˌ kaiˋ nyinˏ tshoiˏ tuṅˏ phenˊ theuˌ loiˌ tauˋ Yaˌ-luˋ-saˎ-laṅˏ kinˏ šaṅˌ.* 2. *Kanˌ yonˋ waˋ: yuˏ tšakˎ nyinˌ tšhutˎ šeˋ loiˌ tsoˋ Yuˌ-t̠haiˋ nyinˌ kaiˋ woṅˌ; kiˌ tshoiˏ laiˋ tšakˎ thanˋ liˏ? Ṅaiˌ tshoiˏ tuṅˏ penˏ khonˋ tauˊ kyaˏ sinˏ syukˎ; soˊ yiˏ thitˎ s̥iˋ loiˌ paiˋ foˋ kiˌ.* Ev. Matth. 2, 1. 2.

Remarks.

The *Hakka* dialect, as spoken in *Hoṅ-koṅ*, has been already reduced by the Basle-missionary Rev. Lechler to the Standard Alphabet, in his translation of the Gospel of St. Matthew (Berlin, 1860) from which we have taken the above specimen. It has one tone more than the *Kwan-hwa*, viz. a high and a low *nyip*-(*ži*-)tone. It has moreover a vocalised *m*, which is to be written *m̥*; but it has, on the other hand, not the vowel *r̥*, nor the consonant *ž*, instead of which it uses *ny*. The *Hakka* dialect, as well as most of the southern Chinese dialects, admits besides *n* and *m* other consonants at the end of words. In fact, all the words having the *nyip* or "returning" tone, end in one of the three consonants *k*, *t*, or *p*. In compound words, however, and in other cases, these final consonants, when preceding another consonant, are not pronounced. If, therefore, we find in the translation of Mr. Lechler the names of *Bethlehem*, *Jerusalem*, *Abraham* rendered by *Pak-li-hen*, *Ya-lu-sat-laṅ*, *A-pak-la-hon*, we have to read: *Palihen*, *Yalusalaṅ*, *Apalahon*. In such cases, we prefer not only to put little lines between the single syllables, but to put the apostrophe instead of the elided consonants: *Pa'ˎ-liˋ-henˌ*, *Yaˌ-luˋ-sa'ˎ-laṅˏ*, *Aˏ-pa'ˎ-laˏ-honˊ*, or to omit even the apostrophe, the elision being sufficiently indicated by the tone.

THAI (Siamese dialect).

–ั	ạ
–ะ –า	a ā
เ–ะ แ– – –	e ę (o) (ǫ)
– เ– – โ–	-ē -ō
–ิ –ี –ึ –ื –ุ –ู	i ī ị ị̄ u ū
[ฤ ฤๅ ฦ ฦๅ]	[ṛ ṝ ḷ ḹ]
ใ ไ เ–า –ำ	ai ei au am̃

1 ก		2 ข	3 ฃ	4 ค	5 ฅ	6 ฆ	7 ง	41 ห	42 ฬ	43 อ	44 ฮ
8 จ		9 ฉ		10 ช	11 ซ	12 ฌ	13 ญ	34 ย	38 ศ		
[14 ฎ	15 ฏ	16 ฐ		17 ฑ		18 ฒ	19 ณ]	35 ร	39 ษ		
20 ด	21 ต	22 ถ		23 ท		24 ธ	25 น	36 ล	40 ส		
26 บ	27 ป	28 ผ	29 ฝ	30 พ	31 ฟ	32 ภ	33 ม	37 ว			

k		kh	x́	k̄	χ	gh	ṅ	k̄	ḷ	'	h
č		čh		č'	ś	ǰh	ń	y	s̈		
[ḍ	ṭ	ṭh		ṭ'		ḍh	ṇ]	r	š		
d	t	th		t'		dh	n	l	s		
b	p	ph	f'	p'	f	bh	m	w			

Tones.

The floating or period tone *(rectus)* . . . . . . —
The higher ascending *(altus)* . . . . a'
The lower ascending or short *(gravis)* . . . . . a̍
The higher descending *(circumflexus)* . . . . . a̕
The lower descending or expectant *(demissus)* . a̖

Remarks.

The letters of the Siamese are derived from the Devanagari. Their present pronunciatiou differs greatly from that of the time when the alphabet was fixed. As in the Mandarin Chinese, the variety of sounds was in former times much greater than now, as the alphabet itself proves sufficiently. It contains on the other hand a certain number of letters which have been subsequently distinguished from one another, as we may conclude from the slight variations of their shape. The Grammarians generally exhibit 44 consonants, to which J. Low adds two other obsolete signs for *th* and *s*. These 44 letters are transcribed by Low (*A Grammar of the Thai or Siamese language.* Calcutta. Bapt. Miss. Press. 1828) and Pallegoix (*Grammatica lingua Thai.* Bangkok. 1850): 1. *k*, 2. *kh*, 3. *kh*, 4. *kh*, 5. *kh*, 6. *kh*, 7. *ng*, 8. *ch*, 9. *ch* (Palleg. *x*), 10. *ch* (*x*), 11. *s*, 12. *ch* (*x*), 13. *y* (*j*), 14. *d*, 15. *t*, 16. *th*, 17. *th*, 18. *th*, 19. *n*, 20. *d*, 21. *t*, 22. *th*, 23. *th*, 24. *th*, 25. *n*, 26. *b*, 27. *p*, 28. *ph*, 29. *f*, 30. *ph*, 31. *f*, 32. *ph*, 33. *m*, 34. *y* (*j*), 35. *r*, 36. *l*, 37. *w* (*v*), 38. *s*, 39. *s*, 40. *s*, 41. *h*, 42. *l*, 43. *a* (*o*), 44. *h*. — They state expressly, that there is no distinctiou in the present pronunciation between the different letters transcribed alike, except that certain letters viz. our letters *kh*, *χ́*, *čh*, *ṭh*, *th*, *ph*, *f̆*, *ṡ̌*, *š*, *s*, *ȟ*, are always followed by a vowel with the high ascending tone. This great uumber of identical sounds, amongst which we fiud 5 *kh*, 4 *ch*, 6 *th*, 3 *ph* would be quite unintelligible and embarrassiug for the linguist, if we did not distinguish them in transcription as well as they are distinguished in Siamese writing, and this is only possible, if we are able to distinguish them at least etymologically; for it would be absurd to suppose that this identical pronunciation existed from the beginning. Now, the alphabet will be understood at once, if we reestablish the aucient order as we have done it above. Taking those letters, which differ only by a slight break in one part of the character, as later variations derived from one and the same sound, we find but five origiual divisions of every one of the five explosive classes, in perfect harmony with the system of the five Devanagari-classes and with the Siamese Pali-alphabet as communicated by Low. The same Indian arrangement is evidently followed in the subsequent letters corresponding with the Sanskrit *y*, *r*, *l*, *v*, *ś*, *š*, *s*, *h*, *ḷ*, to which are still added two other letters อ, the fulcrum of initial vowels (ʾ), and ฮ a second *h*. The fifth column contains the nasal letters aud we learn from it, that the palatal letter ญ, which now sounds only like *y*, was originally the palatal nasal *ń*. The fourth column corresponds with the aspirated medials of the Sanskrit. It seems that even at present this original value has not quite disappeared and that the guttural ฆ at least is still heard as *gh*. The strong aspiration may have misled mauy a foreigner respective the real pronunciation of the first part of these compounds. The third column ought to represent the simple medials *g*, *ǰ*, *ḍ*, *d*, *b* and we do not doubt, that this was originally the case. But, as in the Mandarin-Chinese, where the medials were still pronounced in the 6th century after Chr., they lost their sonant nature, and are now even pronounced as hard aspirates, without any great distinction from those of the second column, which properly correspond to the hard Sanskrit aspirates. The original great force of aspiration inhereut to the letters of the second column has only left a trace in the clevation of tone imparted to the following vowel The proper value of the letters of the first column was that of surd explosives (tenues), and this is still the case with ก *k* and จ *č*. Regarding the three other classes, the cerebrals, dentals and labials, we see sonants and surds distinguished. After the original sonants of the third column had changed into surds, the original surds of the first column entered partly into their place, and were finally distinguished by a slight variation of shape in those cases, when they kept their primitive surd value. On the other hand, the old aspirates of the second and the new aspirates of the third column passed partly, as in many other languages, into their corresponding fricatives, *ph* and *ṕ* into *f̕* and *f*, *č̕* into *ś*, *kh* and *k̕* into *χ́* and *χ*; for we do not doubt, that ข *χ́* and ค *χ* have the value of fricatives, although they are commonly transcribed by English and French writers, who have not this sound in their own language, by *kh*. If this should uot be the case in the present time, we must at least suppose, that this fricative sound existed at a certain former time, when its character was expressly altered for this purpose.

It is indispensable to distinguish also in onr transcription the second and the third column. To this effect, we have dissolved, as in modern Sanskrit, the original aspirates of the second and fourth class into the respective explosives and the following *h*, except in *χ́* and *f̕*, *χ* and *f*, in which the aspiration does not follow, but is inherent. We presume, that *χ́* and *f̕* are only stronger aspirated than *χ* and *f*, and likewise *h̕* stronger than *h*, as indeed the whole second column, as well as the sharp fricatives ห *h̕*, ศ *ś̕*, ษ *š*, ส *s*, manifest their stronger aspiration by their effect on the intonation of the following vowel. The cerebral letters *ḍ*, *ṭ*, *ṭh*, *ṭ̕*, *ḍh*, *ṇ* and the two sibilants *ś̕* and *š* do not belong to the Thai proper, but are found only in Pali words. Hence their actually identic pronunciation with corresponding *d*, *t*, *th*, *t̕*, *dh*, *n* and *s*. Capt. Low has published an old Thai alphabet, in which these foreign letters are not comprised.

With respect to the vowels, they seem to have undergone likewise several changes. We follow in the above exhibited table the statement of the Rev. S. J. Smith, American Missionary, compared with the remarks of the Rev. D. D. Bradley in the Bangkok Calendar of 1860. p. 51. 82. as given orally at Bangkok 1862 to Mr. Th. von Bunsen, of the Prussian expedition to those countries. We can only fix the different vowel sounds existing in the Thai and their regular representation in the Siamese writing. But we must leave their application in the running text, which will occasionally vary, to the Siamese scholars. The vowels *o* and *ǫ* are often pronounced but not written, except that *ǫ* is sometimes irregularly written by the consonantic sign อ '; *o* is mostly pronounced between two consonants. The description of the pronunciation of the vowels ึ and ื leaves no doubt, that they correspond with the Chinese and Tataric *į* and *ī̧*. The sign ำ which is read *am*, or as others say *amn*, is an imitation of the Sanskrit *anusvāra*, and the vowels *ṛ ṝ ḷ ḹ* occur only in Indian words.

There are five tones in the Thai language, mostly represented by the two signs ่, ้ and the diacritical letter ห (*h̄*), the various application of which belongs to the grammar. These five intonations may be compared with the above indicated Chinese tones, and represented alike.

KAMBOJA.

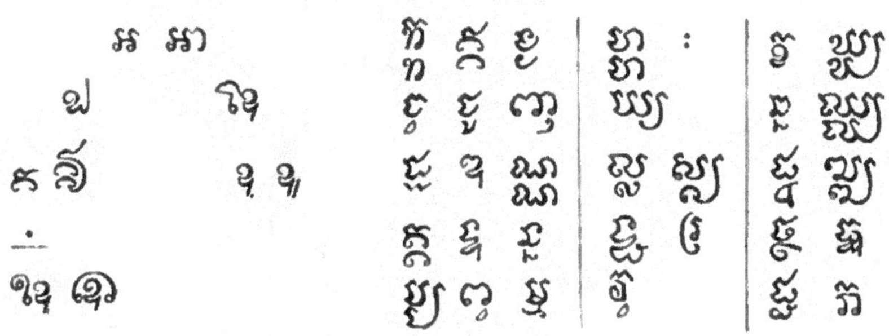

a ā	*k*	*g*	*ṅ*	*h*	*:*		*kh*	*gh*
ē ō	*č*	*ǰ*	*ń*	*y*			*čh*	*ǰh*
i ī u ū	*ṭ*	*ḍ*	*ṇ*	*ḷ*	*r*		*ṭh*	*ḍh*
~	*t*	*d*	*n*	*l*	*s*		*th*	*dh*
ai au	*p*	*b*	*m*	*w*			*ph*	*bh*

Remarks.

The characters are almost the same as the old Pali characters of that kind which is exhibited in the Siamese Grammar of Capt. J. Low.

MRANMA (BURMESE).

Vowels.	Consonants.						
အ အာ	က	ဂ	င	ဟ	း	ခ	ဃ
ဧ ဩ	စ	ဇ	ဉ	ယ	-	ဆ	ဈ
ဣ ဤ အိ ဥ ဦ	ဋ	ဍ	ဏ	ဠ	ရ	ဌ	ဎ
ã ũ	တ	ဒ	န	လ	သ	ထ	ဓ
အဲ ဪ	ပ	ဗ	မ	ဝ	-	ဖ	ဘ

Tones.

The floating or natural tone, not written.
The acute *(an' myīt)* ့
The grave *(syē' pauk)* —း

a ā	*k*	*g*	*ṅ*	*h*	*:*	*kh*	*gh*
ē ō	*č*	*ǰ*	*ń*	*y*	-	*čh*	*ǰh*
i ī ị u ū	*ṭ*	*ḍ*	*ṇ*	*ḷ*	*r*	*ṭh*	*ḍh*
ã ũ	*t*	*d*	*n*	*l*	*ś*	*th*	*dh*
ei au	*p*	*b*	*m*	*w*	-	*ph*	*bh*

Tones: *a a' a`*

Remarks.

The *Burmese* writing is syllabical as the Sanskrit; the inherent *a* is not written; the mark ် placed over a consonant indicates the want of any inherent vowel. The vowel-signs, as given above, are all initial. The vowel called triphthong by Latter, which is composed by the signs of *u* and *i*, and pronounced sometimes "intermediate between *o* and *u*", and sometimes as "a short *oi* or long *i*", seems to be our *ị*, *ī̤* of the Tatarian and Slavonic languages, which we have found also in the Chinese language. The nasalisation (*"anusvāra"*) affects only the vowels *a* and *u*. The pronunciation of the first diphthong is, according to Th. Latter, *ei*, not *ai*. The only Burmese sibilans corresponds with the Sanskrit श *ś* and seems to be pronounced very near like the Polish *ś*. We may therefore write it *ś*, if with any diacritical sigu at all.

The present pronunciation of the Burmese letters deviates in many cases from the received orthography. It seems therefore advisable for missionary purposes to follow the actual pronunciation, whilst in linguistic researches it will be necessary either to transcribe exclusively the old orthography, or to mention it at least in every single case of deviation. Cf. the *Grammar of the Burman language*, by F. Carey, Serampore, 1814. and the *Grammar of the Language of Burmah*, by Thomas Latter, 1845. All pure Burmese words are monosyllabic. Of the peculiar Chinese tones, only three are in use among the Burmans, of which the floating or natural needs not to be indicated.

YUKAGIRIC.

		a			*k*	*g*	-	*χ*		-		
	e̱		*o*		*č*	*ǰ*	*ń*	*š*	*ž*	*y*		
e					*t*	*d*	*n*	-		*r*	*l*	
i		*ị*		*u*	*p*	*b*	*m*	-		*w*		

Specimen.

Omóča ádịl terikadéni léngi. Ke lomdók yonǰúririma? Ponbure̱ oille̱. Kawéik adakún ịnlịčaon kečím. Ke lomdók yonǰúririma? Yonǰóde oille̱. Kawéik kečím adakún monógoχ. Ke lomdók yonǰúririma? Šerežéń móža, oille̱ šerežéń pugalwe. Kawéik adakún čomogína kečím.

Remarks.

The alphabet and the specimen are taken from A. Schiefner, *Ueber die Sprache der Jukagiren*, in the Mélanges Asiatiques t. III. 1859. p. 595 sqq., who there uses already the Standard Alphabet.

CHUKCHIC (ČAUČAU).

			a			*k*	*g*	*ṅ*	*χ*	*h*		
e̱	*e*	*ẹ*		*o*		*č*	*ǰ*	*ń*	*š*	*ž*	*y*	
i			*ị*		*u*	*t*	*d*	*n*	*s*	*z*	*r*	*l*
						p	*b*	*m*	-	-	*w*	

Palatalised consonants:

ǵ χ́ t́ ŕ ĺ

Specimen.

χwaχo, χaχametwa, χ́uči. Miṅkri χịtịrkin? Torekaite geal-lim. Tawaχ warkin? Ketai, mintawaχom. Inan yarsnok hiwut torekaite mịnrestịm. Meṅχostin? Doten χač. Neṅko χịtịrkin? Inege χịlkit. χwaχo iṅki! minχametwamịk kinemal.

Remarks.

The alphabet and the specimen are taken from the treatise of L. **Radloff**: "*Ueber die Sprache der Tschuktschen*", in the Mémoires de l'Acad. Impér. des Sciences de St. Pétersbourg, VIIe série, tome III, n° 10. 1861. The author of this treatise has already employed the Standard Alphabet with a few exceptions. With regard to his *ä* as corresponding to the Russian Я we are not sure, whether this vowel is really different from our *ẹ*.

JAPANESE.

		a			k	g	(ṅ)	-	-	y
	e		*o*		t,ts,tš	d,dz,dž	n	s,š	z,ž	r
i				*u*	(p)	b	m	f,v, h	-	w

| indicates the lengthening of the preceding vowel.

ツ (t) indicates often the shortening of the preceding vowel, or the doubling of the following consonant.

ン *ṅ*, final nasal.

カ	*ka*	ケ	*ke*	キ	*ki*	コ	*ko*	ク	*ku*
ガ	*ga*	ゲ	*ge*	ギ	*gi*	ゴ	*go*	グ	*gu*
ア	*a*	エ	*e,ye*	イ	*i*	オ	*o*	ウ	*u*
タ	*ta*	テ	*te*	チ	*tsi,tši*	ト	*to*	ツ	*tsu*
ダ	*da*	デ	*de*	ヂ	*dzi,dži*	ド	*do*	ヅ	*dzu*
パ	*pa*	ペ	*pe*	ピ	*pi*	ポ	*po*	プ	*pu*
バ	*ba*	ベ	*be*	ビ	*bi*	ボ	*bo*	ブ	*bu*
ハ	*fa,va,ha*	ヘ	*fe,..*	ヒ	*fi,..*	ホ	*fo,..*	フ	*fu,..*
ナ	*na*	ネ	*ne*	ニ	*ni*	ノ	*no*	ヌ	*nu*
マ	*ma*	メ	*me*	ミ	*mi*	モ	*mo*	ム	*mu*
サ	*sa*	セ	*se*	シ	*si,ši*	ソ	*so*	ス	*su*
ザ	*za*	ゼ	*ze*	ジ	*zi,ži*	ゾ	*zo*	ズ	*zu*
ヤ	*ya*	-	-	-	-	ヨ	*yo*	ユ	*yu*
ラ	*ra*	レ	*re*	リ	*ri*	ロ	*ro*	ル	*ru*
ワ	*wa*	ヱ	*we*	ヰ	*wi*	ヲ	*wo*	-	-

Specimen.

col. 2. col. 1.

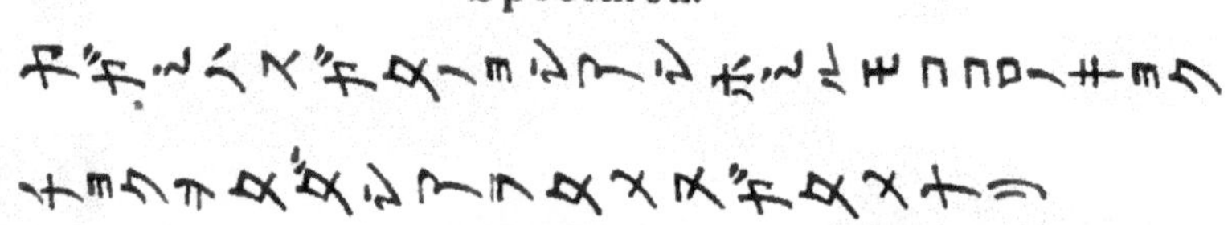

Japanese proverb.

Kagami fa sugata no yosi-asi fo miru mo, kokoro no kĭyokŭ tšĭyokŭ wo tadasi aratamenŭ ga tame nari. Japanese proverb.

Kon̆-nitsĭ wa. Nani-wo o me-ni kake-mašĭyō ka? Mo šŭ-kosi ōki-no-wo o mise. Ki-rō wa nozomi-masenŭ. Hei, zui-bun̆ deki-masŭ. Sore wa Nippon̆-no fi-dori-de ari-masŭka? Si gŭ-watsŭ žĭyū yokka-de ari-masŭ. Fito fako fĭyak kin̆ iri-ni nasare. San fūto-de itsi yāto-ni nari-masŭ (three feet make one yard). *Iš-šĭyakŭ-no tō-wo itsi žĭyō to ī-masŭ.*

J. Hoffmann, Shopping-dialogues.

Remarks.

Of the two Japanese formes of writing, the cursive *Firo-kana* and the more square and distinct *Kata-kana*, we have exhibited above the latter, which has been reduced already to our Standard Alphabet by J. Hoffmann (the learned editor of Donker Curtius's Japanese Grammar, Leyden, 1857.) in his „*Shopping-dialogues in Dutch, English and Japanese*, Leyden. 1861." The Japanese used first for their language the Chinese writing. In the 9th century they derived from it a Japanese alphabet of their own and limited it to 47 syllabic signs. These syllables were put in such order as to form a little poem, the beginning of which *I-ro-fa* became the name of the alphabet. We learn from it, that the Japanese language of this time distinguished only ten consonants, which were composed with the five vowels *a e i o u;* three combinations were left out as not existing in the language, viz. *yi*, *wu* and *ye* (or *we*). The old consonantal system was therefore this very small one:

k	ʾ	-	*y*
t	*n*	*s*	*r*
p	*m*	-	*w*

Afterwards the sonants *g*, *d*, *b*, *z* were distinguished by a diacritical sign added to the corresponding surd letters; *p* was changed into the fricative letter *f* in all Japanese words; it preserved its original sound only in foreign words and was then marked by a little circle. The five letters, which are prononnced at present as pure vowels, seem to have been regarded originally as beginning with a slight guttural nasal *ṅa*, *ṅe*, *ṅi*, *ṅo*, *ṅu*, which afterwards was weakened (as the Tibetan འ) into ʾ *(hamza)*, or disappeared entirely. The assibilation of *t* and *d* before *i* and *u* into *tsi*, *tsu*, *dzi*, *dzu*, as well as the softening of *f* into *v* and even into *h* is of still later origin, and is therefore not indicated at all in writing.

The vowel *u*, inherent in the syllables of our 5th column, is very often pronounced so short as to disappear almost entirely, and the same happens also not unfrequently with the inherent vowel *i*. We propose to represent these vowels in this case (as in the similar one of the Rumanian, old Slovenian and other languages) by *ŭ* and *ĭ*, the more so as we have ouly to follow in this respect the authority of Hoffmann. The syllable *ṅŭ (ŭ)*, *nŭ*, *mŭ* were formerly employed to express the nasal terminations *-ṅ*, *-n*, *-m*, especially in the Chinese words ending with *-ṅ* or *-n*. Afterwards a peculiar sign was chosen for every final nasal, which at present is pronounced sometimes *ṅ* and sometimes *n*, still differing from *nŭ*. We represent it by *ǹ* (cf. the Tamulian). The signs | and ッ indicate, in foreign words, respectively the lengthening and the shortening of the preceding vowel. The latter sign is that of the letter *t (tŭ)* and is apparently chosen in imitation of the southern Chinese dialects, which exhibit, instead of the Mandarin words with the short or "returning" tone, syllables ending with *t*, *k* or *p*. We follow Hoffmann and other European scholars in indicating the shortness of the vowel by doubling the next consonant and transcribe for ex. the Japanese *Nitpon* by *Nippon*. When the syllables *si*, *zi*, *tsi*, *dzi* are followed by the syllables *ya*, *yo*, or *yu*, their respective combinations are contracted into *šya*, *šyo*, *šyu*; *žya*, *žyo*, *žyu*; *tšya*, *tšyo*, *tšyu*; *džya*, *džyo*, *džyu* (or *śa*, *śo*, *śu*; *źa*, etc.). We should prefer to keep, for the sake of etymology, the original *i*, adding however the sign ˇ *(ĭ)* to indicate its disappearance. The change of *f* or *v* into *h* seems to be very arbitrary and, according to certain observations, which the author had the opportunity to make personally during the presence of the Japanese embassy in Berlin (1862), rather a matter of politeness towards the person addressed.

TIBETAN.

(ཨ)		ཀ	ག	ཁ	ང	འ	ཧ			
ེ	ོ	ཅ	ཇ	ཆ	ཉ		ཤ	ཞ	ཡ	
ི	ུ	ཙ	ཛ	ཚ	-		-	-		
		ཏ	ད	ཐ	ན		ས	ཟ	ར	ལ
		པ	བ	ཕ	མ		-	-	ཝ	

a		k	g	kh	ń	ʼ	h				ȧ = e
e	o	tš	dž	tšh	ń		š	ž	y		g̈ = d
i	u	ts	dz	tsh	-		-	-	-		r̈ = d
		t	d	th	n		s	z	r	l	m̈ = n
		p	b	ph	m		-	-	w		ÿ = tš

Specimen.

དེའི་ཚེ་དེའི་དུས་ན་ཡུལ་བཱ་ར་ན་སེ་འདིར་དྲང་སྲོང་ལྔ་
བརྒྱ་ཞིག་གནས་ཏེ། དྲང་སྲོང་དེ་དག་གིས་སྟོན་པ་ཨུད་པ་
ལ་ཞེས་བྱ་བ་དམ་པའི་ཆོས་སློབ་ཅིང་བསྒོམས་པ་ལ་དགའ་
བས་ཀུན་ཏུ་རྒྱུ་ཞིང་། སུ་ལ་དམ་པའི་ཆོས་ཡོད་པ་དེ་བདག་
ལ་སྨྲ་ན། Foucaux, Gramm. sur la langue Tibét. p. 195.

Deʼi tshe deʼi dus na yul Bāranase ʼ-dir drań sroń l-ńa br-g̈ya žig g-nȧ-s te; drań sroń de dag gis s-ton pa Udpāla žes b-ÿaba dampȧ-i tšhos s-lob tšiń bs-gom pa la d-ga-ʼ bȧ-s kun tu rg̈yu žiń; su la dampȧ-i tšhos yod pa de b-dag la s-mrana.

Remarks.

The Tibetan writing is syllabic like the Sanskrit, from which its characters are derived. The orthography of the Tibetan literature was fixed at a time, when the language was still in a very different state. Many letters which then were pronounced, are at present silent. We have the choice, either to give up entirely the old historical orthography, following only the actual pronunciation, or to seek for a compromise between both. We have made a proposition to that effect in the above (p. 233) mentioned treatise, and our specimen will best show what we mean. As almost all the silent letters precede or follow the root, which alone is pronounced, they might all be transcribed, but separated from the letters pronounced in a conventional way, and the altered pronunciation of a few other letters might be placed above those of the old orthography. The brackets as in *bs)gom* = *gom*; *d)ga('* = *ga*; *nå(s* = *ne*, which we formerly proposed, seem to be less convenient, than a separating line, although also this line has in our European writing an other meaning. The change of pronunciation occurs principally in the letters *a*, *g*, *r*, *m*, *y*, which become sometimes *e*, *d*, *d*, *n*, *tš*, and might then be written $\overset{e}{a}$, $\overset{d}{g}$, $\overset{d}{r}$, $\overset{n}{m}$, $\overset{\prime\prime}{y}$. Other minor changes, as the softer pronunciation of *b* before vowels, or the sharper of *d* before *r*, might be omitted. The letter འ was originally a weak nasal, but is now, if heard at all, weakened into the sound of our '. The vowels, except *a* (which is not written), are expressed in the middle of words by the signs known from the Sanskrit, and in the beginning of words they are added to ཨ as their fulcrum; the same letter without any vowel-sign designates, as in Sanskrit, *a*. The quantity of the vowels is not distinguished in Tibetan, except in Sanskrit words, where the long vowels are commonly expressed by adding underneath the letter འ.

GEORGIAN.

ა	ყ	-	-	-	ჴ	ჰ		
ე ო	კ	გ	ქ	-	ხ	ღ		
ი უ	ჭ	ჯ	ჩ	-	შ	ჟ		
ჲ ჱ (ჳ)	წ	ძ	ც	-	-	-		
	ტ	დ	თ	ნ	ს	ზ	რ	ლ
	პ	ბ	ფ	მ	-	-	ვ	

a	*q*	-	-	-	*λ̇*	*h*		
e o	*k'*	*g*	*k*	-	*λ*	*γ*		
i u	*č'*	*ǰ*	*č*	-	*š*	*ž*		
ĭ ē (u̯)	*ṭ'*	*ḍ*	*ṭ*	-	-	-		
	t'	*d*	*t*	*n*	*s*	*z*	*r*	*l*
	p'	*b*	*p*	*m*	-	-	*w*	

Specimen.

წმიდათა და უძლეველთა მოწამეთა დავით და კოსტანტინესი : ესე უძლეველნი მოწამენი იყვნეს ნათესავით ქართველნი, საზღვართაგან აფხაზეთისათა, სანახებთა-გან არგუეთისა. აზნაურნი იყვნეს ტომით, და ნათესავნი ერთმან-ერთისანი, უძლეველნი და ძლიერნი ბრძოლასა, მჴედარნი შუენიერნი და განთქმულნი წყობასა მტერთასა ::

Brosset, Elém. de la l. Géorg. 1837. p. 268.

Ṭ'midata da uḍlewelta moṭ'ameta Dawit da K'ost'ant'inesi. Ese uḍlewelni moṭ'ameni iqwnes natesawit Kartwelni, sazγwartagan Apχazetisata, sanaχebta-gan Aryuĕtisa; aznaurni iqwnes t'omit, da natesawni ertman-ertisani, uḍlewelni da ḍlierni brḍolasa, mχedarni šuĕnierni da gantkmulni ṭqobasa mt'ertasa.

Remarks.

The vowel *ĕ* is described as a very short *e* and occurs especially after *u*: *uĕ*. In the same way *ĭ* mostly forms the second part of a diphthong *aĭ*, *oĭ*, but sometimes it occurs also alone at the end of words, as in *saidumbĭ*; it is rendered in Russian by й or ь. As all the characters and their order are derived, like the Armenian, from the Greek, the sign of the vowel *u* is originally a composition of *o* and *v* (Greek *ov*). The Greek vowel *v* alone does not belong to the original Georgian alphabet, but is added afterwards after *u* (without any numerical value). It is found, however, in a few words, *ǩ;d* (= *ǩwidi*), seven, and may then be rendered by *ụ*: *ǩụd*. About the dry *tenues*, which we write *k'*, *ṭ'* etc., and which are common to the *Georgian*, *Lasian*, *Mingrelian*, *Suanian*, *Abχasian*, and other Caucasian languages, see above in the *Ossetian* alphabet, p. 139. We are not quite sure of the pronunciation of that letter which we have rendered by $\dot{\chi}$. European Grammarians usually write *kh* instead of our χ and *kkh* instead of our $\dot{\chi}$. It seems that the latter is the corresponding fricative to *q*, and that it has the same pronunciation as that Kurd letter, which Mr. Lerch (see above p. 137) has rendered by *ǩ* and which in this case would also be written more conveniently $\dot{\chi}$, the Semitic *ǩ* being of quite a peculiar nature. The pronunciation of the letter called *hae* ჱ is that of a feable *h*. The last letter with a numerical value (10,000) is the letter called *hoe* ჵ, the sound of which is not quite clear. The letter ჶ *f*, and ჷ *ị* seem to have been invented only for the Ossetian alphabet, not for the Georgian, where it is, however, employed by some writers to render several difficult combinations of consonants more pronouncable.

TUŠ.

The alphabet of this Caucasian language has been discussed by Schiefner, Bulletin de la classe histor. philol. de l'Acad. de St. Pétersbourg, tome XII. 1855. p. 103 sqq. It seems, that his letters:

	a		q	-	ẋ	-	ḥ	h			
e		o	k	g	kh	-	x	gh			
i		u	ć	ʒ́	ć̣	-	ś	ź	j		
			c	ʒ	c̣	-	-	-	-		
			t	d	th	n	s	z	r	l	ḻ
			p	b	ph	m	-	-	w		

would correspond with the following letters of the Standard Alphabet:

	a		q	-	q'	-	χ̇	h			
e		o	k	g	k'	-	χ	γ			
i		u	č	ǰ	č'	-	š	ž	y		
			ṭ	ḍ	ṭ'	-	-	-	-		
			t	d	t'	n	s	z	r	l	ł
			p	b	p'	m	-	-	w		

Remarks.

The letters, which we write with ' are apparently the same dry tenues, on which we have just spoken p. 247 (cf. p. 134). On the aspirated ł see above p. 172.

ALBANIAN (*Toskan* dialect.).

		ε̣			-	-	-	χ̇	-	-	
		α			κ	γ̇	-	χ	γ	-	
	ε		ο		κj	γ̇j	νj	σ̈	σ̇	j	λj
ι		υ		ου	τ	d	ν	σ ϑ	ζ δ	ϱ	λ
					π	b	μ	φ	β	-	
					ξ						

		ẹ			-	-	-	h	-	-	
		a			k	g	-	χ	γ	-	
	e		o		ḱ	ǵ	ń	š	ž	y	ľ
i		ṳ		u	t	d	n	s θ	z δ	r	l
					p	b	m	f	v	-	

Specimen.

Kjε νjε̣ μbϱετ νdε̣ νjε̣ βε̣νd ε μbϱετε̣ϱόν, ε ι κjε ϑε̣νε̣ κjε̣ do τε βϱίτειγ νγ̇α νjε̣ νιπ ι τιγ κjε̣ κjε ἀκόμα πα λjέϱε̣. Πε̣ϱ κε̣τέ̣ πούνε̣ σα djε̣μ bέ̣ινε̣ τε̣ dυ̣βαίζε̣ τ' ετίγ, κjε̣ κισ̈, ι σ̈τιγ νdε̣ dετ ε ι μbυ̣τ. Ι τϱέτι djάλjε̣ κjε̣ σ̈τίου νdε̣ dετ, νουκ' ουμbύ̣τ, πο ταλάζι ε χ̇όδι νd' άνε̣ τε̣ dέτιτ, ε ατjέ ε γ̇jένε̣ τσα τσοbένε̣ ε ε μούαϱε̣ νdε̣ σταν τε̣ τύ̣ϱε, ε ε δάνε̣ νdε̣ γ̇ϱα τε̣ τύ̣ϱε πε̣ϱ τε̣ ϱίτουϱε̣.

Popular tale. J. G. von Hahn, Albanes. Stud. II, p. 167.

Ḱe ńẹ mbret ndẹ ńẹ vẹnd e mbretẹrón, e i ḱe θẹ́nẹ ḱẹ do te vriteiγ nga ńẹ nip i tiγ ḱẹ ḱe akoma pa ľẹ́rẹ. Pẹr kẹtẹ́ púnẹ sa dyem bẹ́inẹ tẹ dṳváizẹ t' etíγ, ḱe kiš, i štiγ nde det e i mbṳt. I tréti dyaľẹ ḱẹ štíu ndẹ det, nuk' umbṳ́t, po talázi e hóδi nd' ánẹ tẹ détit, e atyé e ǵẹ́nẹ tsa tsobénẹ e e múarẹ ndẹ stan tẹ tṳ́re, e e δánẹ ndẹ gra tẹ tṳ́re pẹr tẹ riturẹ.

Remarks.

The *Albanian* language is divided into two dialects, the *Toskan* and the *Gegan*. The Toskan write with Greek letters, the Gegan with Roman. We follow the *Toskan* grammar of J. G. von Hahn in his learned *Albanesische Studien*, Wien, 1853. 2[d] P. — In the *Gegan* dialect occurs the french nasalisation of vowels, expressed by the addition of *ṅ*, which we render by the sign ̃ over the respective vowels.

MALAYAN.

								In foreign words.			
ـَ	ق	ء	-	ة	-			ح	ع		
ـَ اـَ	ک	ݢ	ڠ	-	-			خ	غ		
ـِ ىـِ ـُ وـُ	چ	ج	ڽ	-	ي			ط	ظ	ص	ض
ـِ ىـِ ـُ وـُ	ط	ڎ	-	-	-			-			
	ت	د	ن	س	ر	ل		ث	ذ	ش	ز
	ڤ	ب	م	-	و			ف			

ạ	*q*	’	-	*h*	-		*ḳ*	‘		
a ā	*k*	*g*	*ṅ*	-	-		*χ*	*γ*		
e ē *o ō*	*ċ*	*j̀*	*ń*	-	*y*		*ṯ*	*ḏ*	*s̱*	*ẕ*
i ī *u ū*	*ṭ*	*ḍ*	-	-	-		-			
	t	*d*	*n*	*s*	*r*	*l*	*θ*	*δ*	*š*	*ž*
	p	*b*	*m*	-	*w*		*f*			

Specimen.

Makka manʼalūwarkan dīya darripadda karaǰāanna padda bāran siyāpa yan dikahandakīna, dan dimuliyākanna ākan bāran siyāpa yan dikahandakīna danan tānan qodaratna. .Bāran siyāpa mammānuh ōran danan tiyāda sabanar kaqna niscāya diśiksa allah danan āpi nāraka yan āmat hānat.

Schleiermacher, de l'influeuce de l.écrit. sur le langu. p. 602. 604.

Remarks.

The Malays, like the Arabs, distinguish in writing only three vowels, short and long, *a ā*, *i ī*, *u ū*, using the same signs for *i* and *e*, *ī* and *ē*, *u* and *o*, *ū* and *ō*; ـَا is always *ā*, but ـَ is sometimes *a*, and sometimes the indistinct vowel, which might be transcribed *ẹ*, or as we prefer it in this case *ạ*. The pronunciation of چ and ج is described as between our *č ǰ* and *t′ d′*; it seems therefore that our nearest expression for them is *ċ* and *j̇*. We write the merely Arabic sounds as we write them in Arabic. We have followed principally the exposition of the Malayan grammar by Schleiermacher in his book: *de l'influence de l'écriture sur la langue*, 1835. p. 409 sqq. There, however, the two cerebral letters *ṭ* and *ḍ* are not mentioned. They are at present, as it seems, fallen into disuse; but the new invented sign ڎ of the Malayan alphabet proves, that this letter *ḍ* was used, at least in former times. The corresponding *ṭ* was expressed by the Arabic ط, which afterwards was commonly confined to the words of Arabic origin, and replaced in genuine Malayan words by ت *t*.

BATAK.

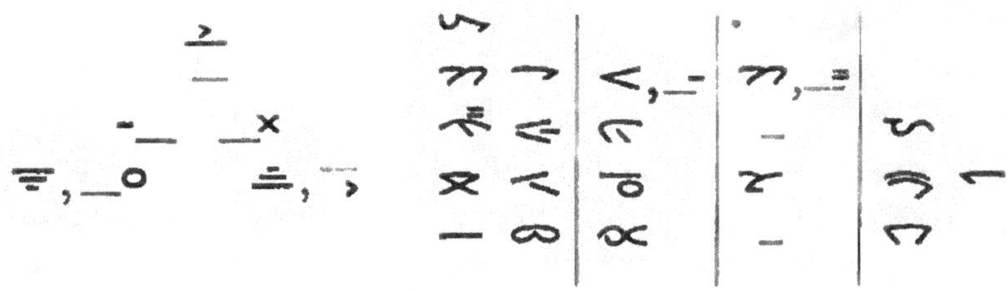

ẹ	(ʾa)			
a	ka ga	ṅa,-ṅ	ha, :	-
e o	ča ǰa	ňa	-	ya
i u	ta da	na	sa	ra la
	pa ba	ma	-	wa

Remarks.

There are three dialects of the *Batak*, which is spoken in the north of *Sumatra*, viz. the *Toba*, the *Mandailiṅ* or *Aṅkola*, and the *Dairi*. The characters given above belong to the *Toba* dialect, except *ča*, which occurs only in the southern branch of the *Mandailiṅ* dialect. In the same dialect is written instead of *ʾa*, or instead of *ha* or *ka*, for *ma*, for *na*, for *sa*, for *ya*, for *i* and (north) or (south) for *u*. The western *Toba* and the *Dairi* dialect use instead of *t*, and instead of *w*. The vowel system in pronunciation and in writing is almost the same as in Javanese. The initial vowels *a*, *i*, *u* have their peculiar signs, the middle or final vowels (except *a*) are expressed by little symbols added to the principal characters. The vowel *a* is not expressed at all, but is inherent in every consonantal character, if it stands alone and is not followed by the sign —\, which indicates the absence of every vowel. As in Javanese, there is a peculiar sign for the final *ṅ* as well as for the feeble final aspiration, both as it seems, in imitation of the Sanskritic *anusvāra* and *visarga*. The letters *ń*, *w*, *y* occur in the *Mandailiṅ*, not in the *Toba* dialect. The *Dairi* has no *ń*; it uses the characters of *w* and *y*, but only instead of , which letter is pronounced *h*. As in other languages the present pronunciation deviates in several cases from the old orthography. *g*, *ǰ*, *b* are pronounced at the end of words *k*, *č*, *p*. In the eastern Toba dialect and in some other parts of the island the *r* is pronounced in a guttural manner, and ought then to be written *ṙ*, if compared with other dialects. *h* in *Toba*, if initial, is sounded *k*; in *Dairi* this is always the case, and in *Mandailiṅ* also, if final or following immediately a consonant. Before *k*, *t*, *p*, *s* the nasals *ṅ*, *n*, *m* are pronounced respectively *k*, *t*, *p*; *n* before *p* becomes *p*, not *t*. In the *Mandailiṅ* alone the nasals are not changed. Before *g*, *ǰ*, *d*, *b* the nasals *ṅ*, *n*, *m* pass into the respective class of the preceding consonant. At the end of words the nasals *ṅ*, *n*, *m* before *h* are pronounced respectively *kk*, *tt*, *pp*, as likewise *k*, *t*, *p* before *h*, with the exception that *t-h* or *p-h* are sometimes pronounced *kk*. *n* before *l*, *r*, *m*, as well as *r* before *l* are changed into the following letter.—All these changements of pronunciation are sometimes neglected in writing, in order to be understood by all the Bataks, and sometimes, they are expressed according to the different dialects. The transcription will follow in most cases, especially for linguistical purposes, the etymological orthography. We owe our remarks on the *Battak*, to Dr. Land, Secretary of the Netherlandish Bible-Society at Amsterdam, the exposition on the subject by H. Neubronner van der Tuuk not being in our hands.

JAVANESE.

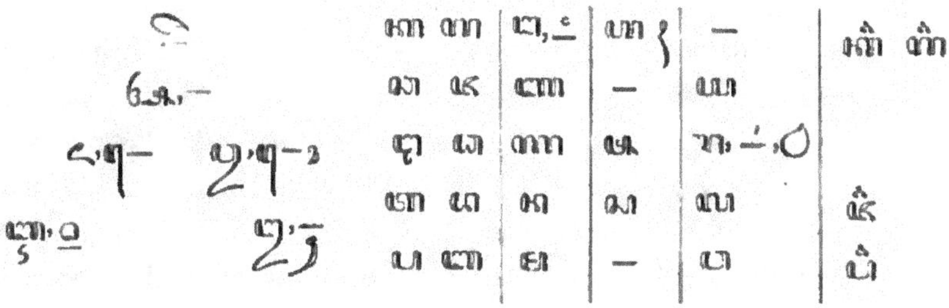

		ẹ			*k g*	*ṅ*	*ḥ ʒ*	-	*χ γ*
	a,ạ				*č ǰ*	*ń*	-	*y*	-
e			*o*		*ṭ ḍ*	*ṇ*	*ṣ*	*r*	-
i				*u*	*t d*	*n*	*s*	*l*	*z*
					p b	*m*	-	*v*	*f*

Specimen.

Negari Bali vontẹn tigań; budinnipun lańkuń denniń rosạ. Padamẹllannipun sabin. Namannipun J̌ạkạ Pirańńon. Mireń χabar, yen nẹgari Mẹssir havis tẹdạ. J̌ạkạ Pirańńon laǰeń kesaʒ datẹń nẹgari Mẹssir; bẹktạ dagańńan pantun hutavi huvos. Sarẹń dumugi nẹgari Mẹssir, kapańgiʒ tiyań dusun hiń Karas.
Javaansche Spraakkunst door Cornets de Groot uitg. door T. Roorda, 1843. p. 68

Remarks.

The system of vocalisation is essentially the same as in the *Dēvanāgarī.* The vowel *ẹ* does not occur in the beginning of words. The vowel *a* which after any consonant is not written at all, has two different sounds, according to certain rules; the one is our pure *a*, the other a somewhat closer and therefore more indistinct *a* approaching to our *o*, as ⌒ approaches to an indistinct *ẹ*. We write therefore those two sounds *ạ* and *ę*. The sign  is described as a final *ṅ*; it seems to imitate in its figure the Sanskrit *anusvāra*, but without its peculiar nature; we prefer therefore, not to distinguish it in our transcription from the full consonantal *ṅ*. The final letter  corresponds with the Sanskritic *visarga s*. About the two cerebral letters *ṇ* and *ṣ* (*š*), we think that T. Roorda is right in what he observes in his edition of Cornets de Groot's *Javaansche Spraakkunst*, Amsterdam 1843. p. 8. As the notation of the final *ṅ*, the different notations of *r* also seem to be imitated from the *Dēvanāgari*, and the two signs  and 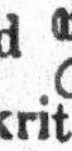 called *Pą-čęrę* and *Ṅą-lęlęt* seem to represent the Sanskritic *ṛ* and *ḷ*. The full vowel characters are sometimes used as initials in original Sanskrit words. Instead of them the letter *h* is generally used with its respective vowel sign. It seems preferable to transcribe this *h*, although it is at present scarcely audible.

DAYAK (Bórneo).

		ą			*k*	*g*	*ṅ*	*h*	-	
		a			*t'*(?)	*d'*	-	-	*y*	
	e		*o*		*t*	*d*	*n*	*s*	*r*	*l*
i				*u*	*p*	*b*	*m*	-	*w*	

Specimen.

Aton olo iďą tempon anake hatuą duą biti. Dan iďąbusu intu ąwen tą hamau dengan bapa: Apaṅ, teṅa akaṅku bagin ramo iďą baris ayuṅku. Dan ią membagi akan ąwen tą penataue. Maka ďaton arą andau limba tą, anak iďą busu menampunan karą ramo, dan hagoet akan lewu awaṅ keďau, hetą ią meṅanan ramoe awi kapapan gawie. Luc. 15, 11—13.

H. C. von der Gabelentz: Grammatik der Dajak-Sprache. Leipzig. 1852. p. 45.

MAKASSAR.

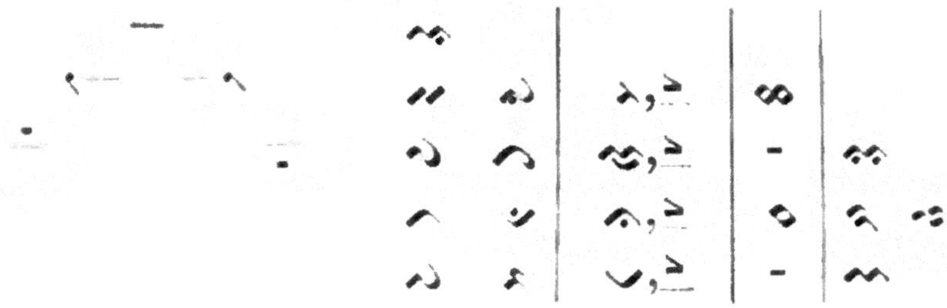

	a		-						
e		o	ka	ga	ṅa	ha	-		
i		u	t'a	d'a	ńa	-	ya		
			ta	da	na	sa	ra	la	
			pa	ba	ma	-	wa		

Specimen.

Iya-minne aṅkána-kánai pau-pauwanna D'ayalaṅkára. Ala siyápa-siyápad'a karáeṅ lompo, a'makéya makóta, a'mináwaṅ irawáṅaṅ parentána D'ayalaṅkára. Na aṅd'o D'ayalaṅkára, tau lámbusu' pamái', na ádele' bit'aranna ri sikamma bone-buttána, siyagáaṅ ri-patarintína, riyanroṅ-kemokanna, ri-pasaribattaṅanna. Pássala'. Na ni-surokána-mo pau-pauwanna. Níya' se're karáeṅ ri parasáṅaṅa, niyáreṅa T'ina-Sumpe. Naíya arenna karáeṅa, nikána Rād'a-Ad'aṅ; ma'lompo kakaraeṅanna, ma'lá'baṅ irateyaṅáṅiṅ, siyagáṅ ri bawa aṅiṅ; na kaleléyaṅ-mo biri'tána ta'sé're-ta'sé're parasáṅaṅ, lambusú'na siyagáaṅ labóna ri-sikamma pákereka, siyagáaṅ ri-tau-kasiasíya.

Matthes, Makassaarsche Spraakkunst. 1858. p. 14.

Remarks.

The *Makassar* language is spoken in the southern part of the island *Celēbes* and partly in the small neighbouring island

Saleyer. The vowel *a* is inherent in every simple character; the other vowels are expressed by points added to their respective consonantal characters. There are no peculiar initial vowel signs, but the character ᨕ serves as a *fulcrum* for every initial vowel. We need not transcribe it. Final nasals are regarded rather as modifications of the preceding vowel and are for this reason usually not written at all, or represented sometimes by a common sign ⩽ placed above the syllabic sign, and pronounced at the end of a word always *ṅ*, and before other consonants *n*, *ṅ*, *ń* or *m*, according to the class of the following letter, imitating in this respect the use of the Sanskritic *anusvāra*-point. Decidedly long vowels occur very seldom in Makassar and almost alone in foreign words. But every vowel, short or long, may be pronounced with a sudden closure of the throat after it, which corresponds very nearly with the Chinese *ži̖* tone (see above p. 232), and which we represent best, as Mr. Land proposes, by adding our *hamza* ʾ after the vowel, as we have done it in those Semitic languages, where א or ء *(hamza)* closes a syllable. It seems, that in Makassar this final ʾ, which is not written, replaces always, as in Chinese, the Samoyetic (p. 219), the eastern Polynesian (p. 259) and other languages, a dropped consonant, especially *k*, which reappears, when a vowel is added, for ex. *ballaʾ* and *a* becomes *ballaka*, whilst *balaṅ* and *a* remains *balaṅa*. The letter *h* is not found in the older Makassar writing; it has been introduced only in later times, and principally used in Malayan or Arabic words, hardly in pure Makassar words. The word-accents may be added on a much larger scale, as it is done in the standard works on the Makassar language by Dr. B. F. Matthes.

BUGIS.

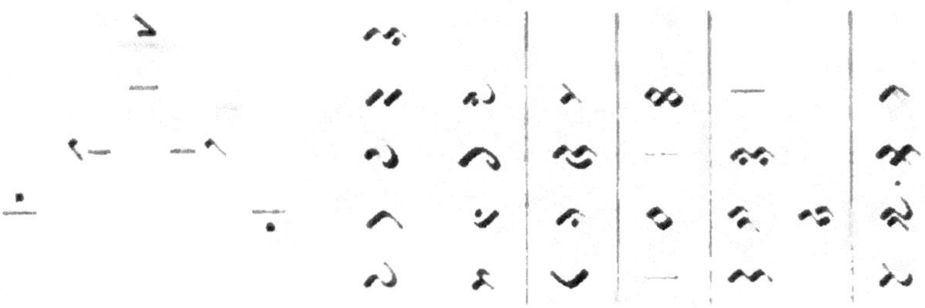

q	-						
a	k	g	ṅ	h	-		ṅk
e o	t́	d́	ń	-	y		ńt́
i u	t	d	n	s	r	l	nr
	p	b	m	-	w		mp

Remarks.

The same sign, called *ańt́a*, which in the Makassar indicates a final nasal, is in the *Bugis* a vowel sign designating an indistinct sound approaching to *a*, and therefore transcribed by us *q*. Four signs are added to the Makassar alphabet to express the combinations of *ṅka*, *ńt́a*, *nra*, *mpa*. There is no *nta*, which seems to be replaced by *nra*. These combinations occur also in the beginning of words and remind us of the same fact in many African languages. *ṅg*, *ńd́*, *nd*, *mb* have no peculiar signs and when they occur in the middle of words, the nasal, as in the Makassar, is not indicated at all. We owe these remarks to the personal information of Dr. Matthes, who is scientifically and practically fully acquainted with the different languages of *Celēbes*, where he has lived many years, as an agent of the Netherlandish Bible Society at *Celēbes*.

EASTERN POLYNESIAN LANGUAGES.

These languages belong to the poorest with respect to the number of sounds they use. None of those which are hitherto known, have the letter *s*, nor *y*, nor *χ*, nor any aspirate, nor even any media, with some rare exceptions. They have the three tenues *k*, *t*, *p*, pronounced rather softly and even of these the *Tahiti* wants the *k*, the *Sandwich* the *t*. But we think that we have to regard not only the *hamza* ʾ as a softening of *k*, but also *v* as the soft correspondent of *p*, and *r* or *l* of *t*; for we find in the language of *New Zealand r* and *d* changing with one another; the *Sandwich* has *l*, but no *r*, the *Raro-Toṅga* has *b*, but no *v*, and other languages have *w* (perhaps *w̱*?) instead of *v*. Most of them have the three nasals *ṅ*, *n*, *m*, and besides *h*. Some distinguish *f* and *h*, which, however, change most frequently with one another; the *Raro-Toṅga* and the *Gambier* have neither. We possess an instructive comparison of several of these languages by B. Gaussin (*Du dialecte de Tahiti, de celui des îles Marquises et en général de la langue Polynésienne*, Paris. 1853). According to this work, we give the following alphabets in our transcription. The vowels are in all the same: *a*, *e*, *i*, *o*, *u*. They are very rarely decidedly long, *ā*, *ē*, *ī*, *ō*, *ū*. Besides the short and long, Mr. Gaussin distinguishes also two accents, which he calls "grave" and "aiguë" without describing them nearer nor designating them by peculiar signs. The consonants of the different languages treated by him are as follows. The feeble guttural, which he calls "explosive pharyngienne" or "postéro-gutturale" seems to be our "hamza" ʾ.

New-Zealand.			
k	-	*ṅ*	*h*
t	*r*,*d*	*n*	-
p	*w*	*m*	-

Raro Toṅga.			
k	ʾ	*ṅ*	-
t	*r*	*n*	-
p	*b*	*m*	-

Gambier.

k	’	*ṅ*	-
t	*r*	*n*	-
p	*v*	*m*	-

Tahiti.

-	’	-	*h*
t	*r*	*n*	-
p	*v*	*m*	*f*

Marquesas,

north-western part.

k	’	*ṅ*	*h*
t	*r*	*n*	-
p	*v*	*m*	-

south-eastern part.

k	’	-	*h*
t	*r*	*n*	-
p	*v*	*m*	*f*

Sandwich.

k	’	-	*h*
-	*l*	*n*	-
p	*w*	*m*	-

The general system of consonants of these different languages would therefore be the following:

k	’	*ṅ*	*h*
t	*r,l,d*	*n*	-
p	*v,w,b*	*m*	*f*

Specimen of the *Tahiti* language.

Ua hoe e toopiti tau ta’ata i tai e hi i te i’a; ’o Roo te i’oa o te tahi, ’o Teahoroa te i’oa o te hoe. Ua tu’u i ta raua matau ’i raro ’i te moana; fifi atura te matau i te rouru o taua atua ra o Ruahatu; parau ihora raua: e i’a; ’ua huti ihora e fa’atata aera ’i te pae va’a, hio ihora raua e ta’ata, te mavera te rouru. Gaussin, p. 255.

ILLITERATE LANGUAGES.

AUSTRALIAN or PAPUAN LANGUAGES.

SOUTH AUSTRALIAN.

(Adelaide.)

	a	*ā*		*k*	*ṅ*	*y*	
	e		*o*	*t*	*n*	*r*	*l*
i			*u*	*p*	*m*	*w*	

ai au oi ui

Remarks.

We follow the work of Teichelmann and Schürmann of the Lutheran Miss. Soc., *Outlines of a Grammar, Vocabulary and Phraseology of the aboriginal language of South Australia, spoken in and around Adelaide.* 1846. The authors conform to the Standard Alphabet with the exception of our *ṅ*, for which they write *ng*.

ANNATOM (New Hebrides).

	a			*k*	*g*	*ṅ*	*h*		*y*	
	e	*o*		*t*	*ð*	*n*	*s*		*r*	*l*
i			*u*	*p*	*b*	*m*	*f*	*v*	*w*	
				tš	*dž*	*ny*				

Vide: H. C. von der Gabelentz, *Die Melanesischen Sprachen.* 1860. p. 65.

Specimen.

Is eteug natimi is ethi, is ero inhalav atamaiṅ o un. Is ika a inharei ehele etman: At ekmak, alupai nyak nahaidži inpaδiaiṅ unyum imtak. Is atiakoai ira rau inpaδiaiṅ o un aien. Is wat ti pan itag noδiat is eti alupat, is astšapig naiṅ nidži itai aseṅa o un a inkarei, um atṅa o un, um apan antaka pege itag agen, is um eδuaraprap inpaδiaiṅ o un aien an neδo auati ahnaṅ.

MARE (Loyalty Islands).

a			*k*	*g*	*ṅ*	*χ*	*h*	*y*		*kh*
	e	*o*	*t*	*d*	*n*	*s*	*z*	*r*	*l*	*th*
i		*u*	*p*	*b*	*m*	-	*v*	*w*		*ph*
			tš	*dž*	*ny*					

See: von der Gabelentz, *Die Melan. Spr.* p. 170.

Specimen.

Kei Makaze dže onome, kei nuponi ko. Inu Yehova ono re Makaze nupo, inu toedžakore nupo wanei Aiphiti, na yara meneṅe. Nupo ake iro ne makaze menu, ekewe ne inu.

Exod. 20, 1.

VITI (Fiji Islands).

a ā			*k*	*ṅg*	*ṅ*	-	-	*y*	
	e ē	*o ō*	*t*	*nd*	*n*	*s*	*δ*	*r*	*l*
i ī		*u ū*	-	*mb*	*m*	-	*v*	*w*	

p, *f*, in foreign words.

Specimen.

E ndua na tamata sa lewe rua na luvenatañane. A, sa kaya vei tamana ko koya sa ñone vei rau: Tamañgu, solia mai vei au nai votavota ni yau sa vota me noñgu. A sa votu vei rau na nona yau. A sa tawa vuñga na boñi sa mari sa soñgonavata na nona yau keδeña ko koya na ñone oñgo, ka lako tani kina vanua vakayawa, ka sa biuta waleña kina na nona yau e nai valavala δidroi. Ev. Luc. 15, 11—13.

Remarks.

The Rev. D. Hazlewood in his *Compendious Grammar of the Feejeean language*, Vewa. 1850. writes *q*, *g*, *d*, *c*, *b*, *j* instead our *ṅg*, *ṅ*, *nd*, *δ*, *mb*, *ǰ*. The vowels are short or long; but they are not distinguished in the Grammar of Hazlewood, nor by H. C. von der Gabelentz, in his work on the Melanesian languages, from which (p. 63) we have taken the specimen. Hazlewood remarks that his *k* and *q* represent two sounds each, the former *k* and in certain cases *g*, the latter *ṅg* and sometimes *ṅk*. The combinations *ṅg*, *nd*, *mb* seem to be only modifications of the respective explosives. We must prefer however to transcribe these combinations of two sounds, according to the pronunciation, by two letters, as we transcribe the same combinations in the African languages.

AFRICAN LANGUAGES.

SUÁHELI (KI-SUAHELI).

a	*k g* .	*ṅ*	*χ h*	
e ẹ o		·	*š ž*	*y*
i u	*t d*	*n*	*s z*	*r l*
short and long.			*θ δ*	
ai (ei) au oi	*p b*	*m*	*f v*	*w(w̱)*
Two clicks.	*tš dž dy ts dz*			

Specimen.

Muánso lalikúa neno, na neno lalikúa kua Muṅgu, na Muṅgu alikúa neno. Hilo ndilo lalikúa muánso kua Muṅgu. Kulla kitu džalifonioa kuakwe; na isipokuái, hakikúa kitu kimoža kilidžo fánioa. Ev. Joh. 1, 1—3.

Remarks.

Krapf, in his *Outline of the elements of the Kisuáheli language.* Tübingen 1850. writes *n*, *c̣*, *ṣ*, *j̄*, *s*, *ṭ*, *ḍ*, *tj*, *j*, *z* instead of our *ṅ*, *χ*, *š*, *ž*, *z*, *θ*, *δ*, *tš*, *dž*, *dz*. Two clicks which have been observed by Dr. Krapf in the *Suáheli* are not written nor described in his publications. We prefer, as we have stated already above (p. 10), to write *tš* and *dž* in the illiterate, especially in the African languages, instead of *č* and *ǰ*, as in the Asiatic languages, because the origin of these compound sounds from simple gutturals is not traceable in all cases, and because there are no simple signs of an indigenous alphabet to be rendered, and finally, because we are now able to quote Grout, Appleyard, Kölle, Schön, Schlegel, Zimmermann, Barth and others as authorities in our favour for the same transcription.

MAKÚA (Mosambique).

Vowels										
a	*k*	*g*	*ṅ*	*h*	-		
e ẹ o	-	-	-	*š*	*ž*	*y*	*l*
i u	*t*	*d*	*n*	*s*	*z*	*r*	*l*
Short and long.	*p*	*b*	*m*	*f*	*v*	*w*	

tš dž ts dz

Remarks.

We give this alphabet from oral communications made by Prof. W. Peters. Cf. *The languages of Mosambique drawn up from the Mss. of Dr. W. Peters* by Dr. W. Bleek. London 1856. In this book our letters *e*, *ẹ*, *ṅ*, *š*, *ž*, *ł* are rendered by *e*, e, *ñ*, *ṣ*, *ṣ*, *hl*. The letter *ł* is not identical with the composition *hl*, but resembles the Welsh *ll*, which we have also rendered by *ł*. The middle tongue touches the hard palate and at the same time the breath is thrust out on both sides of it, producing a similar friction as the letter *χ*.

TŠUĀNA (SE-TŠUĀNA, BE-TŠUĀNA).

				h	.		
a	*k*	-	*ṅ*	*χ*	*γ*	*y*	*ł*
e *o*	*t*	*d*	*n*	*s*	-	*r*	*l*
i *u*	*p*	*b*	*m*	*f*	*v*	*w*	

ai au ei eu oi ou *tš ts.* In foreign words: *dž(j)*

Remarks.

Cf. Appleyard, *Kafir Grammar* 1850. p. 50. He writes *ng*, *kh*, *g*, *c* or *ch*, *j*, *tl* instead of our *ṅ*, *χ*, *γ*, *tš*, *dž*, *ł*. We have the pleasure to state, that on a later occasion, viz. in the *Correspondence between the Committee of the South African Auxiliary Bible Society and various Missionaries and others, relative to the translation, printing and circulation of the scriptures in the native languages of South Africa*, Cape town, 1857. p. 107. Appleyard himself recommends the writing of *tš*, *dž*, *ł*.

KAFIR, *Zulu (Ama-Zulu)* dialect.

a					*h*				
e o	*k*	*g*	*ṅ*	*χ*	*γ*				
i u	*tš*	*dž*	*ny*	*š*	*ž*	*y*			
short and long.	*t*	*d*	*n*	*s*	*z*	*l*	*l*	*ľ*
ai au ao eu	*p*	*b*	*m*	*f*	*v*	*w*			

Clicks:	Pal.	Cer.	Dent.	Later.
	/	!	'	″
	/g	!g	'g	″g
	/ṅ	!ṅ	'ṅ	″ṅ

Specimen.

Uıetšwayo no Mbulazi ukuzalwa kwabo intaṅga inye. Baluke ṅgonina. Uıetšwayo wa zalwa kwa Nıumbazi. Umbulazi wa zalwa kwa Monasi. Kodwa ba laṅgene ṅgoyise; uyise wabo munye. Uyise ka beka ṅkosi pakati kwabo; ṅgokuba ba be isiʹuku, be baniṅgi. U te e se yi beka iṅkosi pakati kwabo, ba se be nako ukuvukelana; ṅgokuba ba se be kulile boṅke.

Grout, Zulu-Grammar. 1859. p. 387.

Remarks.

With reference to the clicks, which the Kafirs have taken from the Hottentots, we have given our opinion above p. 80. 81. We have been sorry to remark that one more has been added to the numerous proposals for the rendering of the clicks. The Rev. H. Hahn, of the Rhenish Mission, having received the commission to send a set of types of his own choice from Europe for the Missionary Press of Cape-town, has added to them his new invented signs for the clicks. As we are unable to discover any particular advantages in these signs, and do not therefore expect their being extensively adopted, we do not feel inclined to recede from our own proposal. We leave it, however, to others to decide whether our strokes should be lengthened a little either above or below, in order to distinguish them still more from the other characters. Beyond the lateral fricative *ł*, which we have already found in the *Makúa* and *Tšuāna* languages, we have to notice in the Kafir at least one lateral more, which we write *ł̣*. This latter one is pronounced in the same way as *ł*, only more forward in the mouth. We may compare the difference of *ł* and *ł̣* with that of *χ* and *χ́*, or with that of *š* and the Polish *ś* (our *ś*). In earlier publications we find our letter *ł* represented by *tl*, *hl*, *'t*, *χ́l*, and our letter *ł̣* by *tl*, *thl*, *dhl*, *hl*, *'t*, *χl*; and in the *Ama-ǁOsa* dialect some writers distinguish even a third lateral fricative, which they render by *khl*, *kχl*, *χl*. The author has only been able to distinguish two sounds in the pronunciation of native Zulu Kafirs (see above p. 80), and agrees in this respect essentially with the observations made by the Rev. L. Grout, Missionary of the American Board, in his valuable *Grammar of the Zulu language*, Natal and London 1851, p. 17, in which he has already introduced the signs *ł* and *ł̣*. Mr. Appleyard, in the above mentioned *Correspondence* etc. p. 108 recommends the sign *ł*, but retains besides the combinations *kł* and *dł*. It seems to us, that the sound rendered by *kl*, *khl*, *χl*, which, according to Boyce, Appleyard and others, is only heard, when the letter *ł* is preceded by *ṅ* or *n*, ought not to be distinguished from the latter. It is a natural phonic effect to hear and even to pronounce *nkł* and *ntł̣*, in conversation, instead of *ṅł* and *nł̣*, and it is the same mistake which has induced others to write *tl* also behind vowels instead of *ł* or *ł̣*. The lateral aspiration might even be uttered without any decided *l*-movement of the tongue; it is then nearly the same sound as the Arabic ض (only without emphasis), a rather difficult letter which the old Arabic orthoepists describe as an "*emphatic aspirated l.*" It might therefore be desirable to fix a peculiar sign for this lateral aspiration, if this did not go beyond our practical wants.

KAFIR, *ǁOsa (Ama ǁOsa)* dialect.

The alphabet is the same as the *Zulu*-alphabet.

Specimen.

Lite ilizwi lika-Tiǁo, ukuǀala kwalo ukuṅgena ema-ǁOseni, laṅgena kwa-ǀṅika; lalipetwe ṅgu-Nyeṅgana, umfo wapešeya kwolwanle. Wayete yena esekwelinye ilizwe, weva kusitwa, Kuko isizwe esiṅgama-ǁOsa. Waza wati kekaloku, wanokuṅga aṅašumayela ilizwi lika-Tiǁo kweso-sizwe. Wasel ecela inlela ke kwabantu abakulu; wasuka wawela ulwanle, wapumela ṅganeno apa Wati, akufika, wanǀedwa kakulu ṅgama-Bulu.

Appleyard, The Kafir language, p. 369.

HERERÓ (O-TYI-HERERÓ).

	a		*k*	*g*	*ṅ*	*h*		*y*	
e		*o*	*t*	*d*	*n*	*s*	*z*	*r*	*(l)*
i		*u*	*p*	*b*	*m*	-	*v*	-	
short and long.			*ty*	*dy*	*ny*	*ts*	*dz*		

Specimen.

Yehova omurise oandye, hina tyi mee hepa. E men dyi rarisa moutsuta uondyoura. E men dyi tsike komeva uokusuva. Omuinyo oandye E ma tarareka; E men dyi tsikire Ena re mondambo yousemba. Ps. 23, 1—3. (Hahn p. 339.)

Etuako ndza ri notyizire ty ovinza ovihuze, mbia s okuya, ka ra ri notyinza otyini. Ozombura azehe va puṅguhire ozombuṅguhiro otyiṅgazo, nu ka za sorere okukohora imba, mbe ze puṅguhirire. Hebr. 10, 1. (Hahn p. 116.)

Remarks.

The Rev. H. Hahn has published two valuable larger works on this language, a Grammar (1857) and Biblical Stories (1861). We regret sincerely, that the orthography of the latter is not only essentially differing from that of the former, but even less acceptable. The question is only about the sounds, which were first written: *n*, *tj*, *dj*, *nj*, *j*, *t*, *d*, *nd*, *s*, *z* by the Rhenish Missionaries, for which Mr. Hahn gives in his Grammar the letters *ṅ*, *ḱ*, *ǵ*, *ń*, *y*, *t*, *d* or *dz*, *n* or *ndz*, *s*, *z*, and in his last publication: *n*, *ty*, *dy*, *ń*, *y*, *ṱ*, *ḓ*, *ṋ*, *s̭*, *z̭*. With regard to *s* and *z* he remarks in the Grammar p. 4, that their pronunciation approaches to the English hard *th* and soft *th*, owing to the custom of the people to cut out the two upper front-teeth in form of an angle Λ. This very plausible explication accounts for the fact, that our common *s* and *z* does not exist at all in the *Hereró*, and justifies us at the same time to retain the common signs of *s* and *z* notwithstanding, instead of *θ* and *ð*, which would else be required according to the Standard alphabet. On a separate leaf printed 1861 Mr. Hahn raises doubts respecting his own former explication, because he had since remarked the same lisping sounds behind *t*, *d*, and *n*, and he uses now a peculiar diacritical sign for *s* and *z* and the compounds *ts*, *dz*, *nz*. We cannot find the reason he gives for this new invention sufficient, and would decidedly prefer the old fashion. On the other hand we adopt his proposal to write *ty* and *dy* instead of *ḱ* and *ǵ*, the more so because we prefer in general, according to our principles, and especially with regard to illitterate languages, to resolve all consonantal diphthongs into their component parts. The natural consequence is that we write also *ny* intead of *ń*. But we keep the distinction of *ṅ* and *n*, as it is done in the Grammar, were it only in order to avoid the very common mistake to pronounce the two letters *ng* as a simple *ṅ*, which latter in many other languages precedes vowels immediately without an intermediate *g*.

FERNANDO PO.

		a			*k*	*g*	*ṅ*	*h*	-	*y*	
	e		*o*		*t*	*d*	*n*	*s*	-	*r*	*l*
i				*u*	*p*	*b*	*m*	*f*	*v*	*w*	
short and long.					*tš*	*dž*	*kw*				
au											

Specimen.

Lue lula bohaho boba pwa, bwaei na a bohah ribi o bunutšu bwabe, ketši o bonutšu bwabe la pulai? atši na batši a takeidi oli, ṅkwai inaba mpio, atši naba o erio a bakoto ata ba boie.

Matth. 5, 13.

Remarks.

The alphabet and specimen are taken from the „*Introduction to the Fernandian tongue*, by John Clarke (Wesl. Miss.) 2[d] ed. 1848. Mr. Clarke writes *n*, *tsh*, *j* instead of our *ṅ*, *tš*, *dž*.

IBO.

			a ā				*k*	*g*	*ṅ*	*h*	-		
		ẹ ẹ̄		*ọ ọ̄*						*š*	*ž*	*y*	
	e ē				*o ō*		*t*	*d*	*n*	*s*	*z*	*r*	*l*
i ī						*u ū*	*p*	*b*	*m*	*f*	*v*	*w*	
ã ẽ etc.							*tš*	*dž*	*kp*	*gb*	*ny*		
ai ei oi													

Tones.

High tone *a*´ *e*´ etc.
Middle tone *a* *e* etc.
Low tone *a*` *e*` etc.

Specimen.

Mbẹ' ya welite anya ya na nde soga ya, ya se' ṅgọ'zi ūnu nde na digi īhinye idži hã ma ūnu nwe' āla'eze Tšu'ku, ṅgọ'zi ūnu nde ne ēbẹ' ūbu'a ma ūnu ga ātšiọ'tši. Ṅgọ̄'zi ūnu, nde āgu' na āgu' ūbu'a, ma afọ' gedžu ūnu. Ṅgọ'zi ūnu, mbe' ma'du ga ākpọ' unu asi', mbe' āgahan ātšọ' unu, na ēbi'rihã ma mebo' ūnu na ihu'n ẹrẹn ākpọ' ūnu aha'n doka ndžọ' na ihi Ọpa'ra wō'ke.

Luke 6, 20 – 22.

Remarks.

We give the alphabet and specimen according to the *Grammatical Elements of the Ibo language* by the Rev. J. F. Schön and the native Missionary S. Crowther's *Isuama-Ibo Primer*, revised by the Rev. J. Chr. Taylor, having changed only their *dš* into *dž*. In the compounds *kp* and *gb* of this and other African languages, the component parts are so intimately connected, that they are regarded almost as guttural modifications of *p* and *b*, in a similar way as we speak of guttural (emphatic) dentals in the Semitic languages. We prefer however to write both letters in the same way as it has been done before us. About the peculiar intonations represented by the accents ' and ', see our remarks on the *Yoruba*.

YÓRŪBA.

ẹ
a ā
e ē ọ ọ̄ ō
i ī u ū
ă ĕ ĭ ŏ ŭ
ã ẽ etc.
au ai ọi ōi ẹi ēi
Tones: *a' a a'*

k	*g*	*ṅ*	*h*	-	-
t	*d*	*n*	*š*	*ž*	*y*
			s	-	*r l*
p	*b*	*m*	*f*	-	*w*

tš dž kp gb

Specimen.

Ọ'kǭri kā' li ọmọ'kǭri mēdži. Ēyi aburo nĭ inọ' wǭ wi fu baba' rè kpē', Baba', fu mi ni iwǭ ogū' ti o tori' mi. O' si kpī ohū ini' rè fu wǭ. Ki isi to' idžọ' mēlokā li ehī ēyi, ēyi ọmọ'kǭri aburo ko' ohū gbogbo ti o' ni džọ', o' si mu ọ'na rè kpǭ lọ'h si' ilu o'kērē; ni ibe' ni o' gbē' na' gbogbo ini' rè ni inakuna.

Luke 15, 11 – 13.

Remarks.

We owe our acquaintance with the *Yórūba* language principally to the valuable works of the native Missionary Rev. S. Crowther *(Adža'ye)* (Grammar and Vocabulary 1852) and lastly of the Rev. T. J. Bowen (Grammar and Dictionary. 1858, published by the Smithsonian Institution). Their alphabet exhibits the letters *ạ*, *ẹ*, *e*, *ọ*, *aŋ(an)*, *ŋ(n, ng)*, *ś (ṣ)*, *ź*, *ç* or *tṣ*, *dź (j)* instead of our *ẹ*, *e*, *ĕ*, *ọ*, *ã*, *ṅ*; *š*, *ž*, *tš*, *dž*. The vowel *ẹ* is not noticed by Crowther; it seems to be very rare and is described by Bowen as the "obscure sound of *u* in *but*, *o* in *mother*." The *ŋ(n, ng)* on the end of syllables "is equivalent to the French *n* in *bon*." This is the same nasalisation of a vowel, which Mr. Schön in *Ibo* has already rendered according to the Standard alphabet by *ã*, *ẽ*, etc. "Before a consonant, that is, at the beginning of a word or syllable, it has a stronger sound, nearly equivalent to the English *ng* in *song*." That is our *ṅ*. The compound *tš* is not mentioned by Bowen and seems to be almost unknown in native words. As to the peculiar intonation of vowels, which is identical with that in *Ibo*, *Ewe* and other languages, "there are three primary tones; the middle tone is the ordinary tone of the voice without inflexion; the acute and grave tones are simply the rising and falling inflexions of elocutionists; in the *Yoruba* and other cognate languages however, they are employed to distinguish words which are spelled alike, but have different meanings."

We find here in a smaller extent the same principle of intonation as in the Chinese. The middle tone requires no expression in writing; the two other tones have been indicated by Crowther, Schön and Bowen, as the rising and falling Chinese tone used to be, by the acute and grave accents ′ and ‵, over the vowel. We have already suggested (p. 231), and more amply discussed in the above quoted treatise, our scruples against this use of the European accents, which have quite a different meaning, and the former of which is indispensable in every language to indicate the common word-accent. Mr. Bowen has met with this very difficulty also in the *Yórūba* language, where the word-accent is entirely different from the intonation. He distinguishes therefore the former from the latter by placing it on the right side of the vowel, ex. *a′daba*, *ẹdà′*, *alufā′*, *á′laśa′ra*, *onì′ba′ta*. In the running text and in the Dictionary Mr. Bowen generally omits the word-accent and it seems that it would not be difficult to fix those cases where it ought to be put and where not. But we should decidedly propose, that the word-accent be placed, also in the African languages, over the vowel, according to the usual custom, and the tones on the right side of the vowel, without altering the shape given to them by Mr. Bowen. We gain by this mode of writing the full harmony with the only languages, which exhibit the same tones, viz. the Chinese and cognate languages, where the *Śań′* or *ascending* tone is represented by the acute, and the *Khyu‵* or *descending* tone by the grave accent, placed on the right side of the vowel (see above p. 232). We should consequently write the above quoted words: *ádaba*, *edá‵*, *alufá*, *á′lašára*, *onibáta*, or if we omit the word-accent, where it is not necessary: *ádaba*, *eda‵*, *alufá*, *a′lašára*, *onibáta*. Mr. Bowen has introduced a new diacritical sign ^ over those vowels, which are pronounced so short as to be scarcely perceptible. We have used in those cases, as in the Slavonic and other languages, the particular sign of shortness ˘.

E Ẃ E, *Aṅlo (Aongla)*-dialect.

e̥
a ā
ę ę̄ ǫ ǭ
e ē o ō
i ī u ū
ă ĕ ĭ ŏ ŭ
ã ẽ ĩ etc.

-	-	-	*h*			
k	*g*	*ṅ*	*χ*	*γ*		
t	*d*	*n*	*š*	*ž*	*y*	
			s	*z*	*r*	*l*
p	*b*	*m*	*f*	*v*	*w*	*ẃ*
tš	*dž*	*kp*	*gb*	*ny*		

Tones.

High: *a'* *e'* *i'* etc.
Middle: *a* *e* *i* etc.
Low: *a`* *e`* *i`* etc.

Specimen.

Se gbli alaklę le kǫẃe deka. Se eẃa'dži vio amę wui eve, na alaklę tǫ deka. Alaklę gblǫ na se, bena enǫvi enye. Eyia devio nǫ alaklę gbǫ fam, oẃa'tu awǫ na alaklę. Eyia gbǭ efa gblǫ na se bena: nuka wogbli amęke le kǫẃe deka mâhą̂? megblie n'anyi le kǫẃea me, eli' vinyeo kpatā.

J. B. Schlegel, Schlüssel zur Eẃe-Sprache, p. 148.

Remarks.

We have applied the same system of orthography, which the Rev. J. B. Schlegel—in accordance with the Standard Alphabet—made use of in his able Grammar and Dictionary of the *Eẃe* language (Stuttgart. 1857). The obscure vowel-sound, of which he speaks p. 6 seems to be the same as the vowel *ạ* of Mr. Bowen in the *Yoruba*. We represent it, as in the *Yoruba*, by *e̥* in the rare cases where it occurs. The letters *χ* and *γ* are remarkable, and still more so the letter *ẃ*, which seems to be met with only in the *Eẃe*,

Akra, and a few cognate languages. The pure breath, says Mr. Schlegel, passes silently through the lips as if you slightly blow off something from the paper before you; the teeth have nothing to do with it, nor is it a sonant, but a mute letter; the mouth takes the position of the German *w̱*. We cannot but approve the rendering of this labial breathing by *ẃ*. Others have tried to substitute *f* as basis; but the entire absence of a dental friction leads us more naturally to *w*. Instead of *dš* of Mr. Schlegel we have to write *dž*.

AKRA (GÃ).

a ā
ẹ ẹ̄ ọ ọ̄
e ē o ō
i ī u ū
ă ĕ ĭ ŏ ŭ
ã ẽ ĩ etc.

k	*g*	*ṅ*	*h*			
t	*d*	*n*	*š*	*ž*	*y*	
			s	-	*r*	*l*
p	*b*	*m*	*f*	-	*w*	*ẃ*

tš dž kp gb km

Tones.

High: *a′ e′* etc.
Middle: *a e* etc.
(Low: *a‵ e‵* etc.)

Specimen.

Osu ni‵ amẹyọ, ni amẹyanu lẹ, akẹ lumo eba; ši ekẹ, ayatſa tũ ahâlẹ. Ni amẹbabua oblahĩ bii lẹ ana. Kẹkẹ ni‵ amẹbayiṅ amẹyatſa tũ lẹ. Beni fe sẹ lẹ, akẹ̄ ayafla lumo lẹ, ni amẹte amẹyaflalẹ. Džetšẹrenọ lẹ, akẹ̄ ayatšẹ onukpai yẹ mõ, ni amẹbayiṅ amẹte. Aso noni akẹo noni akẹẹo, amẹnuu mli eko; ši fe sẹ moṅ fẽdã ni‵ amẹnu asẹmsro, akẹ onia obatšu.

Zimmermann, Akra Grammar. p. 187.

Remarks.

The Standard Alphabet has been already employed by the Rev. J. Zimmermann in his *Grammatical Sketch of the Akra- or Gã-language*, Stuttgart. 1858. We write only *dž* instead of his *dš*, and *ẃ* instead of his f, which would remind rather a dental *s* than a labial *w* (see above). With regard to the tones, he distinguishes only two of them, indicating the elevation of the voice by the grave accent (*à*) instead of the acute (*á*) employed in the cognate languages, and leaving the other without sign (p. 6). He uses the acute (*á*) in its original meaning as word-accent, as we do.

TYI (O-TYI, OJI), *Akwapim* dialect.

		a			*k*	*g*	*ṅ*	*χ*	*h*	*y*
	ẹ		*ọ*							
e		*ọ̣*		*o*	*t*	*d*	*n*	*s*	*z*	*r*
i		*ụ̣*		*u*	*p*	*b*	*m*	*f*	*v*	*w*

Mostly short, sometimes long.

ai ei oi (*ọ̣i*)

Specimen.

Abẹ baakoṅna sei ensa. Wo to adur-a, ebi ka w'āno. Abofra ente n'enna ni n'agya asẹm-a, odi aduaṅ eṅkyinne nim. Tāpo ni abaṅm. Wonim tu-a, tu wo dyọṅ. Ohia na ma odeχe yẹ akoa. Wohū kọtọ ẹni-a, wose: eyẹ duā. Ẹsonno afoṅ-ā, woṅgwa no bergu so. Atyọ abiẹṅ borro vụ. Riis, Grammat. Outline p. 111.

Remarks.

Rev. H. N. Riis, in his *Grammatical Outline and Vocabulary of the Oji-language, with especial reference to the Akwapim-*

dialect, Basel. 1854. writes *ę*, *ǫ*, *ụ*, *ñ*, *c* instead of our *ẹ*, *ọ*, *ü̱*, *ṅ*, *χ*. If he says p. 9: "The combination *wy* is to be considered rather as a simple sound, intermediate between *w* and *y*", this peculiar sound is perhaps the same, which we have written *ẃ* in the preceding languages. He distinguishes (p. 7) "a third class of vowels, which cannot be said to be long, and yet are different from the short vowels. They are sounded more fully and sharply than the latter, but without the sound being prolonged, as in the case with the long vowels." He marks those vowels by the circumflex *â*, *ê*, etc. If by this description he wishes to designate the ascending tone of the cognate languages, we should write it *a'*, *e'*, etc. as in those languages.

TEMNE.

			e̥						*k*	*g*	|	*ṅ*	|	*h*	|	*y*		
			a											*š*				
		ẹ		*ọ*					*t*	*d*	|	*n*	|		|	*r*	*l*
	e		·		*o*									*s*				
i						*u*			*p*	*b*	|	*m*	|	*f*	|	*w*		
ai	*au*	*oi*	*ui*							*tš*				*gb*				

Specimen.

Wani reke katroṅ ka nu, o wo ba tre̥-lomme kemme kin, bi o k'in ka ṅaṅ o sokkar, o mo trei fẹ a tre̥-gba tr'anle trofat tramat ro ṅ'anle ro-kant-i, o mo kọnne treka ten o wo sokkar, hã o sotto kọ i? Ko bi o poṅ sotto kọ, o botr kọ ka e kẹṅkla e yoṅ, o ba ma-bonne. Luke 15, 4. 5.

Remarks.

We give the alphabet and the specimen according to Rev. C. F. Schlenker in his *Temneh Primer*, Stuttgart, 1854, although his transcription seems to be in an imperfect state. He writes *ạ*, *ẹ*, *ọ*, *n* or *ng* or *ngh*, *ṣ* instead of our *ẹ*, *ẹ*, *ọ*, *ṅ*, *š*. The description of his *ạ* (*ẹ*) "like the English *u* in *but* or in *run*" is doubtful; *ẹ* (*ẹ*) has according to him the double pronunciation of the German *ä* in *Väter*—our *ẹ̄*—, and that of the English *ai* in *bait*—our *ẹ̄*; he gives to his *o* only the long sound as in *home* or *old*—our *ō*, and to his *ọ* only the long sound as in *law* or *water*—our *ọ̄*; he writes very frequently *h* at the end of words, as *kah*, *woh*, *ngangh*, *oh*, *moh*, *ih*, *kọh*, *eh*, *yongh* in our specimen, only "to distinguish words which, though sounded alike, have a different sense", a principle which we could not recommend. The quantity of the vowels in the specimen is not indicated, nor is it clear, what is meant by his writing *hā̃*.

VEI.

ạ
a
ẹ *ọ*
e *o*
i *u*
short and long.
au *ai* *ẹi* *ẹi*
ọu *ọu*

k *g*	*ṅ*	*h* *γ*	*y*	
t *d*	*n*	*s* *z*	*r*	*l*
p *b*	*m*	*f* *v*	*w*	

tš *dž* *gb*

Specimen.

Fatōma Sẹ̄ri a ba Tāru Gura a ra wurú difimuro ke mu kĩa sāma gbẹ̄a mu tere gbẹṅ dzérēma kẽa amu mõa Dúru-karọ kérēma dže. Difi biri a were ka ṅkundọ gba. Kẹ dondo. Ṃ́fa sāu afá keṅ-gba-tọ-bọ́rōro-kárọẽwa nĩe Gbombai. Amu Gbombai mōnuẹ Dōaru Sisi sọ Džhondu. Kẹrẹ Dōaru bẹrẹ Tugba Fá misā a džommu a fākẹ, amu a tõa ṃ́fa Sāu bọro. A tā fākumẹ ā fõa Džondu. Kam biri banda ṃ́fa Wónyawere bẹ bọ́rō nu.

Remarks.

We refer to the *Outlines of a Grammar of the Vei language* by Rev. S. W. Koelle, Church Missionary. London. 1853. He writes in this Grammar *ẹ*, *ọ*, *ò*, *n˙*, *ṛ*, *dṣ*, *dṣ* instead of our *e̱*, *o̱*, *o̥*, *ṅ*, *γ*, *tš*, *dž*. He describes the sound of his *ò* as between the *o* of *note* (our *ọ*) and the *u* of *book*. Being uncertain, whether this description would characterise this vowel sufficiently, we shall meanwhile write it *o̥*. Mr. Koelle adds to his valuable work a most interesting account respecting the mode of syllabical writing invented in modern times by the Vei people themselves, and we find the vowel *o̥* (*ò*) distinguished from *o̱* and *o*(*ọ*) also in this *Vei* writing.

SUSU.

		a			*k*	*g*	*ṅ*	*χ*	*h*	*ṙ*
	e		*o*					*š*		*y*
					t	*d*	*n*	*s*		*r* *l*
i				*u*	*p*	*b*	*m*	*f*		*w*
						dž				

Remarks.

Rev. J. L. Wilson, Missionary of the American Board on the Gabun, gives the *Susu*-alphabet in the *Journal of the Amer. Or. Soc.* vol. I, No. IV, p. 365 after the Grammar of the Rev. Mr. Brunton (Edinburgh. 1802). We have no doubt that his *ng*, *sh*, *kh*, *dzh* correspond with our *ṅ*, *š*, *χ*, *dž*; but we are not sure, whether his *rh* is a guttural *r* (*ṙ*) or our letter *γ*.

MANDIṄGA.

Vowels						
a	*k g*	*ṅ*	*h*	*y*	
e ẹ̄ o	*t d*	*n*	*s*	*r*	*l*
i u	*p b*	*m*	*f*	*w*	
ai au oi	*tš dž ny*				

Specimen.

Katuko aryena-mansarö molunta ko buntio mem bota somanda džuna, fo asi dolalu sotto ala wainekuṅkoto. Afaita dolalu fe koppere sai, a wolu ki ala wainekuṅkoto. Abota buṅgoto wonyama wate sabbandžaṅgoto, a dolu dye beloriṅ kensiṅke marseoto.

Ev. Matth. 20, 1—3.

Remarks.

The alphabet and specimen are taken from the *Grammar of the Mandingo language, with Vocabularies*, by the Rev. R. Maxwell Macbrair. London 1837. p. 70.

WOLOF.

Vowels						
ẹ	*k g*	*ṅ*	*χ h*	*y*	
a			*š ž*		
e	*t d*	*n*	*s z*	*r*	*l*
ẹ̦ o̱ o	*p b*	*m*	*f v*	*w*	
i u̱ u	*dž ny*				
ă ĕ ŏ ŭ					

Specimen.

Ben bes goloh-gĕ nẹ: Mọn-na gyẹki tkię lĕlek bel ṅgyent-sou, tẹ du-ma-okĕtu. Lọg-bĕ nẹ ko: Man it mọn-na gyẹki tkię lĕlek bel ṅgyent-sou tẹ du-ma-χẹniku. Nyu di gyẹki thiẹ lĕlek bel dig u bĕkyek. Goloh bọg-nă okĕtu, tẹ am-ul ben mpeχẹ-mu mu-def. Mune lọg: Bĕ-mu-demon tkiẹ χarẹ-bĕ, nyu-dyam mĕ ballĕ fi.

Remarks.

In the *Recherches sur la langue Ouolofe*, par M. le baron Roger, Paris, 1829, our letters *ẹ, ĕ, e, ē, ẹ, ọ, u̱, u, ṅ, χ, š, ž, dž, ny* are rendered by *ë, e, è, ê, é, eu, u, ou, n, kh* or *hr* or *rh, ch, j, dj, gn.*

FŪL (FULAH).

a

ẹ ọ

e o

i u

short and long.

ã õ

ai au ei oi ou ui

								Arabic sounds		
								;	'	ḱ
k	g	ṅ	h					χ		
t	d	n	š	ž	y			ṯ	ḏ	ẕ
			s	z	r	l				
p	b	m	f	-	w					
tš	dž	ny								

Specimen.

Lādi ẹ diri nyaldi be yáldini fī džaka ẹ Augustus Kaisara no be winda dendaṅgal nībube. Ko nduṅ woni tálkuru árwandu o džoni duṅ to Kirēnus lamdo Sāmi. Wali dendáṅgalmabe kayo winde kala gōto ẹmábe hato sáremako. Yahi Yúsufu kade íude Džalíla hato sáremako Názarata to lēdi Yahudiaṅkōbe hato sāre Dāwúda ndeṅ nọtirtende Baituláhami ko doṅ woni sāre Dáwūda ẹ gabílamuwu; kayo be wíndane wóndude ẹ Maryáma gendiráomako kọ doṅ orēdi. Ev. Luc. 2, 1—5.

Remarks.

The Rev. C. L. Reichardt, Church Miss., in his *Primer in the Fulah language*, and in his *Three original Fulah Pieces*, Berlin, 1859, has already used the Standard alphabet. There are many Arabic words in the *Fūl*, which ought to be rendered according to our Arabic transcription. We should also adopt the letter *ǰ* instead of *dž*, if this sound occurred only in Arabic words. The specimen is taken from Reichardt's Primer p. 23.

KÁNURI (BORNU).

ẹ̤ ạ̤
a
ẹ ọ
e o
i u
short and long.
ã
ai au ei oi ọu ui

k	*g*	*ṅ*	*h*	-	*y*	
			š	-		
t	*d*	*n*			*r*	*l*
			s	*z*		
p	*b*	*m*	*f*	-	*w*	
tš	*dž*	*ts*	*(dz)*			

Specimen.

Tátōa sandi kām 'di ganántsān sōbāgáta. Sōbāgatányā, tilō, abāntsẹ gálifū, tilō, abāntsẹ tálaga. Sandi ndi nẹmsóbāntsa tsadin, dúgō, sandi wurágẹda. Wurāgẹdányā, nā kāmubē tsátī. Kẹtẹ́nyā, táta gálifubē lētsẹ, pḗrō kuyáṅgā yāsgẹ nígā tsẹdẹ, gōtšī; kúrū wṓltẹ, kámū kura tilō nígā tsẹdẹ, pḗrōa kām yásgurō fṓktsẹgī.
Koelle, Afr. native literature, p. 7.

Remarks.

We refer respecting the alphabet and specimen to the most valuable works of the Rev. S. W. Koelle, Church Missionary:

Grammar of the Bornu or Kánurī language and *African native Literature*, both publ. London, 1854, in which the Standard Alphabet is already used.

KOṄǴÁRA (DAR-FŪR).

	a ā		*k*	*g*	*ṅ*	*(h)*		
e ĕ		*o ō*	-	*ǵ*	*ń*	*š*	*y*	
i ī		*u ū*	*t*	*d*	*n*	*s*	*r*	*l*
ai au			*p*	*b*	*m*	*f*	*w*	

NUBA.

	a ā		*k*	*g*	*ṅ*	*h*		
e ē		*o ō*	*k̄*	*ǵ*	*ń*	*š*	*y*	
ı ī		*u ū*	*t*	*d*	*n*	*s*	*r*	*l*
ai aú			*p*	*b*	*m*	*f*	*w*	

Specimen.

Inī urrag Yesū Mesih, nōrin tōdin, iṅǵīlnilin. Nebi Isahian fāyisīn nagittā: Adī, ai f-īdēr melaik aṅgā urrag innā, dawig indōro haddereyā. Hissi wē tāk̄in falēlā: Hadderan nōrin dawigā, sallahan sikke tannigā. Yūhannā falēlā gatisōǵa menon, ād-derson getāsiltōn tūbōǵana yā, sembī gafritakkana yā.

Ev. Marc. 1, 1—5.

Remarks.

The alphabets of the *Koṅǵara* and *Nuba* languages are picked up by the Author himself from the natives, the *Nuba* specimen from his *Gospel according to St. Mark translated into the Nubian language.* Berlin. 1860.

AMERICAN LANGUAGES.

INDIAN LANGUAGES OF NORTH AMERICA.

e̥				*h*			
a	*k*	*g*	*ṅ*	*χ*	*γ*		
e o	*tš*	*dž*	*ny*	*š*	*ž*	*y*	*ly*
i u	*t*	*d*	*n*	*s*	*z*	*ʽr*	*l*
ã ẽ ĩ õ ũ ẽ̥				*θ*	*δ*		
ai au	*p*	*b*	*m*	*f*	*v*	*w*	

Remarks.

Few of the American languages have been carefully analysed with respect to their sound-system, and we are not able to trace rightly the alphabets of the *Kri*, *Odžibwa*, *Mikmak*, and others, after the imperfect descriptions and transcriptions which lie before us. We think it therefore advisable to refer to the valuable and well known *Essay on a uniform orthography for the Indian languages of North America* by John Pickering, who describes with acuteness the above given sounds. His transcription differs from ours in the following letters: *e̥*, *ã*, *ẽ*, *ĩ*, *õ*, *ũ*, *ẽ̥*; *ṅ*, *χ*, *γ*, *š*, *ž*, *θ*, *δ*, which he writes: *o*, *ą*, *ę*, *į*, *ǫ*, *ų*, *!*; *n*, *kh*, *gh*, *sh*, *zh*, *th*, *dh*.

GREENLANDIC.

a ā				*h*		
e o	*k̇*	-	*n̈*	*χ̇*	*γ̇*	-
i ī u ū	*k*	*g*	*ṅ*	*χ*	-	*y*
				š	*ž*	
	t	-	*n*			*l*
				s	*z*	
	p	-	*m*	*f*	*v*	-

Specimen.

Nālagaḱ mianeχallugo, taža ilizimaneχmut autlaχniutigšaḱ. Ps. 111, 10. — *Tamažža sukuiautigšā, kunχi-ā! Ḱutziṅneχuwžāχtup peχḱužžutā tažža, piumāχtugšaḱ nālagkawnut kuṅimut. Inuṅit ayagtoχumāχpātit.* Dan. 4, 21. 22. — *Izumaḱaχpoḱ, ḱataṅṅutaiza malugizzagāne, annautigiumāχitik, Gūtip annaukkumaṅmatik.* Acts. 7, 25.

Remarks.

S. Kleinschmidt in his *Grammatik der Grönländischen Sprache*, Berlin, 1851. supplies us with a very learned and accurate description of the Greenlandic sounds, although we must deviate in many points from his transcription of the consonants. Our letters: *ḱ*, *n̈*, *χ̇*, *γ̇*, *k*, *ṅ*, *χ*, *š*, *ž*, *z* are the same as his: *κ*, *rng*, *r*, *r̉*, *k*, *ng*, *g*, *ss*, *ss*, *s*. He calls the first class gutturals, the second palatals, but be describes both classes as uttered deeper in the throat than the same classes in other languages. The second class comes very near to the common gutturals, whilst the first might be compared, as in the *Geʾez* and *Amharic*, to a peculiar developement of the Semitic *q*-class. We distinguish those deep gutturals by adding over them, as in the just mentioned languages, the guttural point, and by doubling it over *n̈*. It is the same misconception which we have met already several times, that he takes the rough friction of *χ̇*, *γ̇*, and even *n̈* as a regular vibration, representing it by the basis *r*. The original explosive *media* is, according to this author, only preserved in the second class as *g*, whilst in the other classes it is either softened, between vowels, into the respective soft fricative (*γ̇*, *ž*, *z*, *v*) or, after consonants, changed even into the hard fricative (*χ̇*, *š*, *s*, *f*). In the latter case he distinguishes the soft and the hard fricative only in the first class (*r̉* and *r*) and in the last (*v* and *f*), but he does not distinguish *ss* = *š* from *ss* = *ž*, nor *s* = *s* from *s* = *z*. It is, however, only consistent, to show fully in our transcription the regular developement of this interesting system of consonants. It seems, on the other hand, that we might easier dispense with the compound letter *dl*, which this author uses for *l* if it follows an other consonant. As to the different accents, which Mr. Kleinschmidt employs, they seem to us not necessary, if we double, after every sharp accented vowel, the following consonant.

MASSATŠŪSET.

a	*k*	*g*	*ṅ*	*χ*	*h*	-
e *o*	*tš*	*dž*	-	*š*	-	*y*
i *u*	*t*	*d*	*n*	*s*	*z*	(*r*)(*l*)
short and long.	*p*	*b*	*m*	*f*	*v*	*w*
ā̆ *ō̆*						

Specimen.

Noošun kesukwut qwuttianatamunatš koowesuoṅk, peyaumooutš kukketassootamoonk kuttenantamooṅk ne ennatš ohkeit neane kesukwut. Numeetsuoṅgaš asekesukokiš assamainnean yeuyeu kesukok. Kah ahkwontamaiinnean nummatšeseoṅgaš neane matšenehikwegeeg nutahkwontamauounonog. Matth. 6, 9—11.

Remarks.

The alphabet is taken from John Eliot: *A Grammar of the Massachusetts Indian language*, ed. by P. S. du Ponceau. Boston, 1822, and the Specimen from Josiah Cotton: *Vocabulary of the Mass. Ind. langu.* Cambridge, 1829. p. 104. There remain still several doubts about the vowels. The letters *r* and *l* are used in cognate dialects instead of *Massatšusett n*. We add *χ* according to a remark of John Pickering, see Cotton p. 6.

IROKWOIS.

a
e *o*
i *u*
ã *ẽ* *õ*

k	-	-	*h*	*y*
t	-	*n*	*s*	*r*
-	-	-	-	*w*

Remarks.

Du Ponceau, in his *Mémoire sur le systême grammatical des langues de quelques nations Indiennes de l'Amérique du nord.* Paris, 1838. p. 103. pretends expressly, that the Irokwois use only the poor alphabet exhibited above. According to Zeisberger (du Ponceau, p. 259) they have also the letters (*g*), *ṅ*, *tš*, *χ*, *š*, *e̱*, *o̤*.

MUSKOKI.

e̥
a
e *o̥* *o*
i *u*
ai *au* *iu* *ui*

k	*ṅ*	*h*		
tš	-	*š*	*y*	*hl*
t	*n*	*s*	*l*	
p	*m*	*f*	*w*	

Specimen.

Tšihofe̥ isti ye̥me̥ ike̥ne̥ ohfulo̥t imĩlhlusit iputsin atote̥tis; mutse̥ istaime̥t oho̥ke̥so̥mi nomo̥t istimilhlaiki kos; hisakite̥ imi yukse̥ sikot in hitske̥ke̥hlis. John 3, 16.

Remarks.

See *A short Sermon: also Hymns, in the Muskokee or Creek language* by Rev. John Fleming, Miss. of the Amer. B. of Comm. f. F. Miss. Boston, 1835. Cf. Winslett, *Muskokee* Hymns, Park Hill, 1851. (Presbyter. Miss.)

TŠAHTA (CHOKTAW).

ẹ		*k*	-	*ṅ*	*h*		
a		*tš*	-	-	*š*	*y*	
e o		*t*	-	*n*	*s*	*l*	
i u		*p*	*b*	*m*	*f*	*w*	
ã ĩ õ ũ ẹ̃							
ai au							

Specimen.

Piki ẹba iš binili ma. Tši hohtšifo hẹt holitopaške. Iš apehlitšika yẹt ẹlaške. Nana iš aiahni ka yakni pakna yã a yohmi kẹt ẹba yakni a yohmi mak õ tšiyuhmaške. Himak nitak ilhpak pim ai ẹlhpesa hoka iš pi ipetaške. Matth. 6, 9—11.

Remarks.

See *The Choctaw Spelling book*, 5th ed. Boston, 1849. p. 36. and cf. *The Choctaw Instructor*. Utica, 1831.

TSALAGI (CHIROKI).

ẹ	-	*gw*	-	*h*	-	
a	*k*	*g*	-	-	*y*	
e o	*t*	*d*	*n*	*s*	*l*	
i u	-	*ds*	-	-	-	
	tl	*dl*	-	-	-	
	-	-	*m*	-	*w*	

hn nah

Ꭰ *a*	Ꭱ *e*	Ꭲ *i*	Ꭳ *o*	Ꭴ *u*	Ꭵ *ę*
Ꮖ *gwa*	Ꮗ *gwe*	Ꮘ *gwi*	Ꮙ *gwo*	Ꮚ *gwu*	Ꮛ *gwę*
Ꭽ *ha*	Ꭾ *he*	Ꭿ *hi*	Ꮀ *ho*	Ꮁ *hu*	Ꮂ *hę*
Ꭷ *ka*	- -	- -	- -	- -	- -
Ꭶ *ga*	Ꭸ *ge*	Ꭹ *gi*	Ꭺ *go*	Ꭻ *gu*	Ꭼ *gę*
Ꮿ *ya*	Ᏸ *ye*	Ᏹ *yi*	Ᏺ *yo*	Ᏻ *yu*	Ᏼ *yę*
Ꮤ *ta*	Ꮦ *te*	Ꮨ *ti*	- -	- -	- -
Ꮣ *da*	Ꮥ *de*	Ꮧ *di*	Ꮩ *do*	Ꮪ *du*	Ꮫ *dę*
Ꮎ *na*	Ꮑ *ne*	Ꮒ *ni*	Ꮓ *no*	Ꮔ *nu*	Ꮕ *nę*
Ꮜ *sa*	Ꮞ *se*	Ꮟ *si*	Ꮠ *so*	Ꮡ *su*	Ꮢ *sę*
Ꮃ *la*	Ꮄ *le*	Ꮅ *li*	Ꮆ *lo*	Ꮇ *lu*	Ꮈ *lę*
Ꮳ *dsa*	Ꮴ *dse*	Ꮵ *dsi*	Ꮶ *dso*	Ꮷ *dsu*	Ꮸ *dsę*
Ꮭ *tla*	- -	- -	- -	- -	- -
Ꮬ *dla*	Ꮮ *dle*	Ꮯ *dli*	Ꮰ *dlo*	Ꮱ *dlu*	Ꮲ *dlę*
Ꮉ *ma*	Ꮊ *me*	Ꮋ *mi*	Ꮌ *mo*	Ꮍ *mu*	- -
Ꮹ *wa*	Ꮺ *we*	Ꮻ *wi*	Ꮼ *wo*	Ꮽ *wu*	Ꮾ *wę*
	Ꮏ *hna*	Ꮐ *nah*	Ꮝ *s*		

Specimen.

Ogidoda galęladi hehi, galęgwodiyu gesesdi dedsadoęi. Dsagęwiyuhi gesę wigananugoi. Ani elohi widsigalisda hadanętesgęi, nasgiya galęladi dsinigalisdiha. Nidadodagwisę ogalisdayędi sgięsi gohi iga. Digesgięsigwono desgidugęi, nasgiya dsidigayódsineho dsodsidugi. Ale dlesdi udagoliyediyi widisgiyatinęstanęgi sgiyudalesgesdigwosgini uyo gesęi. Dsadseligayeno dsagęwiyuhigesęi, dsalinigidi ale gesęi, edsalęgwodiyu ale gesę nigohilęi. Amen.

The Lord's prayer.

Remarks.

The *Chiroki* or, as they pronounce themselves, *Tsalagi* are known by the remarkable fact, that they alone of the Indian tribes use in writing and printing vernacular characters, invented about 1823 by a Chiroki man called *Segwoya* or with his English name *George Guest.* The history of this extraordinary invention, will be found, after an authentic relation in a Chiroki newspaper, in the Notes to the treatise of John Pickering on the Indian languages of America, translated into German by the learned Mrs. Th. Robinson (Talvj). It is interesting to observe, that the inventor, who could not read nor speak any other language except his own, did not proceed to the separation of vowels and consonants, but set up a syllabarium of 85 characters, uniting 15 consonantal sounds with six different vowels and giving besides a peculiar sign to every pure vowel. He omitted those combinations, which he did not actually meet in his language, and he added a character for the syllable *nah* (= *nâ*?), probably because this syllable constitutes the only monosyllable Chiroki word (except some interjections), a second one for the syllable *hna*, perhaps because the aspirated *n* seems to be the only aspirated consonant which occurs in the beginning of words, and a third for the simple vowelless *s*, which precedes several other consonants, for ex. *st*, *sd*, *sk*, *sg*, *sgw*. The sixth vowel (*ę*) has been described as a nasalized English *u* of *but.* It seems not impossible that it may resemble the hard *į* of the Chinese and the Tatarian languages, which would easily be decided by a Russian linguist. We should propose in this case to render it likewise by *į* instead of *ę*. As to the consonants, we are of the opinion, that the *Tsalagi* language has no true sonant *Mediae*, but that our second row contains the real dry *Tenues*, which we ought to write *kw*, *k*, *t*, *ts*, *tl*, and the first row the aspirates *k'*, *t'*, *t'l*. We conform however to the already received orthography, whose deviation from the true pronunciation is all the less important, because no third row has been developped in the *Tsalagi* system. J. D. Wofford in his *American Sunday School Spelling book, translated into the Cherokee language*, New York,

1824. represents all the rows of vowel combinations, also those with *k*, *t*, *tl*, *m*, as cömplete, and adds even several consonantal sounds which by *Segwoya* were not distinguished; for he gives besides *l*, *tl* and *dl* a second *l*, rendered by *'l*, which he compares with the Welsh *ll*, our *l̄*, and which occurs also in the combinations *tl̄* and *dl̄*. Moreover, he uses an aspiration expressed by ʾ before vowels and almost all the consonants (*ʾq*, *ʾgw*, *ʾk*, *ʾg*, *ʾy*, *ʾds*, *ʾt*, *ʾd*, *ʾn*, *ʾs*, (*ʾl*))—except only the labials *m* and *w*—and distinguishes *ʿy* from *hy*. In a single sheet in 4°, containing the *Cherokee Alphabet*, we find the remark, that "in some words *g*, *l*, *n*, *d*, *w* and *y* are aspirated, as if preceded by *h*." We render in our specimen this aspiration provisionally by ʿ. With regard to the vowels, he writes v for the English *u* of *thus*, and *v* for the same vowel nasalized. He employs also occasionally two accents placed over the vowels, *á*, *é*, *í*, (*ó*), *ú* and *à*, *è*, (*ì*), *ò*, *ù*, without, however, any explication. He also gives, besides the consonantal combinations with *s*, several others in his texts, as *kl*, *hy*, *wh*, *nt*, *nd*, *ntl*, *nn*, and we are at a loss to know, how such vowelless consonants might be expressed in the Chiroki writing. It seems, that Segwoya did not provide at all for those cases, but that at present the diacritical sign :— is prefixed before such consonants which have lost their vowel-sound. This is at least the case in the *Cherokee Hymns*, *compiled from several authors*, 8th ed. Park Hill, Mission Press, 1848, as we see from a note added to p. 2 of those Hymns, as well as in *The Gospel acc. to Matthew*, *translated into the Cherokee language*. 5th ed. Park Hill 1850, from which we have taken the Specimen. Chiroki scholars will in these respects complete our transcription.

DAKÓTA.

a	-	’	-	-	*h*	-		
e o	*k*	*g*	*k̠*	-	*χ*	*γ*		
i u	*tš*	-	*t̠š*	-	*š*	*ž*	*y*	
ã ẽ ĩ õ ũ	*t*	*d*	*t̠*	*n*	*s*	*z*	(*l*)	
	p	*b*	*p̠*	*m*	-	-	*w*	

Specimen.

Witšašta wã tšihĩtku nõpa: ũkã hakakta kĩ he atkúku kĩ hetšiya: Até, wóyuha mitáwa kte tši he mitšúwo, eya. Ũkã wóyuha kĩ yuákipam witšáku. Ũkã iyóhakam ãpétu tónana, tšihĩtku hakakta k̠õ he owási wítaya tpahí, k̠a ítehãyã makótše wã ekta ítšimani ya; k̠a hen šiχã́ oχã́yãpi kĩ õ, táku yuhé tšĩ owásĩ hdutákunišni. Ev. Luc. 15, 11 – 13.

Remarks.

The distinction of long and short vowels is not clearly fixed. The sound of ’ in *s’a*, *p’a*, *bot’õ*, *kap’ĩ*, *kaš’ĩ*, etc. is that of the Arabic *hamza*. Of the sounds, which we write *k̠*, *t̠š*, *t̠*, *p̠*, the Rev. S. R. Riggs, Missionary of the American Board, says in his *Grammar and Dictionary of the Dakota language*, Washington, 1852, that they are pronounced "with a strong pressure of the organs, followed by a sudden expulsion of the breath." Others call this pressure a sort of aspiration. We believe that the pronunciation of these sounds is the same as that of the corresponding *Khetšua* sounds, and write them accordingly (see below). The assibilated palatals *tš* and *t̠š* seem to be mostly derived from gutturals. The letter *l* occurs regularly only in the *Títôwã* dialect, replacing *d* or *n* of the other dialects. Mr. Riggs uses *aŋ*, *eŋ*, etc., *ć*, *ḳ*, *ć̣*, *ṭ*, *p̣*, *ḣ*, *ġ*, *ś*, *ź* instead of our *ã*, *ẽ*, etc., *tš*, *k̠*, *t̠š*, *t̠*, *p̠*, *χ*, *γ*, *š*, *ž*.

OTOMI.

ę				*h*		
a ā	*k*	*g*	*ṅ*	*χ*		
ę e o	*tš*	-	*ny*	-		*y*
ı į u	*t*	*d*	*n*	*s*	*z*	*r*
ã ẽ ĩ õ ũ	*p*	*b*	*m*	*f*	-	

Remarks.

See *Grammatica della lingua Otomi* dal conte V. Piccolomini. Roma. 1841.

KHETŠUA (QQUICHUA, PERUVIAN).

a	*k*	*kh*	*k̲*	-	*h*	*h̲*	-	
e o	*tš*	*tšh*	-	*ny*	*ś*	-	*ly*	
i į u	*t*	*th*	*t̲*	*n*	*s*	*s̲*	(*l*)	*r*
	p	*ph*	*p̲*	*m*	-	-	-	

Specimen.

Tšaįpatšapi Jesus yatšatšiskankunamanmi nyirkan: unantšakuna intipi, khilyapipas k̲oįlyurkunapipas kankam; runakunari kaįpatšapi mamak̲otšap tšaunyiįnyinpa pokhtšik̲enkunap kumnyiįnyinpas mantšaįnyinhuan lyakhirayankam. Runakuna tukuį tekkimuįup hahuaman h̲amuk̲unap mantšaįnyinhuan suįaįnyinhuanpas tšakhikuptinku. Tšek̲apunim hanak phatšakunap tekkinkuna kuįukunka. Tšaįpatšapiri hatum atipaįnyinhuan, apukaįnyinhuanpas phuhuįupi hamukhta v i r g e n p a *huahuanta rik̲unkam.* Ev. Luc. 21, 25—27.

Remarks.

The following letters: *i̧*; *k*, *kh*, *k̲*, *h̲*; *tš*, *tšh*, *ny*, *ś*, *ly*; *th*, *t̲*, *s*, *s̲*; *ph*, *p̲*, of our transcription are rendered by Gonçalez Holguin in his *Vocabulario de la lengua Qquichua*, Reyes, 1608, and by Torres Rubio in his *Arte y Vocabulario de la lengua Quichua*, Lima, 1754, *y*; *c* (before *a*, *o*, *u*, *i̧*) or *qu* (before *e*, *i*), *k* (*a*, *o*, *u*, *i̧*) or *qqu* (*e*, *i*), *cc* or *kc*, *h*; *ch*, *chh*, *ñ*, *s*, *ƚƚ*; *th* or *tt*, *tt*, *ç* (*a*, *o*, *u*) or *c* (*e*, *i*) or *z* (before consonants), *ſs*; *p* or *pp*, *pp*; by J. von Tschudi, *Die Kechua-Sprache*, Wien, 1853: *y*, *c* or *k*, *k* or *k̓*, *c̓* or *k̓*, *k̓*; *cȟ*, *cȟ*, *ñ*, *s̓*, *ƚƚ*; *t̓* *t̄*, *s*, *s̗*; *p̓*, *p*. The letters *k̲*, *t̲*, *p̲*, *h̲*, *s̲* are pronounced with a peculiar contraction of the throat, which we can only compare with the guttural emphasis of the Semitic linguals, and which we render accordingly by the same line underneath. The letter, which we write *ś* seems to be more a sharp aspirated *s*, than a full *š*, which latter, however, is substituted in some districts. We are not sure as to the exact pronunciation of the letter written *y* by former grammarians and rendered by us *i̧*; it seems to be always combined with other vowels.

KIRIRI.

		a				*k*	*g*	-	*h*					
e	*e̜*		*o*	*o̜*		*ts*	*dz*	*ny*	*š*	*ž*		*y*	*ly*	
	ẹ			*ọ*		*t*	*d*	*n*	*s*	*z*		*r*		
i		*i̧*		*u*		*p*	*b*	*m*	-	-		*w*		
ā *ē* etc.														

Remarks.

P. Mamiani in his *Kiriri-Grammar*, *translated from the Portugese into German* by H. C. von der Gabelentz (Leipzig. 1852), writes *æ*, *ê*, *â*, *ô*, *ŷ*, *tç*, *hn*, *ch*, *j*, *hl*, instead of our *e̱*, *ẹ*, *o̱*, *ọ*, *į̇*, *ts*, *ny*, *š*, *ž*. *ly*. The vowel *ŷ* = *į̇*, is called by the Brasilian Grammarians the "thick *i*" and is said to be pronounced with a guttural sound. We have rendered it by the Tataric and Chinese *į̇*, to which it seems to approach, as in the preceding languages.

The *General Table of Languages*, which we exhibit hereafter, is added for the convenience of the reader. It rests entirely upon the responsibility of the author of the pamphlet and claims no other authority; the affiliation and interdependence of the dialects of mankind being too wide a question to be allowed to interfere with the practical object, which, especially in its Missionary bearing, the Standard Alphabet has in view. It will hardly be necessary to state expressly, that the names, *Japhetic*, *Semitic*, and *Hamitic*, do not imply the independent origin of those languages, which are not classified under them, but which cannot yet be identified with these three branches. We use them merely as conventional and convenient terms, following in this respect, and carrying out, the general linguistic use, which has long existed with regard to the *Semitic* languages. As to the details of our survey, we pretend by no means to completeness or perfection in all parts; we have used, however, the best authorities and examined the latest researches on the different groups of languages, as far as we had access to them.

GENERAL TABLE OF LANGUAGES.

The languages reduced to the Standard Alphabet are marked by an asterisk.

LITERARY LANGUAGES.

A. GENDER LANGUAGES.

I. Japhetic (Indogermanic) languages.

A. Sanscritic (Arian).

I. Old Indian languages.
1. *Vedic.*
2. **Sanskrit.*
3. **Pāli.*
4. **Old Prākrit.*

II. New Indian languages.
a. General dialects.
1. **Hindī.*
2. **Hindūstānī.*
b. Local dialects.
1. **Sindhī.*
2. **Guǰarātī.*
3. *Marāṭhī.*
4. *Kaśmīrī.*
5. **Panǰābī* or *Sikh.*
6. **Nipālī.*
7. **Bangālī.*
8. *Assam.*
9. **Urīya.*

B. *Paśtō or Afγān.

C. Eranian.

I. *Old Baktrian (Zend).

II. Persian.
1. **Old Persian (Cuneiform).*
2. *Pehlevī.*
a. *Huzvāreś (Pehlevi).*
b. *Pārsi (Pazend).*
3. **New Persian.*

III. *Armenian.

IV. *Kurdo-Luric or Lekī.
1. *Kurd.*
a. *Kurmánǰi.*
b. *Zazá.*
2. *Beluči.*

V. *Ossetian.

D. Lituanian (Lettic).
1. *Old Prussian.*
2. **Lituanian,*
a. *High Lituanian.*
b. *Low Lituanian* or *Żemaitis.*
3. *Lettic.*

E. Slavonic.

I. South-eastern branch (Kyrillian letters).

1. *Sloveno-Bulgarian.*
   a. **Old Slovenian (Church Slavonic).*
   b. *New Slovenian (Windic).*
   c. *Bulgarian.*
2. **Serbian (Illiric), Kroatic (Khorvatic).*
3. **Russian.*
   a. *Great-Russian.*
   b. *Small-Russian.*

II. Western branch (Roman letters).

1. **Cheskian (Bohemian), Slovakian.*
2. **Polish, Polabic.*
3. **Sorbian (Wendic, Lusatian).*
   a. *High-Lusatian.*
   b. *Low-Lusatian.*

F. Greek.

1. *Old Greek.*
2. *New Greek.*

G. Italic.

1. *Umbrian.*
2. *Oskan.*
3. *Latin.*
   a. *Old Roman.*
   b. *Romance languages.*
      a. *Italian.*
      b. *Spanish.*
      c. *Portugese.*
      d. *Provencial.*
      e. *French.*
      f. *Grison (Rheto-Romance).*
      g. **Rumanian (Wallachian).*
         α. *Northern* or *Dako-Rumanian.*
         β. *Southern* or *Macedo-Rumanian.*
4. *Etruscan.*

H. Germanic.

1. *Gothic.*
2. *High-German: Old, Middle, New.*
3. *Low-German: Old-Saxon, Middle-Low-, New-Low-German.*
4. *Netherlandic: Middle-Netherlandic, Dutch.*
5. *Frisic.*
6. *Anglo-Saxon.*
7. *English.*
8. *Scandinavian.*
   a. *Icelandic.*
      a. **Old Icelandic.*
      b. *New Icelandic.*
   b. *Swedish.*
   c. *Danish, Norwegian.*

J. Celtic.
1. *Welsh (Breton).*
a. **Kimri (Cymric).*
b. *Cornish.*
c. *Armorican (Bas Breton).*
2. *Gaelic.*
a. *Scotch (Gaelic).*
b. *Irish (Ers).*
c. *Manks.*

II. Semitic languages.

A. Northern Semitic languages.
1. **Hebrew.*
2. *Kanaanitic, Phœnician, Punic.*
3. *Aramean.*
a. **Syrian.*
b. *Chaldee.*
c. *Samaritan, Palmyric.*
d. *Mandean* or *Sabean.*
4. *Assyrian.*

B. Southern Semitic languages.
1. **Arabic.*
2. *Sinaitic.*
3. *Himyaritic, Ehkili.*
4. *Abyssinian (Ethiopian).*
a. ** Old Abyssinian (Gęʾęz).*
b. *Tigre.*
c. **Amharic.*

III. Hamitic languages.

A. Egyptian.
1. **Old Egyptian (Hieroglyphic).*
2. **Coptic.*

B. Ethiopian.
1. **Beǰa (Bišāri).*
2. *Dankāli.*
3. *Harrar.*
4. *Somāli.*
5. **Orma (Galla).*

C. Libyan.
1. **Ta-Māšeq (Māšiγ, Tuaric).*
2. **Haúsa.*

D. Hottentot.
1. *Hottentot.*
a. **Nama (Namaqua).*
b. *Kora.*
2. *Bushman.*

B. NO-GENDER LANGUAGES.

I. Asiatic languages.

A. Tataric (Ural-Altaic, Tataro-Finnic, Scythian, Turanian).

I. Tungusian.
1. **Manǰu.*
2. *Lamutic.*
3. *Čapogiric.*

4. *Orotongian.*
etc.

II. Mongolian.
1. **Sharra-Mongolian (eastern Mong.).*
2. *Kalmuk (western Mongolian).*
3. **Buryetic (northern Mongolian).*

III. Turkish.
1. **Yakutic.*
2. **Osmanlian (Turkish).*
3. *Nogairic, Kumuk.*
4. *J̌akataic.*
   a. *Uiguric.*
   b. *Usbek.*
   c. **Turkmenian.*
5. *Kirgisian.*
   a. *Eastern Kirgisian (Kirgiz).*
   b. *Western Kirgisian (Kazak).*
6. *Čuwašic.*
7. *Barabinzic, Teleutic, Sayanic.*

IV. *Samoyedic.
1. *Yurak-Samoyedic.*
2. *Tawgi-Samoyedic.*
3. *Ostyak-Samoyedic.*
4. *Yenissei-Samoyedic.*
5. *Kamassic.*

V. Finnic (Chudic, Uralic).
1. *Ugric.*
   a. *Ostyak.*
   b. *Wogulic.*
   c. **Madyaric (Magyaric, Hungarian).*
2. *Permian.*
   a. *Siryenian (Permian).*
   b. *Wotyak.*
3. *Wolgaic (Chudic).*
   a. *Čeremissian.*
   b. **Mordvinian.*
      α. *Erse.*
      β. *Mokša.*
4. *Western Finnic.*
   a. *Lapponese.*
   b. *Finlandic.*
      α. *Yemian.*
         1. *Western Finlandic.*
         2. *Wepsic.*
         3. *Wotic.*
         4. *Esthonian.*
         5. **Livonian.*
      β. *Karelian.*

VI. Dravidian languages.
1. **Tamiḷ (Tamulian).*
2. **Malayāḷam.*
3. **Tuḷu.*
4. **Karnātaka (Kanarese).*
5. **Telugu (Telinga).*
6. *Gōnd.*
7. *Tuda.*

8. *Kōta.*
9. *Ku (Kund).*

B. Monosyllabic languages.

I. Chinese.
1. **Kwan-hwa* or *Mandarinic.*
   a. *Dial. of Peking.*
   b. *Dial. of Nanking.*
2. *Fu-kyan.*
   a. *Dial. of Čaṅ-čeu.*
   b. **Hok-lo.*
3. *Kwaṅ-tuṅ (Canton).*
   a. *Pun-ti (Pen).*
   b. **Hak-ka.*
   c. *Sin-hwai.*

II. Annam.
III. *Thai (Siamese).
IV. *Kamboja.
V. *Mranma (Burmese).

C. Isolated languages.
1. **Yukagiric.*
2. **Čaučau (Chukchik), Koryak.*
3. *Kamchatka.*
4. **Japanese.*
5. *Korean.*
6. **Tibetan.*
7. *Caucasian languages.*
   a. *Georgian (Grusinian), Lazian* and *Mingrelian, Gurian, Suanian.*
   b. *Lesgian, Aware.*
   c. **Tuš, Kistian (Mizje-gian).*
   d. *Čerkessian, Abhasian.*
8. *Lycian.*

In Europe:
9. **Albanian.*
10. *Basque.*

II. Polynesian or Malayan (Oceanic) languages.

A. Western Branch.
1. *Sumatra* and *Malakka.*
   a. **Malay.*
   b. **Batak.*
   c. *Ačin, Rejan, Lampun, Mantawei, (Poggi), Nian, Maruwin.*
2. **Javanese.*
   a. *Kawi* or *Old Javanese.*
   b. *New Javanese: Bhasa-krama, Nyoko, Madliya.*
3. *Borneo.*
   a. **Dayak*, etc.
4. *Sumbava, Timor.*
5. *Celébes.*
   a. **Makassar (Mangkassara).*
   b. **Bugis (Wugi).*
6. *Moluccas Islands.*

7. *Philippine Islands: Tagala.*
8. *Formosa (Taiwan).*
9. *Marianne Islands.*
10. *Caroline Islands.*

B. Eastern Branch.
1. **New Zealand.*
2. *Friendly Islands.*
3. *Navigator's (Samoa) Islands.*
4. *Union Islands: Fakaafo.*
5. **Hervey Islands: Raro-Toṅga.*
6. **Gambier's Islands.*
7. **Society Islands: Tahiti.*
8. *Paumotu Islands.*
9. **Marquesas Islands: Nukahiwa.*
10. **Sandwich Islands: Hawaiyi.*

C. Madagaskar: Malagasse.

ILLITERATE LANGUAGES.

III. Australian or Papuan languages (Negrito, Melanesian).

A. Australian.
1. *Southwest. languages.*
2. *Parnkalla.*
3. **Adelaide.*
4. *Murray river.*
5. *Encounter bay.*
6. *Victoria.*
7. *Tasmania Island.*
8. *Eastern languages.*
9. *Northern languages.*

B. Melanesian (Papuan).
1. *New Guinea.*
2. *New Ireland.*
3. *New Britannia.*
4. *Louisiade.*
5. *Solomon Islands: Bauro, Guadalkanar.*
6. *New Hebrides:* **Annatom, Tana.*
7. *New Caledonia.*
8. *Loyalty Islands:* **Mare, Nengore, Doka, Lifu.*
9. **Viti (Fiji) Islands.*

IV. African languages.

A. Original or South African languages.
1. *Zanzibar.*
   a. **Sudheli (Ki-Suaheli).*
   b. *Nika.*
   c. *Kamba.*

d. Pokōmo.
e. Hinzuan.
2. *Mosambique.*
*a. *Makúa.*
b. Tette.
c. Sena.
3. *Tegeza.*
4. **Tšuāna (Se-chuana).*
a. Suto (Ba-Suto).
b. Roloṅ.
c. Hlapi.
5. *Kafir.*
*a. *Zulu.*
b. ǁOsa (Ma-ǁOsa).
6. *Bunda.*
*a. *Hereró.*
b. Ṅgola (Angóla).
c. Beṅguela.
d. Londa.
7. *Koṅgo.*
a. Koṅgo.
b. Kokoṅgo.
c. Mpoṅgwe.
8. *Biafra gulf.*
a. Kele (Di-kele).
b. Beṅga.
c. Dualla.
d. Isubu.
*e. *Fernando Po.*
9. *Niger-Delta.*
a. Effik.
*b. *Ibo.*
*c. *Yórūba.*
d. Nupe.
10. *Slave coast.*
a. Ewe (Ife).
b. Maχi.
c. Dāhume.
d. Ẃeta.
e. Aṅfue.
f. Aṅlo (Aoṅgla).
11. *Gold coast.*
a. Fanti.
b. Ašanti.
*c. *Akra* or *Gã.*
*d. *Tyi (Otyi)* or *Akwapim.*
12. *Windward coast.*
a. Grebo.
b. Kruh.
c. Basa.
13. *Sierra Leone.*
a. Bullom.
b. Šerbro.
*c. *Timne.*

B. Isolated languages in Middle Africa.

1. *Gōr.*
*a. *Wolof.*
*b. *Fula.*
2. *Mande.*
*a. *Vei.*
*b. *Susu.*
*c. *Mandiṅga.*
3. *Tebu (Teda).*
4. **Bornu: Kánūri.*
5. **Dar Fūr: Koṅgāra.*

6. **Nuba*.
7. *Umále* (*Tumale*).

IV. American languages.

A. North-American languages.
1. *Karalian.*
   a. **Greenlandic.*
   b. *Eskimo* (*Labrador*).
   c. *Eskimo-Chukchic.*
2. *Kološ.*
3. *Athapaskan.*
4. *Delaware* (*Lenape*, *Algonkin*).
   a. *Kri.*
   b. *Ottawa.*
   c. *Chippeway* (*Ojibway*).
   d. *Pottawatomi.*
   e. *Mikmak.*
   f. *Abenakwi.*
   g. **Massatšusct.*
   h. *Mohegan.*
   i. *Delaware.*
   k. *Šawani.*
5. **Irokwois.*
6. *Florida.*
   a. **Muskogi* or *Krik.*
   b. **Tšahta* (*Chocktaw*).
   c. **Tširoki* (*Chirokese*).
7. *Sioux* (*Nadowessi*).
   a. **Dakóta.*
   b. *Kansa.*
   c. *Iowa.*
8. *Pani.*
9. *Arrapahu.*
10. *Komantše* (*Paduka*).
11. *Kalifornian.*

B. Middle-American languages.
1. *Astek* or *Mexican.*
2. *Tolteka.*
3. *Miksteka.*
4. *Zapotcka.*
5. *Taraska.*
6. *Apatše.*
7. **Otomi.*
8. *Maya*, *Pokontši.*
9. *Moskito.*

C. South-American languages.
1. *Moska* (*Chibcha*).
2. *Guarani* (*Carib*).
3. *Tupi* (*Brasilian*).
4. *Botokudian* (*Engerekmung*, *Aimbore*).
5. **Kiriri.*
6. **Khetšua* (*Kechua*, *Peruvian*).
7. *Aimara.*
8. *Guaikur.*
9. *Araukana* (*Moluche*).
10. *Pueltše* (*Pampa*).
11. *Tehuel* (*Patagonian*).

POSTSCRIPT.

The publication of these sheets has been delayed longer than we expected, on account of the increased number of alphabets, from all classes of languages, which had to be reduced to our standard. We hope that this delay will only have been in the interest of the present work, as we have already explained above (p. 19), why we considered it necessary to devote particular care to this Second Part of our pamphlet. We met with great difficulties especially among those languages, which possess from ancient times a native alphabet and a national literature; and yet these are just the most important, as well for Missionaries as for Linguists.

We have now still to complete the list of publications given above (p. 2 sqq.), in which the Standard Alphabet has been adopted. As far as we are acquainted with them, they are the following:

Joh. Andr. Sjögren's *Livische Grammatik nebst Sprachproben, im Auftrage der Kaiserlichen Akademie der Wissenschaften bearbeitet* von Ferd. Joh. Wiedemann, St. Petersburg, 1861. 2 vol. in 4°.

Aug. Ahlqnist, *Versuch einer Mokscha-Mordwinischen Grammatik nebst Texten und Wörterverzeichniss*, St. Petersburg, 1861. 8°.

The same author has published a *Wotic Grammar* in the *Acta Societatis scientiarum Fennicae*, tom. V.

C. F. Schlenker (Church Miss.), *Collection of Temne Traditions, Fables and Proverbs.* 1861.

H. Hahn (Rhen. Miss.), *Omahungi nomambo omatororoa Uomambo oa Mukuru uetestamente ekuru nepe pura oviprente ovingi*, Gütersloh, 1861.

The same: *Omahongise uokoleza Motyi-herero.* 1861.

R. Lepsius, *Ueber die Arabischen Sprachlaute und deren Umschrift, und über den harten ị Vocal.* (Abhandl. der Berliner Academie, 1861.)

J. F. Schön (Church M. Soc.), *Grammar of the Hausa language*, London, 1862.

H. Barth, *Collection of Vocabularies of Central-African languages*, 1st Part, 1862. of the *Kanuri*, *Teda*, *Hausa*, *Fulfulde*, *Soṅγai*, *Lógonē*, *Wándala*, *Bágrimma*, and *Māba*-languages.

Dr. Fr. Müller, *Beiträge zur Lautlehre der Neupersischen Sprache*, Wien, 1862. (from the *Sitzungsberichte der Phil. Hist. Classe der Kaiserl. Akad. d. Wiss.*, vol. XXXIX.)

The same, *Ueber die Sprache der Avghânen (Paχto).* Wien, 1862. (Vol. XL.); IId Part, 1863. (Vol. XLII.)

Dr. W. Bleek, *A Comparative Grammar of South African languages* Part I. London. 1862.

The Standard Alphabet has also been introduced in the great Map in four parts of the Austrian Empire with its manyfold countries of different languages, edited by Artaria in Vienna, 1862; and Prof. Augustus Petermann in Gotha writes to us, that he has the same intention for his own future Maps.

We have also the satisfaction to refer to a detailed review and recommendation of the Standard Alphabet by Prof. William D. Whitney, the eminent Sanskrit scholar, in New Haven, Yale College: *On Lepsius's Standard Alphabet* (from the Journal of the American Oriental Society, Vol. VII. 1862). Some of the deficiencies, which he points out in the first Edition, had been already removed in the present Edition, before his pamphlet reached us.

Dr. Fr. Müller, *Zend-Studien*, Wien, 1863. (*Sitzungsberichte* etc. Vol. XL.)

The same, *Beiträge zur Lautlehre der Armenischen Sprache*, Wien, 1863. (Vol. XLI.)

The same, *Beiträge zur Lautlehre des Ossetischen.* Wien, 1863. (Vol. XLI.)

R. Lepsius, *Das ursprüngliche Zendalphabet*, Berlin, 1863. 4°. (*Abhandl. d. Akad.* 1862.)

The same, *Ueber das Lautsystem der Persischen Keilschrift*, Berlin, 1863. 4°. (*Abh.* 1862.)

In order to inform the reader as to the more or less reliable means, which were at the disposal of the author, respecting the apprehension of the sounds of those living languages, which are discussed in the present pamphlet, the following remarks may here not be out of place. The author has had the opportunity of learning directly from intelligent natives the pronunciation of the *Armenian, Serbian, Russian, Cheskian* (*Bohemian*), *Polish, Rumanian* (*Wallachian*), *Hebrew, Arabic, Coptic, Beja* (*Bišari*), *Galla, Turkish, Madyaric, Japanese, Zulu-Kafir, Kongara* (*Dar-Fur*), *Nuba;* he conversed orally with the following learned gentlemen, who had long resided in the respective countries and were practically acquainted with their languages: on most of the *Sanskritic* languages, spoken actually in India, with the Rev. Dr. Trumpp (see above p. 19); on the *Pašto* or *Afγān* with the same, whose last Indian residence was for several years Peshawer, where he mastered this language completely; on the modern *Persian, Ossetian, Turkish, Georgian* with the Prussian Consul at Jerusalem Dr. G. Rosen, late interpreter at the Prussian Embassy in Constantinople, and author of grammatical Sketches on the Georgian and the Ossetian languages, which he studied in their respective countries; on the *Slavonic* languages with Prof. Miklosich in Vienna; on the *Rumanian* with the highly accomplished Princes Al. and Matth. Stourdza, as well as with Mr. Campianu, the learned author of a

Rumanian Grammar; on the *Welsh* or *Kimri* with one of the best Welsh scholars, Karl Meyer, in Berlin itself; on the *Amharic* with the Rev. C. W. Isenberg, Church Missionary in Bombay; on the *Haúsa* and *Ibo* with the Rev. J. F. Schön, formerly Church Missionary at Sierra Leone, now in England; on the *Mordvinian* with Dr. Ahlquist in Helsingfors; on the different *Chinese* dialects, especially the *Mandarinic*, *Hok-lo*, and *Hak-ka*, with the Revs. J. Gough and T. M'Clatchie, late Church Missionaries in China, as well as with the Rev. Lechler, Basle Missionary, who resided eleven years first in *Tšau-tšeu*, afterwards in *Hoṅ-koṅ*, and the Rev. A. Krone, Rhenish Missionary in China; on the *Thai* or *Siamese* with Mr. Th. von Bunsen, of the Prussian East-Asiatic Expedition, who was kind enough to inquire into this hitherto most obscure language expressly according to our views and at our request; on the *Yukagiric* and *Tuš* with Prof. Schiefner of Petersburg; on the *Albanian* with J. G. von Hahn, the learned editor of the Albanian Researches, the Austrian Consul at Syra, who formerly resided several years in Albania; on the *Makassar* and *Bugis* with Dr. B. F. Matthes, Agent of the Amsterdam Bible Society in Makassar; on the *Makúa* (Mosambique) with Prof. Peters in Berlin, who resided five years in Mosambique; on the *Hereró* with the Rev. H. Hahn, Rhenish Missionary among the Herero; on the *Vei* and *Kánuri* (Bornu) with the Rev. S. W. Kölle, Church Missionary; on the *Fūl* with the Rev. C. L. Reichardt, Church Missionary at Sierra Leone. The author has also been in literary communication on the sounds of the *Kurd* and the *Kazak* or *Kirghiz* with Mr. Peter Lerch; on the *Tamiḷ* with the late Rev. L. B. E. Schmid formerly connected with the Church Miss. Soc. in South India, and for many years resident in Ottacamund; on the *Tibetan* with the Rev. H. A. Jäschke, Miss. of the United Brethren at *Kye-laṅ*; on the *Suáheli* with the Rev. Dr. Krapf, in Kornthal, late Church Missionary;

on the *Ewe* with the Rev. J. B. Schlegel, of the North German Miss. Soc. at Bremen, on the Slave Coast.

Lastly we have to mention that we have been most courteously seconded in our endeavours for exhibiting the Native Alphabets. Besides the types furnished to us by the Printing-office of the Berlin Academy or forwarded to us from Mr. G. M. Watts in London, whose private entreprise in this department must not be overlooked; we have been enabled to make use of the types of Mr. Tettenrode in Amsterdam for the *Battak*, *Mandailing*, *Makassar* and *Bugis* languages. Dr. Land, Secretary to the Netherland Bible Society at Amsterdam, was kind enough to send them to us, accompanied by his explanations. We owe to the Rev. Dan Beach Bradley of the Amer. Miss. Assoc., the *Siamese* types, which he had the kindness to send to us through Mr. de Bunsen. But most of all we have to thank Mr. Alois Auer, Director of the Imperial Printing-office at Vienna, for the praiseworthy liberality, with which he has placed the excellent Collection of foreign types, the result of his intelligent labours since many years, at our disposal. We are obliged to him for the types of the *Pālī*, *Gujarātī*, *Panǰābī*, *Bangālī*, *Urīya*, *Old Slovenian*, *Cyrillian*, *Gẹ̄ẹz*, *Amharic*, *Māšeq*, *Manǰu*, *Mongolian*, *Kamboǰa*, *Burmese*, *Japanese*, *Javanese*, and *Chiroki*.

In the course of the printing, arduous and full of interruptions as it was, several mistakes and misprints have happened, which we will partly rectify here.

P. 1, lin. 18, read: uncontroverted. P. 3, 14: *anrūbútaši*. P. 6, 15: Estnischen; l. 18: Helsingfors. P. 7, last line, expunge: (See—Alphabet). P. 8, 22: cf. p. 71. P. 17, 3: come. P. 26, 12: entirely; l. 13: characterises. P. 27, 19: the *Vei* and the *Bornu*. P. 30, note: Essay. P. 32, 5: recommends. P. 35, 6: *appliquée*. P. 41, 8: *Suáheli*. P. 48, 28: as *ṇ̥*, *ṃ̥*. Expunge note 2. P. 52, 16: *ḁ̆ what, hot*; l. 21: *ŭ hood*. P. 54, note, l. 6:

Manju, Mongolian, Kalmuk. P. 55, 7: See also the *Livonian* p. 223. P. 58, 16 expunge: which—system *l*; l. 28: Slavonic *ł*. P. 59, 18: different. P. 66, 11: modern Greek *γ*, before *α*, *ο*, *ω*, *ου*, and the consonants (*γ* before *ε*, *η*, *ι* being pronounced *ý* = *y*). P. 68, 9 expunge: Sanskrit ष. P. 71, 7: Cf. p. 161; l. 24: Carey. P. 75, 11: see. P. 77, 2 expunge: *z* chin. mandar. *tsz*; l. 12 after (*yain*) add: mod. greek *ἀγαθός*: l. 23 add behind *w* engl. *we*: *w* germ. *Wind.* P. 80, not. 2, expunge: *We cannot* till *x*, and in the last line but one read: work (p. 4. 15. 34). P. 81, note, l. 5: the clicks *before* these letters. P. 82, note, l. 3: declare ourselves. P. 89, 1: into. P. 90, 10: all. P. 94, 8: nasalization; l. 15: We; l. 30: view of the ancient. P. 99, 4: wishes; l. 8: क्ष (*kš*) and ज्ञ (*ǵń*); l. 21: *yazāh* or يزه, *yazzwah*; last l. but one: *Kāyathī.* P. 107, 16: which is derived. P. 109, 4: *Bālbodh.* P. 114, 1: *Paštō.* P. 117 put ? ؟ behind سن ٺ; l. 9: Ligatures. P. 121, 9: C *ý*. P. 123, 24: Cf. p. 311. P. 124, 9: *ya,i,u*; l. 10: *ka,i,(u)* . *ra,i* *ru*; l. 11: *za,(i),u* . *wi*. P. 125, 3[d] l. from the end: *θatiya.* P. 127, 21: the Romance. P. 129, 12: Cf. p. 311. P. 131, 16: *θ*(*s*) *δ*(*z*). P. 136, Spec. l. 1. 2: *bē*, *šē*; l. 9: *e* *ē* | *o*. P. 138, 12: *k'* *ǵ* *k*. P. 143, 1: remarks; l. 15: the *a* and *e* .... are; l. 20: diphthongal, not dissyllabic. P. 144, 16: *ī* = *y* *i* *į* *į*. P. 149, 7 from below: bestows. P. 156, 17: weak. P. 157: Hard vowels: *a*, *o*, *u*, *į*. P. 160, 16: *ń* *ř* *ľ* *p'*. P. 161, 13, affix; l. 19: ancient and modern Asiatic languages. P. 165, 4th l. from below: *Ši a fost.* P. 168, 23: in use. P. 173, 8[t] l. from below: *š* *š*. P. 174, 21: *Wehâvâres*; 6th l. from below: *Wayya'aš.* P. 188, 3: *k'a*, *ga.* P. 189, 2: Himyaritic. P. 191 and 192, write *š* instead of *ś*. P. 198, 16: drops. P. 200, on the end: Matth. 2, 1. 2. P. 202: *ṭ* *ḍ* -. P. 203, 3: descendants. P. 204, 6: *ñ*; l. 15 expunge: *z*. P. 205: *Ta-Mâšeq* (*Mâšiy*). P. 206, 12: *Ta-Mâšeq*, *Ta-Mašeyt.* P. 209, 10: *e* *u* *i*; l. 11: Write (*i*) instead of (*u*), and likewise p. 210; after the Specimen add: Langlès, Alphabet Mantschou,

p. 158, sqq. P. 218, 12: *r ḽ ł*. P. 233, 1: *Yeu₁-thai*. P. 243, 15: it *ṡ*, if. P. 252, 4th L from below: The letters .... where ệ ị̂ is. P. 253. According to Prof. Schiefner's *Versuch über die Thusch-Sprache oder die Khistische Mundart in Thuschetien* in the *Mémoires de l'Acad. des Sc. de St. Pétersbourg*, VI. Sér. Sc. Polit. etc. T. IX, (in which he writes *k̓*, *t̓*, *p̓* instead of *kh*, *th*, *ph*) it seems that his *ć* and *c* belong to our third, *ḉ* and *ç* to our first column. P. 252, 6 f. b.: feeble; l. 1 f. b.: pronounceable. P. 255, 2d l. from below: *θ đ š ž*. P. 271, 5 f. b.: newly; l. 2 f. b.: feel. P. 275, 14: Clarke (Baptist Miss.). P. 276—278: *Yóruba* instead of *Yórūba*. P. 280, 3: blew. P. 288, 4; *Koṅgára*, and likewise l. 4 from below. P. 292, 3 from below: Miss. of the Amer. Board of Comm. P. 295, 23: of the Chinese, the Tatarian and Slavonic languages.

STANDARD ALPHABET, SECOND EDITION 1863.

SECOND POSTSCRIPT.

1) WITH regard to the **DRAVIDIAN (DRĀVIDA)** languages, treated above p. 224—231, we have had the advantage of consulting, soon after our work had left the press, the eminent Dravidian scholar, Dr. Gundert, the successor of the late lamented Dr. Barth at Calw. Dr. Gundert having mastered this branch of languages both practically and scientifically by a special and highly intelligent study of them amongst the indigenous races, during a many years residence as missionary in India, we consider it our duty to communicate in a second appendix to our readers the remarks and rectifications, which he has kindly communicated to us orally and in writing on these languages. He corrects and completes the list of the Dravidian languages in the following manner: *Tamıḻ, Malayāḷam, Tuḷu, Koḍaga, Karṇāṭaka, Telugu, Gōṇḍ, Tuḍa, Kōta, Koi (Kund), Brahui.*

In the **TAMIḺ** the vowel ஐ is nothing else than our diphthong *ei*, which sometimes is pronounced short (very much like *ĕ*) and treated thus in poetry. It represents at the same time also the Sanskrit *ai* and is then often written *ayi.* The diphthong *au* is also found in Tamil words, written ஔ; *avvei* may become *auvei.* The cerebral consonants cause a slight change of the preceding, not of the following vowel. The vowel *e* or *ē* is often pronounced in the beginning of words with a preceding *y.* In old Tamil writings the character ஃ occurs and is pronounced as a harsh *h*, which often is compared with the Sanskrit visarga. It may therefore be transcribed *ꞩ* as the visarga. The correct form for the guttural nasal *ṅ* is ங. The letter which we had proposed to transcribe *ṛ*, as others had done before us, is decidedly different from the Hindi *ṛ*, according to Dr. Gundert, though belonging to the cerebral row, and ought to be represented rather as a peculiar deviation from *ḻ*. In Malayālam the same character, which represents the final ḷ, serves also to express the Tamil ழ, for instance in the word *Tamil̤* itself, which in Malayālam is written with ḷ, in Tamil with the letter in question. We propose therefore to distinguish this new sound by a doubled cerebral point underneath, l̤. The pronunciation of the letter ற, in those cases where we had proposed to write $\underset{r}{ṭ}$ or $\underset{r}{ḍ}$, contains so little of the *r*-sound, that we now prefer, with Dr. Gundert, to give to these new sounds a new diacritical sign, preserving the necessary basis of *t* and *d*, and to write *t̀* and *d̀*. In those cases, however, where the same character is pronounced as a peculiar kind of harsh *r*, we write it *r̀*. The nasal letter of this row, *ǹ*, does not occur in the beginning, but only in the middle of words (not merely before *d̀*) or at the end, whilst *n* is only written in the beginning or before *d*. Though for consistency's sake we write *ǹ* differently from *n*, it will not be necessary in common writing to distinguish them; the less so as in the modern Malayalam alphabet the same letter is used for both sounds. The complete row is therefore *t̀*, *d̀*, *r̀*, *ǹ*.

Each of the six characters க ச ட ற த ப has three different pronunciations, except the third and sixth which have only two. They may be pronounced as surd explosives, as sonant explosives, or as fricatives of their respective classes, according to their position in the word. In the beginning of a word, they are pronounced: *k*, *s* (or *ś*), *ṭ*, *r̀*, *t*, *p*. In the middle of a word, if they are doubled, their sound is: *k*, *č*, *ṭ*, *t̀*, *t*, *p*; if not, they are pronounced after the corresponding nasals: *g*, *ǰ*, *ḍ*, *d̀*, *d*, *b*, between two vowels: *γ*, *s* (*ś*), *ḍ*, *r̀*, *δ*, *b*. Where *b* occurs between two vowels, it changes readily with *v*, which might be indicated by *β*. In Sanskrit words the sounds of initial *g*, *ǰ*, *d*, *b* are often preserved in opposition to the *Tamil̤* laws of change, or indicated by giving the inherent *a* an *e* sound, which is occasionally written. The Sanskrit *h* is omitted in Tamil or replaced by *γ*; Sanskr. *aham* = Tam. *aγam*. At the end of words only vowels or liquids or nasals occur. It is evident that the Tamulian orthographical system precludes entirely any attempt to transcribe only the indigenous characters, irrespective of their different pronunciation; but its fixed rules will almost be sufficient to enable one to reestablish the original text from a transcribed one.

According to the rectifications of Dr. Gundert, we now propose the following Alphabet and Specimen of the *Tamiḻ* language:

	அ ஆ				*a ā*		
	எ ஏ	ஒ ஓ			*e ē*	*o ō*	
இ ஈ		உ ஊ		*i ī*		*u ū*	
ஐ ஔ				*ei au*			

க	ங	ஃ		*k*	*g*	*γ*	*ṅ*	:
ச	ஞ	ய		*č*	*ǰ*	*s(ś̌)*	*ń*	*y*
ட	ண	ள	ழ	*ṭ*	*ḍ*	-	*ṇ*	*ḷ ḻ*
ற	ன	ல }	ர	*t̀*	*d̀*	*r̀*	*ǹ*	} *l r*
த	ந			*t*	*d*	*δ*	*n*	
ப	ம	வ		*p*	*b*	*(β)*	*m*	*v*

Specimen.

Yeǹnattiǹāl-eǹil Parābaraǹ tammuḍeiya orē pēṙāṅa kumāraṅei visuvāsikkiṙavaǹ yāvaṅō avaǹ keṭṭu pōγāmal nittiya sīvanei aḍeiyum paḍikku avareiyē koḍuttu ivvaḷavāy ulaγattār-iḍattil aṅbāy irundār. Ev. Joh. 3, 16.

Kumāraǹ avaṅei nōkki, taγappaṅē tēvanukkum umakkum virōδamāy pāvam seyδēǹ. Iδu muδal ummuḍeiya kumāraǹ eǹdu aḻeikka-paḍuvaδaṙku nāǹ pāttiraǹ alla-veǹdu soǹṅāǹ.
Ev. Luc. 15, 21.

The **MALAYĀLAM** has enlarged its ancient alphabet for the use of the Sanskrit words; but it employs nevertheless the ancient signs in their old manifold significations, following in the Malayālam words nearly the same rules as in the Tamil. The consequence is that the same or very similar sounds are very often differently written according to the origin of the words in which they occur. The chief difficulty is found in the transcription of the Sanskrit sonants, which receive in Malayālam an exceedingly soft pronunciation. These might be distinguished from the stronger Tamil sonants by additional points *ġ*, *ǰ̇*, *ḍ̇*, *ḋ*, *ḃ*; not indeed in all cases, for there can be no ambiguity about the initials; it is only in the middle of words, especially after the nasals, that the distinction becomes desirable. Thus the Sanskrit word *aṅǰanam* occurs in two forms: the assimilated Tamil (or Tadbhava) form, which, being written with ച, we transcribe as above *aṅǰaṅam*; whilst the word in its original garb must be represented by *aṅǰ̇anam* and sounds then almost *aṅṅanam*. The sound of വ is not the English, but the German *w* (*w̱*), which however we may without inconvenience write *v*, as in other languages. There are in the Malayālam two kinds of *u*, one of which is very short and indistinct, so as to be left out entirely in prose writings, and even to slide dialectically into the pronunciation of the inherent *a*. If this second *u* is to be distinguished at all in transcription, it may be written *u̥*. The arrangement of the consonants might therefore be the following:

ക	ങ	-		ഗ	ഖ	ഘ	ഹ	ഃ
ച	ഞ	യ		ജ	ഛ	ഝ	ശ	
ട	ണ	ള	ഴ	ഡ	ഠ	ഢ	ഷ	
റ	ഩ			-	-	-	-	
ത	ന	ല	ര	ദ	ഥ	ധ	സ	
പ	മ	വ		ബ	ഫ	ഭ	-	

k	*g*	*γ*	*ṅ*	-		*g(ġ)*	*kh*	*gh*	*h*	:
č	*ǰ*	*š̌*	*ń*	*y*		*ǰ(ǰ̇)*	*čh*	*ǰh*	*ś̌*	
ṭ	*ḍ*	-	*ṇ*	*ḷ*	*ḻ*	*ḍ(ḍ̇)*	*ṭh*	*ḍh*	*š*	
t̀	*d̀*	*ṙ*	*ǹ*			-	-	-	-	
t	*d*	*δ*	*n*	*l*	*r*	*d(ḋ)*	*th*	*dh*	*s*	
p	*b*	(*β*)	*m*	*v*		*b(ḃ)*	*ph*	*bh*	-	

Specimen.

Yendu̥ koṇḍ-eṅṅāl Daivam taṅdē yēγaǰāδaṅ-āya putraṅē avaṅil viśvasikkuṅṅavaṅ oruttaṅum naśičču̥ pōγāδē nitya ǰīvaṅ uṇḍāyēṇḍuṅṅaδiṅu̥ taruvāṅ takka vaṇṇam yetrayum lōγattē snēhiččū. Ev. Joh. 3, 16.

Appōḷ mayaṅ avaṅōḍu̥, appaṅē, ṅāṅ svargattiṅu̥ nērēyum niṅdē muṅβāγēyum pāβam čeyδ-irikkuṅṅu. Ini mēl niṅdē mayaṅ eṅṅu̥ čollappeḍuvāṅ yōgyaṅ alla eṅṅu̥ paṙaṅṅu. Ev. Luc. 15, 21.

The **TULU** has no ṛ. It was originally written with the Malayālam character, which the Brahmans still prefer. After the conquest of the Canarese however the *Karṇāṭaka* alphabet has been introduced. Of this also the Missionaries make use in their books, in which the *Tuḷu* has been printed for the first time. The number of the *Tuḷu* people is so small, that it will perhaps never possess a literature. The length or shortness of vowels is often hardly distinguishable. For the vowel, which we had proposed to write ḭ, we prefer now, with Dr. Gundert, to employ the indistinct u̥.

Specimen.

Yēsu, Yehūdada Bethlehēmuḍu arasāy Hērōda dinoḷedu̥ puṭṭi bokka indā ǰōtiseru̥ mūḍayiḍuḍu̥ Yerusalēmugu battuḍu̥ Yehūdyeregu̥ arasu āḍu̥ puṭṭināye vōḷu uḷḷe dāyeg anduṇḍa yeṅkuḷu āya boḷḷinu̥ mūḍayiḍu̥ tūdu āyagu̥ ārādhane malpere battā anduḍu̥ paṇḍeru̥. Ev. Matth. 2, 1. 2.

The old **KARṆĀṬAKA** has the letters ṙ and ḹ. In later times, however, they have been replaced by r and ḷ.

Specimen.

Yātakk-endare ātanalli viśvāsa-v-iḍuvavarellaru nāśavāgade nitya ǰīvavannu honduva nimitta Dēvaru tanna vobbanē maganannu koṭṭa hāge ǰagatannu aṣṭu prīti paḍisidanu. Ev. Joh. 3, 16.

Ādare maganu avanige tandeyē paralōkakke virōdhavāgiyū ninna mundeyū pāpa maḍiddhēne nānu innu ninna magan-endu kareyalpaḍa yōgyan alla andanu. Ev. Luc. 15, 21.

In the **TELUGU** (Andhra) the sound of *ṙ* is almost changed into *r*, although the former is still often written.

Specimen.

Yendu vallanante āyanayandu viśvāsamunśēvādevvaḍō vāḍu nāśamu pondaka nitya ǰīvamunu ponde nimittamu Dēvuḍu tana yoka kumāruniččinattugā ǰagattunu prītipallačenu. Ev. Joh. 3, 16.

Appuḍu kumāruḍu āyanatō tandrī paralōkamunakunnu nīkunnu virōdhamugā pāpamu čēsiyunnānu yikamīdaṭa nī kumāruḍani piluvabaḍa nēnu yōgyuḍanugā-n-anenu. Ev. Luc. 15, 21.

2) We have given the alphabet of the **TYI** language (p. 281) according to the Grammar of the Rev. H. N. Riis. The Rev. G. Christaller has since made most accurate researches on the grammar and especially on the sounds of the same language, which he had the kindness to communicate in manuscript to the author. We therefore take this opportunity to give some additional remarks to what has been said above, referring for the rest to the future publications of this excellent observer, to which we look forward with great interest. He distinguishes not only long and short and very short vowels, which latter we may represent, as he does, by the sign of shortness ˘,—for instance in the name of the *Ḁkŭape̥m* dialect, *kŭa* being different from *kwa*—but he shows also, that the *Tyi* language has nasalized vowels, which he represents with us *ã ẽ ĩ õ ũ*, and that it uses besides a certain broken or weakened and indistinct pronunciation of the vowels *a ã e* and *o*, which he indicates by a point underneath *ạ ạ̃ ẹ ọ*, and which we would prefer to write *ḁ*, *ḁ̃*, *e̥*, *o̥*. Moreover he has observed a peculiar and interesting vowel harmony, by which the four rows of vowels 1) *a ã e̥ o̥*, 2) *ḁ ḁ̃ e o*, 3) *ẽ õ e̥ o̥*, 4) *ĩ ũ i u* combine in neighbouring syllables not indistinctly, but according to certain rules. Finally, he has found the same tones in the *Tyi* as in the cognate languages *(Ibo, Yóruba, Ewe, Gã)*.—With respect to the consonants, Mr. Christaller eliminates the soft fricatives *z* and *v*, as well as the letter *χ*, to which latter however the

sound of *h* approaches, when placed before the vowels *e̱*, *e* and *i*. The sound *ŵ*, which in the *Eŵe* language is pronounced between the two lips, but as a surd letter, not as a sonant like the German *w̱*, is not found in *Tyi*.

3) We have lately received the first Part of the most valuable work on the **LETTIC** language by A. Bielenstein, Lutheran Minister at Neu-Autz in Kurland *(Die Lettische Sprache nach ihren Lauten und Formen. Erster Theil: Die Laute, die Wortbildung.* Berlin. 1863*)*. The complete description and scientific treatment, in this work of the sounds of that well cultivated language, and the peculiar kind of vowel-sounds, which we have not yet met with in any other language, induces us to add a few remarks on the manner in which the Lettic sounds might be reduced to our Standard Alphabet. Mr. Bielenstein shows that simple vowels as well as diphthongs have, beyond the pronunciation common to almost all the languages, a second one, which he calls "the pushed pronunciation" *(die gestossene Aussprache)*. It consists in an abrupt uttering of the vowel followed by the same or another, but very short, vowel, or by a liquid consonant, so as to leave between both a minimum of hiatus. He tries to represent this pronunciation in the following manner: *a'ᵃ*, *i'ⁱ*, *u'ᵘ*, *e'ᵉ*, *a'ⁱ*, *a'ᵘ*, *i'ᵘ*, *u'ⁱ*, *u'ᵃ*, etc. The sign of the *hamza* ', however, the same which he employs in his description of the sound would be too heavy for the purpose. He proposes therefore to put in writing only the acute ′ over the "pushed" vowel, and keeps the sign ' only before liquids. When the short *ă* formes the second part of a diphthong as in *i'ᵃ* and *u'ᵃ*, he writes *i̊* and *ů*, and such streched vowels which he describes as a combination of $\overline{{}_{i}e_{a}}$ and $\overline{{}_{u}o_{a}}$ compressed to one syllable, he writes *ẽ* and *õ*. In the Standard Alphabet the acute ′ is exclusively reserved for the accent of the word, and the circumflex ˜ for the nasalization of the vowel; the character *ů* expresses in other languages rather the diphthong *uŏ*, not *uă*. We would propose therefore

to indicate the peculiar "pushed" sound of the vowels by the hitherto unemployed accent ̀, writing *à*, *ì*, *ù*, *è* and the diphthongs *ài*, *àu*, *ìu*, *ùi*, *èi*, and likewise *ìa*, *ùa* instead of *î* and *û*. If the *e* and *o* in the compound vowels $\overline{\textit{iea}}$ and $\overline{\textit{uoa}}$ have the "*pushed*" pronunciation, we should write also *ièa* and *uòa*, or if the beginning *ĭ* and *ŭ* are of little consequence; *èa*, *òa*; if in the contrary there is no slight hiatus between *a* and the preceding vowel, we might write *ēa* and *ōa*. Mr. Bielenstein regards the accented vowels in *ài*, *àu*, *ìu*, *ùi*, *èi* as long, in *ìa* and *ùa* as "almost short" (p. 45), and if they precede a liquid, as short; but there seems to be no great difference of quantity, and if there is any, it is certainly less important than the peculiar "pushed" pronunciation; we, therefore, should not hesitate to write also *à ì ù è* before liquids instead of *a' i' u' e'*. The complete vowel system would thus be the following;

Bielenstein.										Standard.									
a	*â*	*ai*	*au*	*á, a'*	-	*ái*	*áu*			*a*	*ā*	*ai*	*au*	*à*	-	*ài*	*àu*		
i	*î*	*iu*		*í, i'*	*i̊*	-	*íu*			*i*	*ī*	*iu*		*ì*	*ìa*	-	*ìu*		
u	*û*	*ui*		*ú, u'*	*ů̂*	*úi*	-			*u*	*ū*	*ui*		*ù*	*ùa*	*ùi*	-		
e	*ê*	*ei*		*é, e'*	*ẽ*	*éi*	-			*e*	*ē̇*	*ei*		*è*	*èa*	*èi*	-		
				-	*õ*	-	-							-	*òa*	-	-		

If in the Lituanian (p. 141) the same peculiar "pushed" pronunciation of the vowels should occur, we might employ the same transcription.

As to the consonants, they do not contain any new sound, and are all fixed in the Standard Alphabet.

Bielenstein.										Standard.											
k	*k̄*	*g*	*ḡ*	-	-	-	-			*k*	*ḱ*	*g*	*ǵ*	-	-	-	-	-	-		
tsch	-	*dſch*	-	-	-	*sch*	*ſch*	*j*		*č*	-	*ǰ*	-	-	-	*š*	*ž*	*y*	-		
z	-	*dſ*	-	-	-	*ſ̃*	-	*r*	*r̄*	*ṭ*	-	*ḍ*	-	-	-	-	-	*r*	*ŕ*		
t	-	*d*	-	*n*	*n̄*	*s*	*ſ*	*l*	*l̄*	*t*	-	*d*	-	*n*	*ń*	*s*	*z*	*l*	*ľ*		
p	*pj*	*b*	*bj*	*m*	*mj*	-	-	*w*	*wj*	*p*	*ṗ*	*b*	*b́*	*m*	*ṁ*	-	-	*w*	*ẃ*		

4) P. 18, lin. 11. 17. read: *d̀*, *t̀*, instead of *ḍ*, *ṭ*. P. 193, 5: [illegible], not [illegible]. P. 215, 8. 15: ڭ, not ک; *γ* not *g*. P. 216, 10: *oγul.* P. 307, N° 11[b] *Asante.*

CPSIA information can be obtained
at www.ICGtesting.com
Printed in the USA
LVHW100436110522
718424LV00003B/144

9 783375 005054